What the critics are saying...

ℰℐ

Marriage in Moonlust

"Set in a fantasy/medieval world, Marriage in Moonlust is a new take on the concept of vampire romance that fans of the genre will be sure to appreciate." ~ *Sensual Romance*

"Narcisse is the perfect emotionally wounded hero." ~ *Just Erotic Romance Reviews*

Moonlust Privateer

"...a fast-moving combination of swashbuckling pirate story and unique vampire tale." ~ *Romantic Times*

"...loaded with love, death, fighting, betrayal, and honor." ~ *Sensual Romance Reviews*

"This is a fast-paced, action packed book. I enjoyed the story of a swashbuckling Errol Flynn of the Vampires." ~ *Just Erotic Romance Reviews*

Kate Hill

Dusky
Kisses

ELLORA'S CAVE
ROMANTICA PUBLISHING

An Ellora's Cave Romantica Publication

www.ellorascave.com

Dusky Kisses

ISBN 1419953931
ALL RIGHTS RESERVED.
Marriage in Moonlust Copyright © 2002 Kate Hill
Moonlust Privateer Copyright © 2002 Kate Hill

Cover art by Syneca.

Trade paperback Publication July 2006

Excerpt from *Infernal* Copyright © 2005 Kate Hill
Excerpt from *God of the Grim* Copyright © 2005 Kate Hill

Warning:

The following material contains graphic sexual content meant for mature readers. This story has been rated E–rotic by a minimum of three independent reviewers.

Ellora's Cave Publishing offers three levels of Romantica™ reading entertainment: S (S-ensuous), E (E-rotic), and X (X-treme).

S-*ensuous* love scenes are explicit and leave nothing to the imagination.

E-*rotic* love scenes are explicit, leave nothing to the imagination, and are high in volume per the overall word count. In addition, some E-rated titles might contain fantasy material that some readers find objectionable, such as bondage, submission, same sex encounters, forced seductions, and so forth. E-rated titles are the most graphic titles we carry; it is common, for instance, for an author to use words such as "fucking", "cock", "pussy", and such within their work of literature.

X-*treme* titles differ from E-rated titles only in plot premise and storyline execution. Unlike E-rated titles, stories designated with the letter X tend to contain controversial subject matter not for the faint of heart.

Also by Kate Hill

∞

Contents

Marriage in Moonlust

&

Chapter One

ȿͻ

Skeletal fingers of bare treetops pointed at the full moon. The devil's moon, as it was called in Leona's village. From her awkward position, half-drugged and slung like a sack of wheat in the arms of a stinking brute, a devil's moon seemed the perfect description.

She squinted through blurry eyes and felt bile rise in her throat. As the world spiraled around her, she lost consciousness.

* * * * *

Landing with a thud that bruised her back and ribs, Leona awoke in a dim, windowless stone room. The stench of animal droppings left to rot in slime-slicked puddles of water nearly gagged her. She raised herself to her knees, straining to see in the light of the single candle emerging from a puddle of melting wax beside an oak door.

"The others will be here soon."

Leona jumped at the sound of the rumbling voice. Her heart pounded as she spun to face the misshapen fiend who'd carried her there. As monstrous in height as he was in size, with grotesque lumps of flesh and muscle bulging through his black robe, he glared at her with narrow, close-set eyes. His hairless, bloated face reminded her of moldy dough. Narrow lips slipped into a malicious smile, exposing the sharp incisor teeth her people so feared.

It had been terror of the Debray family that sent Leona to the monster's lair as a sacrifice offered by her village. To appease the gory hunger of the family who held legal rights over their land, her own parents had thrust Leona to her wretched fate.

For years unexplained deaths, anemic symptoms of heretofore healthy people, and the detailed dreams of children had been brushed aside and ignored. The Debrays were known vampires, yet as long as the land yielded crops and people remained silent, they issued light taxes and ruled fairly compared to most nobles in the region. Until that summer.

More villagers had died, livestock was found mangled and drained of blood, and taxes increased. Kornel Debray, acting ruler in his brother's absence, had demanded human sacrifices to be made on the last eve of every month. At first the villagers rebelled, but homes were burned, and mothers, sisters, wives, daughters_even beautiful youths_were taken by force. The victims were carted off in a black, steel-wheeled coach, or worse, trapped in the monstrous arms of the Debray family servant, Augustus.

The beast Augustus snarled at Leona as she crawled away from him, her brain still muddled from the herbal mixture her mother had used to poison her, rendering her helpless to fight for her freedom.

"You are so lovely," Augustus seethed, saliva slipping from the corner of his mouth and sticking to his blubbery chin. "I could lick you up."

"Not without the rest of us." Kornel Debray's tall silhouette filled the doorway. Eyes glowing with fiendish amusement, he stared at Leona. The younger of the Debray brothers was as handsome as Augustus was ugly, with wavy chestnut hair cut short about his chiseled face, full lips and large, thickly-lashed eyes that shone blue beneath a tinge of bloodlust red. In spite of his sensual appearance, Kornel Debray reeked of evil. He advanced on Leona, giving passage to the third Debray sibling, their sister, Sabine.

Like Kornel, she was tall and slender with fine cheekbones, wide-set blue eyes and delicate hands that floated gently over her gray silk dress.

"Truly, Augustus, you must wait your turn." She giggled, sweeping past the brute and leaning toward Leona. "She's lovely, Kornel, for a common wench."

"I suppose." Kornel squatted beside Leona, took a handful of her thick, auburn hair and jerked her neck back. "Would you like the first taste, sister?"

"Let go of me!" Leona shrieked, swiping at Kornel with her nails. He laughed and trapped her wrists in his other hand.

Leona fought him with a combination of fury and terror, but he laughed until he grew tired of her flailing and shoved her into Augustus' arms. The brute's slug-like tongue licked the back of her neck. She jammed her elbow against him, but the solid masses of fat and muscle were too strong an armor for mere mortal flesh and bone to penetrate.

"Why don't we all drink of her at once?" Augustus suggested.

"Me? Drink with a lowly beast like you?" Kornel scoffed. "Perhaps when I've drained her nearly dry I'll let you have what's left."

"Kornel, that's enough." Sabine's smile faded.

"Enough? My dear, we've only just begun. I allowed you to join our games because you've pleaded with me for weeks. If you're going to be a bore, then you can go back to visiting babes in cribs and leaving them with the sweet little dreams you're so fond of."

Kornel advanced toward Leona who struggled in Augustus' arms, but Sabine stepped between them. "Kornel, she's afraid. This isn't right."

"Of course she's afraid. If you were going to be ravaged by wolves, you'd be terrified as well. That's the fun of it."

Kornel shoved Sabine aside and lowered his mouth to Leona's throat while Augustus, drooling down the back of her neck, held her immobile.

"Kornel, let her go!" Sabine yanked her brother's arm, her own immortal strength not an even match for his, but enough to deter him momentarily. Leona used the opportunity to lash out at his groin with her foot, hoping that area would be as sensitive to him as it was on human males.

To her satisfaction, he groaned and bent forward in pain. Sabine laughed.

"Shut up, you spoiled wench!" Kornel grasped Sabine's silk-clad wrist and hurled her backward toward the door where she smashed directly into the chest of Narcisse Debray.

Narcisse caught Sabine, holding her against his rain-soaked cloak, while his eyes, gleaming beneath his hood, surveyed the gruesome scene in the dungeon room.

"On the way home I heard stories." Narcisse's voice sounded dangerously soft. "I didn't believe them, but I can see I was wrong."

"We were just having a bit of fun." Kornel shrugged. "It's not like you've never done the same."

Narcisse glared at Augustus until the servant released Leona. She stumbled, but Narcisse caught her. His hood fell from his face, and she gazed up at the most striking man she'd ever seen. Perhaps it was the poison herbs in her blood, or maybe what the legends said about vampire's mind powers were true, but she felt bewitched by his glistening sapphire eyes and smooth, dusky skin. Full lips parted slightly, revealing the tips of his teeth. The chest beneath her palms felt hard, but living, breathing, not death-like, as she had expected.

"Lord Debray, I just want to leave." Leona tried to keep her voice steady. "Please."

He shook his head. "You're in no condition to go anywhere. Sabine, have a servant prepare a room for her."

The vampiress left to obey her brother's request.

"No! I don't want to stay here!"

He swept her into his arms, pressing her to his damp cloak and the warm, virile body beneath. As he strode out of the cell, he glanced over his shoulder to his brother. "We'll talk soon, Kornel."

The younger man nodded, a muscle jerking in his smooth

cheek, his hands clenched into fists so tight that blood dripped from his palms. Beside Kornel, Augustus glanced at his booted feet like a reprimanded child.

Narcisse climbed the winding flights of stone steps to the Castle Debray, as if scarcely noticing the weight of the woman in his arms. Leona, realizing he wasn't about to release her, clung to his neck to avoid being jounced with every step. The heavy tendrils of his damp black hair felt slick against her cheek. His aroma was of the forest and the earth, the fresh smell of the storm, and the comforting scent of leather and horse. Her forearms touched the warmth of his neck, and she felt completely enveloped by strength she had never known before.

"I'm perfectly able to walk."

He raised a skeptical eyebrow. "Highly unlikely."

"You really needn't go out of your way. I'd much rather go home."

"To a family who drugged you so you could be carted off to amuse my brother and his pet ogre?"

"Better to be back in my own village than to spend another second in this demon pit!"

"You won't be hurt again. I promise," he said as they reached the top of the steps. "Once you're well, we can talk about returning you to the village."

"But—"

"But until then, you're my guest. I want to make up for my brother's rudeness."

"You're being just as rude by not letting me go," she ventured, unsure of how much flippancy he would accept from one of his villagers.

"Am I?" He kicked open the door of a chamber at the end of the hallway and stepped into a room where a fire blazed. Several candles glowed on a long wooden table. He placed her amidst warm fur blankets and feather pillows on a canopy bed and added, "Then rudeness must run in my family."

Leona wanted to argue further, but the herbs seemed to drag her into darkness. Her body felt colder than she ever remembered.

* * * * *

"Don't sleep!" Narcisse grasped the woman's arms. Even filthy and drugged, she was beautiful. Her rich auburn hair hung in thick waves about her delicate face. Except for the deadly pallor beneath, caused by the poison, her skin carried a hint of gold, as if touched by the sun. "I'm tired," she murmured.

"The poison you were given makes you want to sleep, but you might die if you give in to it!"

Her eyes slipped shut, and she resisted when he tried shaking her to wakefulness.

There was a way to save her, but after all she'd endured with Kornel and Augustus, it seemed almost too cruel.

"Tell me your name," he said, crossing the room to bolt the door. He tossed aside his cloak and tugged his shirt over his head.

"Leona."

"I like that name." He kicked off his boots and trousers, dropping them in a heap beside the cloak. "Leona!" He spoke as if commanding an army as he sat on the edge of the bed and began unfastening the ties on the front of her dress. His teeth clenched. There were so damn many little knots that she could be dead before he removed the garment! Claws emerged from beneath his human fingernails, and he gently slashed the gown, tearing only cloth, not so much as scratching her tender flesh.

Her eyes opened halfway, and she fought him with her remaining strength.

"Leona," he held her arms at her sides and slid his body over hers while speaking against her lips, "please trust me. I won't hurt you."

She shook her head, eyes terrified beneath their haze. "I don't want to become what you are. I'd rather be dead."

Her words stung, not so much from the insult, but from past memories. If another woman had been so repulsed by his nature, she might have lived. Now this woman might die for the opposite reason. She needn't have worried, however. Narcisse would never again make the mistake he had before. He had no intention of changing Leona. He merely wanted to share some of his strength with her.

"Look at me." He gently grasped her chin when she tried to turn away. Her green eyes held his, and he felt some of her fear melt away when their minds touched. After a moment, he released her from his spell. He'd never taken a woman by the use of magic and had no intention of starting now. He merely wanted to prove to her she was safe with him.

"Leona, if you don't let me help you, the poison will kill you. I swear you will not become what I am."

"Why should I trust you?" she slurred as death sank its fingertips into her soul.

He covered her mouth with his, tenderly, chastely at first. Her lips felt so soft, her breath so human. The tip of his tongue traced her lips, parting them. He explored every heated corner of her mouth while one hand pushed aside what was left of her dress and cupped a warm breast. His thumb stroked her nipple, and she moaned softly. Narcisse smiled. That was not a moan of refusal!

His lips roamed down her neck, pausing at the artery throbbing beneath her chilled flesh. He licked her skin, his heartbeat quickening as his tongue left a wet trail between her breasts and across her belly. Finally, he took one of her nipples in his mouth and drew on it, his tongue flicking over the tip, causing it to swell to a sensitive peak.

She uttered a soft sound of pleasure. Shifting position, Narcisse kissed her again while his fingertips stroked the curling hair above her sex, then slipped into her heated crevice, gathering moisture. His damp fingers found her tight little nub and massaged in gentle circles as he sank his teeth into his bottom lip, drawing blood. His immortal elixir dripped into her mouth. She moaned, licking the shallow cuts on his lips, her hands clutching the hair at his nape, pressing him closer as she tasted his blood.

Her enthusiasm made his heart pound and his manhood swell with desire. He covered her body with his, lips never separating from hers, even as he slipped inside her hot, wet passage. Narcisse felt her delicate feminine barrier tear beneath his probing weapon. He moved as gently as possible, but her hips jerked against his, her long, smooth legs locking around him while her fingertips sank into his shoulders.

She met him thrust for thrust until her body convulsed. Tearing his mouth from hers, he gasped as she cried out in climax.

His own breathing out of control, Narcisse slipped from her and stood, trembling with desire, by the bedside. A faint smile touched her lips as she drifted to sleep, her face no longer pale, but flushed from a combination of his blood and the vigor of their lovemaking.

He dampened a cloth in the basin of water by the bed and cleansed the droplets of blood from her thighs, resisting the urge to lick them away. She'll be fine, he thought to himself. Better than I am at the moment.

Narcisse glanced at his heavy erection. Its thickness shone rosy in the firelight, blue veins creating sensual patterns beneath the velvety flesh. He'd been traveling hard for weeks and hadn't taken any blood during that time. Sharing his own with Leona, feeling her soft, naked body so close to his, had excited him to a pitch of desire he hadn't experienced in centuries.

His body demanded release, but he wouldn't allow himself to take such pleasure in her. What they'd shared that night had been to save her life, but when they made love again_and he had no doubt they would_he wanted her fully aware and completely willing.

Until then, he would find satisfaction_and nourishment_elsewhere.

He covered her with a quilt and brushed her kiss-swollen lips with his, licking away a droplet of blood clinging to the corner of her mouth. Narcisse covered himself with his robe, slung his clothes over his shoulder and picked up his boots. Before leaving the chamber, he cast a final glance at Leona and smiled with sad anticipation. After so many years, he'd found a woman who truly interested him. He knew from experience such attraction could only end in disaster. Perhaps he should simply forget her before he became so enraptured he'd refuse to let her go.

Chapter Two

ɞ

After depositing his clothes in his chamber, Narcisse didn't waste time traveling back down the winding hallways and narrow staircases to the main door. He thrust aside the brown velvet drapes concealing the tall, arched window of his chamber. Stepping onto the ledge, he gazed at the courtyard below. Cobbled pathways created a maze through clipped shrubs and rosebushes cushioned with white, lavender and burgundy flowers. If nothing else, Augustus was a fine gardener. If he could only learn to treat mortals with the same tenderness as his beloved roses.

Taking a deep breath of summer air cooled by the earlier storm, Narcisse glanced skyward. The brilliance of the moon caused his heart to pound. He leapt, wind caressing his face as he dropped to the distant ground below. The jump would have killed a mortal, but Narcisse's vampiric body accepted the impact, the length of his muscled legs bending to a crouch. He remained still for a moment, eyes sweeping the courtyard, before he ran several steps and bounded over the high stone wall.

On bare feet, he raced over the miles of countryside to the village. Most of the thatched buildings were dim, but lights shone from the tavern in the square. The sound of pouring ale, drunken laughter and sex emanated from the tavern. Other sounds reached him as well, people snoring, a random sheep bleating, horses snorting in their stalls and cats mating. The night spoke to Narcisse, and it showed him things mortals often missed. An owl perched on top of a nearby barn stared at him as he moved silently through the streets. A rat, believing itself to be protected by the shadows, scurried along the base of a tree. An old woman squinted at Narcisse through her shutters, her wrinkled brow furrowed in a gesture of fearful rage. He couldn't resist flashing her a fanged grin. The shutters slammed closed, and he continued toward the tavern.

Not bothering with the door, he jumped, catching the window ledge and pulling himself inside.

Peggy, one of the town's harlots, moaned with false pleasure as she bounced atop a naked man whom Narcisse recognized as a local horse trader. The man's head was thrown back in ecstasy as his large, dirt-encrusted hands squeezed Peggy's full breasts.

Peggy's eyes opened, widening as they fixed on Narcisse. With a cry of surprise, she tumbled off the horse trader, landing on her backside on the wooden floor.

"What the hell?" the trader snarled, pushing himself onto his elbows, his glistening erection saluting the ceiling. It shriveled when he noticed Narcisse. He leapt out of bed, stumbling as he yanked on his trousers. "Lord Debray!"

Narcisse lifted his chin, motioning toward the door. The trader wasted no time before racing out, the door slamming behind him.

Peggy stood, gooseflesh visible on her skin in spite of the warm night and stuffy room. Her dark eyes stared at him with a combination of lust and fear. Though he'd never hurt her and always paid her well, she still didn't trust him. Mortals rarely did. Perhaps it was better that way.

"You've been away for a long time, my lord." Peggy approached, a pulse pounding in the pit of her throat. He caught the scent of her desire beneath the stench of the horse trader. "Welcome back."

He caught her hands as she reached for him. "You can welcome me after you've bathed. Order hot water."

Peggy slipped a worn shift over her head and disappeared. Moments later, a young man who worked for the tavern keeper hauled in buckets of water to fill the wooden tub in the corner of the room. When he'd finished, Peggy sank into the tub, scrubbing with a cake of rose-scented soap Narcisse had brought for her one evening along with a silver comb. She had seemed happy with the gifts, telling him she rarely received trinkets from men, and there were some who even tried to slip away without paying her fee. Though Narcisse occasionally used her to relieve sexual tension, part of him pitied her. Peggy's seemed like such a wasted life.

Narcisse spread his robe on the floor and yanked Peggy out of the tub.

She giggled, clinging to his neck. "I wasn't finished, my lord!"

"You're finished enough." He placed her on top of his cloak and loomed above her, hands running over her breasts and thighs, caressing her belly. She watched him through half open eyes as he licked her nipples, the tips of his teeth nipping them, just short of drawing blood. Narcisse's cock swelled at the thought of tasting her blood. His body was already tense with desire from making love with Leona.

Leona! How he wished he was skin to skin with her instead of Peggy! Closing his eyes, he grasped the harlot's wrists and pinned them above her head as he thrust into her. He began a fast, steady rhythm that soon had her moaning with real passion. Her wet sheath clamped around his cock and pulsed with desire as his teeth pierced her shoulder. Narcisse closed his eyes, her bittersweet blood drizzling over his tongue. He pulled away, gasping, not wanting to take too much from her__ or end his own pleasure too soon.

As he released her hands, she mewled, arms clutching him as hard as her mortal strength would allow. The motion of his hips never slowed as he drove her to peak after peak, until she lay exhausted beneath him. She whimpered in protest as his cock drove into her.

Narcisse lowered his mouth to her shoulder again, this time giving in to the bloodlust. His thrusting increased, keeping time with the sucking of his lips on the tiny wounds in her flesh. Vampiric claws sank into the bare floor above her head, splintering wood and clawing ridges in the smooth boards as Narcisse climaxed, his heart pounding. The vision behind his closed eyes was not of the harlot, but of Leona's beautiful face.

* * * * *

In the midst of morbid, frightening dreams, Leona felt strangely comforted by haunted eyes touched with compassion. They urged her away from darkness toward safety, protection and pleasure such as she'd never imagined.

Slowly her eyes opened, and she cuddled deeper into the quilt, the flicker of firelight dancing in the otherwise black room. The drugs had almost completely worn off, yet it took her a moment to remember she was still held captive in the Castle Debray. She jerked to a sitting position, searching the room for any sign of Kornel Debray or his monstrous servant. Instead her gaze met Sabine's.

The vampiress perched on an oak chair in a corner of the room, watching.

Without fear or the influence of herbs hindering her perception, Leona noticed for the first time how exquisite the vampire lady appeared. Glossy black hair hung loose beneath a headpiece of gray pearls. A silk gown draped her slim figure and complimented her aquamarine eyes.

"Don't be afraid. You're quite safe now that Narcisse's home," Sabine said.

Leona couldn't disguise her resentment as she replied, "Forgive me, but as long as I'm behind these walls I will never feel safe."

"I'm very sorry about what Kornel tried to do to you. I never realized the manner in which he played with the villagers. I thought his games were harmless."

"You talk as if we're playthings. We're people. We have families, feelings. You have no right to—"

"Unfortunately, we have every right. By law you belong to us. However with such rights come responsibilities, and Kornel has not fulfilled his. Narcisse is not pleased, and neither am I."

Leona opened her mouth to argue, but realized the lady was trying to be kind and appeared truly sorry for her brother's actions. Not only that, Leona could think of no other noble who would apologize to a commoner, but like Narcisse, Sabine's eyes shone with compassion.

"I should thank you for defending me earlier." Leona relaxed against the pillows. "If it hadn't been for you, I might not be alive right now."

"If Narcisse hadn't arrived when he did, I'm not sure what would have happened," Sabine admitted, her smooth brow creasing with the memory. "Not all of us are cruel. We do require certain contributions from you, but there is no reason to cause you pain in the process."

"You really drink blood?" Leona tried to speak with an air of nonchalance, but couldn't completely repress the quiver in her voice.

"Of course." Sabine shrugged. "You eat the cattle in the field, and we drink of you."

"But we're not cattle! We're people! You look like us, talk like us, but don't you feel anything for us other than thirst?"

"I hadn't really considered it." Sabine narrowed her eyes, tapping her long fingernails on her folded arms. "Our servants are mortal. My brothers have taken mortal lovers. All I know is I drink when I'm thirsty. It doesn't mean I dislike you. It's just my nature."

Leona stared at the vampiress, unsure of how to reply to such complete honesty to a question more complex than she realized.

"It would make an intriguing study, don't you think? How much we're alike and how we're different." Sabine walked to the bed and sat beside Leona, her face radiant with new interest. "While you're here, you could learn about us, and I want to learn about mortals. You could teach me."

"I can't stay here, my lady. I have to go back to the village and be with my family."

"But they gave you to my brother! They knew he was going to hurt you. Narcisse said so. Why do you want to go back to people like that when we could have so much fun here?"

"Because I don't belong here. Your brother tried to kill me. What's to stop him from doing so again?"

"Narcisse would never allow it." The lady lifted her chin. "And Kornel knows better than to disobey him."

"But Lord Narcisse isn't always here. As soon as he leaves again, my life is over, and I want to live. According to legend, you have forever, but someone like me has only a few short years. I want a family of my own. I want to enjoy the time I have."

"Do you like to ride?"

"We don't have a riding horse," Leona said. Her family was too poor.

"We have many. Tonight, after you've eaten and rested, I'll come back for you and teach you how to ride. It will be so much fun, Leona. You'll see. You're going to love living here."

With a swirl of silver-gray silk and floral perfume, Sabine drifted from the room, leaving Leona staring after her in frustration.

In spite of the ghastly circumstances under which she and Sabine had met, Leona admitted feeling an inexplicable fondness for her. Though she had openly admitted the villagers were little more than food to the Debray family, Sabine's enthusiastic nature was difficult to resist. In a different setting, Leona would have welcomed the opportunity for an association with the unusual noblewoman. However she had no intention of remaining at the castle to satisfy Kornel's appetite.

Slipping from the bed, she stretched, grateful for the feeling of her young, strong body completely under control once again. She felt a bit surprised that her bones didn't ache from the rough handling of the previous day, and her ribs and arms bore no bruises. She wondered if Narcisse had done something to her after he'd carried her to the chamber. She scarcely remembered him placing her on the bed, yet she knew he had given her some kind of medicine. It had tasted sweet instead of bitter, and through the herbal haze, she'd felt warmth and strength flood her body. In her dreams, they'd made love. He'd taken her with unexpected gentleness. His lips and tongue had bestowed gifts of the flesh she'd never imagined, and she'd felt loved.

One thing she knew for certain, Narcisse Debray wasn't a bit like his brother.

Leona washed in a basin of water by the bed, then sat by the fire and inspected her wrists. Not a single mark had been left from Augustus' bone crushing grip, and again she wondered what sort of magic Narcisse had practiced on her.

"Are you all right?"

Leona's head jerked up at the sound of Narcisse's voice. The vampire lord approached, and her heartbeat quickened as she realized her attraction to him from the night before hadn't been a result of her drug-muddled mind. In her lucid state, she knew he was even more wickedly handsome than she remembered. Satiny tendrils of black hair grabbed his broad shoulders. His straight-cut evergreen tunic exposed a lean, big-boned frame. Legs of long, thick muscle crossed the room in two strides, the knee-length black boots soundless on the stone floor.

The sight of him caused her mouth to go dry, and she moistened her lips, annoyed with her own weakness toward the beautiful monster. "I'm fine, my lord."

He stooped beside her and took her hands in his. She noted how small and fragile her hands looked in his grasp. When he opened his palms so that her own rested in them, she drew back. For the first time in her life, Leona felt ashamed of her callused skin, prominent veins and sturdy fingers. Yet how could she have the hands of a lady when her life had been one of tedious labor?

"I apologize for what you've endured because of my family. It should never have happened."

"It has been a regular occurrence since your departure, my lord." She met his eyes, a pulse fluttering in her throat when she saw the increased intensity of his dark gaze.

"So I've heard. I've considered leaving the Castle Debray, but that would mean passing my lands to Kornel, and obviously he's not ready for such responsibility."

Leona's eyes widened, and she gripped the edge of her chair. "You can't go, my lord. Since you've been away he's already destroyed our crops and taken the lives of countless villagers. I know there's good in you, in spite of what you are."

Leona drew a sharp breath. Confronting the vampire with his fiendish habit was risky.

He raised himself to the seat beside her, a look of sad amusement in his eyes.

"You stare at me like I'm some sort of animal ready to tear out your throat at the first sign of confrontation."

"Forgive me, but the only experience I've had with your kind is last night."

"Men like Kornel are as dangerous to our kind as he is to yours."

"I hardly think so, my lord."

"No, it's true. We can live in the company of mortals so long as we're discreet, but once a vampire goes wild, once he becomes impassioned with killing, he creates the legends that have forced mortals to hunt us with stakes and torches. We become the devil's minions, and must move on or die. We of the Debray family have been fortunate, as we've remained here for generations with little difficulty."

"I had never considered what life is like for you. It seems that creatures with your power are untouchable."

His smile looked so sorrowful that she wondered about the cause of his unhappiness. To her, he appeared to have everything—power, wealth, beauty, eternity.

"I haven't yet thanked you for helping me last night," she

ventured. "When I return to my village, I'll tell everyone that you've come home and we needn't worry about any further attacks of violence. I'm sure everyone will be relieved to hear you're back."

"You won't be returning to the village."

Her chest tightened with fear. "But it's my home! I have to go back!"

She couldn't remain in this palace of horror for the rest of her life. She wouldn't!

"Why do you wish to return to a village that sacrificed your life so cruelly? Your own mother poisoned you and your father held the door as you were carried off."

"It was either my life or the lives of everyone in the village! The demands of your kind forced my family to make the sacrifice!"

"True," he cupped her cheek with his palm, "but if you were mine, I would not have forfeited you so easily."

"I suppose you'd have given your own life instead?"

"Perhaps, but it would depend on whether you are as worthy as you are beautiful. Something tells me you are more than worthy, Leona."

She wanted to move away from the warmth of his hand, but felt compelled by his dark eyes and his tender touch. "You're wrong, my lord. I'm not beautiful. Your sister is beautiful."

"Sabine is lovely like a portrait on a porcelain vase, but you are like a living rose that smiles at the moonlight and cries with the rain. A man could live a thousand years and not find one such perfect flower, Leona."

"You're mocking me," she whispered, feeling the heat rise in her face at his compliment. Endearments were unheard of in her family. Her parents had always made it clear her purpose in life was to work their farm and, if any man would have a dowerless girl, to provide grandchildren. Her entire life had been spent toiling in the fields by morning and helping her mother with household chores until dusk. She hadn't the time for frolicking with the young men in the village, and even if she had, her parents frowned on such behavior. They'd resented Leona for being born female, the only child to an otherwise barren marriage. Her parents had wanted sons to carry on their plot of land, but had been given Leona instead. "You're no buxom beauty to lure men with your wiles," her mother had often told her. "Other than a great capacity for work, you're useless."

Narcisse leaned closer, his lips almost touching hers. "I never mock, Leona. I've been told I'm far too serious for that."

"Please, my lord," she whispered, though whether she pleaded for him to kiss her or begged him to let her go, she wasn't certain.

He stood abruptly and strode to the door. "A maid will bring you food and a change of clothes. My sister will give you a tour of the castle and grounds so you'll be familiar with your new home."

"I won't stay here."

"You haven't a choice," he said, closing the door behind him.

Chapter Three

ഓ

Narcisse paused in the stable door, watching his brother who lay on his back in a pile of clean straw, one of the castle maids astride him. Kornel's eyes squeezed closed, his hands clutching the woman's rounded buttocks. Her creamy breasts shook as she rode Kornel with a vengeance. Long, blonde hair that had escaped from beneath her white kerchief swirled around the couple, sweaty tendrils clinging to the woman's shoulders and arms. Kornel's sleek body glistened in the darkness, the muscles of his chest and arms beaded with moisture. He gasped, the tips of his fangs catching the moonlight shining in through the door.

He shifted position, pinning the maid beneath him. His claws scraped one of the plump breasts and drew a thin line of blood. The woman cried out in pleasure/pain as Kornel's teeth pricked her nipple, and he sucked hard. The scent of the sweet liquid drifted toward Narcisse. He felt his groin tighten and his mouth start to water in spite of his anger at his brother's treatment of Leona. As his brother began thrusting into the maid's straining body, Narcisse interrupted the moaning, passion-crazed pair.

"Return to the kitchen," Narcisse commanded.

The maid's eyes flew open, and she tried jumping to her feet, but Kornel's body still pounded into her.

"My lord, please!" she whimpered, pushing at Kornel's shoulders.

Snarling, Kornel rolled off his lover and shoved her aside. Eyes scarlet with rage, he turned to Narcisse and snapped, "Don't I look a little busy?"

Tugging on her loose muslin dress, the maid cast a longing

glance at Kornel before scurrying past Narcisse, eyes lowered.

"That is the second time you've ruined my amusement and disrupted a meal." Kornel stood, brushing straw from his hair.

"The first time wasn't a meal. It was an act of violence, and from what I understand, such practices have become commonplace for you."

"How I choose to take my victims is none of your concern."

"When it brings danger upon this house and those under my protection, it is very much my concern. When I left here, the village was flourishing, but I've returned to a pitiful crop yield and stories of brutality."

"It's not my fault the peasants are lazy." Kornel shrugged. "As for brutality, you drink blood just as I do, so who are you to judge me?"

"I am the ruler of this land, and I will not tolerate cruelty. If the way you were treating that girl last night is any indication of—"

"I'm six hundred and fifty years old, Narcisse! I don't need my brother advising me on how to take my victims!"

"Then show better judgment," Narcisse hissed through clenched teeth.

"I know what it is." Kornel grinned. "You wanted Leona for yourself. She's a feisty little wench, isn't she? And you've always had such a liking for vixens, as father did. Don't get too fond of her, Narcisse. You know what happened the last time you fell in love."

Narcisse approached his favorite horse's stall and stroked the animal's dark gray nose. If the timing and circumstances were right, one vampire could create another by sharing blood with a mortal, but the most powerful vampires were born of immortal parents. Such conceptions were extremely rare among their kind. It had taken Narcisse's parents over two thousand years to be awarded three offspring. Like his father, Narcisse had been lucky enough to fall in love with a woman who had conceived his child. She and the unborn babe had died in a riding accident one night while Narcisse was away. She had fallen from her horse and been knocked unconscious as the sun rose, burning her and the fetus to ashes before she could reach the safety of the castle. Kornel had ridden out to look for her. Narcisse had seen the burns on him to prove it. Kornel's search was the only reason he endured his brother's arrogant and unpredictable behavior instead of banishing him as he should have long ago.

"Don't lose yourself to another." Kornel's anger seemed to fade as he rested a sympathetic hand on Narcisse's shoulder. "I know how much it hurt you to lose Ann. Just let mortals be food and pleasure. It's simpler that way."

Narcisse shrugged off Kornel's hand. "There will be no more of these random killings and crop burnings. If you want to remain here, you will obey me."

Kornel's jaw clenched, but he nodded before leaving the stable.

Narcisse continued stroking the horse while his mind churned with a battlefield of emotions. For years he and Kornel had butted one another like territorial rams. When their parents had decided to move on years ago, they had left Narcisse their lands to care for until he chose to leave. After that, the property would pass to Kornel_unless Narcisse had an heir of his own.

At first Kornel had been content to reap the benefits of being a vampire lord without the responsibility of overseeing the Debray lands, but as he aged, his desire for power increased. Instead of outgrowing the brutal passions of a young vampire, his perverted desires rose. Kornel's wild appetites incited many confrontations between the brothers.

Though Narcisse understood Kornel's desire for his own land to rule, he refused to destroy the peace their parents had worked for. The Debray land had been theirs for too long to allow Kornel's violence to ruin it. So Narcisse waited, hoping that Kornel's domineering nature would decrease, creating space for compassion. He knew somewhere deep inside, Kornel was capable of decency, such as he'd displayed on the morning he'd attempted to rescue Ann.

Ann. Narcisse had finally come to terms with her death, though he had not considered taking another permanent lover until he'd seen Leona. Not since his wife, had a woman filled him with such animalistic passion. From the moment he'd seen Leona struggling in Augustus' brutish embrace, he'd imagined her hot, human passion baring itself to him, completely free of fear and anger. When he'd made love with her to save her life, her thoughts had been dulled by poison and his own mind control. He wanted her to offer herself to him in blood, spirit and flesh. He wanted to see genuine pleasure and affection in her eyes.

"Damn!" Narcisse struck the stable wall with the flat of his palm. Leona's face was scorched upon his memory. When he closed his eyes he could still feel her warm, slender arms about his neck, the gentle weight of her body and the exquisite scraping of her nipples against his chest.

Narcisse brushed his horse until the animal's coat gleamed, then guided him out of the stable. He mounted bareback and galloped across the field behind the castle, hoping to forget his frustration and passion in the vigor of the ride.

* * * * *

As promised, Sabine returned to Leona's chamber later that night. She brought a dress of green satin nearly the color of Leona's eyes. The lady's personal maid assisted in grooming Leona to a noblewoman's perfection.

When she finally stood before the glass, Leona could scarcely believe the woman staring back at her was a common farm girl. The green gown contrasted with her reddish hair styled elegantly beneath a gauze veil. Silky material clung to her full breasts and dropped gently over her slender hips.

Somehow the finery made Leona feel more feminine and beautiful than ever before. Her posture automatically straightened, and the slightest smile of pleasure touched her mouth.

"You look gorgeous." Sabine smiled. "Are you ready to go for our ride?"

Leona nodded, glancing at Sabine's image in the mirror.

"I thought your kind didn't cast reflections?" she ventured.

Sabine laughed, a gentle bell-like sound. "More foolishness. You'll learn that much of what the legends say about us are exaggerations, but you'll also witness truths mortals don't know."

"That's only if I stay here."

"You'll stay." Sabine's amused expression faded, and she squeezed Leona's hand. "If Narcisse wills it."

"He can't always get whatever he demands."

"He's the lord here, and even if he wasn't, Narcisse is persistent and strong. It's rare that he doesn't get exactly what he wants."

"There's a first time for everything," Leona muttered. "However, I would like you to teach me how to ride. It's something I've always wanted to try."

Sabine needed no further encouragement. She guided Leona to the stable where they were unpleasantly surprised by two guards awaiting them.

"Lord Narcisse ordered us to ride with you, in case you should try to leave the grounds," said the taller of the two men.

"But where's the fun in being followed?" Sabine huffed. "We'll be in no danger."

"Lord Narcisse wants to be reassured that your guest will be returning."

"I command you to leave us alone!"

"Forgive me, my lady," the second guard bowed to Sabine, "but Lord Narcisse's order stands."

Leona raised an eyebrow. "It seems he does get what he

wants after all."

Sabine snarled, exposing her kittenish fangs before the two women chose their mounts.

Leona took to riding more quickly than either woman expected. She loved the powerful feeling of the horse beneath her and the idea of moving as one with such a graceful, majestic animal. More than once she found herself thinking of how Narcisse must look when riding. Just imagining the sight of Lord Debray's mane of black hair lashing out, shadow-like in the night, while his sleekly muscled thighs controlled the mount beneath him made Leona's own legs weak on the saddle.

Sabine's frustrated voice speaking to the guards suddenly forced Leona back to the harsh reality that she was now Lord Narcisse Debray's prisoner.

"Won't you ride just a little farther back?" Sabine said to the men. "How can we have womanly conversation with the two of you hovering like mindless ogres?"

Jaws tightening, the guards backed away, but not far.

"Now at least we can breathe." Sabine sighed. "Are you enjoying the ride?"

"Very much. And also the dress. I've never worn such beautiful clothes before."

"If you stay with us, you'll have many more dresses, and you can ride every night if you want. You might even like living here."

Leona glanced at the lady and realized in spite of all her wealth and power, Sabine was lonely. Not many people accepted her kind, so she must have been shunned by other nobles who feared the rumors regarding her family.

"It's not that I wouldn't like living at the castle, and I'm honored that you want to be my friend, but your brother, the way he looks at me—"

"I told you Narcisse won't allow Kornel to harm you again."

"I was referring to Narcisse. When he looks at me, I feel almost as if I could lose myself in his eyes." Leona shook her head. "I probably shouldn't be saying this."

"Why?" Sabine smiled. "At first I thought you disliked Narcisse because of his arrogance. I know he can be stubborn and demanding. Then I realized maybe you felt a little for him of what I'm sure he feels for you."

"Feels? For me?" Leona's brow furrowed.

Sabine hesitated as she gazed toward the forest north of Debray Castle. Finally, she said, "Narcisse would be furious if he knew I was telling you this, but I care about him too much not to risk his anger. I feel I can trust you, Leona. I don't think you'd ever willingly hurt anyone. I can sense that you're kind. I think you have the soul of a lady, and Narcisse thinks so too. He's attracted to you."

"Impossible." Leona felt heat rise in her face as she recalled the look in Narcisse's eyes on the previous night as well as during their earlier conversation in her chamber. She remembered her dream of making love with him, of being wrapped in his powerful arms, feeling the beating of his immortal heart against her breasts. The possibility that her dream might come true made her entire body tingle.

"I know my brother. I can tell what he feels by how he looks at you. He wouldn't bother keeping you here, if he didn't feel for you. He could easily wipe your memories of all you've seen here. We have our ways." Sabine edged her mount closer to Leona's and lowered her voice. "Many years ago, Narcisse had a wife whom he cared for very much. She was carrying his child."

Leona felt a pang of sympathy. She'd never considered immortals having children or loving their mates. "What happened to her?"

"She died in a terrible accident. Narcisse has shown no real interest in another woman, until now. I know how much you hate the idea of being forced to stay with us, but I'm asking you to please reconsider your feelings, not only for Narcisse's sake, but also for your own. We'll share all we have with you, and you can be happy. Wouldn't you prefer that to laboring in the fields all day?"

Leona focused on her hand as she stroked the smooth side of her mare's chestnut neck. She knew if she could return to a family who loved her, she would rather spend the rest of her life working in the village than in the luxury of the Debray Castle, but she didn't have such a family. Hers had drugged her and willingly sent her off to be devoured by monsters. By remaining at the castle, she would not only have Sabine's friendship, but could prove to her parents that she was not worthless. If her family didn't value her, she didn't need them any longer.

Sabine's words about Narcisse's wife also piqued Leona's interest. Though she felt sorry for his loss, she now believed there was a man living as one with the vampire. If she reached the man, all the vampire's passion would be hers. Unlike most mortal women were willing to admit, the thought of sharing such a dark, lustful secret intrigued her.

"I know it will take time for you to adjust." Sabine interrupted her thoughts. "All I'm asking is for you to try."

Leona opened her mouth to reply, but nearly tumbled off her frightened horse as a tall, steel-gray stallion brushed past her at full gallop.

"Narcisse! Are you and that glorified plow horse trying to terrify her into never riding again?" Sabine shouted.

Narcisse slowed his mount and turned back to the women.

"Forgive me, Leona." His gaze swept her neatly arranged hair to the soft leather shoes on her feet. He lingered on the voluptuous curve of her breasts beneath the fitted green silk. "You look stunning."

"Thank you, my lord." She smiled, unable to keep her gaze from him. Her fantasy of what he looked like astride a horse was no comparison to the reality. Disheveled black hair mingled with the horse's gray mane in the night breeze. Dark eyes, gleaming with inner-hellfire, stared from beneath a handsome brow slightly creased in thought. His body, all sinewy grace beneath his jacket and breeches, effortlessly controlled the energetic animal.

The sight of his fiendish sensuality made the blood throb in her veins, and she wondered if his keen, immortal senses heard the passionate throbbing of her heart.

"Sabine, would you leave us, please? I'd like to ride with Leona for a while."

"Of course." Sabine flashed Leona a knowing smile before glancing at her brother. "Will you please tell these guards to go away? I'm tired of being followed around like a child."

"You are a child."

"Narcisse!"

"Fine." He turned to the guards. "You may resume your regular duties. The Lady Sabine is more than able to care for herself."

Leona watched Sabine and the guards ride off in opposite directions. Her stomach fluttered as she felt Narcisse watching her, and she turned to meet his dark, alluring eyes.

Chapter Four

ဢ

"Ride with me," Narcisse said.

Leona drew a deep breath as they nudged their mounts forward. Her mare and his stallion plodded easily through the moonlit field.

Leona gazed up at the sky. "There are so many stars and the moon is enormous."

"Nights like this, when the moon is so close, stir our kind more deeply than mortals can imagine."

Leona felt her chest tighten with fear.

As if sensing her discomfort, Narcisse offered her a gentle smile. "For most, it's a good feeling. It heightens our pleasures."

"When you drink blood?" She tried to sound nonchalant.

"Yes. And when we make love. Moonlust, we call it. It's a magnificent passion_when not abused. I guess mortals must feel it a little, too. The moon must affect everyone, even a bit."

Leona gazed upward again. "It is lovely."

"But not half as lovely as you."

Leona's heart pounded at his words. She glanced at his thigh, noting the hard curve of muscle braced against the horse's side. Wet heat seemed to spread through her core, and she shifted in the saddle.

Again, Narcisse appeared to read her mind as his gaze fixed on her groin for a brief moment. Moistening his lips, he turned away, another sad smile touching his face. She longed to see what he looked like wearing a genuinely happy smile.

"Leona, I know you're here against your will."

"It doesn't matter, my lord. You have the right to order me

wherever you choose."

He raised an eyebrow. "It seems your new attire has mellowed your spirit. I think I preferred you barefoot in torn muslin."

"All I'm saying is no matter what I feel, you'll do exactly what you please." Her honesty seemed to amuse him, and he smiled again, this time exposing the tips of his fangs.

Her heart pounded at the sight of the white, pointed teeth.

"I do have the right," he said. "However, I am not a monster, in spite of what people like to think. If you wish to return to your village, you may do so."

"But you'll wipe out my memories?"

"How do you know that?"

"Lady Sabine told me a little about your powers. I don't want my memories taken from me."

For the next moments they rode together in silence. Leona's mind reeled with unasked questions to which she feared his reply. Twice she opened her mouth to speak, but was unable to form the words.

"What is it, Leona?"

"You didn't have to give me this choice, my lord. Do you want me to stay?"

"Yes." His voice reflected the desire she felt. "I want you to stay."

They stopped their horses and stared at each other in the brightness of the moonlit field. Though his face was shadowed to her mortal eyes, she sensed the strength of his emotions. She felt a bit relieved upon realizing he was as apprehensive as she was.

* * * * *

Narcisse's hands tightened on the reins until his fingers ached. He stared into Leona's wide green eyes. Since Ann's death, he'd lived in seclusion, ghost-like in his ventures for blood as he made certain he never knew his victims, except for village harlots whom he paid for their flesh and blood. If he could live his life without closeness to anyone, then the jagged wound that had healed to a seeping ache would never reopen. Leona had reached him somehow, and he no longer wanted to feel alone.

"My lord?" Her whisper drew him back to reality. He heard the throbbing of her heart and caught the scent of her passion on the wind. She inhaled deeply, as if summoning the strength to utter her next words. "I want to stay here."

He slipped off his horse, grasped her waist and pulled her to the ground so they stood inches apart. He took her face in his hands and touched his mouth to hers. His kiss remained chaste until he felt her relax beneath the soft, supple movement of his lips. One of his hands slid through her thick hair to caress the back of her neck while the other moved to her waist, pressing her gently to the length of his body.

Her hands slid up his sides until her palms rested flat against his chest.

When the kiss broke, she murmured, "It seems so strange when I feel your heartbeat. We think of your kind as devils or ghosts, but you're flesh and bone, just like us."

"Flesh, bone and desire." His voice sounded husky, and he kissed her cheek. His tongue traced the delicate shape of her ear. "I'm alive, not dead, Leona. I can feel love and hate every bit as much as you can. I'm not a devil, just a different kind of animal."

She looped her arms around his neck and parted her lips against his. His tongue slipped hot and moist into her mouth and her own reached out to meet it, tentatively at first, then with more confidence and ardor. Her hands clenched his back, and she moaned softly as she melted against him, no longer certain that they were two separate bodies. The kiss ended far too soon.

"My lord," she breathed, looking up at him with passion-filled eyes.

His thumb traced her full lower lip, and she licked the pad with the tip of her tongue, watching his eyes redden with desire.

"Do you want to drink my blood, my lord?"

He shook his head. "No. It's too soon for that. I want you to learn to be happy here. I want to know you, and you to know me."

"Why me, when you can have a woman of your own class?"

"I want you."

She grinned. "And you do always get what you want."

"Not always." Sadness squeezed his chest as he recalled the past.

"May I speak to you freely, my lord?"

"Always."

"What makes you so unhappy?"

"It doesn't matter." He forced a smile. "Only know that when I'm with you, my sorrow is less."

"Is it?"

"Yes." He felt surprised by the truth of his reply. "It is. I can understand why my sister is so taken with you. Though you're mortal, you seem to have the power to look into a person's soul."

"If that's true, then I can see your heart is good."

"Few mortals would think so."

"Because of creatures like your brother—" She stopped. At times her truthfulness was a hindrance, and she hoped that she hadn't risked punishment by insulting a nobleman's kin.

"Don't be afraid." He reached for her hand. "I told you to speak freely. My brother's ways have brought trouble upon the Debray lands. Now that I've returned, I'll try to rectify that. I've already sent new seed to the village as well as supplies for repairing the damage Kornel caused. Unfortunately, all I can't do is bring back the dead."

"You're not like others of your class."

"Perhaps we're not as different as you might think. My father was a warrior in a land of the Far East. My mother was a slave. Against all likelihood, they fell in love, but were killed during a battle. A vampire whom they had never known, and to this day have never seen again, wandered through the field strewn with the dead and dying. He found them, still locked in a final, bloody embrace, and resurrected them from death. Yet he left them to plunder alone through many haunting years as they were forced to move from country to country, village to village, hunted and scorned for what they had become. I was born to them shortly after their change. My first memory is of living in a hut far from the closest village. People burned it to the ground while we fled, chased by men armed with pitchforks, torches and wooden stakes."

"I didn't know that," she murmured, her fingers still entwined with his.

"My brother and sister don't recall such things. By the time they were born, my parents had learned to hide their secret. My father used his warrior's skills to provide for us. Eventually, a king became indebted to him during a darker age when the power of a man's sword arm was far greater than his bloodline. The Debray lands were awarded to us, but as the years passed, people forgot how we received them. Everyone assumed we were nobles by blood. I don't even think Kornel and Sabine quite believe our parents' story of our beginning. They fancy themselves noblemen, and who is to argue that they're not?"

"No wonder you have the compassion so many others lack. Most people either have never endured the hardships you remember, or else they make a point to forget where they came from. Your bloodline doesn't matter, my lord. You have a noble heart."

He caressed her cheek with the back of his hand. A noble heart. He had a noble heart. Would she feel the same when she realized he'd already made love with her? More than anything, he wanted her to continue looking at him with the tenderness he now saw in her eyes. Part of him wanted to hide what he'd done, but he refused to build a relationship based on deception.

"Leona, I must make a confession to you."

Her eyes widened. "What, my lord?"

"When you awoke earlier, did you feel well?"

"I felt better than I expected. I wondered how it was possible that I had no bruises, and the welts on my wrists had faded. I assumed you used some kind of magic. Your kind are known to possess witches' skills."

"It's not witchcraft. It's our blood. A tiny bit of our blood can cure many ills among mortals. The poison you were given was killing you."

"So you gave me your blood?"

Narcisse gazed at the moon, then closed his eyes. "Yes. I gave you my blood to drink."

"Will I become like you?" She didn't sound nearly as fearful as she must have felt.

"No." Narcisse rested his hands on her shoulders and gazed into her lovely green eyes. "It's much more difficult than that to create a vampire."

"So you gave up some of your blood to cure me?"

"Yes, but there's more to it. Do you remember anything at all about the other night?"

A blush rose in her cheeks, and she glanced away.

"Leona, please tell me."

"I don't think I can, my lord. It was only a dream."

"About what?"

"About…us. I dreamed you and… If I tell you, you'll think me wanton."

He smiled, remembering the breaching of her woman's flesh, of how he'd washed the traces of blood from her thighs before he'd left her that night. "I know you're not wanton, at least you haven't been. Wantonness isn't wrong between people

44

who care for each other."

"But it was only a dream."

"Did we make love in it?"

"Yes, my lord."

He felt her blood pounding through her body, as much from desire as from embarrassment. He smiled. "It wasn't a dream."

"What?"

"Blood sharing and making love are almost always one in the same for our kind. For some reason, our blood is most powerful when we're aroused."

"You took me?"

"I'm sorry, but I couldn't let you die."

Leona turned away, one arm wrapped around her middle, her other hand brushing loose wisps of hair from her face.

"I know you must be angry, but please believe I only did it to save your life."

"So everything I felt in the dream was real?"

"Yes. I hope with all my soul it was a good dream."

She stood motionless, her back to him. Sadness and guilt washed over him. He hadn't known her well enough for such a confession. The fragile bond between them was broken, and unless he wanted to invade her mind and possess her will, it would never be repaired.

"I want to feel that way again." Her voice was so low, even his vampiric hearing almost couldn't discern the words.

"Leona?"

She turned to him, a blush staining the ridges of her fine cheekbones, her eyes gleaming with desire. "I've never felt anything so perfect in my life, and I want to feel it again."

Narcisse smiled, elation heating his entire body. He reached for her, his mouth descending on hers with a kiss of raw desire.

"The night grows cold," he murmured against her lips.

"Shall we ride back to the castle and continue in the warmth of my chamber?"

"Yes, my lord."

"Call me Narcisse."

She caressed his face with her hand. "Narcisse."

On the way back to the castle, Narcisse's pulse quickened with every strike of the horses' hooves, and he smiled to himself. Nothing or no one could ruin this perfect night.

Chapter Five

ॐ

Narcisse's chamber was decorated simply with oak furniture and dark tapestries. Furs covered the enormous bed, and the scent of sandalwood candles wafted on the air. Fire crackled in the hearth, warming the room and casting shadows on the stone floor.

If Leona hadn't been so eager to make love with Narcisse, she would have taken more time to admire the room and study the portraits over the hearth.

He closed the door behind them and swept her into his arms, kissing her as he walked to the bed and placed her on it. He loomed over her, and his tongue plundered the warm cavity of her mouth, giving and taking with equal ardor until she was aware of nothing but him.

Eyes closed, Leona clung to him, clenching handfuls of thick, black hair and welcoming the muscular thigh, which slipped between her legs. He hovered over her, supporting most of his weight on his arm so as not to overwhelm her, but she wanted to be overwhelmed. She wanted to feel the same fevered passion of her dream, except this time she would be fully aware of every kiss, every melding of flesh they shared. Leona pulled him closer, her inexperienced mouth learning almost more quickly than he could teach.

His lips traveled down to her neck and shoulder, his hands kneading her breasts. Using his sharp teeth, he bit away the ties of her gown, revealing the shift beneath. His mouth covered one nipple, saliva moistening the thin cotton material, molding it to her breast. His tongue teased her nipple, and Leona panted, her hands searching for the heat of his skin beneath the tunic. He rose to shed his clothes, and she watched him through half open eyes, feeling a fresh wave of lust as he bared his flesh.

As lean and muscular as she imagined, his body looked like it had been chiseled from dark marble. Broad, sinewy shoulders and chest tapered to a lean abdomen ridged with muscle. His skin was smooth, except for a slight trail of dark hair beginning at his lower-stomach and disappearing beneath his trousers. He tugged off the trousers and stood for a moment, allowing her to enjoy the sight of her first nude man. Emerging from a nest of wiry black hair, his cock jutted, thick and ruddy, the round flesh beneath heavy and dusted with random dark hairs.

She sat up, shrugging off the torn dress, and reached out a tentative hand to grasp his cock. The skin felt so soft and warm, and he seemed to swell in her palm.

She explored him with her fingertips, tracing one particularly long vein along the underside, then caressing the smooth tip, paying careful attention to the tiny eye gleaming with moisture. Narcisse drew a deep breath and held it, his lean chest swelling.

"Narcisse." She gazed up at him. His eyes shone scarlet, and though part of her feared his appetite, she wondered what his bite would feel like.

"I won't hurt you." His voice sounded raw, his handsome face tense with desire. "I promise."

"I know you won't." She took his face in her hands, kissing him. He pushed her gently into the pillows and climbed onto the bed, his mouth devouring hers.

Leona clung to him, her tongue exploring his mouth, feeling its heat and warmth. Her body felt weak, yet more alive than ever. As she ran her tongue along his teeth, his incisors pierced it, and she jerked in his embrace. A ragged moan escaped his throat. Obviously the taste of her blood excited him, but instead of hurrying to ravage her as she thought he might, his kisses grew more tender. His hands cupped her breasts, thumbs rolling her nipples. Leona shivered, feeling wetness between her legs. Her groin felt tight, her feminine lips swollen.

Narcisse's mouth moved down her throat, pausing to lap its hollow before leaving a hot trail between her breasts. He took one of her nipples in his teeth and lashed it with his tongue.

"Narcisse!" she panted, the feeling of his mouth on her bare breast driving her insane with passion. "Please. I want you. I need you!"

His hand slipped between their bodies, and he gathered her moisture. His wet fingertips stroked her tingling nub. Using the entire length of one long finger, he rubbed faster until she convulsed, gasping, her hands clutching his shoulders. He slipped into her throbbing body, every contraction drawing him deeper inside her wet heat.

He moved within her slowly, deeply, rekindling her passion. She clung to him with her slight, mortal strength as she arched against him in the throes of another magnificent orgasm.

It was then that she felt the true power of the vampire. Narcisse's teeth pierced the throbbing artery of her neck, and he climaxed. His arms locked about her as he drank. Lustful, animalistic sounds vibrated in his throat while his body surged into hers.

His bite felt so pleasurable that Leona peaked again immediately, uttering a sharp cry and clinging to him tighter. Wild, breath-stealing throbs of ecstasy lasted until he'd taken the final sip of her blood. She lay spent beneath him, drifting between wakefulness and sleep.

* * * * *

When Leona had recovered from their bout of lovemaking, she sat in a tall-backed chair. An embroidered quilt draped her nude body as she and Narcisse shared a silver goblet of wine.

Leona touched the delicate stitches on the quilt, tracing a pink rose. "This is lovely work."

"My mother made it. She always had a fine hand with a needle. Sabine didn't inherit her talents."

"She has other talents, like the ability to comfort others and make them feel welcome, as she did for me."

"She's a kind child, but at times she can be too frivolous and independent for her own good."

"It's a gift for a woman to be independent."

"It's easier for a female of our kind to be independent in the world we live in."

"Yes. You can come and go as you please, take care of yourselves and destroy those who try to harm you."

"You don't seem fearful of us or offended by our way of life."

"The only time I've ever been fearful here is when I was with your brother and that beast."

"Augustus, his pet troll? Such a thing never should have happened to you or any of the villagers."

"Are you ever—" she began, then hesitated. Even though they were physically intimate and he'd told her to always speak freely, she doubted she knew him well enough to be completely candid.

"What?" He reached for her, and her hand disappeared in his large, warm grasp. "Please talk to me, Leona. I want us to know each other. I know this sounds like madness, and I almost think I am mad for saying it, but I feel we belong together." He stroked her cheek, her jaw, and brushed the column of her throat with his thumb. Her lashes lowered as she remembered the feeling of his lips against her neck and the incredible pleasure of his bite.

"Aren't you ever afraid that Lord Kornel will turn on you with his wicked ways?"

"No." He dropped his hand from her face and walked closer to the fire. His back was to her, spine rigid, the backs of his thighs and calves curved with muscle. Shadows danced across his tight, round buttocks, causing her heartbeat to pound with the memory of clutching it in the throes of passion. She shifted in her chair, feeling her nipples harden. Now was not the time to think about pleasures of the flesh. By the tension in his posture and the way his fists clenched at his sides, he was obviously upset.

"I didn't mean to anger you," she said. "It just seems that he is fighting your will. There comes a time when everyone must make a decision about his or her life, just like I did when I chose to remain here. If Kornel's way is to be cruel, then he won't abide by your rules forever."

"Kornel fights with me, yes, but to do me true harm..." Narcisse shook his head as he turned to her. "He once risked his life to save someone I loved very much."

"I was only concerned for you."

"I know that, Leona." He joined her at the table, taking her hands in his. "Tell me more about yourself. I want to know everything."

She smiled. "My life hasn't been very interesting, not compared to yours. My parents are simple farm folk. I'm their only child. They despise me because they wanted a son. The truth be known, they were glad to be rid of me when Kornel came for the sacrifice. No matter what I did or how hard I worked, it never seemed to be enough for them."

"Fools." Narcisse's eyes flashed angry crimson. "From women come life. They should be honored, not abused. If my wife had given me a daughter, I couldn't have been more pleased."

Pain flashed across his eyes as he remembered his loss. She touched his face. "Your wife."

He nodded. Whether or not he noticed her words were a statement rather than a question she wasn't sure, but she listened silently as he spoke.

"She was a distant cousin to the King. A true lady. Like you, she was unafraid of what I was, but relished the power of joining me in immortality. Or so we thought. As you might have heard, most of our kind can't survive in sunlight. Not long after our marriage, she went riding a few hours before dawn and was thrown from her mount. She lost consciousness and burned in the heat of the morning sun. All that was left to mourn were bones and ashes."

"I'm so sorry, Narcisse." Leona slipped her arms around his neck and stroked his hair.

He held her tightly and closed his eyes, soothed by the comfort she offered. "She was carrying our child, and though she died years ago, to me it's like yesterday. Sometimes it seems the pain fades, but the memories never do."

"I know I can't replace her, but I hope I can make you happy."

"Don't think of yourself in the same breath as her."

Leona looked up, stunned and wounded by his words, but she needn't have worried.

He took her hands and raised them to his lips. "You are your own woman, Leona. In you, I'm looking for no reminder or replacement of another. I only want to know you and care for you. You're not one to live in the shadow of someone else, any more than Ann was."

She stroked his face and smiled. "I just need to be sure you're real and not a phantom telling me everything I want to hear."

"I'm real." He slipped the quilt from her shoulders and spread it on the floor, then tugged her to the ground. Stretching out beside her, he kissed her forehead, the tip of her nose, then her mouth. Large, warm hands stroked her ribs and explored her breasts.

It was then that the chamber door thrust open. Narcisse jumped to his feet as Leona covered herself with the quilt.

"What the hell are you doing in here?" Narcisse glared at Kornel who stood in the doorway.

The younger man's chest heaved with fury, and his red-tinged eyes spat hatred at the couple.

"I knew it, you self-righteous bastard!" Kornel snarled

through teeth clenched so hard that his lips bled. "You wanted her for yourself!"

Chapter Six

Leona slunk into the shadows, trying to make herself invisible in the presence of two raging vampires. Then she remembered how well they could see in the dark.

Both Narcisse and Kornel stood only several feet apart, eyes glistening redder than firelight in darkness. Every muscle of Narcisse's magnificent body tensed with fury, and in spite of his vulnerable position, he exuded more power than Kornel did fully clothed in black and carrying a double-edged dagger.

"Leave this chamber immediately, Kornel!"

"Or what? You'll steal another woman from me? Rob me of another meal? You and your honor!" Kornel spat, his face contorted. "You pretend to care about their pathetic lives, but you feed on them like cattle, just like the rest of us!"

Kornel's grip on the dagger tightened until his knuckles looked ready to tear through skin. Narcisse reached him in a single stride and wrenched the blade from his hand.

Kornel shoved Narcisse full in the chest. He staggered into a hip-high vase in a corner of the room. Glass shattered. Blood dripped from Narcisse's thigh and feet.

Leona watched in horror as both vampires glanced at the blood.

"Narcisse!" She rushed toward him, the quilt dropping from her shoulders.

Kornel snarled, stepping in front of her before she reached Narcisse. The younger lord's eyes raked her nude form, lingering on the full breasts that dangled above her slender rib cage. "Fertile looking little thing, isn't she?" Kornel sneered. "I know why you wanted her. I know what you're after. You want a blood heir to rule these lands once you've gone. You want to make sure I never get what's mine! I think I'll take this whore myself and we'll see which of us gets her with child first."

Narcisse's claws sank into Kornel's shoulder as he dragged him away from Leona. His fist slammed into Kornel's jaw, knocking him through the half open door. Kornel landed on his backside, spitting mouthfuls of blood.

Kornel sprang to his feet like an enraged leopard, his own fist flying at Narcisse's face. Narcisse shifted his stance and caught his brother's arm. Using Kornel's own momentum against him, he propelled the younger man head-first into the mantle. Kornel's face smashed into the stone, and he dropped to his knees, stunned.

Narcisse grasped a handful of Kornel's disheveled hair and jerked his head backward, pressing the tip of the dagger to his heart.

"Do it, if you can! Destroy your own flesh and blood!" Kornel sputtered. His wild gaze darted from Narcisse to Leona. "In case you don't know, my dear, a sure way to destroy a vampire is to pierce the heart. Go on, brother. It's what you've always wanted!"

"No, it's not!" Narcisse's broad chest rose and fell with furious breathing. He applied more pressure to the dagger. "I wanted us to live as a family, but I can see that's impossible. I want you out of this room and off these lands by sunrise!"

"You have no right—"

"I have every right!" Narcisse snarled. "Get out before I really do use this dagger!"

Kornel jerked his hair from Narcisse's grasp and stood, backing out of the room. He glared at the couple who stood so close their bodies touched.

"This is how you reward someone who risked his own life to rescue your beloved wife? You betray not only me, but Ann's memory, all for a wench you haven't even known for two nights!"

"Get out!" Narcisse seethed, an artery throbbing in the side of his neck, his fist squeezing the dagger so hard the handle bent.

Kornel's gaze flew to the warped metal, and he drew a sharp breath, as if swallowing a final taunt. Slamming the door behind him, he left the chamber.

Leona dropped to her knees by Narcisse, inspecting the wounds on his legs. "Sit and I'll wash and bandage these. They may need to be stitched. Some of the glass cut quite deeply."

"It's all right." He tugged her to her feet and drew her into his arms. "It's not as if it will kill me."

"Still, it can't be comfortable." She nudged him toward the fire where he sat in a chair as she retrieved a basin of water by the bed.

She glanced at the bent dagger handle as she used the blade to tear off a piece of her dress to bind his cuts. His strength amazed her, and she shuddered to imagine the damage the two vampires could have done, had the fight lasted.

Gently, she pulled shards of glass from his feet. Her hand rested on his ankle, thumb stroking the sparse, curling hair on his calf. "Am I hurting you?" she asked.

He shook his head, watching as she cleaned the cuts which had already begun to heal. His recuperative powers amazed her. Still, she wrapped his feet with the bandages. As she tied off the last one, he took her hands and drew her into his arms. Leona snuggled onto his lap, burying her face in his shoulder.

"I'm sorry," she said. "What happened with your brother can't be easy for you."

"I've known for a long time Kornel wasn't happy here. Maybe this is best for everyone. He has his own wealth and is good with a sword. He'll find his own lands to keep. I only hope Sabine will understand."

"Thank you for defending me."

He stroked her hair and back, his palm warming her flesh. "He had no right to speak to you like that, Leona. No right to say any of those things. I loved Ann, and I've mourned her, but I know I belong with you. The feeling between us is powerful."

"I feel it, too, Narcisse." She moved her head from his shoulder and looked into his eyes. The red rage and bloodlust faded, revealing jewel-like blue. Leona knew it was dangerous to give in to her emotions for a man she scarcely knew–not even a man! A vampire.

"Marry me, Leona." He grasped her hands, still sticky with his blood. They both gazed down at their entwined fingers. "Become immortal. Live with me, share the pleasures of flesh and blood with me."

For a moment she forgot to breathe. Marry him! It was too soon, too ridiculous! Yet she already loved him more than anyone in the world.

"Yes, Narcisse. I'll marry you."

He held her tightly, as if fearful she would fade to ashes and he would once again be left with memories of a brief, sweet love.

"You look tired." He stroked her cheek with the back of his hand, smiling softly. "I need to remember you're not yet immortal. It's been a difficult few days for you."

"Yes, but they've also been wonderful." Her fingertips drew random shapes on his chest. "I love you, Narcisse Debray."

"I love you, too." He carried her to the bed and covered her with the cool sheets. Stretching out beside her, he swept his hand over her body from breast to thigh.

"What's it like, being a vampire?"

"It's hard for me to describe. I've never been human, so I don't know how to compare the differences." He looked thoughtful. "I've always felt powerful. Especially during Moonlust. There are times when I feel I could run, swim, and make love and never grow tired."

"The night is never dark to you, is it?" she murmured, gasping as he took her nipple in his mouth and rolled his tongue over the sensitive peak.

He kissed her stomach. "The night is bright, beautiful. We see things I know mortals can't. Night birds flying in the shadows, the tops of trees, insects caught in spiders' webs." His fingers tickled her ribs, and she laughed.

Narcisse stroked her inner thighs, parting them. He lowered his face to her sex, tongue tracing her soft flesh, thrusting into her heated crevice. Leona gasped, body stiffening beneath his carnal exploration.

"Narcisse!" she moaned, eyes squeezed shut, her head tossing on the pillow.

His gentle attack was relentless. His tongue seemed to know exactly where she wanted to be touched, how much pressure to apply. When she felt about to shatter, he slowed his pace, keeping her on the brink of explosion. He played the sensual game until she grasped his hair, legs locking around his neck, heels against his back. "Please, Narcisse, please!"

Through a haze of desire, she felt him smile against her before placing his tongue on her stimulated little bud and moving it rhythmically. Leona cried out, her entire body convulsing, her legs so tight around him that she might have choked a mortal man.

He continued stroking her, extending her passion until the last, delicate shudder released her body to a deep, contented sleep.

* * * * *

Leona's head rested against Narcisse's shoulder, one shapely leg draped languidly over his. Though he felt the daylight draining his strength into a pool of liquid sleep, he couldn't rest. The sight of Kornel clutching the dagger, utter hatred poisoning his eyes, tormented Narcisse. His parents had left him Debray Castle, confident that he would protect their lands and all who dwelled there. They trusted him to guide Kornel and Sabine, to help them nurture their vampiric side without destroying their compassion. Instead of making his family stronger, he'd broken it apart.

Narcisse disentangled himself from Leona, careful not to wake her. He pulled on a black robe and belted it before slipping from the chamber in search of Sabine.

He found her sitting on a low stone wall in the courtyard, gazing at the last of the night sky as it gave way to sunrise. The hint of dawn made their eyes ache, yet neither moved.

"Kornel told me you've banished him from our lands. He said that you've betrayed us all for Leona."

"Surely you don't believe that?" He rested a hand on her hair.

Sabine turned to him, unshed tears glistening in her eyes. "Of course not. You might think of me as a child, Narcisse, but I'm not stupid. I know both you and Kornel far too well. You're my brothers, and I care for you both, but this time Kornel has gone too far. The way he acts, the wicked things he does... You had no choice."

"Sabine, how could one of you be so good and the other so..." Narcisse lifted a hand and squeezed his temples between his thumb and forefinger. The happiness he felt about his engagement to Leona was tainted with sadness and anger regarding Kornel. Why did life always have to be so complicated? "I tried to teach you both the same lessons our parents taught me. I've seen much more of the world than either of you. I've witnessed evil and have at times turned to evil myself. I thought you could learn from my experience, but I failed Kornel."

"No." Sabine stared into his eyes. "You haven't failed anyone. Kornel made his own decisions. If he has chosen to sever relations with you, then it's his mistake. No matter how much you might like to think you can force your will upon others, in the end everyone must choose for himself. You have no right blaming yourself for what he's become."

Narcisse smiled, resting a hand on Sabine's shoulder. "I've

been wrong to think of you as a child. You have more sense than the rest of us."

"Men rarely notice the good sense in women. Especially brothers." She placed her hands on her hips and cast him a look of teasing reprimand. "As for Leona, don't let Kornel make you feel guilty for loving her."

"I've asked her to marry me."

Sabine clapped her hands, sorrow fading from her eyes. "A wedding! There's so much to plan. Tomorrow you can ride out and speak to the Priestess. She'll be glad to perform the ceremony."

"Good idea. I need to speak with her anyway."

"She'll guide you through these painful feelings. And now you have Leona as well. Everything will be fine, Narcisse, and hopefully Kornel will find his own peace."

Narcisse kissed Sabine's forehead. "Let's go inside. The sun is rising."

"Yes." She squinted toward the graying sky. Neither Narcisse nor Sabine had ever seen daylight. Ann had often told him what she remembered of the sun. Her memories had been pleasant, beautiful. It seemed too cruel that she had been destroyed by the very thing she so fondly remembered.

He thought of Leona sleeping peacefully upstairs in his chamber, of how she was already giving up daylight to share the night with him.

He climbed the stairs to his chamber, his footsteps heavy with impending sleep. As he slipped into bed and drew Leona into his arms, she clung to him. He prayed that by sharing with her the power of his immortal blood, he would not destroy her as he had Ann.

"I love you, Leona," he murmured before sleep claimed him in the blackness of his chamber while outside the sun bathed the world in fiery light.

Chapter Seven

🔊

Exhausted from the chaos of horror, thrills and changes of the previous nights, Leona slept past twilight. When she woke, she stretched and snuggled deeper into the pillow that still carried Narcisse's wild, woodsy scent.

For the first time in her life, she looked forward to leaving the comfort of sleep because her waking hours would not be spent in toil. Tonight she had a lover to talk with, a new home to explore, and a female friend with whom she could plan her forthcoming wedding.

Sabine was the first person to greet Leona when she emerged from the chamber. She explained that Narcisse had gone to arrange the wedding ceremony.

"He's speaking with our Priestess. She's performed many weddings among our kind. She married our parents."

Leona raised a curious eyebrow. "Priestess?"

"Yes. We belong to an old religion, which has been in existence since the beginning of our kind. We worship nature, the moon and the sea, the wind and the wild beasts who share in the cycle of our lives. Our religion speaks of the balance which must be maintained among all creatures, and of the responsibility we have to others as well as ourselves. The Priestess is kind and wise. I'm sure you'll like her."

"I can scarcely believe Narcisse and I are going to be married." Leona smiled. "I thought I might have been dreaming."

"There's so much to arrange before the wedding, but first you'll need a dress." Sabine grasped Leona's hand and led her to her own chamber where several bolts of fabric draped the bed.

The women felt the soft materials and held them up to Leona's face to see which would make the perfect wedding dress. In spite of Sabine's cheerful veneer, underlying sadness shone in her eyes.

"Sabine, I appreciate all you're doing for me, but I know you must be upset about what's happened with Kornel. I can't help feeling guilty. It seems like since I arrived, your entire world has been disrupted."

Sabine's eyes widened. "You and Narcisse! I don't know what to do about the two of you! Kornel is the one who started all of this by abducting and nearly killing you, and then you feel guilty. I don't want to hear another word about Kornel unless it is an apology from his lips alone." The vampiress held a bolt of gold fabric close to Leona's face. "I think this is lovely for a wedding dress. What do you think?"

Leona embraced Sabine. "I think I'm going to be the luckiest woman in the world to have a sister-in-law like you."

* * * * *

Narcisse rode through the overgrown path to the temple built into a mountaintop several miles from Debray Castle. As ancient as the first vampire bloodline, the temple had stood through storms, battles, births and deaths. Set on the highest part of the mountain, the entrance blended into the rock and could scarcely be seen from the path below. To a passing traveler, the temple would have been invisible, but Narcisse had looked up at the curved, jagged mouth many times before. He had hidden in the safety of the sacred place when he and his parents had been chased out of their homeland. He'd nursed wounds there after the ravages of battle. In the temple, alongside his father, he had awaited the births of his brother and sister.

Kornel. How had that once innocent babe become a creature of evil?

Sabine had scolded Narcisse for his feelings of guilt, but Kornel's words had cut deeply. Had he mourned Ann long enough? Was he disrespecting her memory by the intensity of his feelings for Leona whom he had only known a short time? Even if he was, he couldn't bear to give her up. He needed Leona's touch, her love and her gentleness. He could no more refuse her than he could stop the beating of his heart.

As the horse picked its footing carefully up the narrow, rocky ridge to the temple, Narcisse knew the Priestess would help him answer the questions ripping his soul. He would tell her about Kornel and Leona, and he would ask her to perform the ceremony that would eternally bind him and the woman he loved.

Narcisse left his horse at the mouth of the temple. As he stepped through the opening in the rock, he felt like the uncertain youth he'd been during his last visit.

The main room of the inner-temple was a vast cave scented with jasmine incense. A stone altar, as old as the cave itself, stood at the back of the room.

Narcisse bowed before the altar. He picked up the silver knife resting beside a plain but carefully polished silver bowl and sliced his palm, offering several drops of his own blood. It dripped into the bowl, already half-full of the dark red liquid.

He cleansed the ritual knife and returned it to the altar.

"Narcisse Debray, it's been so long." The Priestess stood beneath a narrow archway beside the altar. Clothed in a black robe that blended with her dark skin and hair, she resembled an endless shadow.

"Evi, forgive my negligence." He knelt before her and took her hand.

She laughed. "I know you've had much to contend with since your parents' absence and the death of your wife. I see you've finally accepted her loss. I sense your feelings for her have not lessened with time, but your sadness has been replaced with a new love."

"You always know so much, Evi." He fell into step beside her as they passed through the archway and into a smaller room lit by a single candle in the center of a round wooden table.

The Priestess sat at the table, and bid him to join her.

"When one has lived as many years as I have, she learns to read the eyes and actions of others. Tell me about the changes in your life."

"I've met a woman. A kind, courageous woman whom I very much want to marry."

Evi nodded, her onyx eyes gleaming in her sculpted face. The Priestess' silence was cue enough for him to continue.

"I know it's been years since Ann's death, but I can't help wondering if I'm being unfaithful to her."

"Because you've fallen in love with another? Had Ann lived and you been the one to die, would you have wanted her to continue in grief and solitude?"

"Of course not. I would have wanted her to be happy."

"Then why do you think she'd want any less for you?" Evi narrowed her eyes at him. "I sense deeper trouble in your soul."

"My brother Kornel. I've driven him from the Debray lands."

"There has always been great anger in him. Each of us has an evil side. Since Kornel was a child he has never been able to control his."

"I feel I'm partly to blame. If I hadn't left Debray Castle, he wouldn't have indulged in a spree of violence. When I returned, the village was living in terror, and he nearly killed the woman I want to marry."

"You can't blame yourself for his actions. I can't tell you of the times he and I have spoken. When I became Priestess, I was sworn to respect the confidence of all who come to me, but I must tell you to watch your brother. He won't easily grant the peace you seek."

"What do you mean, Evi?"

"I'm sorry, but I can say no more."

Narcisse nodded. In spite of his frustration, he understood

Evi's vows of confidentiality. "I'll heed your warning. I've also come to ask a favor of you. Will you perform our wedding ceremony?"

"It would be a pleasure. Now you may take me home with you. I want to meet your intended."

* * * * *

Leona spent hours in Sabine's chamber working on her wedding dress, her stomach fluttering with happiness. She never would have imagined falling in love with such a wonderful man, let alone sharing her life with him. She and Narcisse would truly belong to one another forever. She smiled, placing aside the silky material, as her beloved stepped into the chamber. Leona melted into his embrace. "I've missed you."

Narcisse kissed her forehead and turned to the beautiful, dark-skinned woman standing behind him. Draped in black, the woman carried herself with pride, and Leona guessed who she was before Narcisse's introduction.

"Leona, please meet Evi, the Priestess whom I would like to perform our wedding ceremony, if it is agreeable with you."

"Sabine told me about you." Leona curtsied low out of respect to the old vampiress. "If I'm to become one of you, then it's fitting for you to perform our ceremony."

Evi reached for Leona's hand, and Leona couldn't repress a shiver at her touch. The Priestess' hand felt like cool, polished rock. Her touch alone drew forth the story of Leona's past and took from her only the truth.

"You've chosen a pure and lovely soul, Narcisse Debray." Evi smiled, releasing Leona's hand. "I wish you centuries of happiness and the blessing of a child."

Narcisse placed a possessive arm about Leona's shoulders, and she leaned against him, feeling the slow, powerful rhythm of his heart beneath her back.

"I see you're working on a wedding gown." Narcisse looked at the golden fabric. "But where is my lazy sister? She's not helping you?"

"As you said, she cares not for the needle, but she has been helping me cut and fit. She left for a ride just moments ago. She promised to be back within the hour."

"A ride sounds like a pleasant idea." He smiled. "Evi, would you care to join us?"

"No. I'm looking forward to sitting in your courtyard and meditating among those famous rosebushes. I've been secluded in my temple for far too long, and now that I'm out, I plan to enjoy myself."

Narcisse bowed to Evi before he left with Leona clinging to his arm.

Outside he lifted her onto the front of his stallion and mounted behind her. She leaned into his steely chest, her hands gripping his forearms folded beneath her breasts.

"Narcisse, I'd like to ride to the village. I want my parents to know what's happened to me."

"You're still concerned for them?" He repressed the anger that tightened his chest. How could she care for them when they'd tried to kill her?

"No," she glanced over her shoulder, a smile on her lips, "I want to gloat."

He laughed and turned the horse toward the village.

Chapter Eight

&

During the ride into the village, Leona's stomach churned with a combination of excitement and apprehension. Though she would have been content never to see her family again, she wanted them to know that in spite of their efforts to ruin her life, she was happy. Had they treated her with a bit of kindness, they would have enjoyed the benefits of her new station, but she felt she owed them nothing.

For the first time, fate had been generous with her. After a lifetime of drudgery, she had love.

Soon the familiar sight of cottages came into view. The village scent struck her — smoke, rotted scraps tossed out windows, manure and cooking food. Sounds of children playing, the clink of a blacksmith's hammer striking metal, barking dogs and conversation wafted on the air.

"I want to stop at the Reeve's house first," Narcisse said. "The people need to know they're safe again. Actually, I'll have him send for your parents. We can speak with them there." Leona nodded, and his arms tightened around her. "Are you all right?"

"Just a little nervous."

"Don't be. You're soon to be the lady of this land. Let your parents," he sneered the word, "be nervous about seeing you."

As they rode through the town, people stared at Leona with wide eyes. She sensed their shock upon seeing her dressed in finery and sharing a mount with their lord. They bowed as Narcisse's stallion passed, and she heard their whispering when they thought the couple was out of earshot.

"It's Leona."

"She's not dead?"

"What is she doing with Lord Debray?"

Narcisse stopped the horse outside the Reeve's home. A youth hurried forward to take his stallion. The couple approached the door, which flew open. The Reeve, tall and raw-boned, stared at them with surprised gray eyes. He bowed deeply. "Lord Narcisse. Welcome home, and thank you for the seed you sent, as well as the men to help with repairs."

"Winfield, I've come to reassure you that the trouble my brother has caused is over."

"Thank God." Winfield released a sigh, then looked up at Narcisse, startled. "Forgive my impertinence."

Narcisse waved his hand as he strode into the house. "Not to worry. I understand what this village has endured in my absence."

Winfield glanced at Leona. "I'm glad to see you're well."

"Had Lord Narcisse arrived a moment later, I would have been dead."

"You know why we had to give you to Lord Kornel." Winfield looked genuinely sorry, and though Leona understood the town's predicament, she couldn't help feeling resentful.

"It was probably the greatest favor I've ever been given," Leona said. "Had you not sent me, I might never have met Lord Narcisse."

Winfield's brow furrowed with confusion, but before he could speak, Narcisse said, "Send someone for Leona's parents. We have an announcement."

"Right away, my lord." Winfield shouted for the same boy who'd taken Narcisse's horse.

While the Reeve's maid served tea, Narcisse and Leona joined Winfield at the table. Leona sat, lost in her own thoughts, while the men discussed plans for rebuilding the village.

Within moments, the boy returned with Leona's parents. Her mother, wearing a brown muslin dress, and her father, in trousers and white shirt dirty from the field, approached. They stared at Leona.

"I'm taking your daughter as my wife," Narcisse announced, his dark eyes staring hard at the couple.

Winfield and Leona's parents looked shocked, then her mother smiled.

"How wonderful! We've been so worried about her!" She approached Leona, arms outstretched. "My darling daughter."

Leona stood and slipped away. "Spare the performance, Mother. Narcisse knows you drugged me and sent me to Kornel as a sacrifice. He knows how you've treated me."

"What lies have you spun, you ungrateful little wench?" Her father's eyes bulged, teeth drawn back in an angry snarl that reminded her of Kornel. "After all we've done for you!"

"What's the matter? Angry because you've had to work the farm yourself while I've been away?" Years of rage burst forth from the depth of Leona's soul.

"This girl lies!" Her father pointed at her. "She's always been a lazy, conniving little bitch! Can't you see how hard we've worked to support her? Are these the hands of a man who doesn't know hard work?"

Narcisse grasped Leona's own callused hands and held them out. "Well these certainly don't belong to someone who lies in bed all day!"

"Are you forgetting what he is?" Leona narrowed her eyes at her parents. "Lord Narcisse can see into my mind and yours. He knows lies from the truth."

Her father's anger seemed to fade as he glanced at Narcisse with fear. Her mother took a step backward, arms folded across her chest.

"So you've come for revenge then." Her mother looked fearful. "You want to feed us to the Debrays, as we tried doing to you?"

"No," Leona said. "Even if I wanted to, the killing is over.

Narcisse has seen to that. My revenge comes from showing you what you could have shared with me, now that I'm to become a Debray. Had you shown me a bit of kindness—"

"Are you finished with us, my lord?" Leona's father ignored Leona.

"I'm not sure." Narcisse took a step toward him, his tall, muscled body dwarfing the farmer. His black eyes stared the man down. "Leona is a kind-hearted woman. She's tamed the beast in me, so to speak, and hasn't yet seen the full results of my wrath."

Leona glanced at him sharply. What was he doing? This wasn't the loving, gentle man she'd grown accustomed to. His eyes gleamed the same furious red as when he'd fought Kornel.

"What do you want from us, my lord?" Leona's father backed away, the last of his anger fading to terror.

"Please!" Her mother dropped to her knees, clutching the hem of Narcisse's black tunic. "We're poor people. We did our best to raise Leona. It was our duty to teach her the value of hard work."

"So you wouldn't have to do it. I see." Narcisse stepped away from the woman's grasp.

"That's not what I meant!"

"Then what do you mean?

"I'm a fair man. I'm willing to listen to why you've treated your only child with contempt. Why you fed her poison and handed her so easily to killers."

"Your brother inspires terror, my lord!" Leona's father sounded desperate. "We had no choice!"

"Cowardice I can forgive." Narcisse's lip curled, revealing his sharp incisors. Leona's mother trembled visibly, and her father seemed frozen where he stood. Winfield had long since disappeared to a corner of the room, staring at the vampire in terror. "Cruelty I cannot. Leona, what would you like me to do with them?"

Leona swallowed hard, for the first time fearful of Narcisse. She'd never seen this side of him, even when he'd fought with Kornel. He turned so only she could see him and winked, his lips curving upward in a quick smile. Relief flooded her, and she warmed inside. Apparently he thought her parents deserved a little frightening.

"It's enough for me, my lord, for them to know that in spite of how they've tried to make my life miserable, I've been awarded eternal happiness."

"My wife-to-be has a tender heart." Narcisse turned back to Leona's parents, his rage fading to cool disinterest. He waved his hands. "Go. We're finished with you."

They wasted no time in rushing out of the house, Leona's father nearly knocking over her mother in his haste. Neither looked back at Leona once.

"Make a list of any more supplies the village needs." Narcisse turned to the Reeve. "I'll send a servant to collect it and make sure you receive what you ask for."

Winfield bowed. "Thank you, my lord."

Narcisse took Leona's hand as they left the house.

"I think that went well, don't you?" He grinned as they approached the stallion. This time he mounted and pulled her onto the saddle behind him.

"Better than I imagined. Thank you." She slid her arms around him and pressed her cheek to his broad back.

"You can thank me properly as soon as we're out of this village."

Leona's stomach quivered at his implication, and she smiled. "So it's back to your chamber?"

"No. There's a special place behind the castle I'd like to show you."

"Sounds intriguing, my lord."

"I promise you won't be disappointed."

Chapter Nine

രാ

Leona clung to Narcisse as the stallion cantered across the moonlit meadows to a cove at the edge of the forest where the river cut a slender path through the trees.

"It's lovely," Leona said as they dismounted. He tethered the horse and guided her to the shelter of an enormous willow tree. The leaves created a canopy, sheltering them from the warm summer breeze.

Narcisse undressed, his cock swelling when he noticed her hungry eyes studying his body.

She leaned against the tree, a coquettish smile on her lips. "You look like you've been sculpted from dark marble. So strong and handsome."

"I'm a living, breathing creature, Leona." He stepped closer and took her hands, pressing them to his bare chest. His heartbeat quickened just from the sensation of her palms on his flesh.

"I know." She looked at him with tenderness. "Still, I sensed how powerful you are when we made love. It seemed as if you were restraining yourself, like you could crush me if you wanted to."

"Right now you're only mortal." He kissed her forehead. "I can't treat you as I would one of my own kind."

"But when I change, there will be no need for you to worry about hurting me." He heard her heartbeat, and her fingers tightened on his chest. "When I become immortal, I want to feel every bit of your strength. I want you to devour me. I want to draw your very essence into myself and never let you go."

His erection tightened, the engorged flesh trapped between

their bellies as he pressed her closer for a kiss.

"There's no fear in you, is there?" He whispered, his fingertips caressing the soft, pale tops of her breasts just visible above her dress's neckline.

"Only the fear that your love for me is all part of a dream and I'll awaken back in the village where no one cares about me."

"That will never happen, Leona. When you become my wife, everything I have will be yours."

"I want to touch you, Narcisse. I know how powerful you are."

"Take me, my lady. I belong only to you."

She glanced at his long, sleekly muscled body, then back to his eyes. "You belong only to me, my lord, to do with as I please?"

Her mischievous smile ensnared him. "What is it you want to do with me, Leona?" His deep voice caressed each word.

"I want you to lie beneath the frailty of these mortal hands and obey their demands as if they were weighted with iron gloves. I want you to give me complete control over you and let me pleasure you."

Narcisse's pulse leapt, and he bowed from the neck. "I'm your servant."

She sat, tugging his wrists. He sank to his knees, allowing her to push him onto his back against the packed dirt ground. Her lips covered his face with light, delicate kisses, moving down his neck and chest. She buried her face in his shoulder, her soft mouth and moist tongue caressing every inch of his throat while her fingers threaded his hair.

Sitting back on her heels, she traced the lines and planes of his face. She kneaded the muscles of his shoulders and stroked his hair until he felt so relaxed beneath her pleasant touch that he doubted he could move, even if he wanted to. She left him for a moment, and he smiled as he heard fabric rustling as she undressed. Suddenly, her smooth thighs clasped his waist. She leaned forward, kissing him deeply. Her nipples brushed his chest while her tongue thrust into his mouth, causing him to reach for her. She grasped his wrists, her strength nothing to him.

"Remember your promise, Narcisse," she whispered in his ear, her tongue encircling his lobe. He sighed with frustration, dropping his hands from her breasts.

She licked and kissed his neck and shoulders while her palms roamed over his taut, lean pectoral muscles. Her fingers clutched his biceps.

"You are the most beautiful man I've ever seen." Her lustful purr caused his heart to pound harder. Already his teeth ached for her, his entire body desperate for her blood, but she wasn't finished with him yet.

Slow, taunting kisses raked over his abdomen. Sensing where her sensual game was leading, he opened his eyes. He tried to control his breathing as her mouth hovered just above the glistening crown of his erection. She took him into the warm, wet softness of her mouth. Her tongue swirled around the bulbous head, the tip of it teasing the eye. He growled, his body tightening. She drew him deeper into her mouth until he felt the hot, slick back of her throat against his cock's sensitive head.

Unable to restrain himself any longer, he buried his fingers in the waves of her hair and moaned aloud, his head thrown back in ecstasy.

She licked and suckled the length and thickness of him as her hands grasped the globes of soft flesh beneath.

Suddenly he pulled her body on top of his, sliding her wet sheath over his shaft while his hands kneaded her breasts, thumbs circling the hardness of her nipples.

She closed her eyes, head thrown back as she rode him hard, pushing them both to the brink of passion. Placing his hands against her back, he tugged her forward to capture one of her straining nipples. His teeth pierced the tender flesh, and she cried out in surprise and desire. He licked droplets of her blood and sucked hard on her nipple, causing the first rush of orgasm. Her entire body trembled in his embrace.

Rolling her onto her back, he pumped into her as his mouth continued to purge the sweetness of her blood from her quivering breast.

He slowed his movements as the last of her climax pulsated along his cock. He slipped out, stroking hair from her face while she took a moment of rest.

Leona opened her eyes and smiled at him. "I think I liked having control over a vampire."

"You have a slave for eternity." He kissed her fingertips.

"You like this game, then?"

"I'll show you how much I like it."

Leona watched as Narcisse walked to his horse. Moonlight cast shadows on the muscles of his legs and back as he moved. Tendrils of inky hair wafted on the breeze as he took a rope from his saddlebag and returned to her.

"What's that for?" She eyed the rope suspiciously.

"For you, my lady."

"I don't understand." Momentary fear gripped her. What did he intend to do with the rope?

He handed the coil to her and walked to the tree, standing with his back against the trunk. "Tie me up."

She laughed.

"Do it," he commanded. "I'm yours entirely, Leona. Tie me up and do what you will."

"Narcisse, I don't need to—"

"I need you to." His eyes bore into hers, red lust gleaming in their depths. Moonlust. She realized their game truly excited him. Maybe after so many years of having complete power over everyone around him, he enjoyed the illusion of surrender.

"All right." She grinned. He watched as, naked, she mounted the horse and walked the animal closer to the tree. Nodding toward a low-hanging branch, she ordered, "Raise your arms."

She saw his erection leap as he did what she asked. She tied the rope around his wrists. Astride the stallion, she was able to reach the branch, and fastened the rope as tightly as she could, stretching his arms above his head. She tied several knots to ensure the rope wouldn't loosen.

Leona dismounted and stood in front of Narcisse, her heartbeat fluttering at the sight of his exquisite body stretched, bound and awaiting her touch. The muscles of his torso strained. His thighs looked like granite, his calves rounded. Most enticing of all was the engorged staff rising stiff and long from a cushion of dark, curling hair.

Leona took her lower lip between her teeth as she strolled behind him, eyes sweeping his broad back, narrow waist and steely buttocks. Unable to resist, she placed a hand to each tight globe and squeezed. He tried to look over his shoulder at her, but tied as he was, the motion proved impossible. She kissed his spine as her arms slipped around his waist, one fist grasping his balls, the other curling around his cock. She squeezed and stroked, brushing her thumb over the head. The growl dragged from his throat made her smile. Pulsing shaft still in her fist, she swept her other hand from his balls along the crack of his ass. Moving in front of him, she dropped to her knees, clutched his thighs and kissed him from hip to ankle.

Teasing him incited her own lust, and she felt moisture between her legs. Her nipples swelled, and to appease the ache, she rubbed her breasts over his hair-roughened thighs. She rose slightly and trapped his cock between her breasts, squeezing the creamy globes around his hardness.

"Leona," he breathed. She glanced up, heartbeat quickening at the pleasure etched on his handsome face. His eyes were closed, but she knew beneath the fluttering lids, they shone vampiric red.

She chuckled, and he stared at her through half open eyes. As she guessed, they glistened like candle flames against his dark skin. His teeth flashed. She gripped his pectoral muscles and slid up his body. Her tongue flickered over first one nipple, then the other. She nipped one, and he thrust his hips toward her.

Again she sank to her knees and took him in her mouth. Her tongue laved his balls and cock, lingering on the tip. She bit gently, causing him to tremble, his entire body tensing. She licked, sucked and tortured him long past the point when a mortal man would have erupted with pleasure. Yet without the taste of her blood, Narcisse's climax eluded him.

When she finally stood, she noted a sheen of sweat glistened on his smooth, dark chest. Droplets gleamed on his forehead and upper lip.

"Jump on me," he ordered, voice rough.

She hesitated, but he growled again, and she obeyed, leaping upward, her legs locking around his waist, her arms tight around his neck. She felt his cock sliding between her ass cheeks, and suddenly she wanted him inside her.

As if sensing her need, he jerked his hands downward. The thick ropes broke like sewing thread. His hands cupped her buttocks and he lowered them both to the ground.

"So much for restraining you," she panted as he thrust into her.

"It was fun while it lasted," his voice rumbled against her ear.

She couldn't speak again, as he seemed to touch everywhere at once. He nipped her shoulder, sucked and licked her breasts. His cock shot in and out of her from the front, then he rolled her onto her stomach. Wrapping one arm around her waist, he knelt behind her and tugged her hard against him. He took her from behind, thrusting with such strength and speed Leona thought she might faint from sheer excitement. His free hand moved from breast to breast, twirling her nipples and squeezing the warm globes, causing her heart to slam against her ribs. As she neared the end of her endurance, she cried out, her buttocks ramming against him as his hips bucked against her.

They collapsed in a heaving tangle of sweaty limbs. Leona lay gasping, Narcisse's chest pressed to her back, his breath hot against her cheek.

After several moments, he sat up and stroked her shoulders. "Leona."

"Umm." She murmured, not wanting to move.

"We need to go. Sunrise is coming."

She rose immediately, gazing at the dark sky in fear. The last thing she wanted was for Narcisse to be trapped in daylight.

As they dressed, she said, "This has been the happiest night of my life."

"I don't have the words to tell you how happy you've made me, Leona." He kissed her before they mounted the horse and galloped back to Castle Debray.

* * * * *

"Lord Narcisse, the Lady Sabine is missing!" A young guard rode to meet them before they reached the castle gates. "Her horse returned an hour ago, but she was not with it. We've already sent out a search party."

Leona's chest tightened with fear. If Sabine was caught in the sunlight, she'd die.

"It's almost dawn." Narcisse cast a terrified look skyward. "Just like what happened to Ann."

He lowered Leona from the saddle and turned his horse back out of the gates, kicking it to a gallop.

"Narcisse!" Leona shouted, her eyes wide with horror. What if he was caught in the sunlight?

She rushed to the stables, ordered a horse to be saddled, and rode out into the dawn to find him. The thought of losing him when they scarcely had any time at all together was far too painful.

"Leona!"

She turned abruptly at the gates and stared back at Evi. Beneath the hood of a black wool cloak, the Priestess' face looked tense with worry.

"Beware, young one. I sense it is not an accident that prevented Lady Sabine's return."

"Kornel?" Leona asked, trying to keep fear from her voice.

"Take great care."

Leona nodded and galloped off in the same direction as Narcisse.

Chapter Ten

ɞ

As the sun rose higher in the morning sky, Leona's fear for Narcisse mounted. Just hours ago she had rested contentedly in the strongest arms she'd ever known. Now, beneath the brilliance of the daylight, his strength could be sapped, leaving behind only ashes and bones of the beautiful man she loved.

And Sabine! Sweet, lovely Sabine might also be dead.

Urging the horse toward the mountains in the distance, she hoped the brother and sister had found refuge in the darkness of a cave where they could await twilight.

She nearly wept with relief when she heard the whinny of Narcisse's stallion and saw the animal waiting at the mouth of a cave nestled high in the rocks.

Leona dismounted and climbed toward the jagged opening, feeling awed and apprehensive as she stepped inside. This is no ordinary cave, she thought to herself.

The first few feet shone dimly with the sunlight, but she couldn't discern the depth of the cave, since the farthest walls were hidden in blackness.

"Leona?"

Her heart pounded in her breast and she ran forward several steps before stopping, unable to see.

"Narcisse? Where are you?"

"Here." A hand on her shoulder caused her to jump.

She reached for him and heard him gasp, as if her touch caused him pain.

"What is it?"

"Nothing. I'm fine." He took her hand. "Follow me."

She did so, walking with him into utter darkness. His hand felt hot and sticky beneath hers, and though he endured her touch in silence, she sensed his discomfort. "Sit."

She did as he commanded and found herself on a smooth stone floor, her back resting against a rock wall.

"Narcisse, I know you've been hurt. Is it the sun?"

"I've just been burned a little. But I made it here in time. I only hope Sabine was able to find shelter, wherever she is."

"How can I help you?" Leona reached for him, then thought better of it, fearful of hurting him more.

"I'll be fine. We heal quickly." His voice sounded weary. She guessed remaining awake in daylight was difficult, especially when wounded. "Are you warm enough, Leona? I know these caves are always cold."

"I'm fine. I brought my cloak."

"Get some rest then."

"I can't rest when I know you're hurt. Would it help if I gave you more blood?"

More blood! She had no idea how enticing the thought, how much he needed nourishment. He'd reached the safety of the temple before the sun had rendered him too weak to move, but his entire body still throbbed. His face and hands had been so scorched, his flesh had peeled back in places, exposing bone. Her blood could hurry the healing process and end most of his pain.

"I took enough last night. I won't make you sick for my sake."

"A little more won't hurt me, and I'll have all day to rest here with you."

She strained to see him in the dark, her face etched with worry. Love for her overwhelmed him. He'd thought to suffer through the day, his thirst for healing blood almost as painful as the burns on his flesh. Now she sat beside him, offering what he most craved, but he cared too much for her to risk taking another drop of her blood. Not until she recovered from what he'd taken earlier when they'd made love.

"Just rest, Leona," he whispered, the burned skin on his hand and wrist pulling tightly as he touched her face.

She moved closer to him, tilting back her head, exposing her pale throat in the darkness. "Last night you said you were my servant, my lord. I'm also yours. We serve each other through love. Now drink my blood so we can rest today and continue searching for Sabine at nightfall."

"I won't." His eyes squeezed shut, and he turned from her.

Suddenly the aroma of her blood filled the temple. His eyes fixed on the crimson line she'd cut, using the sharp end of a brooch, across the back of her hand. Though the wound wasn't deep, the red blood welling on flesh tempted him beyond endurance. A droplet trickled down her thumb but before the precious liquid could fall, wasted, to the ground, he bent forward and licked her hand.

The blood tasted warm and luscious on his tongue, and as he licked and suckled upon her hand, he felt his flesh healing, the pain replaced by pleasure.

Entranced by bloodlust, his kisses moved to her neck, teeth penetrating the tiny holes left from the previous night.

"Narcisse," she murmured, clutching his head closer and locking her legs around his waist. He caught the scent of her lust as she climaxed, simply from the motion of his lips and teeth on her neck.

Her heartbeat skipped, and he stopped drinking.

"Leona?" He shook her gently, but she lay in his arms, lost in a pleasurable swoon that might have cost her life.

Furious at his own selfishness, he placed Leona gently aside and lit a fire that brightened and warmed the chilly cave. She'd need the heat, particularly after sharing so much blood with him. Narcisse sat with his back against the wall, Leona's head on his lap. He stroked tendrils of soft, auburn hair from her pale face.

"How sweet!" a voice hissed from across the temple.

Narcisse's eyes flew to the doorway behind the altar where Kornel stood, illuminated by the reddish glow of firelight from the Priestess' private chamber. Dressed in black and silver armor and carrying a jeweled sword, he leered at the couple.

"Kornel," Narcisse stood, gently placing Leona aside, "what are you doing here?"

"Waiting for you. I knew when Sabine didn't return you'd come looking for her."

"Where is she?" Narcisse demanded.

"I didn't count on the peasant slut following you, however." Kornel cast a scathing look at Leona. "She's made my life more difficult by giving you back the strength the sun took, but she'll pay for that."

"Kornel, look at yourself. What's happened to you?" Narcisse's brow furrowed as he and his brother circled each other.

"I've finally had enough, that's what!" Kornel raged, his eyes glowing red in the darkness. "All my life I've had to listen to how wise you are and how good you are. What is the point of being good? It doesn't get you anything. No one respects good men. They only tear at their pathetic souls until someone truly powerful takes all they have. Like I'm going to do to you."

"You'll never have the Debray lands." Narcisse moved between Leona and his brother. "Even if I have to live here for eternity, you'll never have them."

"I'm finished being lenient." Kornel snarled. "I've waited, hoping you would go on your own. I couldn't denounce you at the castle. Too many of our worthless people are loyal to you. Augustus was the only one I could tempt to follow me." Kornel ran his tongue over his sharp teeth. "I had to get you alone."

"Get me alone? So that you can kill me? Kornel, we're brothers!"

"Through no fault of mine!" Kornel drew his sword and flew at Narcisse.

Though unarmed, Narcisse was able to dodge his brother's powerful blows. Instead of flesh, the sword struck the temple walls, spraying bits of rock.

"Kornel, this is madness!" Narcisse bellowed, rage devouring the shred of affinity he'd once felt for his brother.

"Why? Because for once I have the power and you must bow to my whims?" Saliva dripped from Kornel's teeth. "What's the point of being immortal if we can't use our strength to instill fear in human slaves? Once I have control over the Debray lands, I'll rule in a manner befitting our kind!"

Kornel lunged at Narcisse who dropped to the ground, kicking his brother off balance. Kornel fell backward and Narcisse leapt on him, wrestling for possession of the sword.

"Augustus!" Kornel bellowed when Narcisse succeeded in pinning him to the ground, the sword flying from both their grasps.

Augustus' huge form emerged from the doorway at the back of the temple, completely overshadowing Sabine who stood locked in his bulky embrace, a sword pressed just below her chin.

"Release me or watch our sister die!" Kornel spat, a malicious gleam in his red-tinged eyes.

Narcisse's lips drew back over his glistening incisors, torn between desire to rip Kornel to shreds and fear of Sabine's fate if he did so.

Augustus' dull eyes watched the brothers, his sword pressing harder to Sabine's pale throat.

"Don't worry about me, Narcisse." Sabine's voice trembled, though with fear or rage Narcisse couldn't tell.

"If you'll excuse the expression, her blood will be on your hands, brother." Kornel smiled viciously.

Suddenly a rock struck Augustus' face. His head snapped

back as blood dripped down his cheek. Though more stunned than hurt, he momentarily dropped his hold on Sabine. She struck the back of her fist into the monster's groin, using every bit of her own vampiric strength. Even a beast like Augustus wasn't immune to such pain. He lurched forward, groaning as Sabine snatched the sword from his loosened grip and raced to Leona who had awakened in time to throw the rock.

Narcisse and Kornel continued struggling. Kornel managed to wedge his knee between himself and Narcisse and tossed off the older vampire. Narcisse crashed into a wall while Kornel scrambled for the sword, reaching it just as Augustus regained himself enough to join the attack.

"Narcisse!" Sabine screamed, tossing her eldest brother the sword she'd taken from Augustus.

Narcisse caught it in time to deflect an overhead blow from Kornel.

"Leona, run!" Narcisse shouted. "Take my horse and go! You'll be safe by daylight!"

"No! I won't leave you!"

"It doesn't matter whether she runs or not!" Kornel taunted. "Once you're dead, I'll find her. Augustus, take those women deeper into the temple. We'll feast on them later. We'll drain the mortal one of her very essence, and when we're done with my sweet little sister, we'll leave her body to burn in the daylight!"

Augustus moved toward the women and Narcisse followed, dodging and blocking the deadly assault from Kornel.

"Split up!" Leona called to Sabine, and the two women rushed to opposite ends of the cave, leaving Augustus pondering over which to chase first.

"The mortal! Get the mortal, you colossal idiot!" Kornel shouted above the clash of swords. He glared at Narcisse. "I want to kill the peasant slut in front of your dying eyes so you can witness what you missed with your last wife. It was a pleasure destroying her."

"You killed Ann?" Narcisse drew a sharp breath, his hand tightening on his sword, his heart throbbing with fury.

"Yes. I wasn't about to let that bitch give you a child to take land that's rightfully mine! But it was even more than that. I enjoyed fucking her while she was tied, spread-eagled in the field. I wonder if she ever cried as loudly for you, Narcisse? She tasted so delicious. Every scream as she died, every plea for her life, I'll treasure forever. My only regret is that I had to watch her burn from the shelter of a cave, and couldn't remain awake long enough to see her flesh shrivel completely from her body."

"You bastard!" The ferocity of Narcisse's attack on Kornel took the other man off guard. The taunting look on Kornel's face turned to one of horror. His eyes gleamed madly like a man who suddenly realized that no creature is truly immortal.

"Augustus!" He bellowed, but the giant had already caught Leona in his arms. The beast lowered his yellow fangs to her shoulder as his rancid breath rushed hot and sour in her face.

Leona clawed at him, but her attack only seemed to entice him. Sabine raced across the cave and leapt on the monster's back. Her claws ripped his scalp, but he reached over his shoulder and grasped her hair. He yanked her off him and flung her to the cave floor.

Narcisse turned from Kornel and rushed toward Leona, striking Augustus in the back of the head with the butt of his sword before the creature's foul teeth pierced her flesh.

Kornel's blade thrust at Narcisse from behind, but the elder Debray dropped to the ground and Kornel's sword sliced through Augustus' heart instead.

The monster's eyes widened in horror and agony before he fell backward onto the stone floor.

Narcisse's blade slashed Kornel's sword arm, and the younger man dropped his weapon. Kornel staggered, holding his arm. Blood dripped into the puddle already spreading from Augustus' body.

"All those years you watched me grieve for Ann, and it was

you who killed her." Narcisse snarled, the point of his sword hovering over Kornel's heart.

"Are you going to kill me?" Kornel goaded, though the wildness in his eyes belied his fear. "Try explaining that to our parents!"

"You were prepared to kill me and Sabine, and I'm supposed to ponder whether or not I should destroy you?"

"Where is your goodness, brother? Your mercy?" Kornel simpered, backed up to the wall and clenched the jagged rock with his good hand.

"You'll get the same mercy you gave Leona, Ann and all your other victims!"

With a final, desperate act, Kornel raked several loose pieces of rock from the wall and tossed them into Narcisse's face.

Temporarily blinded, Narcisse stepped back, swiping tears from his stinging eyes. Kornel drew a dagger from his boot and thrust it at Narcisse's chest.

"Narcisse!" Leona screamed a warning.

Still blinded, he swung with the sword, piercing Kornel's heart just before the dagger struck home.

Kornel dropped to his knees, the blade falling from his hand.

Blinking tears from his scraped eyes, Narcisse released the sword, and backed away from his brother's lifeless body.

Leona crawled to Sabine who sat weeping, tendrils of black hair in disarray about her face. Leona embraced her.

"How could this have happened?" Sabine cried.

Leona raised her sorrowful eyes to Narcisse. He opened his hands helplessly. "Sabine, I—"

"How could Kornel have done that to us? To Ann?" Sabine held out her hand to Narcisse who knelt beside the women, taking both of them in his arms.

"We still have several hours before the sun sets," Leona

said, feeling weak now that the danger had passed. "Perhaps I should ride for help?"

"Absolutely not." Narcisse picked her up and carried her to the Priestess' chamber. Sabine followed close behind as they stepped over the bodies of Augustus and Kornel.

He placed her on the Priestess' austere wooden bed and covered her with a wool blanket. "I want you to rest."

"Narcisse's right." Sabine wiped her eyes with the back of her hand.

"Both of you stay here," Narcisse said. "I'll see to the bodies."

"Narcisse, you're not to blame for any of this," Sabine told him as she slipped onto the bed next to Leona.

He didn't reply. He'd never felt so horrible in his life. Why hadn't he seen the monster Kornel had become years ago? If he hadn't been such a fool, Ann and his child might still be alive. Leona wouldn't have been abducted. But they also might never have met, and she deserved a better life than the one she had in the village.

Leona reached for his hand, and he squeezed hers, gazing into her eyes.

"I love you, Narcisse," she said. He realized her love was enough to truly begin the mending of his anguished soul.

Chapter Eleven

෨

While Leona and Sabine slept, Narcisse tossed the bodies outside.

He watched from the shelter of the cave as they burned, eventually leaving only bones and ashes that were carried away by the wind.

At dusk, the three traveled back to the Debray lands, but were met halfway by Evi. She gazed at them from astride a pale gray mare she'd borrowed from Narcisse's stable. The Priestess' expression alone told them she knew what had happened, but Narcisse still felt compelled to tell her.

"Kornel and Augustus... They died in the temple." He met her gaze in spite of the shame he felt for using a place of worship as a battleground. "I killed Kornel."

"It was a sanctuary. He chose to make it otherwise," Evi said.

"I know how wrong it is for lives to be taken in a religious place," Leona said, "but Narcisse acted to defend us."

"I understand," Evi replied. "Narcisse, unlike his brother, takes his sins seriously. I will pray for the spirits of those who have left us and for those still living."

Leona glanced at Narcisse. "If you feel you want to postpone our wedding, I'll understand."

"Wait not a moment longer," Evi ordered. "The time for hatred and anger is over. A love such as yours should be nurtured, not delayed. Bring forth heirs and raise them to be compassionate as you are. Then the Debray line shall increase in strength while others fall into despair. The likes of Kornel have destroyed the reputation of our kind, but through you, we'll survive and prosper among the mortals who outnumber us in this world."

"I agree," Sabine told the lovers. "It's time for you to be happy. Both of you. No more battles. No more threats."

"I don't think we can argue." Narcisse gazed into Leona's face with a tender smile touched with sadness and joy she well understood.

"Tomorrow evening I will perform the ceremony," Evi announced. "Now I must cleanse my temple, and Narcisse, you must prepare your bride."

"Gladly." He brushed Leona's mouth with a gentle, promising kiss.

"And I have so many preparations to make!" Sabine kicked her horse ahead, calling over her shoulder. "See you later tonight."

"What did Evi mean when she said you must prepare your bride?" Leona slipped her hand into his.

"If it's still what you want, it's time for you to become one of us, Leona."

Her heartbeat quickened with fear, anticipation and excitement.

"Are you certain you're ready?"

"Yes." She locked her arms around his neck and kissed him. "Oh yes."

* * * * *

A bath awaited them in Narcisse's chamber. They discarded their soiled clothes, slipped into the warm, herb-scented water and rested in each other's arms. The gentle lapping of the water on their skin felt soothing as Leona closed her eyes, cheek pressed to Narcisse's chest.

"You're sure this is what you want?" he whispered against the damp, auburn waves of her hair. "Even after you've witnessed the evil our kind is capable of?"

She turned her face up to his, her arms tightening about his waist. "I love you, Narcisse Debray. I know I want to become immortal and spend the rest of my life with you."

"I'll make you happy, Leona. No matter what happens, my heart will always be yours."

"Show me," she whispered, taking his face in her hands and touching her mouth to his. "Show me."

He stood and lifted her in his arms, not caring that they trailed water from the tub to the bed. As he placed her on the cool sheets soon to be warmed by their lovemaking, he kissed her with all the tenderness he felt.

"The making of a vampire is a very delicate task," he whispered close to her ear, his breath a warm caress on her neck. "Everything must be perfect, the timing, the exchange of blood, the emotions. Do you trust me, Leona?"

"With my life." She closed her eyes, her hands threading the hair at his nape.

He kissed her mouth, her throat and her shoulders while his palms cupped her breasts. His thumbs brushed her sensitive nipples to alertness. Gently at first, he let his mind touch hers, as he had on the first night they'd met. He felt her stiffen a bit at the contact.

It's all right, his thoughts reassured her, *this is the beginning for us, Leona. All our thoughts and memories are shared. Know how much I love you.*

Then you must know how much I love you. Her thoughts, soft at first, grew in power as she became accustomed to the mind sharing.

I do. It's a magnificent feeling, your love.

As he touched her, he ignored the lustful demands of his own body, but listened to the rhythm of her heart and felt the surge of blood beneath her skin.

His palm stroked her womanhood before he slipped his fingers inside her, gathering moisture that he used to caress her where she most desired. She moaned softly as he slipped inside her, hips thrusting. He moved within her, his thoughts as well as his body urging her toward orgasm. With their minds joined, he could drive her past the limits of her mortal body and she wouldn't notice any fatigue or pain, only joy. Such was the trick of creating a vampire. He would urge her to the brink of death, then give her a new kind of life. It wouldn't be an easy task, however. He couldn't drink her blood or allow his own release until their bodies achieved perfect union.

He felt her climax, his hips driving into her, pushing her toward a second orgasm before she fully recovered from the first.

Her heart raced, and she clung to him as he pushed her over the edge again, then a third time.

Her heart throbbed harder, faster. His mind caressed hers, sharing thoughts of what his own vampiric climaxes felt like, endless, waves of pleasure more intense than any mortal could feel.

He lost count of how many times she peaked when his own pleasure became so intense that he struggled to keep from taking her blood.

Leona shook beneath him. Sweat poured from their flesh, adhering their bodies and drenching the sheets. He licked her throat, running his tongue along every vein and tendon that strained against her slick flesh. The sound of her panting breath excited him. His cock felt so sensitive the thrusting was almost painful, and he briefly wondered if a vampire could also die from the intensity of creating another. If such was the case, this was the way to perish!

Their heartbeats finally matched in intensity, and he heard hers falter. Her arms, having lost strength ages ago, rested limply on the bed. She whimpered as she reached another orgasm. The moment before her heart stopped, he pierced her throat and drank.

Narcisse felt life flow from her body while her blood rushed, hot and powerful, through him. He knew it was that critical moment when she could either die the death of mortals or share with him the unknown adventures of the long years to come.

He lifted his mouth from her throat long enough to bite the fleshy part of his palm and hold it to her lips, forcing life into her body before her spirit fled to the nether world. Slowly she awakened, clinging to him as she took nourishment with the vigor of a newly made vampire. She sank her teeth into his shoulder, drinking deeply. Narcisse couldn't contain himself any longer. He cried out as orgasm ripped through him, more intense than any he'd felt before.

* * * * *

Leona felt her spirit reclaiming her body, felt her strength return with ferocity she'd never known. Her hands clutched Narcisse's sweat-slicked back, and she gulped his sweet, thick blood.

She kept her eyes tightly shut to experience every new sensation, opening them only when the source of her nourishment slipped from her grasp. She found herself staring at Narcisse, but with new and keener vision.

She gasped in surprise, gazing at the brightness of the room and the beauty of the man beside her.

"Drink, Leona," he said, his voice husky with desire as he tilted his neck, exposing his pulsing, blood-streaked throat. She slipped her hands over his heated flesh, feeling the blood throbbing beneath her fingertips. One of her hands pressed his neck close to her lips while the other encircled his still-engorged cock. She bit him and was rewarded not only by fresh blood flow but by another cry of pleasure as he climaxed a second time, his essence streaking their flesh while his blood washed over her teeth and tongue.

Narcisse tugged her on top of him as she drank until satisfied.

Leona licked the wounds on his throat, her hands loosening

on his shoulders, her nails sticky with blood from the ridges her death grip had carved in his flesh. She had been so lost in the initial passion of bloodlust that she realized she hadn't shown him a bit of the gentleness he'd always shown her. She hadn't concerned herself with his comfort—only with quenching her thirst.

By the depth of his sighs and the pounding of his heart, she realized with relief that he'd felt nothing but pleasure.

She licked the last droplets of blood from his throat and continued licking and kissing down to his navel. While she licked his taut abdomen, her hands stroked the heavy, hair-roughed muscles of his thighs.

"I'm sorry if I hurt you." She looked at him. He wrapped several silky strands of her auburn hair around his fist, gently guiding her mouth back to his.

"You didn't hurt me at all, rather the contrary." His eyes burned into hers. "I want to feel how strong you are, Leona. I can take anything–I mean anything–you have to give me."

"Good." She straddled his waist, sheathing his pulsing erection in her heat and kissing him with lust that was almost animalistic in its nature.

She controlled their pleasure until the moment when her body quaked hotly upon his. Then he pushed her onto her back, his own passion pouring into her. They clung to each other with strength that would have crushed a mortal man and woman.

"I love you, Narcisse." She panted, utterly drained, but more completely satisfied than she'd ever felt.

He rolled onto his back and drew her into his languid embrace. "I love you, Leona. For eternity."

* * * * *

They wed in the courtyard of Debray Castle with a few trusted servants and Sabine bearing witness to their union.

Leona looked beautiful in the dress of gold silk that she,

Sabine, and her maids had spent endless hours preparing.

Leona stood beside Narcisse, listening to the words of the Priestess, her hand enfolded in his.

"Life is a journey of hills and valleys for us and for mortals," Evi said. "We cannot know joy without pain, and we cannot learn without folly. Before me stand two for whom I ask the favor of the shining moon and glowing stars as they are wed for eternity. Woman of the sacred moon, do you promise to love and protect this man and remain true to him, no matter what you might face?"

"Yes." Leona smiled at Narcisse. "I promise."

"Man of the revered stars, do you promise to love and protect this woman and remain true to her, no matter what you might face?"

"I promise." Narcisse's hand tightened on Leona's.

Evi opened her arms wide to the sky. "You are forever wed. Peace and happiness to you."

Narcisse drew Leona into his arms and kissed her beneath the brilliance of the full moon.

"Welcome to the Debray family." Sabine embraced Leona and kissed her cheek.

"Thank you," Leona held her sister-in-law tightly, "for everything."

Sabine hugged Narcisse before excusing herself to see to the wedding feast she'd planned. Soon the newly married couple was left alone in the courtyard, except for the company of the Priestess.

"Evi, thank you." Narcisse bowed from the neck.

"It was my pleasure, as it will be my pleasure to welcome the forthcoming heir in the Debray line."

Narcisse and Leona looked at each other, then back to the Priestess.

"It is true. I'm old enough to sense these things." Evi took each of their hands in her cool grasp, and they felt the reality of her words. "You're carrying his child, Leona, a very rare and wonderful gift for our kind."

The Priestess turned from them and went to join the celebration in the great hall.

For a moment the couple stared at each other in stunned silence, then Narcisse swept Leona into his arms and smiled without a hint of sadness. Leona's belly churned with pleasure. His true smile was every bit as beautiful as she'd imagined.

He kissed her. "I love you, Leona Debray."

"And I love you, Narcisse." She clung to him. "Now and forever."

The End

Moonlust Privateer

Prologue

"We were trapped between silver-tipped spears and sunrise. If we didn't escape within moments…well, you can only imagine what would happen." Narcisse Debray's gaze swept from his wife to his sister as they sat by the fireplace in the great hall of Castle Debray. Both women stared at him, tension heavy on the air.

"So tell us what happened!" Leona Debray edged her chair closer to her husband and clutched his wrist.

"Finish the story, Narcisse!" Sabine flashed fangs in her brother's direction. "Obviously we know you and Captain Donovan didn't burn."

"It was time for desperate measures," Narcisse continued, an amused smile on his lips. "Those islanders were ready to spear us through the heart, then Galen Donovan made the ultimate sacrifice."

"What?" Both women shouted.

"He seduced the tribal Queen and convinced her to let us go."

Leona dropped her hand from Narcisse and raised her eyes to heaven.

Sabine wondered if she looked as disgusted as her sister-in-law. "I'm sure it was a horrible sacrifice, bedding down the tribal Queen."

"I'll take into consideration you two have never traveled to the islands. The Queen had Donovan up for the entire day performing worse than a carnival acrobat."

Leona slapped Narcisse's arm, her face flushed as if she'd just taken blood. "Mind your tongue, my lord!"

"No, it's his friend who'd better mind his tongue." Sabine didn't try to keep the disgust from her voice. "Honestly, Narcisse, the tales you tell about this man are shameful and repulsive."

"But interesting." Leona looked thoughtful. "I rather hope to one day meet Captain Donovan."

"I wouldn't want him near you," Narcisse growled, grasping Leona's forearms and tugging her out of her chair and onto his lap. He nibbled her earlobe until she giggled.

"I certainly have no desire to meet him." Sabine folded her arms across her chest and gazed into the fire. "He sounds like a filthy, arrogant jackass."

"Filthy and arrogant, maybe," Narcisse reached for a goblet of wine and offered the first sip to Leona, "but never a jackass. Together we got through many difficult situations. Galen is not only an excellent military strategist, but fluent in over twelve languages."

"If he's such a wondrous man, then why is he a pirate?" Sabine asked.

"Probably because he has no scruples," Leona said.

Sabine smiled. "Of that I'm certain. Honestly, Narcisse, I don't know how a man of your station could have befriended such a rogue."

"When you're on the high seas, station doesn't matter."

"It would if you let it." Sabine lifted her chin. "And all those women he bedded. They must have been desperate. Even the tribal Queen."

Narcisse shrugged. "Most women find the Captain quite attractive."

"For a bore."

"As attractive as he might be, he must have had difficulty outshining you, my love." Leona slipped her arms around Narcisse's neck and kissed his swarthy cheek.

Lord Debray brushed the tip of his nose against his wife's. "And no tribal Queen could ever possess your charms."

Sabine gazed at the loving couple and sighed. She was very happy her brother and Leona had found one another, but at times she couldn't help feeling a bit jealous. Sabine had never had a lover—even a mortal one. She'd always been content riding, swimming, decorating Castle Debray and designing dresses with her sister-in-law and servants. Though she knew most others of her age and her kind had long since exercised their lust over unsuspecting mortal men and women, Sabine took her nourishment from sleeping children, leaving them alive and well, with pleasant dreams. Killing offended her, and though many strong youths lived in the neighboring village, she hadn't found one with whom she'd like to share a bed as well as blood. Her mother had always told her such feelings would come in time. She was still very young for one of her kind, and there was a whole world of beautiful males for her to search.

"Perhaps I'll see one of those tribal Queens in our travels." Leona's words caused Sabine to turn around in the middle of what she'd hoped to be a discreet exit.

"Travels?" she asked.

"Yes, Sabine, we wanted to talk to you about that," Narcisse said as he and Leona stood. "With our child due in several months, we hoped to travel before its arrival."

"When will you be leaving?" Sabine wondered if her surprise shone on her face.

"The day after tomorrow. We want you to join us," Narcisse said.

Sabine laughed. "No. You were married only a few weeks ago and have yet to have a wedding trip. I will not go with you."

"But we want you to come." Leona squeezed Sabine's hand. "We'll have so much fun."

"Absolutely not," Sabine said. "You should be alone."

"Sabine, it's been difficult for us all since the incident with Kornel. We don't want to leave you here, surrounded by memories of his death—"

"Narcisse, Kornel tried to kill the three of us, and he almost succeeded. Yes, I miss the illusion of what I'd hoped our brother was, but I was wrong about him, and so were you. It's been no more difficult for me than it has been for you or Leona. In truth, I could use the time alone here to sort out my own life."

"You're sure?" Leona narrowed her eyes.

"Yes." Sabine smiled, embracing her sister-in-law. "I want both of you to go and have a wonderful time."

Narcisse looked skeptical. "I don't like the idea of leaving you alone."

"Narcisse, please." Sabine hugged him. "You're a wonderful brother. You've always taken care of me, but how many times have I told you I'm a woman now? I can take care of myself. And even if I couldn't, what could happen to me here on our own lands?"

Narcisse's dark eyes held hers. He touched her cheek. "I can't help thinking of you as a child, but I know I have to be realistic. You're sure you'll be all right?"

"I'm positive. I want you both to have a wonderful journey, and when you come back, everything will be in the same order you left it."

Chapter One
Two Days Later

శ

Sabine tilted her head, a blue-tipped brush dangling between her fingers, and stared at her canvas then to the jade vase filled with luscious pink roses she'd been painting. Firelight flickered beside her, warming her against the castle's chill.

"What do you think, Meg?" Sabine asked the plump blonde woman seated at the table, embroidering. Though a servant of the Debrays, Meg had grown up alongside Sabine. Meg was the only mortal Sabine knew who didn't fear her, and Sabine appreciated the closeness between them—closeness that many of her class would frown upon.

The servant looked up, narrowing pale blue eyes at the painting. "Lovely, miss. The colors look a bit brighter in your work than how the petals look to me, but I see through human eyes."

"And beautiful eyes they are." Sabine's lips curved upward slightly. "If you'd like vampiric ones, however, I can try to arrange it."

"Oh no, miss! Not now, at least. I'm still young enough to stay human for a while. Maybe when I feel time creeping up on me, I'll come to you for the favor."

"You wouldn't want it from me, Meg." Sabine laughed. "When the time comes, we'll find you a handsome man with fangs like a young wolf and arms powerful enough to die in."

"You make it sound almost tempting."

"From the stories I've heard, it can be." Sabine looked far off as she thought about the bawdy tales she'd heard from her deceased brother, Kornel. Most of the time his stories had sickened and embarrassed her, but the times he'd detailed the passion between vampire and mortal, feelings other than embarrassment had caused her to heat. And, on the night Narcisse had made Leona immortal, Sabine had heard their cries of rapture before she'd banished herself for a walk through the vaults below the castle. It hadn't been right to listen to such intimacy.

Sabine was considered quite young for a vampire, but old enough to finally desire a mate, either mortal or vampire.

"Love would be wonderful with the right man, I suppose." Meg shrugged. "Like marriage."

"Speaking of marriage, how are the plans for your wedding?"

"Wonderful. Harold and I will marry in the spring. I'm so pleased you'll attend."

"I wouldn't miss it."

"You have to be there, miss. If it hadn't been for you convincing Kornel not to slaughter me last year—" Meg took her lower lip between her teeth and cursed softly. "I'm sorry, my lady. I shouldn't have mentioned it."

Sabine shook her head and sighed. "It's all right, Meg. We must mention him sometime. Kornel was my brother, but he was a wicked man. Narcisse and I have both accepted that."

"The sun will be rising soon, miss. Would you like me to ready your bedchamber?"

"It's not necessary. Get some rest, Meg. I'm going to finish my painting before I retire."

Meg nodded, collected her embroidery, and left for the servants' quarters. Though many of the servants of Castle Debray were human, they kept the same hours as their immortal masters.

Other than a fat brown cat cleaning himself in a corner, Sabine was alone in the great hall. The heavy velvet drapes had been drawn earlier, but through the cracks, Sabine noted the glow of dawn. She sighed, wondering how it would feel to walk in daylight. She'd looked out at it, seen its almost painful brightness wash over the meadows, but her kind couldn't endure direct sunlight. Their flesh would blister and burn, and with prolonged exposure, would dissolve to the bone.

It wasn't a desperate craving, to feel daylight, but rather a perverse curiosity, like a human wondering how it would feel to slice her own wrists or swallow poison, just to experience those final, intense moments before death.

As Sabine added a few last strokes to the painting, the sunlight bleeding through the curtain dimmed, followed by the sound of rain pelting the castle walls. Thunder rumbled in the distance.

Sabine enjoyed the sound of the storm as she cleaned her supplies and packed them away. By the time she'd finished, the rain had stopped, and the songs of morning birds caused her to smile.

Tapping sounded on the door, and Sabine's brow furrowed. The guards knew better than to allow anyone through the gates at dawn, and if Narcisse and Leona had returned, they would have the key.

The tapping echoed again, and Sabine approached the door. Her heartbeat quickened when she caught the strong scent of another vampire—an unfamiliar vampire. Meg, in her white nightgown, her feet bare, hurried down the stone steps, candle-in hand, but Sabine had already flung open the door. A tall, cloaked figure stood on the cobbled walk. Sunlight caused Sabine to momentarily lose her focus, but after a moment her eyes adjusted and she stared up at her visitor in wonder. His face was pale—far too pale even for one of her kind—but handsome enough to quicken her pulse. Eyes of such dark blue that at a quick glance they appeared black gazed at her through tendrils of drenched sable hair. His nose was straight and well-formed, his cheekbones seemed chiseled by the most talented sculptor. The tips of his strong, white fangs shone against a full lower lip. Most alluring of all was his blood scent. It was so intoxicating, so rich, that Sabine might have thought he bore an open wound.

Meg stood beside Sabine, and by her expression, was as entranced as her mistress by the man's raw beauty. "May we help you, sir?"

"I'm looking for Narcisse Debray." His voice was deep, yet almost musical, the tone perfect for mortal and immortal ears alike.

"Narcisse is away," Sabine said. "Perhaps I could be of help. I'm his sister."

"Sabine?" The man's lips flickered upward slightly. "Narcisse spoke of you often. And your brother, Kornel."

"Kornel's dead."

His smile faded. "I'm sorry."

"Don't be." Sabine stepped aside. "Please come in. The walkway offers little protection against the sunlight."

The man strode past her, and she suddenly realized she had no idea who he was. She'd invited him inside out of empathy for one of her own kind left to burn in sunlight, but she knew nothing about him.

"My name is Galen Donovan. I'm a friend of Narcisse's. I doubt he ever mentioned me."

Galen Donovan! Of all the arrogant, self-absorbed rogues in the world, she would have to choose the worst of the lot to ogle like a puppy in love!

"He spoke of you briefly." Sabine wasn't sure why she lied, but for some reason she couldn't bring herself to admit all the stories Narcisse had told about the men's adventures.

"Would you like a warm drink, sir?" Meg asked. "The fall weather has been terrible this year."

"Yes. Thank you." This time Sabine noted Galen's smile appeared strained as the maid left the hall. He sank into the chair by the fire as if he owned the place. "When do you expect Narcisse to return?"

"Not for at least a month."

The Captain drew a long, slow breath and murmured, "A month."

"I don't believe Narcisse was expecting you."

"This isn't a planned visit. I'm sorry to intrude — especially at this hour."

"I was about to retire, however I'll have a room readied for you to spend the day."

"I'll see to it, miss." Meg had stepped from the kitchen, carrying a steaming mug that she set in front of Captain Donovan. He nodded his thanks, dark eyes meeting the maid's. Meg blushed and curtsied before hurrying up the stairs.

"Prepare the first room on the left in the west wing, Meg!" Sabine called.

"Yes, miss!"

"The west wing." Another smile played around the Captain's mouth. "Sounds appealing, my lady, however I won't stay."

Sabine's eyes widened. "You can't leave now. It's daylight."

"I can and I will, unless you don't mind having a corpse in your guest room."

"What do you mean?"

"I came to your brother for help, but it seems my luck has finally run out. Unless you'd share your sweet blood." Galen slipped a hand from his cloak and reached out to Sabine's cheek. She gasped, noting the fresh blood staining his large, long-fingered hand.

"You're bleeding," she said, the thought of his injury both concerning and arousing.

"I'm dying." He swallowed, Adam's apple moving in a throat that begged to be bitten. "But I won't do it in your hall."

He stood, hand slipping back beneath his cloak and pressing against his ribs. He nearly reached the door when he stumbled to his knees.

Sabine's heartbeat quickened as she slipped an arm around his waist and helped him to his feet. His body felt hard, reminding her of the lean, muscled stallions in the Debray stable. "You can't leave if you're injured. Meg!"

The maid, hearing her mistress's frantic shout, raced halfway down the steps.

"Bring some warm water. Captain Donovan has been injured."

"There's no need—"

"Quiet. I'll help you to your room." Sabine supported him as they made their way up the steps.

"What happened?" she asked.

"It's a long story that I'm not up to telling right now."

"I understand, but at least tell me what sort of injury."

"A silver arrowhead."

By the time they reached the top of the stairs, Galen's breathing was ragged and his face even paler than before. Instead of guiding him all the way to the west wing, Sabine turned toward her own chamber, just down the hall. He eased himself onto the bed and lay still, catching his breath.

Sabine wasted no time before unfastening his cloak. The white shirt beneath was stained with blood, though she saw the outline of bandages beneath. She tugged the garment over his head. He uttered a sharp breath and then fell silent. Sabine tried to ignore his muscled arms and sleek, hair matted chest as she used sewing scissors to cut away the soiled bandage. The man was wounded! How could desire even cross her mind? But it was hard not to think about it when the aroma of his blood permeated the room.

Though the silver arrowhead had been removed, the wound—deep on his left side—festered from the poisonous reaction of the silver.

"From the position of the wound, your heart might be affected—"

"Which is why I'm dying, little miss."

Sabine caught the edge of sarcasm in his voice and, out of pity, chose to ignore it.

"Only one thing can help me now."

Just as they could kill with a bite, vampires could also heal — mortals as well as their own kind. Normally, taking any kind of blood would heal a vampire's injuries, but when the cause included a substance lethal to them, such as silver or certain plants, only the blood sharing with another vampire could save them.

Meg entered with the water.

"Let me help, miss."

"No, Meg. Put the bowl down and you may go back to bed."

"But —"

"Meg!" Sabine's eyes flashed over her shoulder. "I can help the Captain."

Meg's eyes swept over Galen before she left, closing the door behind her.

"Will you?" he murmured, dark eyes half closed. His exquisite chest rose and fell. Blood trickled from his injured side, staining her white sheets. "Help me?"

Sabine's pulse throbbed. Her nipples hardened, pressing against her gown. She could help him. She was a fully mature vampire and possessed the strength required, but to save him would mean giving herself over to him completely. Her flesh and blood would be his, and she'd never shared such intimacy with anyone.

"You don't have to," he whispered. Heat emanated from the raw wound. If she didn't do something, he wouldn't survive.

With trembling fingers, she unfastened her gown. Wearing only a thin cotton shift, she sat on the edge of the bed and placed her hands on Galen's shoulders. Her fingers tightened on the smooth, warm flesh, feeling the steely muscles beneath. "Captain Donovan, you may take my blood."

His half open eyes shifted to her face. "Even though you don't know me?"

"I can't just let you die, can I?"

"You know what this means?

Sabine drew a deep breath and leaned closer to him, her throat against his lips. Her pulse quickened as she anticipated the feeling of his teeth penetrating her flesh. For all the times she *had* bitten, she'd never once *been* bitten.

First came the sensation of his warm lips against her skin, then the smoothness of his teeth. She gasped, eyes widening as his fangs slid into her throat. Her own heartbeat echoed in her ears as she closed her eyes to the sensations. Galen's tongue lapped, his lips caressed and her life flowed into him.

Sabine's hands opened, slid down his arms, then splayed against his chest. Soft hairs tickled her palms, and his pectorals flexed as he shifted position. He rolled her onto her back, groaning, whether from the pain of his injury or the excitement of the bite, she wasn't sure.

She'd never known such pleasure in her life. Her entire body felt like hot liquid. Like passion-drenched vines, her limbs entangled with his. Unconsciously, she slid her hands up his sides and squeezed. Fearing that she'd hurt him further, she tried to pull back, but his grip tightened, and he growled as he continued lapping blood. By feel, Sabine realized his wound had closed. Her blood had healed him quickly, and for him to continue drinking was no longer necessary. Still, she *wanted* him to keep drinking, keep touching her.

Panic gripped her when she started to feel light-headed. "Captain Donovan!"

One of his hands cupped a breast, teasing her nipple through the sheer fabric. Sabine felt her body weaken both from blood loss and the pleasure of his touch. "That's enough! Stop!"

His teeth left her, and she felt near tears. In spite of her words and her fears, she wanted him never to leave her!

"Sabine," he murmured, bloody lips covering hers. She knew she should push him away, but he'd used his incisors to cut his own lip. His hot, delectable blood flowed into her mouth, and her tongue laved the tiny wounds on his full lower lip.

Galen buried a hand in her hair, pressing her face closer to his. His teeth and tongue clashed with hers. A single swipe of his exposed claws ripped her shift down the center. Sabine gasped and jerked her face from his. Her breath quickened. Apprehension and desire battled within her mind, and the depths of his eyes intoxicated her.

"It was your choice, Sabine," he said in a husky voice.

"I chose to help you. Anything more is shame on your conscience!"

A wicked smile touched his crimson lips. White teeth flashed, and he bit her again, this time in the soft flesh between her shoulder and throat. Invigorated by the blood he'd given back to her, she clutched him, her breasts crushed to his chest. She knew she should deny him, that he was taking advantage of her kindness, but she didn't want to. Maybe she was also taking advantage of him. She'd known when she offered her blood to the dying man he wouldn't be able to resist. She also knew blood sharing between a male and female would end in uncontrollable passion. That was why she'd never given in to her desire for a companion. She didn't like the idea of being under the power of another. Once vampires made love, their minds would be as one. Vampires mate for life—no matter how long that life might be. Before one made love to another, they must be *sure*.

"Captain, think about what you're doing!" Sabine gasped, her clinging arms at war with her words.

"What *I'm* doing?" he growled. "Just me?"

"Please, give us both a chance to—" Sabine moaned as a large, gentle hand slipped between her legs. He caressed her inner thigh before his fingers slipped into her heated pussy, gathering moisture that he used to tease her into a frenzy. Unable to control herself, she pierced his throat, her legs clamping his wrist. Waves of climax broke over her trembling body.

An animal sound erupted from his throat as his powerful, hot body pinned her to the bed. She felt him jerk down his trousers enough to free his cock. Velvet hardness pressed against her belly. His hand soothed her thighs and stomach as he positioned his hips over hers. Instead of taking her with the violent desire she saw in his dark, burning eyes, he eased himself into her.

God, you're beautiful, his thoughts rumbled in her mind.

"I—"

His lips silenced her. *Think it, my sweet. Tell me what you want.*

I want you. It's wrong.

Passion like this is never wrong.

Their thoughts lost coherence as he moved within her. All she could discern were their feelings, separate but joined. *Excitement. Desire. Perfection. Yearning for some otherworldly explosion…*

Simultaneously, their fangs sank into each other's flesh. Her legs locked around him as his body drove into hers with a ferocity she craved more than anything she'd ever imagined. Together they climaxed in a mass of slick flesh, panting breaths and throbbing hearts.

* * * * *

Galen lifted his head from Sabine's creamy shoulder. Eyes closed, lips parted, the tips of her delicate fangs gleaming in the dimness, she looked like sweetness and temptation molded into one exquisite being.

When Narcisse Debray had spoken of his younger sister, Galen had gathered she was nothing more than a child. This was no child before him, but a woman of charm and elegance. It surprised Galen that one so passionate and lovely had been pure. The blood of her innocence stained his swollen cock just as the blood of her tempting throat reddened his lips. He felt a twinge of guilt that he'd taken far more than his own life back from her. She'd been kind enough to heal him, and he'd claimed her, marked her, bound her to him forever.

Galen's brow furrowed. He was bound to her as well. He'd know what she felt. He'd always long for her body, her blood and her soul. In all his years of life, he'd avoided making love to a vampire female for that reason, and he'd *never* been stupid enough to change his mortal lovers.

Sabine's eyes opened and her smooth cheeks flushed. She reached for her gown, but Galen jerked it from her hand and threw it across the room.

"You could show a little respect, considering I saved your life!" She snarled, reaching for the sheet to cover herself.

"I could." He rolled off her and got to his feet. She leapt up as he kicked off his boots. Before she reached the door, he grasped her upper arm and flung her back on the bed.

"A scream from me and my guards will kill you," she hissed.

"You're going to scream, little miss, but not for your guards." Galen smiled, though he felt no real amusement. Lust, the likes of which he'd never experienced, consumed him. The scent of her was like the most sumptuous meal. Her pale, flawless skin beckoned him to touch it, lick it, pierce it with fangs that ached liked they'd never tasted blood.

"Consider yourself dead!" Sabine bared her own fangs, but her furious expression and the quickening of her pulse flared his desire.

"If you wanted me dead, you shouldn't have helped me in the first place. Besides, after what we've shared, you'd find my death most difficult. Have you ever seen what a vampire must endure when he loses his mate?"

Sabine's anger faltered and sadness misted her eyes. Galen suddenly remembered how Narcisse had spoken of the horrible death of his first wife. Sabine had witnessed his pain. Again, guilt rolled in his belly. He'd often wondered if he was capable of feeling for a woman anymore. Now Sabine, whom he hadn't even known for an hour, was wrapping her soul around his.

"You're afraid of something, Captain?" A slight smile touched her lips.

Galen yanked off his trousers. At first, he thought Sabine might call for her guards after all. Her lips parted and she moistened them with her tongue as her eyes fixed on his crotch. His cock bobbed ruddy, veined and thick before him. His endowment was a blessing of which he was well aware, and though he doubted Lady Sabine had ever seen a naked man before, his fine weapon wasn't wasted. The scent of her arousal wafted around him. Hard, pink nipples stood out beneath the sheet wrapped around her slender middle.

We've come this far, Sabine. He spoke without words, his eyes fixed on hers, his cock throbbing with the heavy beating of his immortal heart. *Do you really want to stop now? Do you want me to go?*

Would you, if I asked it?

No! His soul cried out.

"I will fight you," Sabine spoke aloud, her cheekbones stained pink in her rage and passion. "You have no right to me!"

"I sense something, little miss." Galen took several steps closer. When he reached out to her, she unsheathed her claws and swiped his hand away, leaving four bloody scratches down the back of his wrist. He licked the wounds, his tongue gently lapping, his eyes never leaving her face before he reached for her again. This time he grasped her shoulders and tugged her close. She rammed her knee upward, and he turned so she struck his hip rather than a more delicate target.

Galen laughed and dragged her onto the bed. One of his long, muscular legs pinned hers while he grasped both of her wrists in one hand and forced them above her head. Using his free hand, he tore away the sheet so they were pressed, skin-to-skin. "I sense you enjoy the fight."

Sabine hissed again, catlike, and her teeth snapped at his throat. The intention of that bite had not been to cause pleasure, but pain. Among vampires, the difference was obvious.

"I won't lie, Sabine." His voice sounded rough with passion. Lowering his head, he took one of her nipples between his teeth. He licked the tip, his tongue tracing the blush-colored areola. His teeth nipped the sensitive flesh before he used a single fang to draw blood from the very center. Sabine's reaction was volatile. Her body trembled and arched, her pulse raced, and she uttered a high-pitched sound of animalistic desire. Galen's erection swelled, almost painful in his lust. He rubbed it against her soft hip. "I want you. I want to give and receive pleasure until moonrise. I want to fuck you until our immortal bodies feel as though they died in paradise."

His finger dipped between her legs, found her plump, moist little clit and circled it with soft, rhythmic strokes. Sabine's flesh heated and she made a kittenish mewl in her throat. Galen kissed her breasts. "I want you, but if you tell me to go, I will. You'll never see me again."

"Never?" she breathed. "I don't think I want never."

"Choose carefully, little miss." He released her hands and slid down her body. He kissed her inner thighs before his tongue lapped her pussy.

"Galen!" she panted, fingers tightening in his hair.

"Choose carefully," he repeated, his warm breath caressing her as he spoke, "because if you ask me to stay now, our bond will be unbreakable. I'll consider you mine."

His tongue continued its carnal work, pushing her to the very edge of fulfillment before he rose and moved away.

"No!" Sabine clutched his shoulders, nails biting into flesh and muscle.

Her eyes were vivid with desire. The blood pounding beneath her flesh cried out to him. For a moment Galen himself felt dizzy with passion.

You want me to stay?

Yes! Stay! Come into me now! Take me! Drink of me! Fill me!

Galen's mouth covered hers in a breath-stealing kiss. His body pressed hers deep into the mattress. Sabine's fangs pierced his shoulder, and she clung to him, her body arching to meet his movements as she gulped his blood. His fast, powerful thrusts gratified her with a quick, quaking rush of ultimate fulfillment. The pounding didn't stop or lessen, but he continued driving her to climax after climax, until their flesh was slick and their breaths came in near painful gasps. With her last shout of triumph, Galen bit her. Orgasm washed over him, so intense he lost sight and hearing and could only feel the intense pleasure of Sabine throbbing around his cock.

Chapter Two

෨

Sabine stirred, her body languid, strangely content. The sensation of a warm body pressed against hers and the wild, musky scent of vampire male made her snap to full awareness. *Captain Donovan!*

Sabine lifted her cheek from his shoulder, her belly fluttering at the sight of his handsome face, eyes closed and peaceful, on their shared pillow. The day's growth of stubble shadowed his jaw, and she resisted the urge to touch his parted lips.

No! Not with him! A common pirate! What have I done?

Sabine leapt, but a powerful arm snaked around her waist and dragged her back into bed.

"Where do you think you're going?" Galen's voice sounded husky in her ear.

"Haven't you gotten enough from me already?"

"Not nearly. It's just begun for us, Sabine."

She braced her hands against his chest, felt the slow beating of his immortal heart through the warmth of hair-dusted flesh. The urge to stroke and knead the hard muscle was almost overpowering. She had to get away from him! "There is no us, Captain Donovan."

"From the moment you climbed into this bed, there was us. Only us. Forever."

Sabine laughed humorlessly. "Oh really? I suppose you've kept every woman you've ever bedded? Come to think of it, my brother did mention something about you and a private harem."

"It wasn't *my* harem." He pushed closer, trapping her arms between their bodies. He nibbled her ear, and she shivered. "It was a harem I was forced into. Long ago."

"Did your master finally throw you out when your obnoxious attitude started to annoy him?"

"No. It was a mistress who managed to get her grubby human hands on me when I'd been injured during a raid. I escaped after killing her—in her bed."

"Is that story supposed to intimidate me?"

"Did it?"

"No."

He lifted his head to stare into her eyes. A smile softened his expression. "Too bad."

"I wish I'd let you die."

"You didn't, so now you have to live with me."

Sabine wanted to scream and claw his flesh, but she realized such a display would be wasted on the likes of him. She wasn't weak, by any means, but she knew her limitations. Her strength was no match for the Captain's. He would take her struggles as incentive to bed her again. She'd heard enough stories about Galen to know all the man thought about was sex and money.

"So Narcisse did tell you about me." Galen grinned.

"Enough for me to know you're the most common of commoners!"

"So that's what's bothering you?" Galen smirked. "Your noble body has been soiled by peasant hands?"

"Yes, if you must know!"

"That's rather a joke, isn't it?"

"I don't see what's funny."

"You wouldn't. Narcisse did say you and your brother Kornel had delusions of grandeur."

"And Narcisse never gave himself — or our family — enough credit. Now get your hands off me!"

"It's not yet dusk." Galen rolled onto his back, holding Sabine tightly to his side. He pressed her cheek to his chest. The sensation was intoxicating. "Unlike most men, I prefer to actually sleep with a woman I've made love to."

"You call *that* making love?" Sabine snorted. "I've seen breeding bulls with more finesse."

Galen laughed. "I think I like you, little miss."

"Oh, I'm flattered. I don't think I can contain my relief and excitement."

"You can't, can you?"

"Are you so ignorant you can't even recognize sarcasm?"

"Are you so deluded that you can't even understand your own desire for me?"

"You're accustomed to whores, Captain Donovan."

"No. A whore wouldn't have reacted with your *enthusiasm*." Galen tilted his cheek against the top of her head. "Quiet now. I want to sleep."

Sabine sank her fangs into his chest.

Galen grunted with pain and wrapped his hand in her hair, tugging her head gently until her throat arched. He kissed the white, throbbing flesh. "Shall I create a muzzle for you, little miss?"

"Only if you want to sleep in peace!"

"I don't appreciate threats."

"Then let me out of this bed!"

Galen smiled. "No. I prefer the muzzle."

"You wouldn't!" She snarled.

He reached a long arm to the floor and slipped a leather belt from his trousers.

"No!" Sabine kicked him hard and lunged for the door, screaming. He was on her in an instant, a large hand clamped over her mouth, another wrapped around her waist.

Her heel stomped on his bare instep, and Galen grunted in pain. He dragged her onto the bed and sat with her struggling in his lap. Her elbow jabbed his ribs and he cursed. Sabine felt the leather belt wedge between her lips, preventing her from screaming. Tears of frustration blurred her vision. No one had ever treated her in such a manner—except when her brother and his wicked servant had abducted her as bait to lure Narcisse to his death. And even they hadn't plundered her, body and soul, as Captain Donovan had done.

Suddenly the belt was tugged out of her mouth and she was shoved toward the door. Sabine stared at him, seething hatred, surprise, and to her dismay, lust for the tall, lean body bending the floor to retrieve her gown. She watched the tightening of the long muscles of his thighs when he moved, the tautness of his buttocks. Braids of muscle flexed in his back and shoulders as he picked up the garment and flung it in her face.

"Go!" he snapped.

"This is *my* room!"

Galen growled, eyes glowing reddish in vampiric rage, fangs exposed. She noted for the first time his fangs were thick and white, wolf-like. The sight of them made her legs weaken, but she yanked the dress over her head and fled down the hallway.

She'd nearly reached the end of the hall when Meg and two guards, barefoot and shirtless but armed with swords, raced to meet her.

"What's wrong, my lady?" one guard asked.

"We heard you scream." Meg's eyes were wide with concern.

All three stared at Sabine, and she realized the sight she must be with her wrinkled dress and disheveled hair.

"Nothing. I'm fine." She spoke calmly, posture straight, chin lifted. "You may go."

After a moment's hesitation, the guards walked slowly down the steps, one yawning, the other scratching the back of his neck.

Only Meg remained, arms folded beneath her plump bosom, her nightcap nearly covering her eyes. "What happened? Is everything all right with your guest?"

"Yes. Captain Donovan is doing well. I'm guessing he'll be rested enough to leave in the morning."

"You healed him, then?"

Sabine nodded, willing herself not to blush.

"And?"

"And that's all I'm going to say, you nosy woman." Sabine narrowed her eyes and wrinkled her nose at her friend.

The blonde stared at her, eyes almost as penetrating as a vampire's. "You're certain you're all right? We all know blood sharing can be as unsettling between vampires as between vampires and humans."

"I appreciate your concern, Meg, but it's best if you keep your curiosity out of such business. I can handle Captain Donovan."

"Will he be staying the night in your room, then? If so, I can stoke a fire in the guest room for you."

"It's not necessary, Meg. Go back to bed."

The maid nodded and disappeared to the servants' quarters. Sabine stood alone in the dark hallway, her eyes fixed on her chamber door. She must have been insane, for she felt the nagging desire to walk back and crawl into bed beside Galen.

Shaking her head, she continued to the west wing and sparked a fire in the guest room that had been prepared for Captain Donovan. Settling into a chair, she watched the flames. As she drifted to sleep, she thought she saw his face dancing in the firelight.

* * * * *

Shortly after dusk, Sabine entered the great hall. Moonlight created an eerie glow through the rectangular, square-cut windows high on the walls, and candles burned in low-hanging chandeliers—more for the servants' sake than for Sabine's. Maids carried on their chores, and the scent of cooking food wafted from the kitchen.

Sabine walked to the long oak table and sat, sipping strong tea and buttering a slice of fresh bread. She glanced at the steps, her pulse quickening as she thought of Captain Donovan. Apparently he was a late riser. All the better. If she hurried, she'd be out on her ride before he departed and wouldn't be forced to look at the vile bastard. After the appalling manner in which she'd acted last night, she didn't think she could look him in the eye. The memory of lying naked in his arms made her face heat and her stomach churn so much she didn't risk taking a bite of food. Solid food didn't appeal to her at all when she remembered the smooth, rich taste of Galen's blood.

Sabine stood, leaving the plate of food, and headed for the door.

"Leaving without greeting your guest?"

Sabine spun. Galen stepped from an alcove in the far corner of the room. Narcisse used the space as a miniature library, containing a single cushioned chair and two shelves filled with rare manuscripts. One of the leather-bound volumes rested snug in Galen's long-fingered hand. He wore a billowy black shirt, the ties unfastened at his throat and black trousers tucked into soft leather boots. A gold-handled dagger in a simple leather sheath hung from the belt about his lean waist. The outfit was a perfect complement to his dark eyes and glossy black hair hanging loose about his shoulders. The man was disgracefully handsome, which seemed to make Sabine hate him all the more.

"I thought you were asleep," she said. His eyes swept her from head to foot in a manner that made her feel naked. She drew a deep breath, willing herself to meet his gaze, unfaltering. "If you're awake, why are you still here?"

"You really didn't expect me to go?"

"You have what you came for. Your life restored." She wondered if he noted the emphasis she placed on the last sentence, as if impressing guilt for his crude behavior toward the woman who'd rescued him.

Galen smiled, revealing those wolfish fangs, the sight of which nearly melted her with desire. "You might not believe it, but I am grateful to you."

"An appreciative man wouldn't overstay his welcome."

"I don't think I am."

"I'm telling you, you are. I want you out of my house."

Galen replaced the book on the shelf and approached Sabine. She stood her ground, tilting her head to meet his eyes, his tall, big-boned frame shadowing her face. His scent was strong, thrilling. "No you don't. What you want is quite the contrary. If you wanted me gone, you would have sent your servants after me last night. Not that it would have done them much good. They're only mortal."

"Trained by a vampire lord, unless you've forgotten."

"I'm sure Narcisse trained his guards well, but I know he's intelligent enough not to give away all our secrets, should his servants' loyalty turn."

"You think like the pirate you are!"

Galen grinned. "I'm not a pirate."

Sabine snorted with contempt as she turned away.

"At times, I'm a privateer." Galen fell into step beside her. "There is a difference."

"Like what?" She didn't try to keep the disgust from her voice.

"Pirates don't attend affairs of nobility and they enter an empress's bedchamber through a window rather than the door."

"Just because you collect your gold from nobility doesn't make your deeds any less bloody or degrading. Do you know how I define privateer, Captain Donovan?"

"I can hardly wait to hear."

"As a whore."

"A whore. And you would know, of course." He grasped her upper arm and tugged her toward the table. "Sit and eat with me."

Sabine jerked from his grasp and hissed, causing two maids walking through the hall to glance at the couple with wide eyes.

"Do try to control yourself, little miss, and leave the foreplay for the bedroom," he said loudly.

The maids looked away and hurried from the hall, leaving Galen and Sabine alone.

Galen sat at the table and began eating the bread Sabine had buttered. She tore it from his hand before he could take a bite. "I want you out of my home. Now!"

"And what do you think would happen if I went?" He leaned back in the chair, studying her. "You'd continue wanting me, Sabine. Just as I want you. We've *mated*, dearest. You can't just dam up such feelings or hope they'll go away. Last night, we both made a decision."

"If you leave, right now, our bond will fade."

"You really believe that?"

"Yes. I've heard stories of —"

"You've heard stories of everything, haven't you, Sabine? Stories about me, stories about blood sharing between our kind. Always stories. But what have you actually *experienced?*"

"Enough to know peasant dung when I see it!"

He stood. "Come riding with me."

The man was impossible! "Haven't you heard a word I've said to you?"

"Come riding with me and afterward, if you still want me to go, I will."

"You can save yourself time. I will want you to go."

One ride. Just the three of us — you, me and the lust-inspiring moon.

"I don't…"

Don't use impersonal words, little miss. Talk to me how we were meant to communicate.

No matter how we talk or what we do, I'll never be yours.

You are mine.

"No. Not now. Not ever." Sabine gritted her teeth, fists clenching. "We'll go on your ride, but it won't make a bit of difference."

Sabine slipped her hand into his extended palm. His fingers, warm and strong, closed around hers, and side by side, they strolled to the stable.

In the stable, Sabine dismissed the groom who offered to saddle her horse. On occasion, she allowed servants to prepare her mount, but she loved everything about horses and preferred to groom and saddle her own. She approached her favorite dapple-gray mare and rubbed between the horse's eyes.

"Good evening, Pearl," she said to the animal.

An unfamiliar whinny caused her to glance over her shoulder to where a tall, blood bay stallion dropped his finely-shaped head over the stall. The animal was spirited, by the look in its dark, gleaming eyes. Galen stroked the horse's sleek neck.

"Beautiful horse," Sabine said. "Where did you steal him?"

Galen laughed. "You love being a bitch, don't you? And I'm shocked to see you tending your own mount. Are you sure it's appropriate for a *lady* to perform such a menial task?"

Sabine cast him a disgusted look, but continued grooming the mare. As she worked, she cast looks at Galen as he brushed and saddled the blood bay. She almost couldn't decide which was more beautiful, the sleek, muscular stallion or the sleek, muscular man. Grudgingly, she had to admit the man won the contest.

"What's his name?" Sabine nodded toward the horse.

"Desert Angel."

"I like that." Sabine smiled.

Galen paused, one hand on the stallion's back. "You're even lovelier when you smile."

Sabine released an exaggerated yawn and turned back to Pearl. She guided the mare out of the stable and mounted, Galen and Desert Angel behind her.

Sabine urged Pearl forward, and the mare's long legs swallowed the field. Within seconds, Desert Angel galloped alongside her. Galen glanced at her through wind-tossed black hair, his eyes flashing as he grinned.

You're wondering why I call him Desert Angel. Galen's thoughts were like a mental caress. Sabine's belly tightened. He continued, *He was a gift from a Sheik. A very special gift.*

Payment you mean, Sabine replied. *Probably for some foul deed.*

Wade deep enough through my thoughts, and you may find out.

Immediately Sabine cleared her mind and urged Pearl faster. She concentrated solely on the ride. She didn't want to delve into Galen's mind—or maybe the idea was too appealing. After the ride she'd be rid of him.

Sinking her fangs into her lower lip, she shook her head. Even she didn't believe that. A terrible fear and horrid yearning snaked throughout her insides as she began to sense Galen was right. They were linked forever, and nothing, not lies or separation, could destroy the bond forged between vampire mates.

* * * * *

Galen glanced at Sabine from the corner of his eye as his stallion galloped neck to neck with her mare. For all her refined, human appearance, she possessed a vampiric spirit. She and the horse moved like a single being, a shared soul—one as wild as the other.

Shared soul. Just like us.

Sabine's eyes met his before she turned her horse sharply toward the forest. He followed, and together they disappeared into the trees, slowing their mounts to avoid being lashed by low-hanging branches.

"Where are we going?" he called to her.

In reply, she grinned to him over her shoulder.

They traveled deep into the forest, so the trees blocked the moonlight. Still, vampire eyes saw every stone on the path below, each night bird clinging to aged branches. They followed a brook, the sound of trickling water mingling with scurrying animals. Forest aromas blended with the alluring scent of Sabine. As Galen stared at her straight shoulders and narrow waist, his groin tightened with anticipation of lovemaking to come.

Her outward denial meant little to him—not when he could read her soul. If there had truly been no attraction between them, he would have left Castle Debray in an instant. Even if it had meant sacrificing his own life, he wouldn't have taken the blood of a woman whose heart could never belong to him. The mating ritual was too serious—*too final*—between two of his kind. Playing games with mortals was one thing, but once the decision was made to either change a human companion or take a vampiric one, the two lives were *sealed*.

In spite of her inexperience, Sabine had known the gravity of their decision. Until Galen had stepped into the hall and met her eyes, he'd considered himself immune to true mating. He'd bedded many, had never denied the moonlust innate in all vampires, but none had ever seduced him into eternal joining. This young woman, in all her innocence, had succeeded where ancient vampiresses had failed. Already the idea of sex with anyone but her was almost enough to shrivel Galen's cock.

The woods thinned and the brook widened until they reached a pool in a clearing. Sabine dismounted and tugged off her boots. Barefoot she walked to the edge of the water.

Galen joined her. He tossed aside his own boots and reaching for her. She slipped away from him, though her eyes burned with desire.

"Turn around," she ordered.

He stared at her for a long moment before turning his back. Perhaps he was being stupid. The woman was so far in denial she might just plunge a dagger through his back to prove to herself she didn't want him.

The ripple of water caused him to turn around. Sabine, her hair piled high on head, swam to the center of the pool. Her gown and shift were spread on a rock on shore.

"You're not making it easy to get rid of me." He smiled, tugging his shirt over his head and pulling off his boots and trousers. He noticed her eyes fixed on his cock, and his heartbeat quickened. He waded in, swimming in her direction.

"This reminds me of my favorite clearing on my island."

"Your island?" Sabine lifted a water-slicked eyebrow.

He nodded. "In the tropics. Even the rain is warm there. The flowers are breathtaking."

"And it's *your* island?"

"You said yourself I'm a pirate." He winked. "Every pirate has an island to keep buried treasure."

She squinted at him. "I knew you were lying."

"I'm not. I do have an island. You'll like it."

"You make it sound like I'm going to see it."

"Of course you'll see it." He reached for her arm, but she swam away.

Sabine floated on her back, eyes closed, the blush-colored tips of her creamy breasts glistening above the surface of the water. Galen almost groaned aloud. The woman was a shameless tease.

Galen ducked underwater and swam beneath Sabine. He indulged in a glance at her firm buttocks before surfacing, his arms wrapped around her.

He held her to his chest. They floated, wet skin to wet skin, legs brushing as they treaded water. Droplets of moisture glistened on Sabine's lashes, and her warm breath caressed his lips.

"Put your arms around my neck," he said. She stared at him, unmoving. "Do it."

Her hands slid over his shoulders before she did as he asked.

"Now kiss me," he ordered.

Her dark eyes reflected moonlight as she tilted her head closer. Her kiss was soft at first, a slight brushing of moist lips. He made no motion, difficult when he wanted to plunder her delicious mouth. Patience. In time, she would grant him all the passion he ever dreamed of. As he'd discovered the previous night, she was an elemental creature. Her lust was untamed, fresh. After she'd left him alone in the chamber, he'd been unable to sleep, but had lain awake, wishing she was beside him. His mind had ventured to touch hers, to see if he could reach her through the castle's stone walls, in spite of the newness of their bond. He'd sensed her fury and her desire.

Perhaps he should have felt guilty, but he didn't. Galen had always been a man who pursued his desires. When he wanted something, he usually got it. And he'd wanted Sabine from the moment he'd seen her. Even wounded, near death, he'd felt a spark of desire for her. When she'd offered herself to him, he couldn't have refused if he'd wanted to. The pull between them was almost magical.

Galen's arms tightened around Sabine as her kiss deepened. Her tongue slipped into his mouth and fenced with his. Their fangs nipped each other's lips, drawing trickles of warm blood that were greedily licked away. Sabine suddenly took his lower lip between her teeth and bit roughly. A guttural sound escaped his throat, and his erection swelled. He leaned backward, dragging her with him as he guided them toward shallow water. The rocks were smooth and slick. He lay on his back, small waves licking his face and chest. Sabine straddled him, her sleek thighs clasping his hips. He took her hand and wrapped her small fist around his growing cock. She squeezed, stroking him almost too gently.

Galen used both hands to cup her breasts. His thumbs rolled over her nipples, teasing the hard peaks until her eyes slipped shut and she sighed deeply.

"Place me inside you," he continued his orders in a low, husky voice.

He heard her heartbeat in his ears, or was it his own heart? His pulse raced like a mortal's, and his entire body tingled. His fangs sank into his own lips as she guided him into her liquid pussy.

"Galen," she whispered, fingers clutching his chest as she began the rhythmic movement that drove them both toward bliss.

"I love how you say my name."

She moaned, movements increasing. He fondled her breasts, pushing her over the edge. Her knees clamped his waist and her body quaked over his.

Eyes closed, he enjoyed the intoxicating sensations of her climax. Before the last contractions rippled through her, she began the sensual gyrations again.

Galen sighed deeply, his body seeming to melt into the water as she rode him. Her vampiric claws slipped from beneath her human nails and raked his chest, drawing rivulets of blood that she licked clean. Like his, her immortal body didn't tire easily. He lost count of how many times she attained perfection before he finally lost control. He rolled her onto the rocks, his teeth sinking into her shoulder as he lunged into her with hard, fast thrusts. Breathing ragged, he collapsed onto her, his body pinning hers to the rocks as water slapped their skins.

He sat back on his knees and tugged her against his chest. Kissing her hair, he said, "That position couldn't have been comfortable for you."

"Not with you lying on me like a big oaf."

Galen's teeth snapped, and he growled. He picked her up, carried her out of the water, and placed her on top of her dress. He stretched out beside her, leaning on his elbow, one hand stroking between her breasts. She studied him, and he smiled.

He traced her belly and hips before dipping his hand between her thighs and caressing her clit. Sighing, she wiggled against his hand. He changed position slightly so he could kiss her breasts. First he took one nipple between his lips, tongue rolling the pert little bud. His fang pierced the tip, and he drank until she quivered. With a final kiss to that breast, he moved to the other and paid it equal homage. Tongue trailing down her torso, he kneaded her inner thighs and kissed her between the legs as deeply as he'd kissed her lips and breasts. He licked her clit, first using the tip of his tongue to caress her in small, circular motions. Then he laved the swollen nub with long, sweeping strokes that brought her almost to the edge without allowing her to pass it. Finally he sucked and licked in a quick, steady rhythm, gently using his teeth until she convulsed, moaning and sobbing his name.

Sabine's fingers clutched handfuls of his thick, wet hair, riding the waves of climax until she lay panting and trembling beneath him.

He'd waited, keeping his own pleasure at bay until he was certain she was utterly satisfied. When he thrust into her throbbing cunt, his heart pounded against his ribs and his teeth ached with desire. He pierced her throat and drank. In a final burst of pleasure, Sabine's legs locked tightly around him. Her nails sank into the flesh of his shoulders, drawing blood. His orgasm, so intense he nearly lost consciousness, broke over him like waves on a capsized ship.

He sank onto the rock beside her, his face buried in her shoulder and thought how much like a storm she was; wild, thrilling and savage in her quest for pleasure.

Smiling, his arms tightened around her. They'd make an incomparable match, the lady and the privateer.

After a moment, she stirred, raising herself onto her elbows. "Galen?"

"Umm."

"Do you smell smoke?"

He lifted his head, brow furrowed as he inhaled.

"Yes." He stood, reaching for his clothes. It didn't seem to be smoke from a mere campfire, but heavier—like a mass burning.

He doubted the fire was in the forest, since there were no signs of animal panic.

"Seems to be coming from the village." Sabine tugged on her dress and ran for her horse.

Galen was already on Desert Angel.

Together, they rode out of the forest as quickly as they could. As soon as they cleared the trees, they saw smoke on the air, coming from the direction of Castle Debray and the neighboring village.

They drove the horses to a gallop. When they reached the crest of the hill, Galen sensed Sabine's panic. The village wasn't on fire. It was the castle!

Chapter Three

ജ

Random flames smoldered on the corpse-littered meadow surrounding smoky Castle Debray. Exhausted-looking villagers wandered amidst the rubble, buckets in hand. Several sat by the river while others had begun digging graves for those who had perished in the flames.

"Lady Sabine!" One of the guards, his face blackened by smoke, uniform ragged, approached her.

"Roger!" Sabine dismounted before the horse stopped prancing. "What happened?"

"We were attacked. A terrible army. Evil night creatures…" The man paused, face growing pale. "Forgive me, my lady."

"A vampire army?" Sabine murmured, glancing up at Galen who stood beside her.

His dark eyes, which had been sweeping the grounds, fixed on hers.

"They were looking for you," Roger said to Galen. "When we said you weren't here, they attacked the castle and village. We drove them off, but we've lost many of our guard."

"Was there a swarthy man among them? One with dark hair and a beard?" Galen asked.

Roger nodded. "His eyes were like burning coals, and his teeth—"

"I know," Galen said.

"He killed most of the palace servants."

"Meg?" Sabine's eyes welled with tears as she raced through the field, searching the corpses of people she'd known all her life. She ran inside the castle, smoke stinging her eyes, the fire-scent burning her throat. Though the flames had been doused, their effects shone in rubble, ashes and bodies of the dead.

She found Meg in an upstairs corridor. The smoke must have killed her, for her face and form hadn't been scorched. Sabine knelt beside her, searching for any sign of life, any spark she could grasp and resurrect in vampiric form.

"Sabine." Galen rested a hand on her shoulder.

She looked up at him, not caring that tears streamed down her face. "They were after you."

"I'm so sorry."

She glanced at his hand, then shrugged it off. "What do they want with you?"

"It's a very long story."

Sabine glanced back at Meg and stroked her cold face.

"We have to bury these people," Galen said. "Then we can talk on the way home."

"Home?" Sabine narrowed her eyes at him.

"I'm taking you with me. It's the only way you'll be safe."

She stood, baring her fangs. "I'm not going anywhere with you! Ever! If it hadn't been for you, these people would still be alive! I can't even stand to look at you right now, let alone go *home* with you!"

Stomach twisting, Sabine shoved Galen hard in the chest before fleeing the castle. She stood outside, gulping night air and staring at the moon. *Narcisse, why couldn't you have been home?* No! She didn't want Narcisse or Leona home. They would probably be dead, too.

All this because of Galen. In spite of her words, she was far more furious at herself than at him. She had left her people to suffer because she'd wanted to be alone with Galen. Because she'd wanted to make love with him!

"I'll never forgive myself," she whispered, hugging her waist. "Never."

She glanced across the field and saw a tall, slim figure in white gliding toward her. *The Priestess.*

"Sabine." The Priestess placed firm hands on the young woman's shoulders.

"Evi." Sabine accepted the woman's embrace.

"I came when I caught the scent of smoke. I—" Evi stopped speaking and stared across the field. Sabine glanced over her shoulder to see what had nabbed the Priestess's attention, but she only saw Galen walking toward them, shovel in hand, as he prepared to assist in the grave digging.

Galen stared at the Priestess. Though his expression remained guarded, Sabine sensed his surprise and discomfort. Almost immediately, an unfamiliar barrier seemed to thrust her thoughts out of his mind.

How did he do that? I thought there was no way to avoid each other's thoughts, now that we'd mated.

"Galen." Evi further surprised Sabine by bowing her head.

"Evania."

Evania?

"I thought I recognized your scent when I approached, but—"

"How do you know each other?" Sabine interrupted.

"We met long ago," Galen spoke before Evi. "There's little time for conversation now. There's work to do, and you and I must leave as soon as these people are buried."

"I said I'm not going anywhere with you!" Sabine snarled.

"Sabine, if he comes back looking for me, he'll know you and I are connected. Our scents have mingled, our…"

Sabine's jaw dropped, and she blushed as she glanced from Evi back to Galen. "Why don't you just announce our private lives to the world?"

"I'm an old woman." Evi met her gaze. "I understand the ways of our kind even better than you, child. What Galen says is true. If someone is pursuing him, they can force you to reveal his whereabouts, or harm you in the process."

"They've already harmed me when they destroyed my home and my servants!" Sabine stared hard into Galen's eyes. "You knew you were being chased. You knew you were putting us in danger, but you came here anyway. And you stayed, even after I asked you to leave."

"You really seemed serious about having me leave, didn't you?" Galen snapped.

Sabine struck Galen hard, her nails leaving four bloody scratches across his cheek. "I said I'm not going anywhere with you!"

Furious, she stalked across the field and joined the villagers in dragging bodies out of the rubble.

* * * * *

Galen wiped his bleeding face on his forearm, teeth clenched as he glared after Sabine. His grip tightened on the shovel, and he did his best to uphold his mental barrier against her onslaught of emotion. She seethed with anger, sadness and utter loss. Though he felt empathy for her—so much that he longed to pull her into his arms and soothe her anguish—losing himself in her emotions wouldn't help either of them. And he had his own guilt to contend with. His enemy had followed him here. *His enemy.* Galen had never expected him to find him so quickly, or else he never would have spent the night at Castle Debray. In spite of how the situation appeared to Sabine, it hadn't been his intention to harm anyone. He just needed another vampire to replenish his health so he could return to the one place he'd be safe to regroup his own army—the one place where he could now protect Sabine.

"You've changed, Galen," Evania continued, "but your soul is still wild."

"Still reckless, you mean."

"I've heard about your deeds, about your life since leaving home."

"Have you."

"You've apparently made a significant enemy."

"You haven't heard as many stories as you pretend—I've made far more than one enemy."

"The bitterness in your voice betrays your true self."

"You wouldn't presume so much in the face of a High Priest."

Evania smiled in a familiar, all-knowing manner that had always infuriated Galen. She'd been little more than a child when they'd first met—even younger than Sabine—but even then Evania had observed every action and emotion.

"It's been a long time, but I remember you well." Evania held his gaze. "I learned so much from you, High—"

"Don't say it." Galen hissed, eyes narrowed in rage. "I am no longer that man!"

"I don't presume to have ever felt the pain you've endured, but I do understand it as well as why you've spent years denying your true self."

"My old self." Galen sighed, running a hand through his hair. "Do you still trust me, Evania?"

"Of course," she replied, "but I'm concerned for Sabine."

"I can protect her. I wouldn't suggest taking her with me if I thought she'd be safer anyplace else."

"You bonded quickly."

Galen stared past Evania to Sabine who sat on a fallen log, her arm around a weeping village woman. "She shares my secret."

"You mean you told her?"

He shook his head. "I mean she possesses the same ability—she doesn't know yet. Another reason why I've decided to take her with me. Otherwise, I never would risk taking her onboard ship. Should an accident occur and we sink by daylight — but that won't affect us."

"If I tell her to go with you, she'll listen to me."

"Even if I have to take her by force, I will. However, it would be much easier if she chooses to accompany me. You will talk to her?"

"I will if you tell me what danger you're in, who is after you."

"A Northern King. He hired me, but I didn't perform to his expectations."

Evania studied him then nodded. "I see."

"No, you *think* you see."

"My only concern is Sabine's safety. "

"Then convince her to come away with me."

"I will." Evania sighed. "But should anything happen to her, you may find me joining the Northern King in hunting you down."

Galen smiled. "Not you, Evania."

"You might not be the only one who's changed."

I don't doubt it.

* * * * *

Galen wiped his perspiring forehead on the back of his hand and squinted skyward. The night was nearly over, and he could already see the sun forcing its way through the darkness. He, Sabine, Evania, and the villagers had worked throughout the night, tending the wounded, digging graves and sorting through rubble.

In the distance he saw Sabine, giving water to a villager. Her dress was torn and soiled, the sleeves rolled up to her elbows. After tossing the last load of dirt on a fresh grave, Galen leaned the shovel against a tree trunk and approached her. He noted Evania had already disappeared within the castle walls.

Like the vast majority of their kind, she couldn't abide sunlight. To her, exposure meant death.

Sabine now stood by the well, filling an empty bucket. Galen tried to take it from her, but she jerked away from him.

"Evi told me I should go with you." Her voice sounded flat.

"And?"

"And if she says I should go, I trust her." Her furious eyes fixed on his. "She seems to think the village will be safer with me gone, now that we're *connected*."

"You make it sound like a disease."

"Isn't it? All the poison that's touched your pirate's life is infecting me and those I love."

"I can't change what's already happened, Sabine."

"No. You can't."

"But I can try to prevent future destruction. Coming with me is the best decision you can make."

"I lost the chance to make the best decision when I restored your life."

Galen's jaw tightened. The bitch was trying to make everything seem like his fault. She was the one who gave him her bed. She was the one who undressed that voluptuous body of hers and offered her treasure-filled arteries. She was the one who had just seen her home demolished. She had every right to feel anger and pain. That he knew first hand. If he were any kind of a man, he would have to keep quiet and allow her to grieve. Well, according to his reputation, he wasn't much of a decent man, but he'd have to forfeit reputation—at least for a while.

"I realize this isn't the turn you expected your life to take."

"Amazing! Did you get that information by reading my mind?"

"I'll tolerate your sarcasm because you're in mourning."

"Don't do me any special favors, Captain Donovan! Lord knows, I've had enough of those from you already!"

"Really? Well prepare yourself, little miss, because there's plenty more where those came from!" He dragged her roughly into his arms and kissed her, his tongue tracing the shape of her mouth and slipping between her lips. For a moment she seemed to melt against him, then she grasped two handfuls of his hair and yanked.

Growling, Galen pried her fingers loose and shoved her so hard she nearly toppled into the well. "Be ready to go within the hour."

"Within the hour? You're insane. It's almost dawn. There's no way we can travel in daylight!"

"Yes." He glared at her over his shoulder. "*We* can."

* * * * *

"No!" Sabine snarled. "Absolutely not!"

"If I thought it would harm you, do you think I'd suggest it?" Galen placed his hands on his hips and stood, feet braced apart, a short distance from the castle's entrance. The door had been broken down during the raid, but Sabine stood beside Evania in the dimness of the hall.

Sabine still couldn't believe Galen was standing there, the sun illuminating his vampiric body without a sign of pain or blistering.

"I already told you, most of our kind react badly to sunlight, but few of us aren't affected," Galen said. "You know I'm a vampire, Sabine."

"It must be some kind of trick, some evil magic!"

"There is no evil magic!" Galen snapped. "I'm standing here because sunlight does not affect me—other than making me a little sluggish and my eyes sore."

"How can you be sure I'm like you?"

"Because I can smell it. There's a scent in your blood that I've recognized in every vampire I've ever met who can walk by day."

Sabine glanced at Evi. The priestess's face looked serious. "If he says you can step into the sunlight, then you can, Sabine. You may believe me when I promise he wants to protect you."

"Please, Sabine. It's dangerous to remain here much longer." Galen extended his hand.

Sabine's stomach quivered. She'd seen the affects of sunlight—Narcisse's first wife had died beneath its rays. Common sense told her that no vampire could walk without cover by day, but Galen was doing just that.

"Sabine," his voice was low, gentle, yet stern, "I thought you were fearless."

"But not stupid!"

Shaking his head, Galen walked into the hall. By the time Sabine realized his intention, he had dragged her into his arms.

"No!" She clawed at his face, but he flung her over his shoulder. Other than a few muffled grunts, he ignored the fists slamming his back. Once in the sunlight, he dropped her onto the scorched grass.

Sabine's heart pounded wildly, and she scrambled to her feet, heading back to the castle.

"Are you burned?" Galen demanded.

Sabine paused before stepping through the door. Trembling, she glanced at her hands and touched her own face.

"Well?"

Sabine looked from Evi to Galen and shook her head.

"Then we're ready to be on our way," he told her. "I'll bring the horses. Prepare yourself to go. My ship will be waiting."

Sabine watched him cross the field, his posture pole-straight, sunlight gleaming off his dark hair.

"I loathe him," she whispered.

The Priestess's hand gently squeezed her shoulder. "No, Sabine, you don't."

Sabine turned to Evi and sighed, "He's not really a peasant, is he?"

"His past isn't mine to reveal. I can only tell you this, you'll find no better protector than Galen. If he's promised to defend you, he will sacrifice his own life to do so."

Sabine snorted. "What pirate would sacrifice his life for anyone? I don't even care if he was a king in his past. He's chosen to live as a renegade, and I can never respect him."

"You judge quickly and harshly."

"When your own brother betrays you, trusting anyone else becomes difficult."

Evi studied Sabine. "Why did you save him?"

"Because I felt sorry for him."

"That doesn't explain why you mated with him."

"I have to go." Sabine hesitated before stepping into the sunlight. She still couldn't quite believe she could walk by day. She'd never heard of any vampire possessing such ability.

"Good luck!" Evi called.

Lord, I'm going to need it.

Sabine walked though the burned courtyard, imagining what the roses might have looked like in the sun. Not a single rose remained among the rubble.

Sabine squinted, the unaccustomed sunlight harsh on her nocturnal eyes. It took her several long moments to adjust to the glare.

When she left the castle, Galen awaited her, holding Pearl and Desert Angel. He and Sabine didn't speak, but exchanged glances. Strange that before that moment, there had never been apprehension between them. Anger and desire, yes, but not this questioning.

"What makes you think your ship will be there?" Sabine asked as they rode toward the shore. "Perhaps the Northern King destroyed it, too."

"Doubtful. I sent them off and told them to return today."

"Protect your own, do you?" she said bitterly.

He held her gaze. "Always, as you'll soon discover."

"Understand this, Captain, I'm not yours and I never will be."

"You are mine. You knew what would happen when you mated with me."

"I can't believe I'll be punished the rest of my life for one mistake."

Galen's jaw tightened visibly. "You didn't seem to think it was such a mistake when you were draining my blood and shrieking my name."

Sabine clenched her teeth and urged her horse ahead. Galen caught up to her and continued, "You can't change what happened between us, Sabine. Neither of us can. We're both stuck, so to speak, so you'd better accustom yourself to —"

"Accustom myself? To you?" She laughed with venom. "Never in my wildest dreams did I contemplate mating so far beneath me!"

It was Galen's turn to laugh. "Your delusions are beginning to annoy me."

"Good. If I have to suffer your company, you'll suffer mine."

You don't want to anger me too much, little miss. You have no idea how unpleasant I can be.

His mental voice caressed her mind, soothing her in spite of his threatening words. Sabine shook her head clear and said, "I'm sure I know as well as every other woman unlucky enough to be rutted by the likes of you."

"So you must make a habit of swimming naked with men who don't appeal to you."

"I never said you didn't appeal to me," Sabine admitted.

He edged his horse closer to hers and grinned. "That's more like it. Tell me what appeals to you."

"I give up." Sabine raised her eyes toward heaven.

"Oh no, little miss. Don't disappoint me. I didn't expect such an easy surrender." His gaze shifted toward the shore where a ship waited. "There she is. The Scarlet Dragon."

Sabine stared at the vessel. Built for speed, its sleek shape seemed ready to sever water and devour wind. A red dragon's skeleton was sewn into the black flag that whipped above the white sails. She noticed only two men on deck. The shorter, dressed in baggy tan trousers and a leather vest, waved. Galen lifted his hand in response.

"Come," he said, kicking his horse toward the water.

Sabine felt a bit dazed as they boarded the ship. She sensed the two crewmembers who met them were vampires, and felt the presence of others as well, though she guessed they were hidden below. Most likely, the rest of the crew couldn't walk by day.

"Who's she?" The vested man nodded in Sabine's direction, pale green eyes switching from her to Galen. She noted he wasn't quite as tall as Galen, and more thickly built, his features rugged. Though not as handsome as Galen, he possessed rough charm that Sabine knew many women would appreciate.

"Lady Sabine Debray. She's coming home with us."

"You're bringing a woman on board? You know what they say about women being bad luck on a ship."

Galen lifted an eyebrow. "Drake, we, of all people, shouldn't listen to old wives' tales."

Drake shrugged. "I'll wager you're right about that. I'm surprised her brother let you take her, with the Northern King after you."

"Narcisse wasn't there."

The second crewmember—tall, dark and sinewy, had been observing from the rail. A black patch covered one eye, and the other stared at Sabine like a sliver of slate rock. He turned to Galen. "If Narcisse wasn't there, then who healed you?"

At Galen's silence, both crewmembers exchanged looks, then smiles.

The taller said, "I see. At least now we know why Lady Sabine is aboard."

"Wipe those wolfish expressions off your faces or I'll rip them off." Galen bared his teeth. "I'm telling you and will inform the rest of the crew, Lady Sabine is to be treated with the utmost respect. Any insult to her will be punished by me, and I will savor every lingering moment."

The men exchanged glances, and the taller said, "We were starting to think you were immune, Galen."

"Mind your own affairs, Sofian, and take the lady's horse below with mine."

"Yes, Captain." Sofian smiled at Sabine as he took her horse. Something in his expression made her want to shiver. The man looked all pirate — unlike Galen who could pass for a decent person, when the mood took him.

"Drake, head for home. I'll show the lady to my cabin and then join you. We have much to discuss."

"That's for certain." Drake folded his arms across his chest, and Sabine felt his eyes upon them as she and Galen made their way below deck.

In the ship's dark holds, men slept among sacks of supplies and cargo crates. Several stirred, gazed at her through half-open eyes, then returned to slumber upon seeing their Captain walking beside her.

"All vampires?" Sabine whispered.

"The entire crew. Unfortunately they haven't the ability to face sunlight. Only Sofian and Drake can help me run the ship by day."

"I've never been on a ship before," she admitted. The rocking motion felt a bit unsettling to her.

Galen smiled. "You'll get used to it."

"What if I don't?"

"Then you'll have a miserable voyage."

"A comforting soul, aren't you?"

"I'm accustomed to pirates and mercenaries, Sabine. They don't often require comfort."

"I'm not a member of your crew, Galen."

"You are now. There's no free ride on this ship, little miss."

Sabine snarled. "I knew I never should have come with you!"

"I forgot a high born lady like yourself must be above working to earn her keep."

"It's not as if anyone here has ever earned an honest wage in his life!"

"Then I guess it's up to you to teach us rogues integrity."

"I suppose you want to stick me in the kitchen?"

He grinned. "It's called the galley, and no, somehow I don't think the cook would appreciate you destroying his workshop."

"What do you mean destroying? How do you know I can't cook?"

"I can read your mind, remember?"

Sabine wondered if she looked as annoyed as she felt. "So what do you expect me to do? Scrub the decks?"

"Maybe. At least that way I could watch your cute little ass sway while you mop." Sabine hissed, and he laughed. "All right. No mopping. I'll think of something, but now you can relax in my cabin."

"You want me to stay in your cabin?" Her lip curled, though her heartbeat quickened at the thought of living with him in such close quarters.

"Unless you want to bunk with the rest of my crew."

Sabine shot him a look which she hoped told him exactly what she thought of *that* proposal.

Galen opened the door to his cabin and motioned for her to step inside.

The room was sparsely furnished with a bunk, desk and brass-rimmed trunk in a corner.

"Nothing fancy, but you'll find it comfortable enough."

Sabine approached the bunk and sat, one hand caressing the woolen blanket. Galen dropped beside her, one long leg stretching nearly the length of the room, the other bent. "You'll like the island, Sabine."

I miss home, she thought.

I am sorry, little miss, his silent voice penetrated her mind. *You'll enjoy our time together. I'll see to that, if you let me.*

Sabine stared into his eyes, dark as the midnight sea.

Galen placed a hand to the back of her neck, drew her face to his and kissed her. At the first soft touch of his lips, Sabine closed her eyes. She should be ashamed for weakening toward him so often, but there was little difference now. She was forced to remain with him, so she might as well enjoy the few pleasures he had to offer.

"I have to go topside," Galen murmured against her lips. "Rest, and tonight I'll introduce you to the rest of the crew."

"What kind of work will you have me do?"

"Don't worry," he smiled over his shoulder as he left the cabin, "I'll make sure you earn your keep."

Before she could think of an appropriate retort, he closed the door and left her alone.

* * * * *

Galen inhaled the invigorating scent of salty ocean air as he stepped on deck. Drake was steering the ship, and Sofian watched from the crow's nest. He'd known both men for almost more years than he could count. Both were seasoned warriors with values similar to Galen's own. Drake was a good seaman and a decent man, though not the most intelligent of creatures. Sofian's mind was quick and shrewd. His single eye saw more than most men with two, which was why Galen had made him his first mate. Together they had accomplished more than Galen had imagined when they'd started their vocations.

Galen approached Drake, and the man grinned at him. "So who's the lady really?"

"Someone who needs protecting."

"Always the same story." Drake shook his head. "But I guess it's what we do."

"He almost found me."

Drake's head jerked in Galen's direction, his eyes touched with a hint of fear. "He tracked you quickly."

"Too quickly for my taste," Galen muttered. "He destroyed Sabine's home — killed her servants — her friends."

Drake shook his head and whistled. "Too bad for the lady. I suppose that does sort of make her your responsibility, doesn't it?"

Galen nodded, lips set in a grim line. Drake's words made his belly clench. The ruin of Castle Debray, the deaths of those people, were on his soul — again. Even worse, part of him was still glad he'd stopped there and met Sabine. He was a selfish son of a bitch when it came to her, and they scarcely knew each other. What would happen when their bond deepened?

"Does she know about him?" Drake asked.

Galen shook his head. "Not the details. She doesn't know about us, either, and I want to keep it that way."

Drake shrugged. "You're the captain. Though I don't understand why you'd want her to think —"

"You don't have to understand. The woman is my business."

"Aye, Captain."

Galen walked to the bow and gazed out at the churning waves. He thought of Sabine lying alone in his cabin. Her soft curves, her creamy skin.

He shook his head and gripped the wooden rail. The woman was like fine wine. Luscious taste that steals the senses. He must have lost his own senses to have dragged her into his dangerous world. Silently, he cursed. The more he grew to love her, the more he would grow to hate himself for what he'd done to them both.

Chapter Four

ॐ

Sabine awoke to the ship's gentle rocking, the cabin pleasantly dark. Unfamiliar scents greeted her, salt, leather, wood, horses and the crew. Vampires in particular noticed the individuality of each person's scent, the scent of other vampires being especially strong. Sabine recognized Galen's aroma among the others, clean and sharp as the ocean, musky as a mythical beast in heat.

She swung her legs over the side of the cot, her bare feet against the rough wooden floor. Though concerned about the state in which she'd left her home and worried about what Narcisse and Leona would think when they returned to ruins, she felt an odd stirring in the pit of her stomach. Already she loved the ship, and the adventure spread before her made her tingle. She'd never been far from her homeland before. She'd never been swept away by a man like Galen.

"I'd better not let him know how I really feel," she muttered, then shook her head. How could she hope to hide her thoughts, let alone her feelings? He slipped into her mind as easily as his flesh slid into hers.

Sabine stretched and stood, washing in a basin of water on the trunk. She brushed and braided her hair and was about to venture on deck when a leather-bound book on the desk nabbed her attention.

Knowing the book was none of her concern but unable to resist a quick look, she opened the cover and glanced at the dark, elongated script.

Day 112

We unloaded the remainder of the King's cargo this morning. By now he must know what we've done. I might give half the gold he paid me just to have seen his face when he discovered the truth.

"Truth?" Sabine murmured, taking a seat at the desk. "What truth? And who's this King everyone keeps talking about?"

Day 113

Clear sky and strong winds speed us on our way. It might be wiser to turn homeward, but one last opportunity awaits us in a village on the coast. I know the crew longs for the islands, and so do I.

It's unfortunate that he is on our heels, or while in this part of the world I might have visited Castle Debray to see if it's as my old friend Narcisse described. We'd have much to reminisce about, and it would be interesting to finally meet that family of his.

Sabine's brow furrowed. It felt strange reading about her family in Galen's log. She turned the page, and the writing changed to a bolder, straighter hand.

Day 114
First Mate's entry

The Northern King's men awaited us in the coastal village. There was no point to our mission. All were dead and pillaged.

During the fight that ensued, many good crewmembers were lost. Against my warning, the captain led our enemies inland. Our orders are to meet him again in two days' time. If he doesn't appear by high noon at our rendezvous, we're to assume the worst and sail for home without him.

Sabine had been so absorbed in reading that she scarcely realized Galen's scent had grown stronger until he opened the door. His brow furrowed as she slammed the log shut.

"Glad to see you've made yourself at home." He approached, taking the book and flipping through the pages.

"Who is the Northern King?"

"Just a man of royal blood. A man of strong convictions."

"What is he to you?"

His eyes fixed on hers, Galen placed the book back on the desk. Grasping her upper arms, he tugged her to her feet, so close she could count his lashes. "You read the log, so you must know."

"He paid you to steal for him."

Galen gave a slight shrug. "In a manner of speaking."

"You took his money but didn't deliver his goods. No wonder he wants to kill you. Keep up tricks like that and you won't be a privateer for long."

His lips curved upward in a wicked smile that exposed his wolfish fangs. "I've been a privateer centuries longer than you've been alive, little miss."

"Then you must have far more enemies than the King, yet he frightens you and your crew." Sabine was already afraid of the King and his army, after seeing what they'd done to Castle Debray. Still, she knew Galen had faced more evils than she had in her short life. If this Northern King worried Galen and his crew, he must be even more formidable than she'd imagined. And what sort of place was Galen taking her to, if he felt they would be safe there?

"You're right in thinking he concerns me."

"Frightens," Sabine corrected, feeling his irritation. She narrowed her eyes at him. "You don't like being afraid, or should I say you don't like someone accusing you of having fear."

He dropped his hands from her shoulders and strode across the cabin. Sitting on the cot, he leaned backward, shoulders resting against the wall, legs stretched out in front of him and crossed at the ankles. "I'm not so stupid I don't understand the value of fear, Sabine. It's wise to be leery of certain situations—and certain people. However fear can't rule your life. I certainly don't let it rule mine."

"Of course not. You're too much of a man for that—too experienced a vampire." She'd tried keeping the bitterness from her voice, but didn't quite succeed.

"Your own lack of experience bothers you," he observed. "You're the youngest in your family and have been treated like a child all your life."

"I'm not a child."

"Obviously." This time his smile looked roguish. "No child makes love with such passion and grace."

"Are you mocking me? I know you've slept with thousands of women."

He laughed. "Thousands! Goodness, Narcisse can exaggerate, can't he?"

"Narcisse didn't give a number, but I could tell by his stories that you have little self control when it comes to making love."

"Really? And I thought I'd controlled myself enough to pleasure you into semi-consciousness."

"You enjoy annoying me, don't you?"

"You're gorgeous when you're irritated. Your eyes glow as if in the throes of moonlust. Speaking of that, it's a clear night and the moon's beautiful. Come on deck with me, and we'll look at it."

Sabine tingled at the thought of watching the moon with him. Even below deck she felt its pull and could scarcely wait to make love with Galen again.

By his expression, she knew he'd infiltrated her mind.

"On the second thought," he said, "why don't we observe the moon later. Come here, Sabine."

Arms folded across her chest, she made no motion to obey.

He tugged off his clothes and tossed them aside. "I said come here."

Sabine laughed. "Who do you think you are?"

You know who and what I am to you, little miss. Now come here and let me pleasure you.

Sabine's pulse leapt. Teeth clenched, she took a step toward him, then another. As she neared the bed, he suddenly snatched her wrists and tugged her on top of him, his mouth covering hers.

Sabine's hands roamed over his chest, feeling the hard muscles beneath a cushion of hair. She opened her mouth to his probing tongue and her own, darted out to meet it.

That's right, little miss. Keep touching me, kissing me. We belong to each other. Always.

Always, she thought, burying her fingers in the thick hair at his nape and pressing him closer.

His lips moved to her neck and the plump tops of her breasts visible above her dress's deep, square neckline. His fangs pierced the soft flesh, and Sabine gasped, eyes tightly shut as she pressed his head closer. One hand slid over his ribs before grasping his cock, fingers squeezing, stroking, caressing.

He groaned deep in his throat as he continued drawing blood from her breast. Sabine's body felt weak yet powerful at the same time. Her teeth ached for his skin, her tongue longed for the sweet, erotic taste of his blood.

Fangs slipped from her breast, leaving her trembling, needing, on the verge of ultimate satisfaction. Whimpering in protest, she tugged him closer. Galen chuckled and began undressing her. When she lay naked on the cot, he kissed her from ankle to forehead then back again. Sabine wrapped her fingers in his hair.

"You are so beautiful," he said, easing his body over hers. "Eyes as black as the darkest cave and holding just as many secret treasures."

"I don't think I could keep a secret from you," she said. "You know my thoughts and feelings."

"As you know mine."

Sabine stroked his chest and throat. "You seem able to hide your thoughts from me."

"I'm older and have had more practice being secretive."

"Maybe someday you won't need to keep secrets from me," she whispered against his lips. One thing Sabine knew was that men in the heat of passion often released their guard to gain pleasure.

"I hope so."

Sabine nipped his full lower lip and sighed as his rich blood flowed into her mouth. She felt his large hand cup her head, pressing her closer and deepening the kiss. His teeth sank into her lips and his tongue sparred with hers, exploring every crevice in her mouth. Sabine broke the kiss to tease his earlobe with her teeth and tongue.

Galen sighed, uttering an incoherent sound of pleasure.

"Tell me," she whispered in his ear, "who is the Northern King?"

He didn't speak, but she felt him smile.

"Please." She kissed him, one hand clasping his cock. She stroked him, running her thumb over the tip, spreading the first droplets of moisture from the tiny eye. "Tell me."

With a growl, he covered her body with his, licking her breasts and dipping his fingers into her cunt. Sabine gasped as his strong, gentle fingers immersed themselves in her wetness and rubbed her hard little clit.

"Galen, please," she breathed.

"Please what?"

"Please tell me."

He grinned. "You're stubborn, but so am I, little miss."

He kissed her from breast to groin. Burying his face between her legs, he used his lips, teeth and tongue on her delicate flesh until she trembled and strained in the throes of orgasm.

"For one so innocent, you've learned to use your wiles well." He kissed her belly before drawing her into his arms as he rolled onto his side. "But I'm too old to fall for that trick."

"If I was innocent, I'm certainly not any more, thanks to you."

"Funny, you don't sound all that grateful."

"I never imagined losing my virginity to a pirate."

"A privateer."

"I know, I know. To me, it's still the same thing."

He kissed her hair before leaving the cot and reaching for his clothes. "I have to get on deck."

Sabine glanced at him, stroking her own breasts. "Don't you want to pleasure yourself?"

He winked. "I plan on it, but the anticipation will make climax all the better. Be prepared for later."

She smiled. "Sounds threatening."

"Good. Now let's go topside."

* * * * *

Galen glanced at Sabine as they stepped on deck. He smiled at her expression as she watched the crew. Drake was at the wheel, several men were mopping the deck while others practiced hand-to-hand combat or fought with swords. A small group emptied nets and cleaned fish.

All eyes found Sabine, some discreetly, others with blatant curiosity. She didn't seem to mind the attention, but lifted her skirts and strode alongside Galen in a queenly manner that made him smile.

"It's a fine night," Galen observed, nodding to several of his men who voiced greetings. "We should be able to make good time." He shouted orders for them to raise the sails and pick up speed.

"In a hurry to reach your island?" Sabine asked.

He nodded, taking her hand and tugging her toward the rail. He pointed to the dark water ahead—not so dark to vampiric eyes. Two dolphins broke the surface, leaping above the waves.

Sabine smiled. "I've never seen anything like that."

"There's much more than that in the ocean. I knew you'd love it."

"How did you know?" She looked up at him.

He shrugged. "Just a feeling. You have the spirit of the sea."

"I'll take that as a compliment, Captain Donovan."

"As it was intended. Come on. We can't watch dolphins all night. There's work to be done."

As they made their way across the deck, Sofian climbed down from the crow's nest, dropping lightly to his feet in front of them.

"No sign of him."

"The King?" Sabine asked.

Neither Sofian nor Galen so much as glanced at her, let alone replied to her question.

"I doubt he'll follow us to the island. He's not that stupid."

"What do you mean? Why would he be stupid to follow?" Sabine continued.

"I still say we watch our backs," Sofian said.

"That's common sense."

"Why wouldn't he follow you to the island?" Sabine demanded, and Galen sensed her impatience. He nearly smiled. If he didn't acknowledge her in the next few seconds, she'd cause a scene neither he nor the crew would likely forget.

"Because it's too well protected, Sabine, and he never goes where he might not win," Galen told her.

"But his army is so powerful. Castle Debray had a well-trained guard and we were nearly demolished."

"There were too few of them, and they were mortal. The island is different. There are no mortals. It would be one vampire army against another."

"And you believe yours would win?"

Galen's gaze held hers. "I believe no one would win. The King doesn't fight for honor or the good of his people. He fights for power and wealth."

"But a man like you would never fight or kill for such things?" Sabine mocked, folding her arms across her chest and narrowing her dark eyes.

If he was the sort of scum who struck women, he might have felt like slapping the arrogant look off her face. Then he forced himself to calm. It wasn't her fault she thought of him as little better than a common thief. How could she know any different? Of course, he could tell her, as Drake had suggested earlier that day while Sabine had slept. With just Galen, Drake and Sofian running the deck by day, the three often discussed important matters, both business and private. At least Drake would discuss private matters. Coaxing Sofian to talk about anything not directly related to their mission was like asking a wolf to disclose the whereabouts of his den. Still, he trusted Sofian more than anyone on board the ship. The man possessed integrity, and they'd saved each other's lives on many occasions.

"I'll send Pete up to watch," Sofian said. "Then I'm training."

"I'll join you as soon as Sabine is settled."

Sofian nodded to them both, his one silvery eye gleaming in the moonlight.

"Settled doing what?" she asked.

Galen motioned for her to follow him to the helm. As they passed a stocky man of middling height, Galen called, "Nils, come with us."

The man grinned at Sabine and rubbed his short brown beard as he followed them to a pile of rope. He picked up two lengths, tossed one to Sabine and the other to Nils. "Teach her how to tie good knots, then I'll have her help tie down the cargo when we move it."

"Finally going to look for those rats burrowing below?" Nils asked. "Cook's been complaining so much I could stake him through the heart myself."

"Rats?" Sabine wrinkled her nose. "I slept down there with rats?"

"Even palaces have rats, Sabine." Galen winked at her. "You see, they don't differentiate between peasants and nobles. Enjoy yourself with your new task. I'll see you when I'm through training with Sofian."

"I'll take good care of her, Captain."

Galen backed Nils into a barrel and glowered down at him, fangs flashing. "You better, boy."

Nils' amused expression faded and his lips jerked upward in a nervous smile, exposing the very tips of his own cat-like fangs. "You have my word, Captain Galen. I won't let a thing happen to a hair on her pretty little head."

Galen growled, teeth gnashing, before he turned away from Nils and strode across the deck.

Chapter Five

ౠ

"Not bad at all, miss." Nils took the knotted rope from Sabine's hand and examined it.

"I'm surprised," she said. "Usually I'm not very good with my hands. I never was one for sewing and embroidery."

Nils chuckled. "This is a bit different from sewing."

"Not all that much. It's still tedious."

"I agree it's not the most exciting part of sailing."

"How long have you been a seaman, Nils?"

"Let's see now." He raised his eyes toward the sky and counted rapidly on his fingers. "Have to be about six hundred years, give or take a decade."

Sabine narrowed her eyes. Being the youngest in her family, she could not yet imagine existing so long.

"My father was a shipbuilder," Nils continued. "So you might say the ocean is in my blood."

"How about Galen?" Sabine asked, wondering how much information she could gather about her lover from the crew. "How long has he been at sea?"

"Can't say I know for sure, miss. I met him about a century ago, but I know he's much older than that."

"How old do you think?"

"I don't rightly know."

Sabine stared across the deck to where Galen and Sofian practiced swordplay. Both men moved with swiftness and grace. Galen was slightly heavier than Sofian, though both men were tall and well muscled. She noted that Sofian's blind side didn't seem to hinder his skill as he fought. He and Galen were well matched, and each man seemed to know it. They pressed each other to their limits, battling with ferocity Sabine wouldn't have expected between friends.

Taking another length of rope to knot, she asked, "How would you describe Captain Donovan?"

"I'm not sure I know what you mean."

She sighed, keeping her patience. This man was either well trained or as stupid as he looked. "What sort of man is he?"

Nils held her gaze for a moment. "A strong one."

"Strong in body or in mind?"

"Both. And you'd do well not to play with him, miss. I know how women can be, but Galen Donovan is not one to annoy."

"I'm not afraid of him. Do I look like a coward?"

Nils eyes flashed, and he appeared offended. "It has nothing to do with cowardice, miss, but with common sense. Treat him right, and you'll find no more loyal companion than the Captain. But you treat him wrong, and—"

"And what?"

"And I think I should show you how to tie another kind of knot. You've got that one down well enough."

"Is he older than you."

"I don't rightly know."

Sabine raised her eyes to the heavens. "What *do* you know, Nils?"

"How to make good knots."

For the next few hours, Sabine and Nils spoke of trivial matters, the weather, their homelands, favorite foods that they wouldn't have until they reached land again. Finally Sabine stood, fingers sore and neck stiff from tying knots. She walked across the deck, closer to where Galen and Sofian practiced. They had been fighting for several hours, but like most vampires, their energy seemed boundless.

They locked swords, bodies straining against one another's. Galen's black shirt and Sofian's white clung to their sweat-soaked bodies, and the sea wind tugged at their damp locks of dark hair. They broke from each other and nodded before Sofian walked to the hull while Galen joined Sabine by the rail. The ties of his shirt had opened, exposing his chiseled, hair-matted chest glistening with perspiration.

She tried to appear indifferent and said with sarcasm, "That was quite a display of manly prowess."

"But a necessary one. Skills that aren't kept sharp will lead to death. And now," Galen winked, "I'm ready to claim the pleasure I'm owed from earlier."

"Oh are you?" Sabine almost hated the way her belly tightened with anticipation.

He nodded, reaching for her hand. His fingers folded around hers. His hand felt hot and moist, though not unpleasantly so. She actually longed for those hands to touch every part of her.

That's what I want, too, he thought. *Come below with me, and I'll touch you anywhere and everywhere. I'll kiss those beautiful white thighs and devour your lovely breasts. I can already feel my teeth slipping into you, my cock driving you to irresistible pleasures…*

Sabine's hand tightened on his, and she found herself dragging *him* below deck.

* * * * *

In his cabin, Galen slammed the door shut behind them and allowed her to shove him onto the bed. She bound his wrists with a length of rope she still carried. It was long enough for her to fasten his arms to each side of the bed. He stared at her with curious blue eyes as she knelt between his legs and massaged his calves, working her way up to his thighs. His breathing quickened in spite of her soothing massage. Perhaps if he hadn't known what was in her mind, he would have relaxed, but it was impossible when he caught her mental vision of lustful tortures to come.

One of her hands cupped his crotch through his trousers. She kneaded, causing him to sigh. Her hands slipped beneath the sweaty shirt and caressed his abdomen, ribs and chest. Heartbeat thudding in his ears, he felt his cock harden.

Sabine's teeth tore open the shirt. She lapped the ridges of muscle in his stomach while she tugged down his trousers. The tip of her tongue traced the sensitive place where smooth flesh met pubic hair. Suddenly she buried her lips at the base of his cock and licked the length of him. The ruddy head slipped deep into her mouth while her tongue teased and tormented. Tiny incisors pierced his aching flesh, and he gasped, every muscle tightening in his body. She sucked, lapping blood and calling forth his essence with a force that drove him to rip the rope to pieces so he could bury his hands in her hair.

"Sabine!" he panted, heart drumming against his ribs. She bit deeper, sucked harder, and the pleasure nearly blinded him. "Merciful heaven!"

There is no mercy, she thought. *Not for a pirate. Not from me.*

Finally, a woman who might just match me.

I don't intend to match you, but to surpass you.

One of her fangs sank into the small eye at the head of his cock and for a moment Galen thought he might faint from sheer pleasure. Damn the bitch! She might just surpass him after all.

It seemed he'd created a beautiful, perfect monster.

* * * * *

"Sabine," Galen murmured, squeezing her shoulders gently.

Though she didn't open her eyes, she stirred, pressing a kiss to the hard, warm chest where she'd rested her cheek in sleep.

"I have to go topside," he said.

"Yes. The crew must be wondering where you are."

He chuckled. "Oh, I think they know exactly where I am."

Sabine felt a moment of embarrassment, replaced by excitement. Passion among vampires was normal. They were creatures of lust and emotion, and for too long she'd lived under her family's protection, ignoring her lustful side. She only wished she'd chosen a man who hadn't caused suffering and death to people she cared about.

"It will be forever between us, won't it? What he did to your people." He tilted her face up to his. She felt his sadness and saw it reflected in his ocean blue eyes. "I don't blame you, Sabine."

"How did he know you'd come to Castle Debray?"

"Simple." Galen left the bed and pulled on his trousers. "I was betrayed by someone on this ship."

Sabine's eyes widened. "Betrayed?"

"I told no one where I was going, but as you read, I mentioned Castle Debray in my log. The only people who have access to the log are on board this ship."

"I guess thieves like you can't even trust each other."

"Are you really one to talk with a brother like Kornel?"

Rage nearly blinded Sabine as she leapt from the bed, teeth and fists clenched. "You bastard! How can you compare this ship full of pirates to a family?"

"The inhabitants of my island and the members of this crew are my family, Sabine. A child like you couldn't begin to understand the centuries of work and struggle we've endured together."

"Funny you didn't call me a child when you were rutting me like some maniacal goat!"

Galen grinned. "You're gorgeous when you're angry. Your eyes gleam like they do in moonlust."

"If it hadn't been for the damn moonlust, I never would have slept with you in the first place!"

"Or the second or third or fourth—"

"Stop it!" Sabine shoved him hard in the chest. He grasped her arms and kissed her roughly, his teeth pricking her lip. She shivered with passion as he licked the blood away.

He shoved her gently onto the bed and headed for the door.

"Wait!" She chased him and grasped his forearm. "If you were betrayed, what are you going to do about it? Whoever did it is dangerous to you."

"I'll bide my time. Eventually, he'll give himself away."

"What if he tries to start a mutiny?" Sabine tugged on his arm as he reached for the door handle. "You think it couldn't happen?"

"Anything can happen, Sabine."

"What does it take to stir you?"

"Your lovely mouth on my cock."

Sabine's lip curled in fury and disgust. She dropped his arm, picked up her dress from the floor and tugged it over her head.

"Captain!" Drake shouted from outside the door. "Captain, come quick! One of the King's ships is almost on us!"

Sabine's heart pounded with fear, and she turned to Galen, but he was already out the door.

The King again! Memories of Castle Debray in ruins made her hands tremble as she followed Galen to the deck.

The crew was assembled, weapons poised and ready for battle. The King's ship flew a black and red dragon flag, similar to Galen's, except their dragon, instead of bones, was covered in scales and breathing smoke. Sabine's vampiric eyes noticed fangs glistening in the mouths of the enemy crew. They also clutched swords, daggers and bows.

"Shall we try to outrun them, Captain?" shouted the man at the wheel.

Sofian, who had appeared beside Galen, shook his head. "We can try, but it won't work. They've got a faster ship."

Galen narrowed his eyes toward the deck of the King's ship. Their archers loaded flaming arrows and let them fly toward the Scarlet Dragon's sails.

Galen ordered his own archers to fire, then muttered a curse.

"Get below!" he barked at Sabine.

"But—"

"Go! And don't move unless you're sent for!"

"I can help!"

"You will. You and Cook will have to care for the casualties."

"Casualties!" Sabine breathed, climbing below deck. She was not a nurse! She had little idea what to do.

You'll be fine, Galen's voice sounded in her head. *We're going to need you, Sabine. You won't disappoint us.*

I'll do my best, she thought, before he broke contact with her as the battle began above.

"Cook?" Sabine stepped into the galley.

The cook, a tall, slender man with gray hair tied at his nape, placed a hand on her shoulder. "Come with me. We'll need bandages. How are you with a needle?"

"Terrible."

"You'll learn. I'll show you how to sew up a wound."

"Are you a cook or a doctor?"

"Either one, depending on whether there's a battle or a banquet."

"How comforting." Sabine helped him tear clothes into strips. Both raised their eyes as the wooden beams above them seemed to shake.

"Murdering bastard," Cook hissed. "Never enough kill for him."

"The Northern King?"

"King of Death."

"Who is he exactly?"

"Someone the Captain shouldn't have bargained with."

"You mean someone whose booty he shouldn't have tried to claim for himself."

"You might not say that if you knew what the booty was."

"No one tells me anything!"

"And I don't agree with that, either, but it's what Galen wants."

"Why does Galen always get what he wants?" Sabine snapped, but the sound of footsteps dragged her thoughts from Galen and the King to the matter at hand.

Nils burst into the galley, a bleeding crewmember slung over his shoulder. He dumped the man on the floor and said, "More are coming. I don't know how the bastard found us this time."

Probably the same way he found Galen at Castle Debray, Sabine thought. If Galen didn't do something soon, his betrayer might just kill him before he gave himself away.

Chapter Six

ഔ

"What in hell's name is going on up there?" Sabine concentrated on holding down an injured crewman while the doctor removed a broken arrowhead from his shoulder.

"Just keep your mind on what you're doing!" Cook ordered.

"It feels like the ship's going to capsize."

"If it does, you needn't worry. You can drift all day. The sun doesn't affect you like it does most of us. Hold him still!"

"I'm doing my best!"

"You bastard! You're killing me!" the crewman snarled, fangs bared. "You're a better cook than a doctor!"

Sabine struck the crewman in the face with her elbow, knocking him unconscious.

Cook's eyes widened for a moment, then he continued his task. "We'll need to work on your bedside manner, young woman."

"He's still, isn't he?" Sabine wiped her hands on her skirt and picked up a bucket of water.

Stooping beside a slender red-haired youth who'd suffered a chest injury, she dipped a rag in water and bathed his face.

"This one needs blood badly," Sabine called to Cook.

"Every able body is up on deck, and I can't spare any of my own right now. I need strength and concentration to help the others."

Sabine rested her hand on the redhead's shoulder. He gazed at her through glassy eyes and murmured, "Diana?"

"Who's Diana?" Sabine asked gently.

"My wife. I want to see her."

"You'll see her," Sabine told him.

He shook his head, and she realized he sensed his own approaching death. Strange for a creature who was thought to be immortal.

"Yes you will." Sabine sat beside him. "When you get home, she'll be so glad to see you."

"Tell her I love her."

Sabine's stomach clenched. The way his injury was positioned — far better than Galen's had been when he'd arrived at Castle Debray — all he needed was blood, and he'd have a chance to recover from the silver poisoning. Thus far, every injury had been caused by silver weapons. Sabine knew Galen's men were armed with silver, so she might have guessed the Northern King's warriors would also fight with weapons meant to destroy others of their kind.

"Sabine, I'm going to need more water," Cook said.

She stood, bucket in hand and glanced over her shoulder at the redhead. "I'll be right back."

After bringing Cook the water, she returned to the youth, knife in hand, and made a shallow cut on the back of her wrist. Crimson droplets welled against her pale skin, and before they dripped wasted to the floor, she pressed her bleeding flesh to his lips.

For a moment, she thought him too weak to accept the nourishment she offered. Then she felt the coolness of his teeth tearing deeper into her wrist. His tongue lapped her skin, and he made a desperate sound deep in his throat. Though simple blood sharing wasn't as intense as mating, she was still able to sense his emotions, if not his thoughts. Lust mingled with the need to survive. As his injury healed and strength returned, he grasped her arm, tugging her closer as he drank.

Sabine's eyes slipped shut, and she tried to ignore their synchronized heartbeats, tried to thrust aside the tinge of desire that heated her belly. Galen! She focused on Galen, imagining it was his teeth inside her.

"Diana," the youth murmured against her wrist.

Sabine shook her head clear. She wasn't Diana, and this boy certainly wasn't Galen. She'd done her part, and it must end before either of them did something they'd regret.

"That's enough." Sabine pushed him away, but his grip was solid. "No!"

The redhead's eyes opened, dazed, and he fell back against the wall. "I'm sorry."

She shook her head, forcing her own breathing under control and willing her body not to tremble.

"Thank you, Lady Sabine."

She smiled, nodding, before she stood and joined Cook who was setting a crewmember's broken leg.

"What can I do?" she asked.

"Rest a minute. You'll need it after that. Casualties seem to have slowed down," he replied without taking his eyes from his work. "I was wrong about your bedside manner."

She smiled. "No you weren't. I've never been a nurturing kind of woman. Perhaps femininity was wasted on me."

This time Cook glanced at her, his eyes sweeping her before returning to his patient. "I doubt that."

* * * * *

After the initial exchange of arrows, the King's men attempted to board the Scarlet Dragon. Galen's crew successfully held them off for a time, but the King's ship was much larger and they were outnumbered three to one.

The first men climbed on deck, clashing with Galen's crew. The sound of steel on steel echoed above waves slapping the side of the ship.

Galen fought, a sword in one hand, a dagger in the other. Four armored warriors flew at him across the slippery deck. He blocked and thrust, his weapon finding chinks in mail even as he felt the tip of a sword slash his upper arm.

From the corner of his eye, Galen saw one of his crewmen — a tall, thickly built man — pick up one of the enemy soldiers and fling him across the deck. Galen ducked before the body struck him. As he spun, knocking aside an enemy blade, he caught sight of Drake fighting alongside two of the King's men. The bastard had turned traitor, and now Galen had no doubts as to who had told the Northern King of his whereabouts. Drake edged his way toward the ropes hanging over the side of the ship.

Son of a bitch! Galen's teeth ground with rage. He'd known Drake for centuries! As if sensing the Captain's glare, Drake glanced in Galen's direction.

"You bastard!" Galen snarled, blocking an overhead blow and kicking his attacker over the rail. He fought his way toward Drake, and the man skidded toward the safety of the ropes.

Suddenly Sofian dropped from one of the masts, closer to Drake than Galen. The men traded sword swipes.

Lightning ripped across the sky and the ship tossed on the stormy water. Cold rain washed the blood-streaked deck and Galen cursed. Just what they needed on top of everything else, a storm!

The next streak of lightning struck the mast. The thick wood fell, causing Sofian and Drake to leap apart to avoid being crushed.

Men surrounded Galen, and as he dispatched them, he noticed Drake had reached the ropes. Before climbing over, he pulled a dagger and aimed it at Sofian who was busy fighting off another group. The blade flew, and Galen shouted, but the dagger struck Sofian in the back. He staggered, the tip of an enemy blade slicing his face.

Galen spun, blocking a sword thrust, and dropped to the deck, extending one leg and knocking the legs out from under his attacker. Leaping to his feet, he flung his dagger at Drake before the man disappeared over the edge of the ship. The blade struck home, piercing his heart. Drake dropped into the dark water, his death cry mingling with a clap of thunder.

"Sofian!" Galen shouted as he reached his friend who had collapsed on the rain-slicked deck.

He fought off two more men, thrusting one through the heart and knocking the other overboard.

The King's men dwindled, those left alive scrambling over the rail, in spite of the raging storm.

"Sofian!" Galen grasped his friend by the shirt.

Blood streaked Sofian's face, soaking the black patch over his eye. His other eye looked unfocused. Still, with Galen's help he struggled to his feet. "Forget about me, and watch your back!"

"Will you shut up and stop playing the lone wolf for once?" Galen snarled, lugging Sofian below deck.

Injured crewmen sprawled in the holds and galley. Galen's eyes instantly riveted to Sabine. Sleeves rolled up to her elbows, her once fine dress streaked with blood, she changed the bandage on a man's shoulder. If he hadn't so much on his mind, Galen might have smiled. In spite of Sabine's soft, overly protected upbringing, he'd sensed the independence and compassion in her soul. He'd known the moment he'd seen her that she didn't belong cooped in that castle. *Not that she belongs risking her life on the Scarlet Dragon, either,* he thought, struck with guilt.

Sabine's gaze met his, and she stood, approaching as he dragged Sofian to an empty space beside a cheese barrel.

"He got hit on his blind side," Galen said. "I need to get back on deck."

"We'll take care of him." Sabine had already reached for bandages. "He's bleeding badly. Get Cook before you go."

Galen nodded, picking up Cook's scent among the others and following it to the deepest hold.

"Cook, Sabine needs your help in the galley. Sofian's hurt badly."

"On my way." Cook stood. "How is it up there?"

"Over, but the storm's knocked down a mast. Of all the ships we had to run into, why did it have to be the biggest one in the bastard's fleet?"

"Because that's how life goes, don't you know that yet?"

"Apparently not."

As Galen made his way topside, he glanced in the galley and saw Sabine kneeling beside Sofian. His stomach warmed in spite of their desperate situation, then he felt a hint of fear. Was he falling in love after so many centuries?

A voice inside his head screamed danger, but the warning came too late. He should have listened long before he'd mated with Lady Sabine Debray.

* * * * *

Sabine glanced at Cook as he nudged her aside to inspect Sofian's back.

"He's bleeding horribly. Must be the silver."

"No, it's the wound itself. Silver doesn't affect Sofian."

"You mean not all of us are affected by silver any more than we are affected by sunlight?"

"He's different than we are. I need another cloth."

Sabine brought him more supplies. "What do you mean he's different?"

"His father was mortal."

Mortal! Sabine had never heard of such a thing. Still, if vampires could produce children together, why not vampires and mortals?

"Then what is he? Human or vampire?" Sabine asked as she assisted. Her curiosity increased when she noticed several scars marking the first mate's back. Her kind usually didn't scar.

"Some of both. He requires blood and isn't affected by silver or sunlight, but his injuries don't heal as quickly as ours. You can check his face. I can handle his back myself."

Sabine reached for the eye patch to further inspect the damage, but Sofian weakly grasped her wrist and murmured, "No."

She was shocked that he was still conscious, especially since he hadn't uttered a sound while Cook worked on his back.

"I need to see the wound." She tugged away from him.

"Now's not the time to worry about that dead eye of yours," Cook said.

"Let me help you." Sabine spoke gently, surprised the first mate wasn't quite as invulnerable as he'd seemed. She should have realized, after sensing Galen's affection for him. Captain Donovan might be obnoxious and arrogant, but somehow he'd retained a degree of warmth, and she couldn't imagine him seeking friendship with someone completely unfeeling.

She removed the blood-soaked patch and began cleaning away the gore. Relief flooded her when she realized the injury had just missed his eye. She pressed a cloth to the wound to stanch the blood flow, and his eye flickered opened. The iris was such pale blue it almost blended with the white, giving him a zombie-like appearance from one side.

"Not pretty, is it?" Sofian's words ended in a grunt of pain as Cook scrubbed his wounded back.

"You didn't strike me as a vain man, Sofian," Sabine said.

His lips twisted in what might have been a smile. "I'm starting to understand Galen's fondness for you."

"Just what I needed in my life. A pirate's fondness."

Sofian fell silent while they worked on his injuries. Sabine watched as Cook placed delicate stitches on the facial wound, relieved that he'd decided to do the job himself. Her stomach churned at the idea of performing such an intricate task. She'd need far more experience. Experience! Had she actually decided to spend more time aboard the Scarlet Dragon? To her surprise, the idea of traveling with Galen and his crew appealed to her, even after the horror of battle. Even though the storm above caused the ship to toss violently.

"As soon as the first uninjured man comes below, make sure he gives Sofian some blood."

"I can."

"You've given up enough already." Cook walked away.

Sofian had fallen into a light sleep, so Sabine visited others, doing what she could to make them comfortable. Gradually, the ship's rocking gentled, and she guessed the storm had subsided.

Before venturing above, she checked the first mate. Unlike most of the others, his condition hadn't improved, but Cook had said he didn't heal as rapidly as a full vampire.

Sabine touched a hand to his forehead, stunned by the heat. She bathed his face with water, and his eye flickered open, his blind one swathed in bandages.

"How is it above?" he asked.

"We haven't heard, but the storm seems to have subsided."

"Galen will have his work cut out for him." Sofian tried to adjust his position, and she guessed his injured back was causing him pain.

"How are you feeling?" she asked.

"Like I'm on fire."

"It's the fever," Sabine muttered. She glanced at the cut on the back of her wrist that was almost completely healed. Cook said she'd given enough, but that was hours ago. She certainly didn't feel weak. Sofian, on the other hand, was worsening.

She took the knife from the box of healing supplies Cook had given her and reopened the wound.

"What the hell are you doing?" Sofian demanded.

She offered him the blood, and when he refused, she said, "So you're going to waste it?"

Tossing her an irritated look that almost reminded her of Galen, he accepted several mouthfuls of the rich liquid.

As she bandaged her wrist, she felt his gaze upon her.

"Thank you," he said.

"You're welcome." Sabine sat beside him, resting her head against the wall. She'd begun drifting to sleep when Sofian's words caught her interest.

"You've done something for me, Lady Sabine, so I feel I should do something for you."

"What do you mean?"

"I know you've been curious about Galen and the Northern King."

Sabine sat up, staring into Sofian's silver eye. "Please go on."

"The cargo Galen stole from him was human. The King ordered him to destroy a coastal village and deliver the inhabitants to him as slaves."

"Why?"

"Because he's a hateful bastard and they refused to give in to him. Galen was paid to carry out the order. Instead he freed them."

"Freed them?" Sabine's heartbeat quickened. Galen wasn't the despicable pirate she thought him to be! Yet he'd made a bitter enemy out of a madman. "The King won't stop until he gets revenge, will he?"

"I doubt it."

"Then why doesn't Galen attack him first? Supposedly his island is home to a vampire army powerful enough to keep the King away."

"I can say no more about the King and Galen."

"Then why whet my appetite?" Sabine folded her arms across her chest, frustrated.

"Because I wanted you to know there's more to Galen than greed."

Sabine lowered her eyes. Deep inside, she'd known Galen wasn't so terrible. No man who helped bury the dead at Castle Debray could have been purely wicked.

"But there seems to be so much more between Galen and the King."

"Anything more is for him to disclose in his own time." Sofian settled back and closed his eyes.

Yawning, Sabine did the same. It seemed like forever since she'd rested, and giving up her blood had tired her more than she realized. Moments later she drifted to sleep, not waking until she felt herself being lifted up in strong arms and cradled against a warm, hard chest.

She opened her eyes slightly. "Galen?"

"I'm taking you to bed, little miss."

"But the others—"

"No longer need you. They've all been given blood and are healing well." Galen kissed her hair. "You were a great help."

She smiled slightly and cuddled closer to his chest as he carried her to his cabin and closed the door behind them.

* * * * *

Galen placed Sabine on the cot and began undressing her. Within moments, she lay naked atop the sheets, Galen's hands stroking her torso with soothing motions.

"Cook told me how much you did for my crew last night. Thank you."

Sabine smiled. "To tell you the truth, I wasn't sure I had it in me. Other than the incident with my brother, I've led a very spoiled life."

"Such an incident is enough to mature anyone—and there's nothing wrong with being spoiled, provided you still retain your compassion. Actually, I intend to spoil you as often and as much as I can for as long as we're together."

Sabine's smile faded, and she glanced down at Galen's hands resting on the gentle curve of her belly. Her thoughts echoed in his mind.

"You like it here." He touched her cheek.

"Why should I like this floating dung heap?"

"I don't know why, but you do. Maybe it's because life at sea excites you. It's always excited me."

"I'm not some pirate scum like you."

"That insult is getting old." Galen touched his lips to the smooth flesh beneath one of her breasts. "Try to think of some new ones, would you, little miss?"

Galen tugged his shirt over his head and discarded his trousers and boots before slipping into the cot and tugging her on top of him. He cupped the back of her head and pressed her to his chest. "You gave up much of your blood, so replenish. Drink of me, little miss. Drink."

Her teeth sank into his chest, and Galen's eyes slipped shut. His head arched back as pleasure built in his loins with each lap of her tongue, each sweet tug of her lips as she sucked his life's essence.

"Sabine," he murmured when she finally raised her bloody lips, "I have to go topside. It's nearly dawn, and I'm the only one who can run this ship, now that Drake—the rotten bastard—is dead and Sofian is injured."

"I can help you."

"No. I want you to rest and let my blood do its work. There will be plenty for you to do when you wake."

She closed her eyes as he covered her with the blanket. Galen dropped a kiss on her parted lips before he tugged on his clothes and returned to the deck.

The day was as difficult as he'd imagined. Sailing a ship the size of the Scarlet Dragon alone wasn't easy, and in between sailing, he did his best to work on repairs. At dusk, most of the crew had recovered and several took over sailing while he and the others worked on repairs throughout the night.

It was close to midnight when Sabine joined him on deck, offering him food.

"Cook's back in the galley." She smiled. "Only Sofian and a few others are still below. I think Cook tied Sofian down. He's been trying to come topside all night."

"Tell him if I see his face up here before he's recovered I'll blind his other eye." Galen took a long drink of water then wiped his lips on his bare forearm. The weather had grown hot, and like most of the crew, he'd discarded his shirt and only wore his trousers.

"You should come down and rest," she said. "It will be morning soon, and you'll be alone up here—except for me."

"I might just teach you how to run this tub after all." He winked. "I need someone to replace Drake."

"Do I look like a good replacement for Drake?" She placed her hand on her hip in mock anger.

Galen kissed her cheek. "Far prettier than he could ever have hoped to be."

"Come below for a while." She looped her arms around his neck and nuzzled his chest.

"There's too much to be done. We can't do full repairs until we reach land, but we can do enough to get us to the island. Get below and I'll see you at sunrise." He slapped her buttocks as she headed below deck.

The look she flung him was both angry and lustful. A shiver ran through him as he imagined making love with her again. Still, he couldn't think about that now. Later, that he vowed.

* * * * *

When the crew retired for the day, Sabine and Sofian joined Galen on deck.

"I said you were to stay below until you're healed," Galen snapped at the first mate.

"I'm healed enough to help you up here. Do you plan to stay awake day and night until you collapse?"

"Just until the work is done. And who's the captain, me or you?"

"He gave me his word he won't do too much," Sabine said.

Galen glanced from one to the other, a hint of jealously creeping into his soul. "So you have an understanding, do you?"

Sabine stroked Galen's forearm and said, "I thought you were going to teach me how to run this ship?"

He grunted in reply, and sent them both to work, feeling annoyed at his own emotions. He could tell by the amused look in Sabine's eyes she'd sensed his envy of any relationship that might have developed between her and Sofian.

For the remainder of the day, there was little time to ponder romance, however, and less time for talk. By dusk, several days and nights of hard work and no sleep began to catch up with Galen, and he longed for a few hours in his cot with Sabine wrapped in his arms.

Shortly after moonrise, he was giving final orders to the crew when she appeared beside him and took his hand.

"Shall we go below?" she murmured.

He followed her, feeling almost like a puppy following his mistress. The thought annoyed him, but she seemed to have a hold over him that increased each time he gazed into her dark, beautiful eyes.

In the cabin, they discarded their clothes and fell onto the cot. Galen closed his eyes and buried his face between her breasts, loving the scent and texture of her skin.

She sighed when his lips fastened on a nipple, his tongue rolling over the hardening peak.

"You taste so good," he murmured. "We belong together, you and I."

"We should never have been. We're as different as the sun and the moon."

You won't always have to pretend to hate me, Galen's mind spoke to hers since his mouth was busy with her breasts. *I know you like being here, in spite of the violence, storms, betrayal.*

"Betrayal!" Sabine sat up, and Galen moved away, his eyes on hers. "There's still someone aboard this ship who wants to see the Northern King destroy you. You have to find him, Galen, before something terrible happens!"

"Worried about the crew or just me?" He wiggled his brows.

"Both. The King is evil. You were trying to do a good thing, and he—"

"What do you mean I was trying to do a good thing?" Galen's heartbeat quickened, and he grasped her shoulders a bit harder than he'd intended.

"I know what cargo the King paid you to retrieve."

Galen gritted his teeth. "Which one of my loyal crew has been talking? Was it Nils? The little pipsqueak was enamored by your beauty from the moment he saw you. Or perhaps it was Cook? He's always appreciated powerful women."

"It was neither of them. And I'm so glad you noticed I'm powerful." Sabine cast him a coquettish glance so irresistible that he kissed her. She buried her hands in his hair and pressed him close. Her blood cried out for him, and he needed nourishment. The past grueling days made him desperate for blood. He'd been so busy, he hadn't realized how hungry he was until now.

He sank his teeth deep into her shoulder and drank. She gasped, hands clutching his back as her legs wrapped tightly around his waist. He thrust into her hot cunt, his cock, trapped by her soft wetness, felt ready to burst from desire. God, he needed her in body, mind and blood!

"Oh Galen!" she moaned, her pulse leaping when he reached between them to stroke her clit as his cock rammed her. Her blood ran sweet and warm over his teeth and down his throat. He growled as he felt her orgasm, her pussy clutching him deeper. Never had he dreamed passion so molten could feel so soft.

Suddenly he slipped from her and rolled her onto her stomach, pressing kisses down her spine and over her smooth buttocks. One hand slipped under her, fondling her clit while the other grasped her breast and kneaded. He lay on his back and tugged her on top of him, his hands still teasing and caressing. The squirming of her buttocks against his crotch aroused him, and he bit her neck, feeling her blood rush over his lips while her body shook as she came again.

When he'd drank his fill and sated their desire, he stretched out on his side, holding her close, and murmured, "Sabine?"

"Umm?"

"Who told you about the cargo?"

She folded her hands on top of his chest and propped her chin on them, staring into his eyes. "Your first mate."

"Sofian!" Galen sat up, shocked by this revelation. Of all the people aboard the Scarlet Dragon, Sofian was the last he'd expect to gossip, let alone disclose information strictly forbidden by Galen.

"Don't be angry with him."

"I won't—until he's recovered enough to defend himself."

"Galen!"

"What else did he tell you?"

"Nothing, though I questioned him. I want to know more about this King."

"Once we get to the island, he won't affect your life, so you needn't worry about him."

"Won't affect my life? He's already destroyed my home, and he wants to kill you!"

Galen smirked. "Why should it bother you that he wants to cut out the heart of a worthless pirate?"

"You know why."

"I'd like to hear you admit it."

Sabine tried to leave the cot, but he held her fast. Her smooth bottom wiggled against his lower abdomen, a delicious torment to his semi erect cock nestled between their bodies.

"It's bad enough you can sense what I feel. I'll never give you the satisfaction of hearing the words."

"But you admit I mean something to you?"

"We've mated."

"You sound disgusted."

"Why shouldn't I be? You're a—"

"Peasant? A pirate? The man who makes you scream in ecstasy?"

"You're insufferable!" She tried to tug away, but he'd wrapped his arms around her and nuzzled her neck.

"You're gorgeous, Sabine. You're sweet, caring, tender."

"And stupid to have tied myself up with the likes of you!"

"If you hate me so much, then why does it bother you that the King wants me dead?"

"Because he's more evil than you are."

"You seem sure of that."

Sabine raised her gaze to the ceiling. "Of course."

"When I first arrived at Castle Debray, you seemed quite certain of my evil."

"I didn't know you as well then."

"It was only a few days ago."

"You said yourself, once we mate, we're part of each other. I can hear your thoughts and feel your emotions, just as you can mine. Oh, you might be more experienced at blocking them from me, but I can still sense them. And I've witnessed the King's wickedness."

"Perhaps I've been just as wicked. My past stretches beyond your comprehension."

"Don't be so sure of that. I might be young, but my parents weren't, and neither is Narcisse."

"Knowing and experiencing are two very different things."

"One thing I do know, whatever you might have done in the past, you made up for some of it by freeing those people. You've made a terrible enemy, though."

"The King and I go back much further than that incident."

Sabine held his gaze, concentrated on sensing his thoughts and emotions. He eluded her for the most part, but couldn't entirely mask his pain, anger, and sorrow.

"What is he to you, Galen? And don't just say he's a royal who hired you."

"That's as good a description as any."

"No. It's not."

"You want to know what we are to each other, Sabine?" He spoke through clenched teeth. "We're enemies. Bitter and seething in rage."

"That's not the whole truth."

"Damn it, Sabine, will you just let it go? I'm tired." That much wasn't a lie. He needed a short sleep before returning to the deck.

With a sigh, she relented and rolled onto her back. She stroked his hair as he rested his cheek against her breasts and closed his eyes.

"I won't give up until I get an answer."

"Later."

"I'll hold you to that."

"Much later."

"Galen!"

He made a contented sound deep in his throat before drifting into slumber.

Chapter Seven

ം

Galen's vow to discuss his relationship with the King "much later" was certainly no exaggeration, Sabine thought as she stood on deck, gazing at the moonlit water. They'd been at sea for weeks — or was it months? — and he'd evaded the subject each time she mentioned the King. His only remarks about his enemy were during tactical discussions with his crew.

Frustrated by his secrecy, Sabine practiced tapping into his thoughts and feelings. To her irritation, Galen seemed to enjoy this.

I love the feeling of you in my mind, he'd tell her. *Especially when we're making love.*

When they made love seemed to be the only time he couldn't pick and choose what he allowed her to pluck from his mind. Unfortunately, she was also too wrapped in emotion to take advantage of his weakness. Even more alarming, she adored their mental link. It felt comforting to be wrapped in each other's thoughts, as if one person in the world could truly understand her needs without explanation.

"Wishing on the sea?"

Galen interrupted her thoughts, and she turned to him as he leaned on the rail. Her gaze trailed across his bare chest before focusing on his eyes. Since they'd sailed into warmer waters, closer to his island, he and many crewmen had taken to wearing only trousers. Sabine found no complaint in this, especially since most were fine vampiric specimens — Galen and Sofian standing out among even the most attractive. Though Sofian was a bit leaner than she preferred — or maybe it was simply that in her eyes, no one could outshine Galen. Just thinking of him made her wet with desire, and when she looked deeply into his eyes—as she was now—all she could think of was bedding him.

The scent of his passion wafted on the breeze, mingling with hers. She knew he smelled it, too, by the spark igniting his eyes.

He touched a hand to her cheek, brushing away a random wisp of hair. "What were you wishing for?"

"You'll never tell me."

He smiled, raising his eyes to the stars. "Not the King again?"

"All right. I won't ask this time. I'll tell you my second wish," she said, and he leaned closer, attentive. "I wish I could have said goodbye to my brother and sister-in-law. I'm sure they'll be worried."

Galen's smile faded. "I suppose you're right. There's no forgiveness for breaking up a family."

His manner concerned her, as did the pained expression in his eyes. She felt the depth of his sadness for a brief moment before his mental barriers rose against her probing. She rested her hand on his forearm. "Galen—"

"I'm sorry, Sabine. Truly sorry. "

He turned away, but she grasped his arm. "Galen, what's wrong?"

"You never should have been involved."

"I don't regret it." She spoke before she could stop the words. Was she insane, admitting that she *wanted* to be with him?

"You've made your regret plain every day of this voyage—at least in words. And I don't blame you, but I can't completely blame myself, either." He glanced over his shoulder at Nils and two other crewmembers who were listening to their conversation with interest. Galen growled at them. "Don't you have work to do?"

"Aye, we're mending this sail."

"Without looking at it?"

"Sorry, Captain," Nils muttered.

"Come with me." Galen grasped Sabine's hand and guided her below. In the cabin, he closed the door and pinned her against it with his body. He kissed her neck, tugging her dress off her shoulders and kissing her smooth flesh.

"Galen—"

"I couldn't completely blame myself for taking you. The moment I saw you, I wanted to devour you, and after I sipped your blood—after we mated—I *needed* you. The pull between us was strong. You could feel it, too, Sabine. I know you could."

"Yes," she admitted breathlessly as he slipped the dress down her torso and sucked a plump nipple, "I felt it. I didn't want to."

"Of course not. Why should you? I'm everything your parents told you to avoid, aren't I?"

"Yes."

"The opposite of your noble bloodline."

"But—"

"But you still *craved my touch.*"

"We're mated."

"For life, Sabine. No matter how long that life might be. That's why I had to take you with me. You're my family now, and I'm yours."

"I'll always be a Debray!"

"I can't take away your bloodline, only merge it with my own. We are one, little miss." He spoke against her parted lips. "And nothing can ever change that."

"I'm yours only as long as I decide to stay and amuse myself with you."

"Is that so?"

"Yes, that's so."

He grinned and kissed her hard, his tongue plundering her mouth while his one hand fondled her breast and the other stroked her damp cunt. She whimpered, on the verge of exquisite climax, when he dropped his hands from her body and tore his lips from her mouth. Through half-open eyes, she noticed the rise and fall of his chest and the color on the ridges of his sharp cheekbones. He wanted her as much as she wanted him, but he'd torment them both just to prove his point.

"I liked you better when I hated you," she whispered, teeth clenched.

He merely smiled and left the cabin, slamming the door behind him.

Sabine slammed her fist against the door so hard the walls rocked beneath her vampiric strength.

"Bastard!" she hissed. What was wrong with him? He was twisted, but she'd known that when they'd first met. She'd heard all Narcisse's stories. Galen was a pirate, a rogue, a man who used his body in battle as well as to manipulate women. Of all the men in the world, she *had* to fall in love with sea scum!

Still, something had troubled him. She'd seen his expression when he spoke of family. He'd never mentioned his own blood family, only his crewmembers and the inhabitants of his island. Where was his family? Who were they? She wished she'd have asked Narcisse more questions about Galen when she'd had the chance. Yet how was she to know she'd end up in his bed, on his ship, traveling to his island?

Anything can happen, her mother had always told her.

After watching one of her brothers kill the other for betrayal, she should have realized that and not given herself so easily to Captain Galen Donovan.

* * * * *

Sabine's first impression of Galen's island was of black sand beaches and green velvet mountains. It was morning when they arrived, so they circled the island until dusk, when the others emerged to help them dock.

As they began unloading supplies, Sabine heard hoofbeats in the distance, and soon another group of men with wagons emerged from the jungle.

"What do you think so far?" Galen asked, brushing past her, a trunk slung over his shoulder.

"I never imagined any place being so hot." She blew a wisp of damp hair from her eyes.

Galen winked. "You'll get used to it."

"And what if I don't?"

He tossed her a look that said he wasn't about to waste time thinking about it. "I'm giving orders for a crew to gather and sail back to Castle Debray to help your people with repairs."

"Thank you."

"It's the least I can do." She sensed a twinge of guilt as he stalked off to speak with some of his men who had begun dismounting.

Cook and Nils took turns introducing her to the islanders and started helping with the supplies. She noted by scent they were all vampires and wondered exactly how many lived on the island.

The sack of food she'd been carrying was suddenly taken from her arms. Galen tossed the sack into a half-filled wagon. He extended his hand, and she took it. "Let's get our horses and ride ahead. Sofian has everything under control here, and I want to show you the house."

After mounting their horses, Sabine followed Galen into the jungle. They rode down a twisting path, surrounded by lush vegetation. Sabine inhaled deeply as her gaze roamed over the vine-covered trees. She tried to discern thousands of new scents, flowers, trees, insects, birds and a variety of animals.

Galen smiled over his shoulder at her. "Exciting, isn't it, having someplace new to explore."

"It's not as if I've never been away from my own village, you know."

"Just about, I'll wager."

Sabine raised her eyes to heaven. "I can tell you the last place I'd have picked to visit would be this sticky excuse for an island."

"You like it."

"Do I sound like I like it?"

"No, but you can hardly contain your appreciation of its beauty. Don't concern yourself, Sabine. It's exactly how I feel when I look at you."

She flashed her teeth at him with a snarl. It seemed so unfair that she wanted to both strangle and make love with the same man.

The jungle seemed to twist on for miles until moonlight shone brighter as they emerged from the trees. Sabine nearly gasped at the beauty spread before her. Tall green mountains pierced the night sky. Two cascades emptied into a river that cut through a valley surrounded by jungle. Several stone houses scattered the valley's green floor, the largest situated at the foot of the tallest mountain. Instinctively, she knew the house belonged to Galen.

"Let's go." Galen kicked Desert Angel to a gallop, and Sabine, mounted on Pearl, followed close behind. Men, women and children were scattered throughout the valley, going about their nightly work. The village looked no different from the one her family ruled—except all the inhabitants were her kind. Sabine's heartbeat quickened at the thought. She'd never expected to see such a place. It reminded her of the stories the Priestess told her about the old days, before vampires and humans learned to fear one another.

As they neared Galen's house, a slender young man approached and took their horses.

"Carlos, this is Sabine."

The youth bowed from the neck, his pale blue eyes fixed on hers. "A pleasure. Captain Donovan has never brought a woman to the island before."

"Really?" Sabine tossed him a coquettish look. She couldn't deny that Carlos' words pleased her.

"Flattered?" Galen's voice rumbled close to her ear.

Sabine shrugged. "I suppose."

"You should be."

"Did you ever consider expressing how you really feel instead of clinging to that arrogant persona you've created?"

"Lady Sabine," Galen placed a hand over his heart in mock emotion, "if I thought you truly cared I might do just that. However, I know you too well to leave myself that vulnerable."

"What do you mean?"

"You're just waiting for some poor, stupid man to bare his soul so you can rip it to shreds."

Sabine smiled sweetly. "There are some men who deserve to have their souls shredded."

"That's true." Galen's teasing expression faded.

He took her hand as they stepped through the tall double doors and into the hall. It was much cooler inside the stone walls, and Sabine glanced around the room. Two little girls played with dolls in a corner, under the care of a group of women bent over needlework at the long, rectangular table in the center of the room. The women smiled at Galen in greeting, and a plump red-haired woman approached, sleeves rolled up to her elbows, her white apron stained with blood.

"Just skinnin' dinner, Captain." The woman grinned, revealing a dimple in her cheek and two sharp little fangs. "Who's the lady?"

"Sabine, this is Monica, our cook."

"I thought Cook—"

"He only works the galley."

"Because he hasn't got talent enough for a proper household," Monica huffed. "He's a fine doctor, though. Taught by the best." She winked at Galen. "You two look like you could use a nice bath."

"Sounds wonderful," Sabine said.

"I'll have one sent up to the guest room."

"Don't bother. I'm taking Sabine to the lake," Galen said. "And besides, she'll be sharing my room."

Monica's smile broadened, and Sabine gritted her teeth.

"You and the lady have married then?"

"No." Sabine and Galen spoke in unison.

"Not yet," Galen added.

"Not ever."

Monica looked confused, and Sabine opened her mouth to explain, but Galen interrupted, "We'll make arrangements with Cass later."

"What arrangements?" Sabine demanded. "And who's Cass?"

"I'm afraid he's still at the forge," Monica said. "You know how he is when he starts on his weapons."

"I know. I'll meet him there once Sabine's settled."

"I can settle myself. And who's Cass?"

"He's of an old religion—similar to your Priestess. He'll marry us. I'll talk him into it."

"You'll have to talk me into it first."

Galen took her chin in his hand and brushed her lips with his. "I'm sure you'll see things my way, little miss." He turned to the maid who watched them curiously. "Sabine will be back before dinner. I'll be late."

"Joining Cass?"

Galen nodded and guided Sabine toward the steep staircase on the wall to their right.

"I'll show you our room."

Our room. The thought made Sabine shiver with desire. In spite of her initial refusal, part of her wanted more than anything to be his wife. Still, another part denied any union with the infamous privateer. She wondered which side of her soul was the stronger and where it would lead her.

* * * * *

From the sleek lines of the understated dark wood furniture to the picture window open to the warm night breeze, Galen's spacious room reflected its owner.

Galen stood in front of the windows and drew a deep breath. He extended his hand to her. "Look at this."

Sabine approached, and he placed his hands on her shoulders, guiding her in front of him. He wrapped his arms around her waist from behind and held her close as they stared at the view.

Tree-covered mountains pierced the starry sky. The moon cast its golden light on the cascades and gazed at its own reflection in the rippling lake. Two long-legged birds walked along the water's edge, dipping their heads past the dark surface to retrieve fish. The scent of tropical flowers and herbs wafted throughout the room.

Had it not been for memories of her family, Sabine might have pretended the outside world didn't exist.

"Are we going to swim in that lake?"

"No. We're going into the jungle. There's a spot I love." Galen paused as a solitary howl broke the soft sounds of chirping insects and the blowing wind.

Sabine furrowed her brow. "I've never heard a wolf sound quite like that."

"You're far from home, remember that."

"Still, a wolf is a wolf."

"Do all horses have the same whinny? Do all dogs have the same bark? Do—"

"I understand Galen." She smirked up at him.

They remained silent as the howling continued.

"I only hear one," she murmured.

"Do you?"

"Shh!" She held up her hand, vampiric ears straining as the howls continued. "You're telling me you only have one wolf on this island? Everyone knows they travel in packs."

"Doesn't sound like that one's traveling." Galen bent to nibble her ear. "He sounds settled to me."

"You know what I mean." She squirmed, giggling as his tongue tickled her ear.

"Let's go to the lake. We both need a bath."

Sabine wrinkled her nose. "That's true enough. I smell like fish."

"That's because you spent too much time with Cook in the galley."

"I like Cook."

"You seemed to like most of the crew," he muttered.

Sabine smiled. "You sound jealous."

"You'd like that, wouldn't you? Vixen."

"You have a nice crew."

"Nice? They're nice, but I'm a pirate?"

Sabine slipped from his arms and headed for the door. "I thought we were going to bathe?"

"Of course, my lady." He offered a mock bow before opening a trunk at the foot of his bed and withdrawing two dark blue robes.

She stepped closer to him and ran her hand over the silk. "So beautiful. And the design is unusual."

"They're from the east."

"The east? My parents were from the east."

"Were they?" He ran his finger across her full lower lip. "Where are you parents now, Sabine?"

She shrugged. "I'm not sure. They still don't know what Kornel did — or that he's dead."

"I'm sorry, for all of you. Nothing is as painful as losing a child to evil or death." He shook his head, an unexpected look of sadness on his face. She felt his pain like a branding iron across her soul and reached out to him.

Galen gathered her in his arms, burying his face in her neck. Still, she felt his thoughts withdraw from hers, and when he stepped away, his semi-smile had returned. "Come, little miss. We're wasting the night."

Chapter Eight

ഏ

Galen guided Sabine through the woods, smiling when the wolf scent faded as they neared his favorite clearing. At least the wild one still remembered his manners.

"Even the nights are hot here," Sabine said as they pushed aside vines. She nearly jumped into his arms upon realizing one of the green and yellow vines was a snake as thick as her wrist.

Galen smiled, his arm tightening around her. They changed direction, traveling down a path barely visible through the vegetation. Aside from the wolf, Galen was probably the only member of his settlement who used this particular path.

After another half a mile or so, the path opened into a vast clearing where the river emptied into a lake. A great black cat had been swimming, but upon seeing them, headed for shore and disappeared into the forest.

"Jaguars, wolves." Sabine smiled. "It seems that vampires aren't the only predators on this island."

Galen grasped her shoulders and spoke against her lips, "But we're atop the hierarchy."

A deep growl turned into the longest howl yet.

Sabine cocked a sleek eyebrow. "He didn't seem to like what you said."

Galen laughed outwardly, but thought, *She doesn't know how right she is. I'm sure I'll be lectured later. He'll most likely drone on for at least an hour. Maybe I won't go to the forge tonight, after all.*

The pressure of Sabine's hands against his chest prevented Galen from deepening their kiss.

"What's wrong?" he asked.

"The wolf is close."

"Don't worry about him."

"But—"

"It's my island, remember? I'm familiar with everything on it. The wolf won't interfere. In fact, I think he'll be leaving the area soon." Galen's voice rose as he spoke the last sentence, and the wolf's scent faded along with the howls.

Sabine smiled, revealing the tips of her fangs. "I'm starting to wonder if there's anything you don't know—or command."

"Not bad for a peasant." He winked.

She took his face in her hands and covered his mouth with hers. Galen swept her into his arms and walked into the water. Warm waves lapped at their skin.

He placed her on her feet, his palms splayed against her smooth, water-slicked back. Sabine's arms slipped around his neck as their teeth locked. She bit his lower lip and licked away the blood until they both shivered with desire.

Growling, he pressed her body closer, his cock trapped between their bellies.

"So beautiful," he murmured, trailing his tongue across her cheek and tickling her ear. Her hips shifted, and he sighed, tugging her closer to shore where he lay on his back on the smooth rocks. She clutched his stiff cock and guided him deep inside her as she straddled his hips. His hands spanned her waist while she rocked upon him.

Dipping his hands into the water at his sides, he grasped two pebbles, worn smooth by the water, and touched them to her nipples. She gasped, his name a broken cry on her lips as he moved the pebbles in gentle circles over the sensitive peaks. Her movements increased until she exploded, the throbbing heat of her climax nearly driving him over the edge.

"Sabine!" he groaned, sitting up so that she tumbled onto her backside, one leg still draped over his. She stared up at him with wide eyes, lips parted slightly, chest rising and falling in the aftermath of passion. He picked her up and carried her to one of the trees. Placing her on a rock near the trunk, he shifted into her with a powerful thrust of his lean hips.

"Galen!" she gasped when he grasped both of her wrists in one hand and pinned them to the trunk above her head. Her lush body trembled against his. He heard her heartbeat mingling with his own and increased his movements. At first he'd thought to savor their lovemaking, but at the moment he wanted her so much his desire was a physical ache. The only healing balm was within her strong, lovely body. As he released her hands, she cried his name again, wrapping her arms around his neck and her legs around his waist.

He impaled her over and again on his steely cock. Her nails sank into the flesh of his shoulders, and when her neck arched in ecstasy, he pressed his lips to her straining throat and bit.

I want to share this with you forever, he thought.

Forever and ever, her voice repeated in his head, then his senses reeled as orgasm washed over his body.

* * * * *

When they returned to their room, dinner awaited them. Together they ate the savory fruits and rare meat, washing it down with goblets of red wine spiced with animal blood.

"I have to go to the forge." Galen finally stood and dropped a kiss on her forehead. "Explore the house and the island, but be in my bed at dawn."

"I don't take kindly to orders."

"Then consider it a request." He leaned closer, one hand braced on each arm of her chair, and spoke against her lips. "I want to sleep the day in your arms, little miss."

He heard Sabine's heartbeat quicken and felt her pleasure at his words. Still, she played her role with nonchalance and said, "I'll see if I can accommodate you, pirate."

"Don't disappointment me." He kissed her, his tongue tracing her lips, then he pulled on worn dark brown trousers, boots, and a tan vest that exposed his muscular arms and broad, hair-roughened chest.

"You're going to the forge?"

Galen grunted in affirmation. "Cass has been overseeing the forge, as well as the rest of the island, in my absence."

"I thought you said he was a priest? Why is he working in your forge?"

"He's the finest craftsman on the island, and yes, among his people, Cass was a medicine man—a healer and practitioner of the Old Religion."

"Can't I come with you and meet him?"

"There'll be other times. The forge is hot and dirty. You wouldn't like it."

"Your ship was hot and dirty, but I liked it very much."

Galen ran a fingertip over her full lower lip before kissing it. "This is different. Trust me. I'll see you at dawn."

Sabine's jaw worked and she folded her arms across her full breasts. He touched her cheek and said, "Don't be angry."

"Why not? You think you can order me around like a member of your crew."

"Believe me, Sabine, you're no ordinary member of my crew."

* * * * *

She stared after Galen as he left her alone in the chamber.

"If he thinks I'm doing everything he says, the man is a raving fool."

Do as I say, Sabine, Galen's amused voice warned in her head. She successfully blocked him out while she dressed in trousers and one of his billowy shirts. She had exploring to do.

Sabine rode Pearl to the beach, then circled the island. In a cove, she discovered several women hauling fishnets and digging for shellfish. She exchanged greetings with them before asking the way to the forge.

One of the women, a tall blonde, pointed into the forest. "Take that path. It's the first cave to your right."

Sabine nodded, following the woman's directions. Rather than winding and overgrown with vines, like the path she and Galen had traveled earlier, this one was well-cleared and wide enough for a wagon. As the fisherwoman had described, she heard the sounds of metal striking metal as she neared the cave. If she strained to listen, she heard the metal workers' heartbeats. The scent of metal, smoke and sweat wafted on the air. She slowed her horse and tethered it alongside Galen's.

After taking several steps toward the cave, she paused, sniffing the air. A familiar scent struck her — the wolf.

"Lady Sabine?"

She spun, facing a shirtless, tawny-haired man carrying two buckets of water. He was tall enough to make a presence, though not nearly as tall as Galen or Sofian. The sharp contours of bone and muscle of his slender frame gleamed with sweat in the moonlight. A braided leather choker encircled his neck, and small silver hoop earrings dangled from his right ear.

"Lady Sabine?" he repeated.

She shook her head slightly. The man's scent was all wrong.

He placed the buckets on the ground outside the cave and extended his hand to her. "I'm Cass."

"Oh yes." She slipped her hand into his, and he bowed over it with unexpected gallantry. "The Priest."

He offered an amused smile. "Among other things. I've been curious to meet the woman who has so enamored our Captain Donovan."

"I don't know about that." Sabine wondered if she blushed.

His greenish eyes never left hers. "Yes you do. You know his heart rests in your charming little fist and all you have to do is squeeze," his hand clenched into a fist, then relaxed, "or caress."

A strange feeling—not quite fear—crept through Sabine. Cass was odd, and she wasn't sure she liked him. Why did he seem to exude a wolf scent? She knew he must be a vampire, since his scent was not remotely human, but where were his canines?

"I'm looking for Galen," she said.

"Then I should take you to him." He extended his hand toward the cave mouth before he picked up the buckets. Sabine followed close behind Cass. She noted his hair was long and bound at his nape with twine. Thick strands clung to his perspiring shoulders and back that seemed to ripple with every supple movement. No, he was not human, but he wasn't vampire, either.

"You're wondering about my scent?" He glanced over his shoulder at her. Those eyes of his never seemed to lose their amusement. He was like a smaller, stranger version of Galen—yet in many ways nothing like her lover at all.

"Yes, actually. I imagine you're a different bloodline. Galen said he could smell the difference between our blood and other vampires. That's how he knew I could endure sunlight."

"That's quite a problem for most of your kind, isn't it?"

"It's not for you?"

"Wolves have little problem with the sun, though I admit we're probably even more a slave to the moonlust than your kind."

"Wolves?"

"Werewolf, though I find the word a little distasteful. That word merely scratches the surface of what we are."

"Werewolf. I've only heard about you in stories."

"We'll have to talk. See what crazy myths you've picked up."

Sabine and Cass fell silent as she followed him deeper into the cave. The sound of metal working grew louder, and against the fire lit cave walls, she saw dark silhouettes of men striking metal.

They stepped into an adjoining cave several feet away, and Sabine tried to draw a deep breath, finding it nearly impossible until she adjusted to the heat.

"First time in a forge?" Cass smirked.

"How can you tell?" she replied, matching his sarcasm.

He laughed and placed the buckets aside while Sabine glanced around. Two tall men, their bodies glistening, shoveled coal into the enormous hearth at the farthest end of the cave. Other men sat at a long table, using pincers and metal to construct shirts of mail. More workers stood before anvils, using hammers to pound steel into shape.

Weapons, helmets and chain mail hung on the cave walls or lay in piles throughout the large room.

"This is just one of the workrooms," Cass explained as he and Sabine walked to another corridor.

They passed a lanky man carrying a mace. His skin was covered with sooty sweat so only his teeth gleamed white in his bearded face. Upon seeing Sabine, he licked his lips and reached for her. "Pretty."

Sabine's lip curled, as she backed away, but Cass had already grasped the man and tore the mace from his hand. For a slim man, Cass seemed to possess a great deal of strength.

"This is Lady Sabine." A growl rumbled in Cass' chest, and Sabine noticed long, thick fangs slide from his upper gums as he snarled at the worker. "She is Donovan's woman. Do you comprehend what I'm trying to tell you?"

"Galen's woman," the man repeated. Sabine could tell from his speech and wide-eyed expression he wasn't the swiftest of Galen's company.

"What are you doing away from your station?"

"Needed some fresh air. Too hot in there."

Cass released the man, shoving him roughly and motioned with his head for him to go.

When they were alone again, he said to Sabine, "You should be careful when you come here. Some of the workers aren't the most pleasant of your kind, and they can be dangerous. I'm sure Galen warned you to stay away, but now that I've met you, I can tell you aren't about to listen to him."

"Excuse me?"

"Am I right?"

"Yes," she feigned annoyance, "but you didn't have to say so."

"Don't worry, Lady Sabine. I'm on your side. Give him hell. Most vamp males are far too arrogant."

Sabine smiled. "But wolves wouldn't be that way."

"Of course not."

They made several turns before stepping into another cave. There were only two men working there, and Sabine's eyes immediately riveted to Galen. Shirtless, he stood over an anvil, one hand wrapped around a clamp that held a red-hot blade, the other clutching the hammer that repeatedly struck the metal into shape. Though his hair was tied at his nape, sweat soaked tendrils matted against his shoulders and neck. Beads of perspiration glistened beneath the mat of hair covering his chest and gleamed on the thick muscles of his arms. His long legs were covered in tan trousers, the waist dark with moisture.

Sabine's mouth went dry at the sight of him, and her own body temperature rose to nearly unendurable heights.

He didn't stop hammering as he spoke. "I told you not to come here, Sabine."

"And you expected her to listen?" Cass picked up a half-finished dagger and a clamp. He approached the hearth where Sofian, clad in a vest and baggy trousers, stood shoveling coal. The pirate glanced at her with his one good eye and winked.

"What am I saying?" Cass continued in a droll voice. "Of course he expected her to listen. Everyone listens to the Captain. Aye, sir, aye!"

Galen's lip curled slightly in Cass' direction as he plunged the sword into a bucket of water. It sizzled, and Sabine approached staring at the workmanship.

"I didn't know you were so talented," she said.

"Not really," he admitted.

"Don't be modest, Captain," Cass grinned. "You're not as good as me, but you're far better than Sofian here."

"What Cass lacks in stature he makes up for in sarcasm," Sofian stated.

"Oh you detected that? Very good." Cass took a quick step backward as Sofian tossed a hot chunk of metal into the bucket by Cass' leg, nearly striking the wolf.

"Cass is a master craftsman." Galen examined the hilt of the sword he was fashioning. "If he wasn't, I'd have killed him long ago."

"You could try, though I don't know how successful you'd be." Cass picked up a hammer and walked to an anvil to pound.

Sabine found the exchange between the men amusing. She sensed deep friendship among them in spite of their insults and threats.

"Has your curiosity been satisfied?" Galen ran his thumb across Sabine's cheek. "I told you it wasn't pleasant here."

"My curiosity is piqued." She approached a wall filled with tools. "Explain these."

Galen raised an eyebrow. "You're interested in working in a forge? Isn't that beneath you, my lady?"

"Perhaps, but I want to learn."

Sabine ignored his sarcasm, though part of her admitted he was right. A few weeks ago, she never would have imagined learning about metal work, but the idea of shaping a hunk of metal into a fine dagger or perhaps even jewelry, intrigued her.

She'd never been good at feminine crafts such as weaving and needlework. Perhaps her vampiric nature cried out for a more physical task.

"Will you teach me?" she asked.

"Teach you?" Cass snorted. "He still has a lot to learn."

"Then will you teach me?" Sabine turned to Cass.

Galen grasped her arm and tugged her to his chest. "I certainly know enough to pass on what I've learned."

"But I thought you didn't want her in the forge?" Cass asked innocently.

Galen's chest rumbled as he growled.

Cass smiled at Sabine. "It's just my sense of humor. You'll find no better teacher than Galen — except for me, of course."

"Of course." Sabine smiled sweetly at the wolf and her belly tightened as the sensation of Galen's jealous irritation struck her.

It seemed life in the forge might be far better than she imagined.

Chapter Nine

ॐ

Cass approached Sabine and examined the dagger she was working on. She credited him with not so much as smiling — let alone laughing — at her work.

"Not bad for a first," he said. "It's actually better than some of the atrocities Sofian and Galen create after years of practice."

"If you tried to say something decent, I think you'd choke to death," Sofian said to the wolf.

"Touchy." Cass glanced at Sabine. "That's what happens when too much smoke gets in his eye."

Sofian's hands shot out, clamping around Cass' throat. He flung the smaller man into the cave wall filled with armor. "I've had enough of your mouth!"

Cass pushed himself off the wall, flexing his shoulders and rubbing the back of his head. "I've told you a hundred times, Sofian, that temper of yours is going to get you killed."

Before Sofian formed a reply, Cass sprang, pinning the pirate on his back atop one of the anvils.

Sabine's heartbeat quickened at the battle unfolding before her. It seemed wolves were a bit quicker than her kind — and stronger, too.

Sofian forced his knee between his own body and Cass'. He thrust Cass backward, almost into the fire.

Galen stepped between them. "Enough! Don't you have anything better to do than bicker like two old maids?"

Cass and Sofian returned to their work, but not before Sabine noticed a muscle twitch in the pirate's taut jaw. Cass wore an amused expression, and Sabine wondered if anything affected the wolf.

"It'll be morning soon." Galen's voice softened as he approached Sabine. He brushed a lock of damp hair from her perspiring face.

She smiled at him and wiped her brow on her forearm. "We need a bath."

"We can stop by the lake before retiring."

"I can't wait to come back tomorrow."

"You genuinely surprised me, Sabine. The last place I thought you'd want to spend time was the forge. What would your family think?"

"I don't know, and I don't care."

Across the room, Cass laughed. "I like this woman, Galen."

"Just don't forget who she belongs to," he growled.

Sabine felt her attraction for him bristle into irritation. "I belong to myself. Don't forget that."

As she brushed past him, he reached for her arm, but she shoved him away and joined Cass.

Galen took a step toward her, his eyes gleaming with fury. Sabine's heart throbbed. She expected him to pick her up bodily and carry to the lake. Instead, he began cleaning his tools.

"I know you're a lady of independence," Cass said in such a low voice even Sabine's vampiric ears almost couldn't hear him, "but you might want to think twice about pushing him too far."

"I'm not afraid of him."

"I don't mean for that reason."

"Then what?"

"True love doesn't happen very often. Throwing it away would be foolish."

"You know, I'm starting to understand why you annoy Galen and Sofian so much."

Cass placed a dramatic hand over his heart. "I'm wounded, my lady."

"You're almost more incorrigible than Galen."

"Somehow I doubt that."

"I don't," Galen called. He glanced over his shoulder at Sabine and winked as their eyes met. Sabine's belly warmed with affection, and to her irritation, the idea of obeying his order didn't seem so terrible. It actually felt wonderful, to imagine the love play they'd share that day.

It feels wonderful to me, too, little miss. The sooner we finish here, the sooner the day begins.

Sabine hurried through the clean up, all the while sensing that Galen was as anxious for lovemaking as she was.

Together, Galen and Sabine traveled the jungle pathways to his favorite clearing. They peeled off their filthy clothes and waded into the water. They ducked beneath and chased one another until Sabine found herself locked in Galen's embrace.

"I don't think I've ever seen a woman look more beautiful than when you were working in the forge."

Sabine gave a snort of mocking laughter. "I'm sure I looked absolutely gorgeous all dirty and sweaty."

"Far more than you realize." He kissed her before she could reply.

Her arms slipped around his neck, and she moaned as their kiss deepened. Before she realized what was happening, Galen's long, sleek body pinned her to the smooth rocks in the shallow water by the bank.

Sabine clutched his shoulders, her teeth sinking into his full lower lip, drawing blood until they both shivered in the throes of passion. Afterward, they lay catching their breath as the water lapped their skin.

The sun had risen, causing Sabine's eyes to ache with its brightness. Still, it felt good to enjoy the day's brilliant beauty without fear.

Galen lifted his head from her breast and smiled at her as he traced her hairline with his fingertip. "Want to go to bed?"

She kissed the tip of his nose and sat up. "That might be a novel idea. Still, I'm becoming accustomed to you ravishing me in the water, pressed against tree trunks, and who knows what else you'll think of?"

"I hardly think I've ravished you, Sabine." He grasped her upper arm and pulled her onto his lap. "You've enjoyed every minute."

"Oh have I? That marvelous a lover, are you?"

His gaze held hers as he gathered her into his arms and stood, heading for the pathway.

"Galen, what about our clothes?"

He paused and glanced at the heap of material.

"Don't even think about carrying me to your house naked!"

"Ahh," his eyes narrowed, "the thought is *so* appealing."

"Galen, no! I have my pride!"

He hugged her close before returning her to her feet. They dressed quickly, and then hand in hand walked to the house.

Sabine noticed the field was empty, since most of the vampires couldn't abide daylight. A distant howl wafted on the breeze, and Sabine gazed toward the mountains several miles off.

"Cass must be lonely," Sabine said. "Being the only wolf among us."

"I've been called a wolf every now and then," Galen teased, nuzzling her face with his stubble-roughened cheek.

She giggled. "You need a shave."

"I'll take care of it as soon as we get to the house."

When they reached the house, Galen escorted her through the back door that opened to the kitchen. There they gathered bread, cheese, fruit and wine and carried it up to his room.

Galen drew the dark curtains while Sabine arranged the food on the table. Again, they undressed, and as Sabine reached for one of Galen's billowy white shirts to cover herself, he took a razor and moistened it in a bowl of fresh water on the table near his bed.

"Over here," Sabine said, taking the razor from his hand and pushing him onto the bed. He sat on the edge, dark blue eyes studying her. She stepped between his legs and tilted his face upward. He remained still as she shaved him carefully.

As she swept the blade over his face, careful not to scrape the flesh, she noted how smooth his skin was, how striking his angular bone structure. The perfect straightness of his nose reminded her of a marble statue, yet he wasn't remote in his beauty. Galen was warm, his expression full of fire.

He took the blade from her to finish those places harder to shave, then dried his face on a towel. Running a hand over his smooth jaw, he glanced at her. "Better?"

In reply, Sabine rubbed her cheek against his, purring like a contented kitten.

"I never imagined you'd be like you are," he breathed. "All those times Narcisse talked about his little sister, I had no idea she was so beautiful in so many ways."

"Galen—"

"It's true." He took her face in his hands. "You can feel what you do to me."

"Yes," she grinned, reaching down to grasp the bulge in his loose cotton trousers, "I certainly can."

"That's not what I meant, but I'll take it," he breathed as she reached inside his trousers, grasped his cock, teasing him with her small, deft hand.

Sabine kissed him, tongue searching his mouth as she continued to tease his cock, squeezing and pumping, her thumb caressing the sensitive head. She absorbed his gasp of pleasure before moving her lips down his throat, chest and abdomen.

His heartbeat quickened as she licked every inch of his steely cock from base to top. She loved his taste, his scent, the smoothness of his flesh. Fingers tightening in her hair, he groaned, a sound of such pleasure that Sabine's belly tightened and she felt herself growing wet with desire. Drawing him deep into her mouth, she sucked and laved, keeping him on the brink of passion. When she felt his fingers trembling against her scalp, she used her fangs to pierce the crown of his erection. He gasped her name, hips thrusting forward, blood pounding through his body. She mewled with pleasure as she continued sucking, tasting the bitter-sweetness of blood and semen.

She'd only been on the island a short time, but the wildness of the place—the vampiric freedom—had rooted deep inside her. Since her life entangled with Galen Donovan's she would never, ever be the same again.

* * * * *

Sabine's eyes opened halfway, and she stretched, fingers reaching high above her head, toes pointing toward the foot of Galen's enormous bed. Moonlight shone through the open window, and a warm breeze rustled the drawn curtains.

Galen's scent, though strong, had faded enough for her to know he'd left the room several hours ago. She walked to the window and realized by the position of the moon that she'd overslept. Galen must already be at the forge, and she felt eager to join him and continue learning the craft of weapon building.

After washing in a basin of water and dressing in one of Galen's shirts and a pair of trousers belted with a rope at her narrow waist, she hurried downstairs. Monica sat at a long wooden table, chopping a variety of fruits and piling the sweet-smelling slices into a large wooden bowl. She smiled as Sabine approached.

"How about something to eat, love?" the redhead asked.

"Sounds wonderful. I'm starved. Where's the kitchen?"

"Right this way." Monica stood, and Sabine followed her through the door at the far end of the room. The kitchen was spacious and airy. Several large windows surrounded the room, bathing it in moonlight. Sabine shivered at the carnal beauty of the moon and realized she was even hungrier for Galen than she was for food. Still, she devoured the bread and fruit Monica provided.

"Have you seen Galen?" she asked, licking mango juice from her lips, wishing it was her lover's delectable blood. *Soon. Very soon.*

"He left at twilight."

"Gone to the forge?"

Monica shook her head. "Ritual, I believe. But he should be returning to the forge soon."

"What kind of ritual?"

"Couldn't tell you." Monica waved her hand. "The vampires native to this island perform many rituals. I don't quite understand their religion, but Galen has lived among them for so long before he brought us here that he's adopted many of their ways."

"Where in the forest do these rituals take place?"

"I don't know. Never seen one myself. The few times I heard the chanting and drumbeats gave me the chills." Monica shivered, the tips of her fangs visible as she grimaced.

Sabine's interest was piqued, and she hurried to finish her meal before searching for Cass or Sofian in the forge. She found the tall, dark-haired vampire standing by the well outside the forge. Bucket in hand, he gazed at the moon and drew a long breath. Apparently the moonlust was affecting him as well. Sabine wondered if Sofian also had a lover on the island to appease the feelings of desire the nighttime stirred.

"Sofian, do you know where Galen is? Monica said he was engaged in a ritual with the islanders."

"He is."

"Would you take me to him?"

Sofian's single eye studied her carefully before he walked to the mouth of the cave and passed the bucket to another man waiting there. He picked up a machete and fastened it to the belt around his lean waist. Turning back to Sabine, he gestured for her to follow him down the path winding through the jungle.

The drumbeats started suddenly, a sultry echo through the trees.

"Monica said the drums are part of their rituals." Sabine glanced up at Sofian.

He stared straight ahead as he walked, his face expressionless. Being on the side of his eye patch, she couldn't discern the look in his eye, but when he spoke, his voice sounded clipped. "The have many rituals. Most of them useless."

"I take it you're not part of them, as Galen is?"

"In many ways I'm more a part of them than Galen will ever be."

Sofian's words raised her curiosity, but she guessed from his attitude he didn't want to discuss any connections he might have to the natives.

They'd walked a couple of miles when Sofian turned off the well-trodden path to one littered with overhanging vines. After slipping the machete from his waist, he began slicing through the vines, shoving them aside. Sabine wrinkled her nose as the vegetation tumbled into her face in spite of how he tried to clear her path.

"Isn't there an easier way than this?" She spat a leaf from her mouth and slapped at the enormous black bug sticking to her shoulder.

"No."

"If Galen and others travel for these rituals, why are the trees along this path so overgrown?"

"Because they take the river."

"Why didn't we do that?"

"Because fighting that current is far worse than slicing these trees."

The jungle grew thicker, darker, yet pleasant to vampire eyes. The land steepened, until they were forced to use their hands as well as their knees and legs to climb. Sabine blinked sweat from her eyes and gazed downward. Her heartbeat quickened. The drop was so severe that one false step could possibly mean death—even for their kind. She imagined tumbling miles downward, a branch piercing her heart as she landed with enough force to break every bone in her body.

"Don't do that," Sofian told her.

"What?"

"Look down."

Swallowing, she took his advice and stared up at him. Using one hand to grip the vine-covered mountainside, he continued wielding the machete with the other, his muscled arm glistening with perspiration. Sofian had obviously inherited the power of his vampire side. If his human half tired, he certainly didn't reveal it.

Suddenly he stopped, and Sabine narrowed her eyes at the ridge above them.

"Get up there," Sofian ordered, sheathing the machete and turning his body so Sabine could pass. She climbed over him, her claws digging into the dirt. His hand clasped her arm, guiding her upward until she pulled herself onto almost flat ground. Sabine grasped his arm, but he waved her away and tugged himself up while she stared at the view in wonder. The entire island lay before her, the jungles, part of the shoreline and the village with Galen's house by the cascades far in the distance.

"It's so beautiful up here," she murmured.

Sofian didn't reply, but took a moment to gaze at the view before walking across the mountain's flat top. Drumbeats continued, filling the island with their rhythm. They grew louder, accompanied by the sound of deep, male voices chanting unfamiliar words. Sabine followed her guide down a not-so-steep path and across another mile or so of trees, rocks and reeds.

The drums vibrated in her ears, and she caught the scent of fire, incense, herbs and other vampires. Galen's scent was strong, and her belly clenched with anticipation of seeing him again, though her infatuation should have faded. She began to wonder if he'd ever stop thrilling her, even if they both lived a million years.

Smoke rose in the distance, and firelight glowed through the trees as they approached a clearing.

A large group of men, bodies bare save for brown leather loincloths that hugged their crotches and left their buttocks exposed, danced around what looked like an enormous mortar standing above a blazing fire. Feathered masks covered their faces, exposing only their eyes and mouths. Symbols painted in henna marked their chests, arms and thighs, and Sabine noticed each wore a narrow sheath about his waist, concealing dagger blades. She stared at the array of male flesh as they danced and chanted. Some were tall, others shorter, all dark-skinned and muscular. Smoke rose from the mortar, thickening as several men danced closer, tossing in handfuls of incense. The pungent, carnal scent wafted on the air, and Sabine inhaled deeply.

She tried to find Galen among the masked group. Her eyes fell on the tall, sleek body she'd know anywhere. Facing her across the fire, Galen squatted, then leapt, muscles rippling in his incredibly long legs. A henna painted snake wound its way from his shoulder and wrapped around his chest and waist, its tail disappearing in the waistband of his loincloth.

Sabine couldn't tear her gaze from him as the dancing continued. Already she could discern his deep voice from the others as the group chanted louder, faster, words interspersed with throaty groans and growls. Suddenly they stopped, ripping the masks from their faces and using both hands to thrust them high above their heads, as if offering them to the moon.

One of the men, even taller than Galen, his dark body of thick muscle glowing in the firelight, spoke in a rumbling voice. Sabine didn't understand his words, but Sofian translated.

"Powerful Moon, Deity of Light, granter of fertility, keep us in your brilliant light. We offer blood in the hope of your return and thanks for your life gift."

The masks fell from their hands, and in a swift motion, each man unsheathed his dagger. Simultaneously, each raised a glistening blade to his chest and carved a single line from armpit to armpit. Sabine drew a sharp breath, her pulse racing, moisture gathering between her legs as she watched Galen's blood run in winding streaks down his chest and abdomen, staining the rim of his loincloth. Suddenly his eyes fixed on hers. They burned with all the desire she felt.

Her nipples peaked, brushing the softness of her loose shirt, as the crowd dispersed. Several of the men remained behind to douse the fire and clean the mortar.

"Sabine," Galen approached, "what are you doing here?"

She shrugged. "I was curious."

"Satisfied?"

"Not hardly. I have so many questions, I—" She stopped suddenly, following Galen's line of vision to the empty pathway beside her where Sofian had stood only moments before.

"He doesn't like your rituals much," she said.

"He has his reasons. His father's people are related to this group. He has family issues."

"Where are the women?"

A smile flickered around Galen's mouth. "Most likely engaging in their own ritual on the other side of the island."

"They don't live together?"

"They do, but this is a special ritual in which they celebrate apart, then join in the hope of gaining children. This is the night of the Fertility Ritual, Sabine."

"Fertility?"

217

"We pray that moonlust will make us fertile." He touched her cheek, and Sabine glanced from his penetrating blue eyes to the blood streaking his chest. She noted his nipples stood out hard on his muscled chest, and his loincloth bulged with the weight of his excited cock.

Sabine moistened her mouth that had suddenly gone dry and said, "Does the ritual work?"

"I was hoping we could find out."

Her hands slid up his chest, feeling the enticing slickness of his blood. He pressed her palms close, and she felt the wild beating of his heart as he bent to kiss her. Suddenly he swept her into his arms and carried her into the jungle.

"Where are we going?"

"Someplace nice."

Sabine's belly quivered at the expression in his eyes. Fertility Ritual. Suppose it did work? She tightened her arms around his neck and rested her head against his shoulder, smiling at the thought of how wonderful a child of Galen's would be.

Chapter Ten

ଉ

Galen had caught Sabine's scent as she'd approached the clearing, and even amidst the ritual, his gaze had riveted to her as soon as she stepped through the trees.

Sabine had been beautiful when he'd first seen her, dressed in the finery of a lady, yet seeing her gorgeous body clad in the freer, masculine style clothes excited him even more. The rustic clothing was a sharp contrast to her classic beauty, yet it reflected her vampiric strength and wild sexual urges.

He carried her through the mouth of a small cave hidden in the trees and placed her on a soft bed of moss.

"Galen," she murmured as he lifted the oversized shirt over her head and took one of her nipples between his lips. Both of their bodies were moist from the jungle heat, and the anticipation of making love caused their hearts to race.

He suckled both nipples, then licked her ribs and belly, causing her to quiver with desire. After tugging off her boots and trousers, he slipped out of the loincloth, his erection springing free. He loomed over her, rubbing his cock over her smooth thighs and belly.

Galen longed to plunge into her liquid heat while lapping blood from her throat, but he also wanted to pleasure her exquisite body until she begged for him to take her. Covering her mouth with his, he used his tongue to explore every wet corner, every bit of soft flesh. He traced the shape of her incisor teeth, piercing his tongue on their tips. Both groaned at the taste of the salty/sweet liquid. After tearing his mouth from hers, Galen covered her face and throat with kisses while his hands kneaded her breasts, thumbs circling her hardened nipples. He licked and kissed her abdomen, feeling it tighten and swell with each of her deepening breaths. Heart throbbing with desire, he paused, lips hovering over her clit. He breathed on the swollen little nub and felt her fingers tighten in his hair. Smiling, he pressed kisses from her inner thighs to her ankles. His mouth covered her clit, tongue teasing, lips tugging. When she moaned his name, he pricked her stimulated flesh with the tip of one fang. She shrieked, her clit throbbing in his mouth as he continued sucking and licking. Unlike a mortal woman, Sabine's climaxes, under the influence of such direct stimulation, seemed endless. When she lay panting and sweat drenched beneath him, he allowed himself to thrust into her quivering body and release his own almost uncontrollable desire.

Her name erupted in a raw cry before his teeth pierced her throat and orgasm washed over him as her blood ran hot and thick over his tongue.

He collapsed on top of her, their hearts throbbing in unison, skins slick and legs entwined.

"I love you, Galen," she murmured, threading her fingers through his hair.

For a moment he forgot to breathe. He raised himself on his forearms, staring into her eyes, allowing the depth of his feeling for her to penetrate her mind.

"I love you, too, Sabine," he spoke in a hushed tone before kissing her lips. "I told myself I never would love someone this much, but I do."

"I said I could never love a pirate, but I can't help it." The expression in her luminous eyes tugged at his heart. It was his own fault she believed him to be such a rogue, undeserving of a true and decent lady. "The truth is, I don't care what you are anymore, Galen. I know you have goodness in you. That's why you freed those villagers instead of turning them over to the King."

"You love me?"

Yes, you can sense it.

I can. Her love warmed him, yet he felt a twinge of guilt.

Sabine, I have a confession to make.

He felt her tense and her eyes widened.

"What is it, Galen?" She rested a hand at the base of his throat.

"I'm not what you think I am. Not exactly."

"What do you mean?"

"I am a privateer, but not for the reasons you think."

"What? Power and riches?" She chuckled, looping her arms around his neck.

"The riches I steal are only from those who can well afford it. They hire me to stab each other in the back, anyway, so I really couldn't care less what I take from them."

She shook her head. "This is supposed to convince me you're not as bad as I think you are?"

"Hiring myself out to nobles provides me with the information of where their cargo is going, how much is there and often where they got it from. I take back much of what they steal and give it to those who need it more. My crew and I have been doing it for years, under the guise of pirating."

Sabine held his gaze for a long moment while his heart pounded in his chest. Only when she broke into laughter did he push himself away from her. "What's so amusing?"

"Galen, sometimes I think you'll do or say anything to get what you want. I already said I love you. There's no need to make up such a wild story."

"It's not a story! You can feel that I'm telling the truth!"

"I know you're much better at mind manipulation than I am."

Galen stood and began pacing the cave, his head brushing the craggy top. "I don't believe this! How can you doubt me?"

"How can I believe you?" She stood, still smiling. "You must think me a completely naive fool. My brother told me all sorts of stories about your pirating."

"Narcisse! He knows what I do. Like all members of my crew, he promised to keep it a secret!"

"Even from me?"

"He understands the importance of the work we try to do, Sabine." He took her hand. "You know I freed the villagers from the Northern King."

"Yes, and it was a wonderful gesture, but surely you don't expect me to believe that you pretend you're a rotten thief when all along you're some kind of saint—"

"I'm no saint, nor am I trying to be! But I'm not lying to you, Sabine! Go with what you feel, listen to your heart!"

She paused, staring into his eyes, her smile fading. "I want to believe you, Galen. I really do."

"You can." He grasped her hands and pressed them to his chest.

"Why would you do such things?"

"I have reasons."

She studied him for a long moment, her mind searching his. Only when she arrived at the door which he needed to keep locked did he thrust her out.

"This has to do with the King, doesn't it?"

"Let it go, Sabine."

"You told me this much, why continue the mystery and the lies?"

"I don't want to lie to you anymore."

"Then don't."

"Sabine," he sighed, pulling her into his arms, "I just need some time. Then I'll tell you everything."

"Tell me now, Galen!"

"I can't." He rested his cheek against the top of her head. For a brief moment, she'd reached out to him, but his continued secrecy threatened their newly created bond. He hadn't wanted to fall so deeply in love, but he could no longer deny he was lost to Sabine Debray. Part of him wanted to tell her all that darkened his soul, yet another part was terrified at how she would react. It was true most of his pirating concealed vastly different duties, but she had guessed correctly that his lifestyle was related to the King.

"Galen, if we can't trust each other, how can we possibly spend eternity together?"

"Sabine, please," he touched a fingertip beneath her chin, "allow me the time I ask for."

She looked ready to argue, but after a moment nodded. "But don't expect me to be patient forever, Galen."

"I won't. I swear it. Now we should start back for the house. It will be sunrise soon."

"Too soon." Sabine pulled on her clothes, body still tingling in the aftermath of lovemaking. "The moon is perfect tonight."

"Much like you."

She smiled, brushing his mouth with a kiss before leaving the cave.

* * * * *

"How did you learn to block your thoughts so well?" Sabine asked.

Midday approached, and other than Cass hammering deep within his private workshop, she and Galen were the only ones left in the forge.

Galen finished pounding a blade into shape, cooled it in a bucket of water, and wiped his brow.

"Years of studying meditation. Centuries of learning to focus. If you can believe it, Sabine, I was once a peaceful man."

"That is hard to believe."

"And chaste."

She laughed long and loud. "Even harder to believe! Now you really are telling me stories."

"No, it's the truth." He approached, brushing a tendril of damp hair behind her ear.

"What happened to you then? From the stories my brother told, you're a master of the carnal arts."

"Master of the carnal arts." Galen's lips curved upward, revealing the tips of his fangs. "I think I like the sound of that."

"Just so long as it's only true when you're with me, from now on!" Her fingers squeezed his hair-roughened pectorals.

"Since meeting you, little miss, I've thought of bedding no one else."

Sabine folded her arms across her chest and wrinkled her nose in a manner he found most endearing. "Should I be a fool and believe you?"

"You've never been a fool."

Her thoughts were both pleased and disbelieving. He didn't blame her. Since they'd met, he hadn't given her much reason to have faith in his integrity.

"Teach me more about how to shield my thoughts," she said.

"You have something to hide from me?"

"Everyone likes some privacy once in a while. Why do you block me out at times?"

His smile faded and he tugged her into his arms. "You're right. Another reason why I like to control my own thoughts every now and then is to keep someone I might love—such as you—safe."

"How?"

"You know my life can be dangerous, Sabine, especially with me and the King constantly hunting one another. Should I be caught by an enemy—any enemy—I wouldn't risk them threatening you to punish me."

"I hadn't thought of that." Her brow furrowed. "Teach me how to better control my thoughts."

"We'll start working on it tonight. Right now I want to go home and fuck you until you can't walk."

Sabine's stomach clenched and an excited shiver ran up her spine. She snapped her teeth close to Galen's throat. "As long as you feel you're up to the challenge."

He replied with a slow, wicked smile.

* * * * *

After several weeks of working in the forge, Sabine could scarcely remember what it felt like not to be working metal. Everything about living on the island seemed to be part of her now—especially Galen. She didn't know when she began to consider the island home, yet like him, it had wound its way into her soul.

She straightened from her anvil and stretched the taut muscles in her shoulders and neck as she glanced at Galen. Shoveling coal into the flames, his bare torso glistening, he looked like a sensual god of the underworld.

He paused for a moment and glanced over his shoulder, winking at her. Sabine smiled and was about to return to the sword she was fashioning when the scent of a strange vampire wafted through the cave. Her gaze fixed on the doorway through which strode a tall brunette. A brown leather vest revealed the chiseled muscles of her shoulders, arms and abdomen. Her skin was dark but her eyes such pale green they seemed to glow.

Sabine was struck by a momentary wave of jealously as she glanced at Galen. To her relief, she sensed no lust from him.

"Natassja," Galen approached, "how are you?"

The woman growled and waved her hand. "Be better when I get back from Dragon's Peak."

"Natassja's a tribal guardian," Galen explained to Sabine. "This year, her Queen will mate, and her duty is to escort her husband-to-be from an island further north called Dragon's Peak."

"You're a warrior?" Sabine's curiosity was piqued.

"I am." Natassja stepped closer, her gaze sweeping Sabine who stared with equal boldness. "And you're Galen's new woman?"

"New?" Sabine folded her arms across her chest.

Galen lifted an eyebrow. "Thank you, Natassja."

"I meant no harm." The warrior woman held up her hands in mock defense. "I only came to use your forge, if that's agreeable. I needed to get away from that village for a while. Since the Fertility ritual last night, it's no place for a woman alone."

"They tried to attack you?" Sabine asked.

Natassja snorted. "Not if they want to live. The sounds and smells of their lust annoy me."

"Then you shouldn't mind your upcoming assignment," Galen said.

"I can think of much better things to do with my time than travel across sea and land in the company of a virgin consort."

Sabine grinned. "Virgin consort? This sounds interesting."

"Hardly." Natassja raised her eyes skyward. "I didn't expect Galen to mate with a forger. Perhaps his taste is improving."

"I've only started this craft since arriving on the island," Sabine said.

"Really?" Natassja approached, examining the blade Sabine had been molding. "You have talent."

"Thank you. I—"

"You know, Sabine, if you're interested in meditation and thought control, Natassja is accomplished in both. Part of her training to be a tribal warrior involves intense meditation and focus. When I'm busy with the crew, she might help train you."

"Learning to block your thoughts from him, are you?" Natassja offered a sly grin. In spite of the woman's gruff manner, Sabine liked her.

"Doing my best." Sabine winked.

"I'd be glad to add to your training. Besides, it's good to find another woman who enjoys the forge. It seems we have much in common, Sabine."

"Perhaps. So tell me more about this virgin consort."

* * * * *

While Galen and Sofian left the forge to attend nightly business on the dock, Natassja invited Sabine to visit the meditation cave in her village.

Sabine had been curious to visit the tribal village since witnessing the fertility ritual, but Galen and the forge had taken up so much of her time that she had procrastinated asking him to take her there.

It was close to midnight when they neared the village. Sabine caught the scent of other vampires, of smoke, cooking food and the luscious aroma of blood. Animal blood.

"Our hunters drain the animal blood when they clean the meat. Not much nourishment to it, but it makes great spirits."

Sabine rarely drank animal blood. Her parents had considered it a nasty habit, and Narcisse didn't encourage the act, either. However, since meeting Galen, she'd learned how many different cultures the world possessed. The variety and richness stimulated her yet made her hungry for more knowledge.

"How long have your people lived on this island?" Sabine asked.

Natassja shrugged. "Always. Our caves still bear the marks of our ancestors from thousands of years ago."

"May I see them?"

"Of course. There are many in the meditation cave. Stop!" Natassja grasped Sabine's arm and thrust her behind her as a tall man wearing leather trousers, dagger in hand, leapt from a tree and landed in front of them.

Natassja barked out words in her own language, and the man stepped aside, his gaze sweeping Sabine as they passed into the village. Stone houses with thatched roofs were built on rocks extending high above a brook running through a vast clearing. Men, women and few children performed various tasks expected in a tiny settlement, fishing, building, hauling water, cooking, dancing, playing games and caring for domestic animals. Sabine noted several pens with chickens as well as exotic birds, horses, goats and pigs.

As they trudged through the village, some of the people waved and spoke to Natassja. She replied, introducing Sabine who could do little more than smile in greeting before Natassja urged her quicker upland.

"We can bathe here before entering the cave." Natassja paused in a remote pool hidden by overhanging trees. As the women undressed, Sabine glanced toward the mouth of a cave through which wafted the scent of incense on warm air.

"The cave is considered a religious place," explained the warrior woman. "That's why we cleanse ourselves before entering. Besides, a good swim always helps me focus."

"Do you have a mate, Natassja? Is that how you've perfected blocking your thoughts?"

Natassja made a face which told Sabine exactly what she thought about binding herself to a man. "No mate. Just a good fuck every now and then to soothe the nerves."

Sabine laughed. "There are some good things about having a mate, you know."

"Outweighed by the bad — at least from my point of view. You're lucky, though. Galen is a good man, and he's hung like a bull."

"Natassja!" Sabine felt heat rise in her face, then her brow furrowed. "How would you know?"

"Just by seeing what's in his loincloth. Don't worry. The Captain and I have never bedded down."

"It wouldn't have mattered," Sabine lied. "What he did before we met doesn't interest me."

Natassja cast her a knowing look. "Uh huh."

"Well—maybe it interests me a little."

The warrior woman grinned and shrugged off her vest. Sabine removed her own shirt, and the two women leapt, naked, into the water.

"You can walk by day, can't you?" Sabine asked.

"It's a requirement to be a tribal Queen's guard."

"Before meeting Galen, I didn't know any of us could endure sunlight."

"In your part of the world, such vampires are very rare. Not that they're all that common here. Most of us never leave these islands."

"I imagine it's a good feeling to know only our own kind live here. Don't you miss drinking human blood, though?"

"Some might. But don't you find the blood of other vampires more satisfying? Especially if it's your lover's blood."

Galen's blood did have the most delectable taste. If Sabine closed her eyes and imagined her teeth on his throat, she could almost taste his sweet blood. She sank deeper beneath the water, her hands cupping her own breasts, thumbs caressing her nipples as she imagined Galen touching her.

"Are you ready?"

Sabine's eyes snapped open at the sound of Natassja's voice. The warrior stood on the bank, supple body gleaming wet in the moonlight. Sabine noticed her full, firm breasts, rounded hips and chiseled muscles of her arms, legs and stomach. She almost envied Natassja's look of combined power and femininity. Then Sabine smiled. Since working the forge, her own body was changing, her muscles becoming more defined, enhancing the already enchanting beauty of her curves. Galen didn't seem to mind the changes. Actually, when she sensed his thoughts, she knew her appearance aroused him more than ever.

As she stepped from the water, she forced her mind off Galen. Her studies with Natassja were to help block her thoughts from him, not to call him to her.

The women picked up their clothes and carried them to the mouth of the cave. There, Natassja bowed her head in reverence, and Sabine followed her action. Waves of heat, even more intense than the rest of the island, struck her at the entrance and increased as she stepped inside. Moisture collected on the walls. Incense, burning in clay pots on an altar carved into a rock wall, filled the air with its herbal scent. Two thick pillar candles also burned on the altar, sticks of fresh incense resting beside them.

"Leave your clothes here." Natassja bent to place her vest, trousers—even her weapons—in a large basket below the altar. When Sabine did the same, she noticed several other articles of clothing and jewelry, which she guessed belonged to those visiting the cave. The warrior woman chose an incense stick and lit it using one of the candles. Incense in hand, she beckoned Sabine to follow her.

The women stepped through a smaller opening next to the altar and walked down a narrow corridor. Sabine noticed smaller caves branching off on both sides. Some she was able to see into and noticed men and woman lying on wooden tables or seated on the floor, eyes closed, in deep meditation. Most of the caves contained small steamy, pools.

"A hot spring runs below the cave," Natassja explained as they walked. "That's why the caves are so humid. It's relaxing and aids in meditation."

And hot. Sabine thought, realizing the rivulets of moisture coursing down her and Natassja's bodies were no longer from the cool water of the pool, but from their own sweat.

At the end of the corridor, they stepped into one of the smaller, empty caves. A large rock hid the center of the room from the corridor, so no one passing by could see inside.

A pool filled half the cave, the water lapping the rocky edge that sloped upward to the center of the room. Two low wooden tables stood side by side, a steel-rimmed trunk between them. Natassja opened the trunk and removed two thick towels, an incense burner and a small glass bottle. While Sabine spread a towel on each table, Natassja placed the incense in the burner atop the trunk and opened the bottle, causing a floral aroma to mingle with the incense.

"Scented oil. Lie on your stomach," Natassja ordered.

Sabine complied, and moments later felt Natassja's hands on her back, massaging the oil into her skin. Eyes slipping shut, Sabine enjoyed the feeling of the woman's strong fingers on her shoulders, back, buttocks and legs. Natassja rubbed the oil into her ankles and feet, and Sabine resisted the urge to sigh with contentment. The only thing better would be if Galen were performing the sensual massage.

"Don't think about him," Natassja said.

"How did you know?"

"Don't worry, I can't read your mind. It was simple deduction. Preparation for meditation can be very arousing. I know it seems like a contradiction, but it's true. It would only be reasonable that you would imagine your lover with you right now."

"And who do you imagine, since you don't have a lover?" Sabine snapped. Natassja's wisdom as well as her obvious dislike of men was irritating, in spite of how much Sabine enjoyed her company.

"I'm past the point of imagining anyone. I know how to control my thoughts."

Sabine fell silent. Perhaps she deserved the rebuke.

"Turn over."

Rolling onto her back, Sabine watched Natassja pour more oil into her palms. She rubbed her hands together, then began the massage all over again at Sabine's feet. As Natassja worked her hands up her calves and legs, Sabine's eyes closed halfway. Oiled palms caressed her hips and inner thighs, and Sabine tried to force her mind off sexual thoughts. It was another woman who touched her! She shouldn't be aroused, but the motions were so stimulating.

Her eyes closed as Natassja rubbed oil into her belly, then used her whole hand to knead her breasts. Sabine's breathing deepened as Natassja's fingers circled her nipples. She felt perspiration roll down her ribs and temples, both from the steamy pool across the room and the hot touch of the hands on her body.

Natassja worked the oil into Sabine's temples through to the ends of her hair. Suddenly the hands were gone, and Sabine opened her eyes.

"My turn." Natassja held the oil out to Sabine who sat up, stretching her shoulders. Natassja smiled. "How do you feel?"

"Very good. Relaxed yet energetic. Centered."

"Excellent. That's exactly how you should feel."

Natassja stretched out on her stomach, sleek body glistening with moisture. Sabine poured the oil into her own palms. Brushing aside the woman's thick chestnut braid, she rubbed the oil into her nape, across her shoulders and down her spine. Natassja's body felt hard and supple, strong as steel, yet there was nothing masculine about her beauty. Sabine had so many questions for her, but they could wait until later. It felt good to have a female friend again. She'd missed Leona and Meg's company greatly. A pang of sadness touched her when she thought of Meg's death. She would have liked to meet Natassja. The two would have gotten along well. Sabine still had the hope that one day Narcisse and Leona would know the vampires of Galen's island.

She shook her head. Her thoughts always seemed to revert back to Galen. Perhaps that was part of love.

Sabine poured more oil into her hands and kneaded the backs of Natassja's thighs and calves, then her feet. The warrior woman turned onto her back, eyes still closed. After working the oil into her flesh from toes to belly, Sabine paused at Natassja's firm breasts. A wicked thought ran through her mind when she noticed the warrior woman's breathing hadn't increased, nor had her heartbeat. It annoyed Sabine that she had felt so aroused when Natassja truly was advanced enough to accept such ministrations as a meditation technique.

Again Sabine oiled her hands, then caressed Natassja's breasts. She massaged slowly, paying careful attention to her dusky areolas and pointy nipples. She rolled the hard nubs of flesh between her thumb and forefinger until she felt her own arousal peaking again. Suddenly a shiver coursed through Natassja from head to toe. The woman sat up, an annoyed expression on her face that turned to a sheepish smile when she noticed Sabine staring at her.

"I see why Galen is so taken with you," Natassja said. "You've got much spirit. Go back to your own table and lie down. It's time to begin our meditation."

Natassja guided Sabine through meditation using imagery, fields, forests, oceans, candle flames. At first Sabine found it difficult to focus for long on a single image, and next to impossible to bury thoughts of Galen. However, she eventually relaxed, mind clear, thoughts of Galen still present, but hidden somewhere deep in her soul.

She wasn't sure how much time had passed when Natassja's voice gently broke her thoughts, guiding her back to reality.

Slowly Sabine opened her eyes. She felt completely relaxed, her body languid yet energized.

"You seemed to do very well." Natassja sat up, rolling her shoulders.

Sabine wiped her damp brow on the back of her wrist and swung her legs over the side of the table. "I enjoyed that—even though I couldn't completely forget about Galen."

"Did you sense his mind in yours?"

"No."

"Then you must have succeeded in blocking him out. How does that feel?"

Sabine thought a moment, then grinned. "It feels rather good. Not that I don't love his thoughts mingling with mine, but at times it irritates me that he knows how to manipulate our joining and I know so little about thought control."

"You'll learn. You're off to a great start. Do you know one thing that feels better than blocking out a lover—or so I'm told?"

"What?"

"Summoning him."

Sabine laughed. "I think I can do that well enough."

"Go ahead." Natassja gestured for Sabine to lie back down. "He said he was working at the Southern dock. That's only several miles outside this forest. Call him."

"Now?"

"See if he comes."

Sabine lay on her back and closed her eyes, clearing her mind of everything except thoughts of Galen. Hands resting at her sides, every muscle relaxed, her breathing deepened.

Galen.

She imagined both of them immersed in the natural pool that heated the room, bodies touching, flesh hotter than the water. She imagined exploring his mouth with her tongue, running her hand over the slick muscles of his chest. Her fingertips traced his ribs, and she felt his long eyelashes tickling her face. Her body tingled for him, spreading moisture through her cunt.

Sabine, stop! His voice echoed in her mind, and she smiled inwardly.

In her wakeful dream, she slid her hands over his taut buttocks, tugging him closer so she could feel his cock press against her hip.

Damn it, woman! I'm trying to get work done. Do you have any idea what you're doing to me?

Haven't you done enough work for today?

She imagined herself sinking below the warm waves. Underwater, she took his cock in her mouth and laved the head with her tongue.

Sabine!

She sensed his urgency and shivered, excitement coursing through her. Fearful of breaking such perfect mental contact, Sabine forced herself to calm. It was so difficult when her body and spirit cried out for him.

Galen, I want you so badly! Come to me. Satisfy this desire before I'm lost.

* * * * *

Galen left the dock with only a quick word to Sofian.

Sabine's lure was irresistible. Her thoughts called to him, caressing his mind and stimulating his body until he must either thrust her out entirely or satisfy the carnal urge taking over his entire being.

Work needed to be done, but if he rebuked her, she would be hurt—and his need wouldn't be satisfied.

He used his vampiric speed and strength to advantage as he tore through the jungle, ignoring lashing branches, seeing the smallest pathways in the darkest jungle. Galen scaled a thick tree trunk and leapt from tree to tree, claws sinking into bark, supple arm muscles swinging him across miles of jungle.

Dropping to his feet in the clearing just outside the meditation cave, he noticed Natassja watching him from where she leaned one shoulder against the cave entrance, an amused smile on her lips.

"They say lust is powerful," the warrior woman commented.

"Not nearly as strong as love," he replied, brushing past her, the humidity of the cave enveloping him as he followed Sabine's scent to the last room at the end of the corridor.

Galen's heart pounded in his chest, partly from his run, mostly from the sight of Sabine reclining naked on a wooden table. Her eyes closed, curvaceous body sheened with sweat, she was beautiful. His groin ached with passion as he watched the rise and fall of her chest. Her nipples stood out in arousal, and her stomach swelled, as if from intense desire.

Sabine.

I want you, Galen. I want you to fuck me.

He tore off his clothes and leapt onto the table, forearms on either side of her head, supporting his weight. Galen buried his lips in her throat, and Sabine's arms slipped around him, clutching him in a fierce hold.

Fingers entangled in the hair at his nape, and she tugged him upward until he kissed her. His tongue circled her lips, then slipped into her mouth, teasing hers while his hand cupped her sex and kneaded.

"Galen!" she panted as he dipped fingers into her wetness and rubbed her engorged clit. He heard her harsh breath and the quickening of her heartbeat. His own raced along with it. Galen felt feverish with passion, yet part of him was in no mood to rush their lovemaking.

Steeling himself against desire soon to come, he thrust into her hot, wet body and pumped with long, fast strokes as he bit her shoulder, drawing rivulets of blood. The taste of her blood combined with the marvelous heat of her body hurled him into a passionate frenzy, still he forced his breathing to slow. His name became a chant on her lips as he drove her to one quick climax, then another. As ripples of pleasure squeezed his cock, he thought for a moment he might climax. His entire body begged for release. She'd been tempting him for so long with her erotic visions, and her body felt incredible enveloping his cock. Shudders coursed through him from head to feet. Blood throbbed inside him with every punch of his wildly beating heart.

As Sabine's body quaked in another orgasm, Galen could have screamed from pure and unfulfilled lust. He felt her claws sink into his shoulders and rake his back and buttocks as her mind shrieked to his.

Galen!

He continued pleasuring her, bestowing seemingly endless climaxes exclusive to vampire females. Reaching the end of his limits, Galen's body pinned hers to the table, his hips pumping fast into her. He groaned with pleasure as his orgasm satisfied him like desert rain.

For several moments they lay, sweat-drenched and panting. When Galen opened his eyes and raised himself, he found Sabine staring at him.

"You came," she said.

"Harder than I ever recall."

Sabine giggled and slipped out from beneath him. "I meant you heard me calling you."

"Heard you?" He snorted. "Your carnal little vision had me working on ship repairs while trying to ignore an erection the size of a tree trunk."

"Tree trunk, eh?"

"The mental picture of what you were doing to me underwater—"

"Liked that, did you?"

"We didn't get to finish in your thoughts."

"Then let's finish now." Sabine grasped his wrist and tugged him toward the pool. Galen smiled, already feeling his cock start to tingle again. Splashing playfully, they waded deeper into the pool, until Galen's back pressed against the rock wall.

Sabine sank below the surface and found his engorged cock. He shuddered as she took him in her mouth and ran her tongue over the velvety head. When she took his cock so deep into her mouth that the sensitive head rubbed against the back of her throat, he cried out her name, both in his thoughts and aloud.

Beneath the waves, she suckled his manhood and sank her teeth into the velvety flesh.

Sabine, you've bewitched me.

No more than you've bewitched me.

I love you! He thought as his body jerked forward and trembled in orgasm.

I love you, too, Galen. Always.

Chapter Eleven

℘

"I can't wait for you to get back," Sabine told Natassja before the warrior woman boarded one of Galen's ships, captained by Nils.

"Neither can I." Natassja curled her lips. "I just hope we don't get stuck in bad weather. I don't want to spend any more time than necessary with this virgin consort."

"Maybe he won't be such terrible company. You said he was of the warrior class."

"A warrior with tribal leaders' blood. They're never treated the same as the rest of us. I can imagine him now, puny, soft and more of a woman than I'll ever be."

Sabine laughed. "Then maybe he can interest you in things like jewelry and hair arrangement."

"Are you saying my appearance is lacking?"

"I'm saying you're a gorgeous woman who could have almost every man on the island tripping over his feet for your favor if you'd use just a portion of your beauty and wiles."

"I have no wiles, Sabine, but you've got enough for both of us." Natassja placed a friendly arm around Sabine's shoulders. "Remember to keep practicing your mind control while I'm away. And try not to wear Galen out, will you?" The warrior woman winked before she slung her travel pack over her shoulder and boarded the ship.

Sabine waved from the shore as the ship sailed into the dark horizon.

She and Natassja had spent much time together over the past few weeks, and Sabine would miss her companionship.

Even Galen admitted how much her mental powers had improved since working with the tribal warrior.

Sabine mounted her horse and followed the shoreline for several miles before turning back to Galen's house. Their house, she smiled. The following month they planned to marry. Natassja would be home by then, and Sabine wanted her present at the ceremony, which Cass had agreed to perform.

Sabine!

Galen? What's wrong?

She sensed his urgency, and her heartbeat quickened with fear.

Meet me at the north dock. Now.

Sabine turned the horse and kicked her to a gallop, obeying Galen's command. His thoughts had been partially concealed, but his concern struck her, making her own mind race.

When she reached the dock, she noticed men boarding his fastest ship, The Scarlet Dragon. Galen leapt from the deck and met her on shore, his expression tense, and eyes gleaming.

"I have to go for a short time."

"Go? Where?"

"There's something I need to do, Sabine. Hopefully, when I return, it will be the last of our partings."

Sabine's heart sank to her belly, and her mouth went dry. "It's the King, isn't it?"

Galen nodded.

"I'm coming with you."

"No. You're not. You'll stay here until I return."

"Galen, I'm not some fragile human maiden who needs your protection—"

"And the King isn't some weak mortal man whom you can drain of life with a kiss. He's one of us, and he's a brutal killer. I have no time to waste arguing, Sabine." He bent to kiss her, but she slipped from his grasp. Galen placed his hands on her shoulders, his eyes desperate. "Sabine, please. Don't make this any harder than it already is. I love you. I want you safe."

"That's what I want for you! Can't you stop all this fighting and pirating?"

"Sabine, what I must do is urgent. If it wasn't, I wouldn't leave."

She lifted her chin, jaw stiff, and gazed at the crewmen loading the ship with trunks and barrels. Suddenly an idea struck her. She slipped her arms around his waist and pressed her cheek to his chest. "I love you, Galen. Please be careful."

She felt his arms around her, his warm body enveloping hers. "You're concealing your thoughts from me, Sabine."

"You have secrets, so I have a right to my own, wouldn't you say?"

"We'll discuss it when I get back."

"Discuss it! There's nothing to discuss! You don't own me, Galen. My thoughts are my own. If I choose to share them, you arrogant bastard, you should feel privileged!"

Galen smiled and squeezed her tighter. "That sounds like the woman I love."

"Please be careful, Galen."

"I will."

"I love you." She stood on tiptoe and kissed him. He held her so tightly she felt his heart pounding against her. In spite of his teasing manner and calm actions, he was afraid. Very much afraid. If the King could instill such fear in a man like Galen, he must be even more powerful than Sabine imagined. Common sense told her to listen to Galen and remain behind. Common sense rarely guides the heart, however.

When he boarded the ship, she took a moment to collect herself and her thoughts, then she headed for the cargo still piled on shore, waiting to be loaded on the ship. If vampires' sense of smell wasn't so keen, she could have stowed away in one of the trunks.

There had to be a way!

Sabine wrinkled her nose as she passed several oversized barrels reeking of fish oil.

That was it! To a mortal woman, one of the barrels full of oil would have been nearly impossible to move, but Sabine easily dragged it behind one of the wagons. She glanced in all directions to ensure no one watched her, then removed the top and tipped the barrel. The stinking oil soaked into the sand. Sabine hoped that sealing herself in the barrel still reeking of its contents, would conceal her from Galen until they were out to sea.

Drawing a deep breath of the last fresh air she'd inhale for who knew how long, she was about to step into the barrel when Monica's voice caused her to jump.

"Sabine! What are you doing?"

"N-Nothing."

Monica, two sacks dangling from her hands, stared at her in shock. "You were climbing into that barrel?"

"Shh!" Sabine hissed, glancing around, hoping no one had heard. "I'm tired of Galen hiding things from me. This time, I want to now exactly what's happening."

"I don't think stowing away is a good idea. It's the King they're fighting. You know how dangerous—"

"I don't care. I'm going to find out what's between Galen and the Northern King."

"Don't do this, Sabine. It will end in disaster."

"I have to. And swear to me you'll keep silent about what I'm planning."

"But—"

"No buts! If Galen won't tell me the truth, then I'll find it for myself. I'm not going to marry a man and not know his secrets."

"Some secrets are better left hidden."

"For him or for me?"

"Perhaps both."

"Swear to me you won't tell."

Monica's brow furrowed.

"Swear it!"

"Oh…all right."

"Good. Now what are you doing here, anyway?"

"I just brought some sacks of herbs for Cook to use on the journey. He's probably in the galley, so I'll bring them to him. Sabine, please be careful. The Northern King is a dangerous man."

Sabine nodded, grateful for the woman's concern, but desperate to discover what Galen had been hiding since they'd met.

* * * * *

Galen shifted on his cot, unable to rest. The Scarlet Dragon had set sail the previous morning. By sunset, they would reach their destination, and he wanted to be rested for the difficult fight sure to come.

A messenger from an island several leagues north of Galen's had arrived with a message that his land was under attack. The King was slaughtering, looting and collecting slaves. Already he'd destroyed most of the villages on the island and ripped out the tribal leader's heart.

Galen sighed, forcing his eyes shut. Heart ripping was the King's favorite means of execution.

I will rip out your heart. Those had been the King's words to Galen the last time they'd met. Galen didn't doubt one day he would—one way or the other.

Thoughts of the King weren't all that kept sleep at bay. Since leaving the island, Galen had thought often of Sabine—so much that her scent still seemed to linger on board.

He stood and tugged on his boots. If he couldn't rest, there was no use wasting time lying there.

"Strange, Galen." Cook's voice stopped him before he climbed topside.

Galen glanced over his shoulder. "What is?"

"Your lady's scent. Did she give you a token before you left?"

"Token?" Galen grinned. "I'm afraid you're still living in the past, my friend. I haven't heard that expression for years."

"Do you have something of hers?"

Galen shook his head. "I want no reminder of her. Not with the King so close by. If he ever discovers her, I don't want to think about what he'll do.

"He's a bitter enemy. You're right to protect Sabine from his evil."

Galen's stomach knotted as he continued toward the deck. Clouds masked the moon, darkening the night even to vampiric eyes. He glanced at the fleet of ships—his ships—behind him, then searched the deck, wishing for a moment Sofian was aboard. However the pirate was leading a second fleet to the opposite side of their island destination. Together, they would surround their enemy in the bloody battle to come.

Thoughts of the King had been troubling Galen more than usual, and Sofian was the only one who knew the truth about the hatred between them. The bearded pirate might not be much of a talker, but he was an excellent listener.

So many times Galen had wanted to confide in Sabine about the King. She would not only offer him sensible advice, but also give him the comfort he longed for. Even after so many years, past wounds still felt raw. Still, he couldn't risk Sabine— not with the likes of the King stalking him.

"Galen!" Cook bellowed from the hatch. "Come down here! Quickly!"

"No! I didn't want him to find out this way!" screamed an all-too-familiar feminine voice.

Sabine! Galen's pulse raced as fast as his legs as he hurried across the deck and leapt below.

* * * * *

Sabine's heart pounded as she met Galen's furious eyes. He advanced on her, fists clenching and unclenching at his sides, and she tried to hide behind Cook.

Damn Cook! Why couldn't he have kept his silence like she asked him to? This was not the way to approach Galen!

"How dare you stow away on my vessel, and—" Galen paused, sniffing the air. "Sabine, you stink like Hell's asshole!"

"It's the fish oil," she explained.

"Fish oil?"

"I hid in an empty barrel. Galen, I've been there for almost two days with just a few moments to stand up." She widened her eyes and whined—just enough to sound helpless and pathetic. Maybe if she could soften him up, he wouldn't glare at her like he meant to stake her through the heart.

"Sabine, you should *not* be here. Do you have any idea how dangerous this voyage will be? We're going into battle, woman!"

"I know it's dangerous, but some things are more important than self protection!"

"Like?" he raged.

"Like finding out the truths you refuse to tell me! Like trying to know—I mean really know—the man I'm going to marry!"

"Sabine." He stopped, running a hand through his hair and sighing. She noted he looked tired, as if he hadn't slept in several nights. Perhaps he was as restless as she was after all. "We have to talk. Cook, will you tell Jacob to take over for me until I come topside?"

Cook nodded, ignoring the angry look Sabine fired at him.

"Don't be angry with him," Galen said. "You really didn't expect him to hide you, I'm sure."

"I would have revealed myself when the time was right."

"And when would that be?"

"When you were calm enough to handle this."

He snorted with mocking laughter. "Then you were planning on staying in the barrel for the entire trip?"

"Galen!"

"Sabine." In two strides he reached her and tugged her into his arms, kissing the top of her head. He grasped her shoulders and held her at arms' length, wrinkling his nose. "You really stink."

"I know." Sabine's brow furrowed. In truth, she felt near tears from boredom, filth and cramped limbs.

"Come on." He swept her into his arms and carried her on deck. He strode to the wooden rail. Before she fully understood his intention, he'd dumped her overboard.

Sabine shrieked from anger and shock as she splashed in the rough, salty waves.

"Galen, you bastard!" she bellowed.

Grinning, he lowered her a rope and hauled her up.

As soon as she reached the deck, Sabine balled her fist and jabbed it toward his face. He moved his head slightly, her blow just grazing his jaw, before he jerked her into his arms again and began carrying her to his cabin.

"I can't believe you did that to me!" In spite of her anger, Sabine clung to him. "I love you so much, Galen. Heaven knows why, after dumping me in the middle of the ocean, but I do."

"I love you too, which is why I wish you hadn't come."

"But—"

"No, Sabine. This is more dangerous than you know."

"I'm not a fool, Galen. The King destroyed my home, remember? I know what a savage creature he is, but I know if anyone can stop him, it's you."

Galen sighed, placing her on the cot and sitting beside her. She sensed sadness from him, and something else she couldn't place since he did his best to block his thoughts surrounding the King.

"Someone has to stop him," Galen murmured.

"You will. I know it."

Before conversation continued, he kissed her. Deeply. One of his hands cradled the back of her head while his other arm snaked around her waist, holding her close. His tongue explored her mouth, tasted her. Their teeth pierced each other's lips. The taste of blood caused them both to clutch each other tighter.

Galen unlaced her billowy shirt and broke their kiss, just long enough to tug it over her head and remove his own. Sabine mewled with pleasure as her bare breasts, cooled by the ocean, pressed against his hair-roughened chest.

"I've missed you so much," he spoke against her lips, his voice husky with desire. "It's only been a few days, but it seemed like centuries."

Sabine smiled. Though she felt the same, she enjoyed knowing she had power over this free-spirited man. Still lying on the bed, she wiggled out of her trousers while Galen stood and jerked his down, kicking them aside before his body covered hers.

For a moment they lay still, eyes on eyes, his hands pinning hers above her head, their fingers entwined.

Love me, her mind told his.

Forever, Sabine.

His kissed her temple, then her throat. Burying his lips in her shoulder, he bit gently—just enough to draw two slender streams of blood that he lapped away. His kisses rained over her breasts and down her stomach until he reached her tingling clit. She gasped as he pleasured her with his mouth, his warm lips tugging, his tongue lapping.

Suddenly she felt his chest against hers as his thick, warm cock slid into her. Mouth covering hers, his hips thrust with such urgency, it seemed as if they had been parted for centuries. Sabine clung to him, eyes closed, her arms and legs clutching with all her vampiric strength.

"Sabine, God!" He groaned, tearing his mouth from hers. His tongue circled her earlobe and she shivered. Suddenly she could wait no longer. Her teeth sank into his shoulder, and his sweet, salty blood flowed over her teeth and tongue.

She throbbed and moaned, loving the taste of his blood, the strength of his big, steely body, and the gasps of pleasure as he took her sweet crimson essence and came so hot and hard.

* * * * *

Pounding on the door roused Galen and Sabine from the pleasant, semi-sleep following their lovemaking.

"Captain, come quickly!" one of the crewmen bellowed. "The King's men!"

Galen leapt from the bed and dragged on his trousers. He'd left the cabin by the time Sabine threw on her clothes. Her heart pounded as she hurried on deck. She'd seen the results of the King's attacks and wasn't anxious to witness another.

"What did you expect when you followed him?" Sabine muttered to herself. As soon as she reached the deck, the glow of flames from a distant island caught her attention. The silhouette of many ships surrounded the isle.

Galen and several crewmen stood by the rail and stared toward the island. She approached Galen and glanced up at his face. His expression was unreadable, but she sensed the turmoil within him.

"The bastard," Cook murmured under his breath. "Everything he touches ends up in ruins."

"All he knows is destruction," snarled a crewman. "I don't know where he came from, but he must have been coughed up by the devil himself. No blood mother or father for him either human or vampire. Ain't that right, Captain?"

Galen turned back to the deck. "Everybody prepare for battle! Enough standing around! Sabine, get below with Cook."

"Galen, I—"

"Just do what I tell you!" He spun, snarling, hands clasping her shoulders. "Damn it, Sabine, I wish you'd have been smart enough not to follow me."

She shoved him away. "And I wish you'd tell me what you're hiding!"

He looked about to speak, but instead drew a deep breath. "I don't have time for this. Just do what I tell you and we'll talk later."

"Later," she muttered. "What if there is no later."

Don't even think that way, Galen thought to her. *I love you, Sabine. No matter what happens, always remember that.*

She took a step toward him. "Galen—"

"Get below." He strode across the deck, and Sabine resisted the urge to follow him. Though he kept his secret well hidden, she sensed it was terrible. It regarded the King. Something he wasn't telling her—

"Sabine, come with me." Cook grasped her arm as they headed below. "We need to prepare for casualties. Wherever the King goes, death and destruction follow."

"I know that well enough."

Below deck, Sabine followed Cook's orders in turning the cargo holds and the galley into an infirmary. As they worked, Sabine thought of Galen, of how much she loved him but how little she really knew about him.

"Were you always a doctor?" Sabine asked Cook.

"I was a monk first. At that time, monks and doctors were often one in the same. Galen was my first teacher in the healing arts."

"Galen?" Sabine looked surprised. "It's hard to think of him as anything but a warrior."

"I think it's hard for him to remember the days before he went to sea. At least that's what he told me when we first met. At that time, I was living in a secluded village with several other monks. The eldest, who had been instructing us in the healing arts, died after a brief illness. We met Galen by chance, and he taught us all he knew." Cook pointed across the galley. "Put the fresh bandages over there."

Sabine did as he asked, feeling both curious and a bit hurt. Why did Galen keep so much hidden from her? He claimed to love her, and she didn't doubt that he did, but his secrecy hurt her. Why didn't he trust her?

"Where did he learn?" she asked.

"He spoke very little about his past. All we knew was we needed his skills and he seemed to need the seclusion our village offered. One thing about Galen, he always seems to have something to ponder, something to burden his thoughts."

"I wish he'd just tell me."

Cook glanced at her. "I think in many ways he's a luckier man than he realizes."

Sabine's lips flickered upward.

Suddenly the ship seemed to lurch.

Sabine grasped the doorframe. "What the hell was that?"

"Just guessing from experience, we've been rammed by another vessel. Most likely some of the King's men are trying to board us."

Sabine's pulse raced and she raised her eyes upward, wondering exactly what was happening on deck. Though she knew Galen traveled with a fleet and Sofian was approaching with a second fleet from the east, it didn't mean they couldn't be captured or destroyed.

The first of the casualties arrived moments later. Only two injured crewmen who were able to return to the deck as soon as they were bandaged. From the two, they learned that several of the King's men had boarded the Scarlet Dragon, but Galen's' crew had defended well, either killing the invaders or tossing them overboard. They were headed at full speed toward the island where the Northern King had already burned most of the villages.

"He knows Galen's island is close by," Cook said to Sabine. "Galen should never have started this battle."

"He did the right thing," Sabine said. "If it hadn't been for him, all those people would have been murdered. The King needs to be stopped."

"Even if it means Galen's life? All our lives?"

"The King and his men can die just as we can. Don't you have faith in your own people?"

"You're very young, miss. Good doesn't always win over evil."

"And bowing to evil doesn't make it go away."

Cook smiled. "Good reply."

The ship lurched several more times, and Sabine guessed they'd docked and crewmen were rushing to shore.

Casualties trickled in, and Sabine learned that once ashore, it was nearly impossible to return to the ship. Sofian's ships had arrived to join in the fight, and it seemed the battle would be long and bloody. Galen's men were outnumbered—not impossibly so, but enough to cause some worry.

Sabine had just finished wrapping a man's injured arm when she was struck by a pained feeling from Galen. It vanished quickly, causing her even greater concern. Was he dead? Why had the feeling ceased so abruptly?

"Sabine, where are you going?" Cook bellowed as she grasped a sword belonging to one of the wounded warriors and hurried on deck.

Weaving her way through the working crewmen, she leapt into the shallow water below and joined a group fighting their way to shore. Though the warriors surrounding her were also vampires—and male—months of working the forge had increased her own considerable strength, and she'd always been accustomed to handling weapons, if only for sport.

Her blade clashed with that of a tall, bearded warrior who was quickly distracted by another of Galen's crewmen. When she reached the shore, she noticed a horse nosing around a rider who had fallen to the sand, a silver arrow protruding from his chest. Sabine mounted the horse and headed toward what appeared to be the remains of a burning village.

Through the smoky night she saw Galen battling a tall warrior in black and silver armor. A helmet concealed the man's face as he and Galen attacked one another with unimaginable ferocity.

The Northern King, Sabine suddenly realized, as her horse approached.

As Galen spun to deflect one of the King's blows, he noticed Sabine. In his moment of distraction, the King slashed his sword arm.

Galen grunted in pain, but turned his body in time to avoid a second, deadly blow.

Sabine kicked her horse directly toward the King, her own sword poised to kill.

The King deflected her blade, and Galen leapt on him, wrestling the sword from his grasp. He struck the King in the head, knocking him onto his back, then raised the sword.

What's wrong with him? Sabine thought in horror. *Why the hesitation?*

The King's booted foot shot out, striking Galen in the knee. As Galen stumbled, the King leapt to his feet and onto the back of Sabine's horse. His mail-covered arms clutched her so tightly she could scarcely draw a breath.

"The spoils of war, Galen!" the king bellowed, his voice laced with wicked laughter.

Galen sprang at them, and the King ripped the sword from Sabine's hand. The point of it pierced Galen's side. When he dropped, the King forced the horse to rear and trample Galen with its powerful front hooves.

"No!" Sabine shrieked, struggling in the King's grasp. He held her immobile, chest rumbling with laughter. Just before he struck her in the head, rendering her unconscious.

Chapter Twelve

ෂ

Sabine awoke to a rough tug on her hair that jerked her neck backward. Her head throbbed and her bleary eyes took a moment to focus on her captor who held her across his lap. Frigid blue eyes stared into hers, and she knew immediately it was the King who held her, naked, in his arms.

"Awake, my beauty?" There was a mocking edge to his deep voice.

Sabine tried to struggle, but his hand tightened on her hair, threatening to snap her neck.

"I'm pleased with my prize," he continued. "Galen's woman. What a rare jewel to crush."

"I was never Galen's woman!" Sabine hissed. In spite of her confusion, she realized the King would pit her and Galen against one another, should he realize the affection between them.

"He seems to think differently. When you rode into the village, he lost all concentration. Emotions are Galen's downfall, you see. I know that well enough," muttered the King. "When it comes to feelings, he's worse than the gentlest woman."

"I never would have guessed." Sabine tried to make her voice as cold as the King's. "All he seems to care about are the spoils of war. How do you think he got me?"

"He took you?" The King narrowed his eyes. "I find that hard to believe."

"Do you think I'd have gone with him willingly? Why would I taint my noble blood with that of a commoner? Worse than a commoner—a pirate!"

"Yes, he is common." The King relaxed his hold on her hair, and Sabine sat up on her knees, touching a hand to the back of her head. She gazed around at a captain's cabin—rather spacious for a ship. The bed on which they sat was large and cushioned in black satins and silks. A table stood against one wall, a brass-bound trunk against another.

"You're not common, though, are you?" Sabine took her lower lip between her teeth, the tips of her incisors digging into them, just short of drawing blood. She noticed the King's eyes flicker toward her mouth. Something about his face was so damn familiar! She'd imagined he'd appear as ugly as the horrors he'd committed, but to her agitation, he was rather handsome. His cheekbones were high and sculpted, nose straight, and lips full. A trimmed black beard covered the lower half of his face, and when an icy smile touched his lips, thick fangs glistened between sparkling white teeth. She noted the breadth of his shoulders and the strength of his neck and chest exposed beneath the open ties of his billowy black shirt. Fitted black trousers tucked into calf-high black boots hugged the muscular length of his long legs.

"So, you claim he took you, wench?"

"He did." Sabine made a conscious effort not to appear inhibited by her nudity. Though she longed to use her arms and hands to conceal her breasts and the thatch of dark hair between her legs, she knew a man like the King would thrive on humiliating her further. The more wanton she appeared, the better she'd survive.

"And you don't feel anything for him at all?"

"Only disgust."

The King smiled. "Then you won't mind when I execute him."

Sabine's belly dropped and her heart pounded. The King raised an eyebrow. She knew he heard her pulse quicken and smelled her change in emotions.

"You do mind," he continued, grasping her upper arm, his claws digging into her flesh until she winced. Trickles of blood streaked her flesh and dripped onto the bed covers.

"I was hoping you'd let him last for a while. Why put him out of his misery so quickly?"

"You suggest torture?"

"I suggest imprisonment. You know how a man with a spirit as free as Galen Donovan's would detest being chained."

"Too mild." The King thoughtfully scratched his beard. "But I like the way you think—what do you call yourself?"

"Sabine."

The King smiled. "Sabine. He was too soft for you, wasn't he? Too gentle. I understand you just by meeting you this one time. Unless I'm wrong—and I'm rarely wrong—you're much like me. You'll make a fine addition to my slaves."

"Slaves?"

"You might even become a favorite. Would you like that, Lady Sabine? To be a favorite of a King?"

"Yes, oh yes." She edged closer to him, using every trick of mind control Galen and Natassja had taught her. She could not allow herself to think of Galen. The only way to keep him alive and gain the King's trust enough to form a plan for escape would be to convince him that she was willing to play his evil game.

"Not so quickly, my eager little slave." The King grasped her upper arms and shoved her so hard that she knocked into the headboard. Sabine hissed, but her rage seemed to excite him.

The King grasped her calves and dragged her down the bed before covering her body with his. She felt his erection pressing against her belly as he kissed her so hard she cut her lips on her own incisors.

"I'm going to enjoy you, my beauty, but first I want Galen to know what's happened to his favored prize." He stood and walked to the trunk where he lifted the lid, chose one of his long, white, full-sleeved shirts, and threw it at her. "Dress. We're going to the brig."

Sabine slipped on the shirt. In spite of its length, the cotton was so thin it left nothing to the imagination. Her nipples and the triangle of hair on her crotch were visible through the fabric. Gods, he was going to parade her around the ship dressed worse than the cheapest whore!

"Shall we go, Lady Sabine?" Again his voice possessed a mocking edge.

"Of course." She followed him out of the cabin, heart pounding. "What if I aspire to be more than your slave?"

He chuckled. "One step at a time, my beauty. One step at a time."

* * * * *

Galen awakened to a sharp pain in his side. As his eyes snapped open, he jerked his hands downward, but they were bound above his head. Had it not been for barbed manacles slicing into his wrists, he would have broken the bonds.

Beyond the King's powerful scent was that of Sabine. At least she was alive, but in what condition? If the bastard had harmed her—

"Silver barbs." The King grinned. "Comfortable?"

Galen's eyes fixed on the King's. "Aren't you tired of this yet?"

"Of our hunt, you mean? Quite tired. I had intended to execute you, but somebody convinced me otherwise."

The King stepped aside and extended his hand toward the brig's entrance. Sabine stood, wearing nothing but a flimsy cotton shirt open to her belly and just grazing her knees. Galen resisted the urge to touch her mind. Though he needed to feel her, he knew that revealing his love for her before the King would cause her greater harm than whatever she'd already suffered.

"So, my beauty, do you like him in chains?" the King asked.

Sabine's lips slid into a smile, revealing the gleaming tips of her fangs. She sauntered close to Galen and gently rested her palm against his cheek.

"Sabine—" he began, but was interrupted when she slapped him hard. He gazed at her in surprise, his face stinging, though not nearly as painful as the poorly tended sword wound in his side.

"Do you know how long I've dreamed of you in this position?" Sabine snarled, her fingers sinking into his bare chest.

"It seems your little slave doesn't like you any more than I do, Galen." The King leaned his shoulder against the wall, close to Galen. "It was her idea to torture you, and I think it will be a good one."

"Just remember to keep him alive." Sabine smirked. "We wouldn't want our amusement to end too quickly."

"Of course not." The King looked thoughtful. "There are so many ways to cause magnificent pain without threatening life."

"I think I like this ship already." Sabine took a step closer to the King who tugged her into his arms and kissed her. Galen's stomach clenched with fury. He struggled against touching Sabine's mind. She was an intelligent woman and probably realized it was best to act as if she hated him. At least that's what he hoped.

* * * * *

Several hours later, Galen was certain Sabine despised him as much as she claimed. Any woman with a bit of feeling for him couldn't have stood by so coolly while the King performed fiendish torments that left his body throbbing in agony and his spirit numb.

The King has used tiny silver needles to pierce pressure points from neck to foot. He'd used flaming hot pincers to mar his vampiric flesh and watch it heal. All the while Sabine had remained at the monster's side, watching, grinning and teasing the King with sexual innuendoes.

Galen sagged against the wall, the torturous manacles supporting his limp body as the King tugged the last needle from his neck.

"There's nothing quite as painful as silver, is there?" The King grasped a handful of Galen's hair and jerked his head upward. "I'm so tempted to kill you now."

"Not yet." Sabine slipped between Galen and the King. Galen's half open eyes searched her face and his exhausted mind attempted to touch hers. He needed to know the truth. Then he could hate her. If he hated her, he could gather the will to survive. Still loving her, the torture was unbearable.

She stood on tiptoe and bit his mouth, drawing blood that both disgusted and aroused him in spite of his weariness. She trailed her tongue down his chest and abdomen, pausing at his flaccid cock that, quite against his will, stirred to life. She took him in her mouth, her tongue laving the head.

Galen shuddered, lowering his eyes, trying to avoid the King who stared intently, a half smile on his lips

"Sabine, stop," Galen murmured.

She clutched his hips, drawing him deeper into her mouth until he felt the back of her throat, slick and wet, against his cock head.

He closed his eyes tightly, resisting the urge to thrust into her mouth. He didn't need to. She performed with such skill that within moments he erupted. She pulled away, spitting his creamy essence and dragging a graceful hand across her lips.

"You are a perfectly evil slut, my beauty." The King's voice bubbled with laughter. "You give me a marvelous idea. Guards!"

Two tall, bulky men stepped into the chamber, thick fangs resting against their lips.

"Chain the prisoner in my cabin."

"Yes, Highness." The guards spoke and bowed in unison.

"Now, the real fun will begin." The King grasped Sabine's upper arms hard and dragged her to her feet. He licked her lips.

Galen felt both furious and sick. He never imagined hating Sabine, but at that moment, had he been free, he probably could have killed both her and the King.

Sabine trembled inside. She lay on her back on the bed in the King's cabin, making an effort to appear relaxed and ready for the disgusting assault soon to come. She'd scarcely recovered from the sick feeling of watching Galen tortured. Execution might have been less cruel, but she was too selfish to lose him. She could have ripped the King's throat out. She would, if she got the chance. What puzzled her was why Galen hadn't killed the King on the island? His sword had hovered right over the bastard's heart, yet Galen had hesitated.

At the moment, Galen was bound to the wall across from the bed. She tried not to look at him, not to see the dried blood covering his body and the torn expression in his eyes.

His position would give him clear view of the performance between his betrothed and the King. *His betrothed!* She had to stop thinking of him in that way. Though the King couldn't read their minds, she didn't doubt he would observe their emotions. The man's sapphire eyes seemed to notice everything.

"Now, my beauty, the fun shall truly begin." The King grinned from where he stood at the foot of the bed. He dropped his trousers and ripped off his shirt. Sabine's gaze swept his body. To her shame, the attraction she knew shone in her eyes wasn't completely feigned. She detested all the King stood for, but she had to admit he was handsome. Tall, long limbed and muscular, he seemed almost familiar. Now that he and Galen, both naked, stood so close together, she noted a similarity between them.

She shook her head. It was just her mind playing tricks on her. The thought of being with the King was so terrible that she imagined he resembled Galen, just so she could survive the sexual humiliation to come.

"We go well together, don't we, Galen?" the King sneered. When Galen didn't reply, the King turned and struck him in the ribs.

Galen groaned, teeth clenched, and glared at his enemy. "I should have killed you long ago, Alexis."

The King yawned. "Same story over and again, Galen."

"I won't make the same mistake again."

"You won't get the chance." Alexis spat in Galen's face before approaching the bed.

Sabine's fists clenched at her sides. In the face of his wickedness, the King's masculine beauty faded. Still, she would play her role until she and Galen were free—and if she could destroy their tormentor along the way, she would do so willingly. Whatever Galen's reason for sparing the King, it had nearly killed him—might still kill him if she couldn't find a means of escape for them both.

Before Sabine could plot any further, Alexis' body covered hers in a motion so swift she gasped.

"Make this hard for me, beauty," he said against her lips. He licked her throat. Tongue trailing over her breasts, he slipped down her body, his hands rough as they shoved apart her thighs. Alexis took one of her nipples between his teeth and bit. Sabine arched against him, knowing she needed to play her part to the fullest. She struggled against his hand, clamping her legs shut. Still, he pried them apart and cupped her sex.

"Don't worry, Sabine. I'm not a fool." Alexis' voice sounded husky with passion. "I have no intention of filling you with my cock, no matter how it aches for your hot, wet cunt. I wouldn't mate with a woman of our kind and bind my thoughts to hers. I'm going to torture us both, my beauty, and each moment shall be magnificent."

Sabine could have cried with relief. At least now Alexis would never learn of her and Galen's love.

"Alexis, you son of a bitch!" Galen snarled across the room. He strained against his manacles, the scent of fresh blood filling the cabin as the bonds sank into flesh scarcely healed from earlier. "Sabine, if you do this, we are through!"

She forced a seductive smile at the King as she called to Galen. "I hope that's a promise."

The King glanced over his shoulder at Galen and smirked before clasping Sabine's hips in his hands, pressing his face between her legs and lapping her clit.

Sabine moaned, hands impulsively sinking into Alexis' long, curling hair. Her body responded to his tongue and lips. Her clit throbbed and her insides quivered. When she came, the exquisite release was tainted by feelings of shame and hatred. How could she gain any pleasure from a man she loathed?

The King lifted his head, licking his lips, and loomed above her, a knee on either side of her hips. He rubbed his long, thick cock over her smooth belly and thighs. His heartbeat quickened. She heard it and smelled his desire. He shifted upward, the thick, ruby head circling her breasts. He grasped her hand and forced it around his cock. It felt so thick and hard, the veins bulging beneath velvet skin. Sabine almost closed her eyes to pretend it was Galen she touched, but Alexis' eyes bore into hers. She clutched his cock harder, digging in her nails, hoping to turn him away. Instead, he gasped, eyelids lowering, though he didn't close them completely. She watched his throat move as his excitement grew. His breathing became so ragged it was almost hard panting. Suddenly he jerked away, sitting on his knees beside her, arms braced against the headboard, the cabin filled with the scent of his desire.

She stared at him, thinking for a moment he might come all over the bed, yet within moments he'd regained control of himself.

Alexis grinned. "You're a marvelous piece of work, beauty. You could definitely end up being a favorite. No wonder Galen wanted to keep you for himself."

Galen!

Sabine glanced across the room. Galen's face looked as if it had been chiseled from rock. His eyes, gleaming with fury, stared from beneath matted tendrils of hair.

"I'll wager you'd like me to share her again, Galen. You can wait for eternity. She's mine now. Isn't that right, Sabine?"

"What do you think, Highness?" Sabine maneuvered herself beneath him and licked his belly, one hand clutching his balls. She was about to take him in her mouth and bite his cock off, but he was as intelligent as he appeared and shoved her away.

"Oh no, you wonderful little slut. Not yet. I have to trust a woman implicitly for that. Can you believe a bitch once tried to bite off my cock?"

"Imagine that?" Sabine feigned horror.

"She's a dead bitch now."

"So if you don't make love and you don't allow a woman to pleasure you with her mouth, how do you —"

"I have human slaves for that."

"One day you will trust me enough, Highness." Sabine straddled his waist as he lay on his back. Her hands splayed across his lean, hair-roughened chest.

"Perhaps," he grasped her upper arms and pinned her beneath him, "but don't wager on it, my beauty. Now, let's see how long we can hold off your pleasure."

The King took one of her nipples between his teeth while he struck his cock repeatedly over her excited clit. His hands and mouth felt harsh yet stimulating, and her body reacted to his carnal torments. She closed her eyes tightly, imagining it was Galen who touched her. Yet the feelings weren't the same. This was physical excitement without affection. It was pleasure she couldn't fully enjoy since her heart belonged to another.

In the distance, she heard Alexis' mocking laughter.

Sabine's gaze swept the cabin as she lay on her back, Alexis' sleeping form sprawled across her body. He'd bound her wrists to the bed with manacles too strong for even her vampiric power. If he'd seemed to possess a single redeeming quality, she might have pitied a creature who could trust no one.

Galen's head lifted from where it sagged against his shoulder, and she felt his mind touching hers. She thrust him out, not only for fear of the King discovering their true relationship, but out of shame. Though she had little choice but to play Alexis' games, she hated the small pleasures she'd gained from him, and she felt certain Galen must hate her, too.

Even from their brief mental encounter, she sensed his anger and pain — pain that went far deeper than physical. He felt betrayed, more so than she'd have imagined. How could he not? If their roles were reversed, she would have despised him and the woman seducing him.

Alexis stirred, lifted his head from her breast and stared into her eyes. "Not tired? We'll see what we can do about that."

Sabine quivered. She was tired, but too upset to sleep. Alexis took her shiver as one of desire, and he smiled, the tips of his fangs gleaming in the dark cabin.

He buried his face in her shoulder, teeth piercing her flesh in a manner that was both painful and arousing. She felt his cock growing hard against her thigh, and he shifted position. For a moment she thought he'd enter her, but he'd apparently told the truth when he said he wouldn't risk losing so much of himself by mating with one of his own kind. Alexis' hand dipped between her legs, to where she was so wet and wanting. He stroked her, and she clung to him. Over his shoulder, she saw Galen watching him, his eyes blazing and teeth grinding. He looked at her, and she saw hatred and coldness such as she'd never imagined. Never had he looked like such a stranger, and never had she contemplated sexual stimulation with another man.

As she came, her eyes slipped shut. Alexis growled with satisfaction, though he'd yet to climax once with her. Part of her envied his self-control.

Suddenly he stood, and Sabine stared up at him, tugging the sheet over her body. "You're leaving, Highness?"

He touched one of his vampiric claws to her chin and left without speaking a word.

As soon as the cabin door slammed shut and she heard his footsteps grow softer and eventually fade away, Sabine leapt out of the bed and approached Galen.

Are you all right? She communicated mentally, fearful that the King might discover any verbal conversation between them.

Now that she'd opened her mind to his, his fury and pain struck her with such force that she braced a hand against the wall to keep from staggering.

Tell me you're not enjoying him, Sabine!

I'm doing it to save our lives! Do you think I want him pawing me? He's like an animal!

You're either a superb actress, darling, or else you are taking pleasure in his crude ministrations!

I'm flesh and blood, Galen! You saw what he's like, what he does to me! If you'd just killed him when you had the chance —

I couldn't!

Why? He's evil!

If he's completely evil, then part of me must be just as evil!

What are you talking about? Galen, what have you been hiding from me all this time? There's something between you and Alexis. What is it?

"God, it's him!" Sabine whispered aloud, leaping across the cabin and onto the bed. She and Galen parted minds as the King stepped inside.

"That position looks so uncomfortable, Galen." Alexis stood before him, arms folded across his chest.

Again Sabine stared at the two men. Suddenly the resemblance between them seemed uncanny. They could have been brothers. *Brothers!* Was that what Galen was hiding? If so, she understood why he'd hesitated in killing Alexis. She knew how difficult it had been for Narcisse to kill Kornel. Even though their younger brother had been wicked, taking his life still tormented Narcisse.

Of course Galen and Alexis were brothers, too!

"Would you like to lie down for a while?" Alexis' lips curved upward. "I'm sure Sabine and I could make arrangements."

"I'd rather hang here for eternity!" Galen snarled.

Alexis' smile broadened. He lifted his hand, five sharp claws slipping from beneath human nails. He placed his hand over Galen's heart, his claws sinking into his flesh, creating shallow wounds that caused several small droplets of blood to course down Galen's chest, creating sanguine patterns through the dark, curling hair.

"Forget about him." Sabine stood, slipping her arms around Alexis' waist and resting her cheek against his broad, smooth back. "Can't you have him put back in the brig?"

"Want to be alone with me, beauty?"

"Yes."

Alexis removed his claws from Galen's chest. "I once promised to rip out your heart. Am I doing a good job?"

"You've been ripping out my heart for centuries." Galen stared at Alexis.

The King's smile faded. To Sabine's surprise, he took a step closer to Galen and kissed his cheek. "You haven't changed much, Galen, still soft as a woman. Still a fucking liar."

"I've never lied to you, Alexis—"

The King turned his back on Galen, lifting his elbow and jabbing it into Galen's face.

Sabine winced as she heard the crack and saw blood spurt from Galen's lips. He spat a mouthful of it on the floor. As Alexis strolled to the door, Sabine made a motion toward Galen, but he glared at her and shook his head slightly.

Sabine tore her gaze from his bleeding face and slid back into the bed, watching as Alexis summoned several guards who unchained Galen and dragged him to the brig.

"What are you going to do with him?" Sabine asked.

"Save him for execution when we return to my fortress. Or maybe I won't kill him. I could just keep him locked away. It would serve him right, you know."

"What did he do to you, besides free villagers you wanted to enslave?"

"He breathes! That's reason enough for me to loathe him."

"But surely—"

"Enough." Alexis grasped her upper arm with one hand and picked up the shirt she'd worn with his other. He shoved both of them outside and slammed shut the door.

Sabine stood, shivering, as she hurriedly slipped on the shirt and fastened the ties. Glancing over her shoulder at several men who stared at her, she prayed they wouldn't attack her.

They must have feared their King, since none touched her as she made her way through the ship, trying to find better clothing—at least some trousers or a blanket.

"Here." A tall, sandy-haired woman stepped through a small, round door. She tossed a tunic-style dress at Sabine. The woman's scent was fainter than the vampire crew—a human scent.

"Thanks," Sabine muttered. As she dressed, the woman folded her arms across her chest, leaning a shoulder against the wall, and watched. Sabine noticed her body looked strong and well muscled. Something about her reminded Sabine of Natassja and she felt an immediate kinship with her.

"Irritated him, did you?" the woman asked.

"I suppose things could have been worse."

"That's true enough. Alexis really is a monster."

"What are you doing here? Are you his slave?"

"One of many. I'm Calypso." She extended her hand which Sabine clasped in a firm handshake.

"Sabine."

"Follow me. I'll introduce you to the other women."

"He travels with his women?"

Calypso's lips curved in a humorless smile. "Can you imagine a man with his appetites doing otherwise?"

Sabine pondered the truth of Calypso's words as she followed her deeper into the belly of the ship.

They approached a hold from which emanated the scent of perfume and the aroma of mortals and vampires alike. Calypso opened the door and Sabine followed her inside.

Six women mingled in the hold, three lounging on pillows and blankets sprawled across the floor, two munching bread in a corner while watching another buxom slave dance. All eyes fixed on Sabine, and Calypso introduced her.

"Another victim of the handsome bastard," said the dancer, the tips of her incisors sparkling against her dark face.

One of the women munching bread tossed aside thick tendrils of kinky black hair and smiled. "If you want to call her a victim. I, for one, can think of worse places to be."

"That's because all you think about is mating," the vampire dancer spoke again.

"Well he can certainly keep a woman's body happy!" the black-haired woman retorted.

"Some of us prize freedom." Calypso sauntered to one of the oversized pillows and flopped onto it, leaning back on her elbows.

"You'll be the last to get it," the dancer told her, continuing with her fluid arm movements, her hips swaying gently. "Everyone knows he prefers you to any of us, Calypso."

"Not according to him."

"Calypso, what a man says and what he thinks are usually two different things," another woman—a slender redhead—said.

"Rumor has it you were enslaved by that man in the brig." Calypso's large aquamarine eyes fixed on Sabine.

"I don't want to discus him. I'd rather learn what I can about my newest captor."

"King Alexis." The black-haired woman smiled. "Ruthless, cunning, insatiable."

"Not quite insatiable, Ariana," Calypso muttered.

"This mortal claims to have pleasured him to climax." Ariana cocked an eyebrow. "When the vampires among us have not. And you, Sabine?"

Sabine's brow furrowed as she sat on the floor, her back braced against the wall, and studied her new companions. Had these women been love slaves for so long that they were able to openly discuss intimacies shared with a man, even a warlord? She took a moment to reply as all eyes remained focused on her. "No, he has not—climaxed—with me."

"He never would with one of us." The dancer dropped to her knees. "A man like that would never risk mind sharing. He knows that to mate with one of his own kind—or to change a mortal—would mean another person could know every thought churning in his evil mind. That would be too great a weapon for anyone to hold against him."

"He sounds cunning."

"Very cunning," Calypso said.

"And why does he hate Galen Donovan so much?"

Ariana shrugged. "Some say they were close once, and betrayal occurred. King Alexis trusts no one, so I find it difficult to believe anyone could truly betray him."

"Whatever the reason, they've chased one another for years. Then one day Captain Donovan approached in reply to a rumor that the King sought a privateer for a particularly hideous attack on a small northern village, which refused to supply him with armor. The idea of hiring a man he hated to do his bidding appealed to him, except Captain Donovan didn't fulfill his end of the bargain."

Ariana added. "Since then, Alexis has sought to destroy him with more of a vengeance than ever before. I don't envy Donovan the death that must be planned for him once we return to the King's palace."

Then I must find a way to free us before then, Sabine thought. *Perhaps free us all from the monster.*

For the next several weeks, Sabine only saw the King from a distance. She'd approached him soon after meeting his women, but he'd grasped her hard, shoved her aside and ordered her to stay out of his sight until he sent for her.

She also learned he'd seemed to have forgotten about Galen who remained locked alone in the brig. Calypso discovered he was being fed and supplied with water, but no blood. Sabine wanted to touch his mind, but for the first few days after arriving on the ship, was fearful.

Finally, she could bear no more and let her thoughts drift to his. She sat in a tiny supply room between the women's hold and another empty hold, which she'd never seen anyone enter. There she closed her eyes while her mind searched for Galen's.

Galen, if you can hear me, please answer. Galen?

Sabine, have you been harmed?

No. And you?

I don't matter. I'm sure not to you.

Galen, please don't accuse me of wanting him again! I can't —

Do you have any idea what you've done, Sabine?

What I've done! He's taken me by force!

Not quite by force, was it?

Galen!

You enjoyed what he did! I saw —

How can you blame me? If it hadn't been for you, none of this would ever have happened! None of it!

Suddenly his thoughts stilled — except for pain and guilt. *I know. Forgive me, my love, but the sight of you with him —*

He's your brother, isn't he? Don't deny it. I can see the resemblance.

He's not my brother. He's —

Sabine's concentration was suddenly broken by a loud bang. The scents of Alexis and Calypso mingled and she heard movements in the empty hold beside her. Dim light shone through a small crack in the wall, and Sabine pressed her eye to it, staring into the lantern-lit hold. She realized then it wasn't empty, but was sparsely furnished with a bed and a trunk.

Calypso stood in the center of the compartment, arms folded across her chest while Alexis locked the door.

"You've left us alone of late," Calypso said. "I thought you might finally have realized how much you're despised."

Alexis took a long stride and caught her hands in his. Their fingers entwined and the King's arms slipped around her, trapping Calypso's hands behind her back. She tilted her face up to his. From where Sabine watched, she could see Calypso's face clearly. Though her jaw was set in an angry line, her eyes didn't appear hateful — rather quite the opposite.

Sabine felt surprised. She'd been under the impression Calypso hated the King as much as she did.

"I thought it was obvious I don't care who despises me." Alexis lowered his mouth to hers. "I take what I want."

"My people believe all you do comes back to you."

"Your people," he snickered. "Warrior women."

"One day you might know the vengeance of my clan, so I wouldn't be quick to mock."

"If the rest of your clan is as lovely as you, their vengeance might be welcome."

"I could make this very unpleasant for you."

Pressing her body even closer to his, Alexis turned so Sabine could see his grin. "You could try. It might be something we both enjoy."

When he bent to kiss her, Calypso turned her face away. Rather than being discouraged, Alexis kissed her temple, then her throat. Sabine watched the tip of his tongue stroke Calypso's neck. When he released her hands, Calypso's arms slipped up his back, palms pressed flat against bone and muscle.

Alexis' hand swept down her rib cage and rested on her hip as he kissed her neck, then her mouth. His eyes slipped shut, and Sabine caught the scent of their lust.

"Tell me to stop, and I will," Alexis whispered against Calypso's lips.

"You always make that same promise."

"But you never ask me to go away."

Calypso tried to pull away in anger. She grasped the front of his shirt, and he raised one of her hands to his lips and kissed the back of it.

"I'm stuck here, so why should I deny myself pleasure, even if it is from you."

Alexis' wicked grin broadened to a smile as he shoved her on the bed, grasped the waist of her masculine trousers, and tugged them off, along with her boots. Calypso jerked open the ties of her shirt and flung it over her head, her eyes fixed on Alexis as he undressed and approached the bed.

Sabine knew she should look away, but felt compelled to watch as Alexis knelt on the floor at the foot of the bed, grasped Calypso behind the knees and dragged her to the edge. He lowered his head so that his mouth hovered over her clit. Calypso's eyes slipped shut and she grasped handfuls of the King's hair as he lapped her. His lips tugged at her moist, pink lips until Calypso moaned with pleasure.

Within moments, the woman was writhing and trembling beneath his carnal attack. He used his mouth on her for several long moments, bringing her to climax after climax. Sabine heard Calypso's heartbeat quicken with each orgasm. She caught the scent of the slave's desire as well as that of the King. Alexis' eyes seemed to glow with vampiric lust. When he finally stood, his erection bounced thick and hard before him.

Calypso raised herself on her elbows and inched backward on the bed, spreading her legs for Alexis who climbed onto the bed and covered her body with his. Muscles flexed in the King's long legs and rock hard buttocks. Sabine noted that if the brothers shared nothing else, their bodies were of like perfection. Muscles bunched in the King's broad shoulders and back, which Calypso clung to. The slave's sleek legs wrapped around him as another orgasm overtook her.

"Alexis! Alexis!" she panted.

He didn't speak, but as his mouth covered hers, an animalistic groan sounded deep in his chest.

Sabine noted the intricacy with which he kissed her. His tongue traced the shape of her mouth, roaming over each lip, the tip of it dipping between the bow of her top lip. Then his mouth seemed to fuse to hers. The King's eyes were closed, and Sabine realized he never once closed his eyes when they were together. It was as if even while engaged in sexual play, he watched for attack. Calypso engrossed him thoroughly, however, and Sabine's brow furrowed. So it seemed the King could feel at least *something* for *someone*.

As Calypso quivered and jerked in yet another orgasm, the King stopped thrusting and lay on top of her, his breathing ragged, his entire body tense. The slave woman relaxed, dropping her arms and legs, her face peaceful in the aftermath of fulfillment.

Alexis rolled onto his back, his cock still pole hard and pointed skyward. He closed his eyes again and drew a deep breath then released it, his throat moving as he swallowed.

Calypso pushed herself to her knees and crawled between his legs. One of the King's hands touched her shoulder to hold her away from her intended target. For a moment, their gazes met, and he slowly raised his hand to her head, stroking her sand-colored hair as she buried her face at the root of his cock and kissed the length of it. Her tongue laved the head, and once again Alexis' eyes slipped shut. His breathing quickened as she licked every inch of his sizeable erection. She took him deep in her mouth and drew upon him.

"Ahhh," he moaned, the sound dragged from the depths of his dark soul. Perhaps some light burned there after all. His hips shifted and both hands stroked her head as she suckled his cock. His heartbeat echoed throughout the cabin, reaching Sabine who still stared, wetness seeping between her own legs. She calculated ways to use the King's obvious affection for his slave against him—without actually harming Calypso, of course. If Sabine was careful, she might even convince the slave to help her overthrow the King.

"Calypso! Oh God!" he growled. The slave tugged away only to straddle him and envelop his glistening cock. Alexis repeated her name over and again in a husky whisper until he suddenly tossed her onto her back and covered her body with his. While his hips moved in a blur, he lapped her shoulder before sinking his fangs in deeply. Calypso shrieked with pleasure/pain and came again. Groaning like a wild beast, Alexis came hard. When he'd squeezed the last bit of pleasure from both their bodies, he withdrew his teeth and rested his head against her shoulder, eyes closed, breathing slow and even.

"You're a weakness I don't want to obliterate," he murmured. "You might be the death of me, mortal bitch."

"The world wouldn't be so lucky," Calypso said as she drifted to sleep, a smile on her lips.

* * * * *

For over a month the King's fleet sailed, leaving the tropical waters for the cold northern ocean. Clothing and food were provided for the slaves, and Sabine grudgingly admitted the King treated members of his harem well. *And so he should*, she often thought. He sent for at least a woman or two on a nightly basis. Sometimes he'd take up to five a night—often all at once. Sabine knew the extent of Galen's carnal appetite, but the King never seemed to tire of sex. He was insatiable, even for a vampire. Thankfully, he saved his viciousness for battle and not the bed. His brutality in war as well as his earlier torture of Galen still terrified Sabine. She was grateful that he seemed to have forgotten about her lover. During their mental conversations, she'd learned that though chained, Galen was allowed to walk and lie down in the tiny brig. He was given scanty meals and water, but except for what he could take from the rats aboard ship, was starved for blood.

He fears you, Sabine thought to Galen one night as she lay, wrapped in blankets, among the other women in the slave's quarters.

Not in the way you think.

Galen, I know he's your brother, but how can you possibly feel for him after all he's done?

Sabine, I've tried to keep this from you — from everyone, but —

What, Galen? After all we've endured, you could at least confide in me.

It's so difficult. He's part of me. I hate what he's become, but some part of me —

Loves him. I know. I can feel it. How?

He's my son.

For a moment Sabine forgot to breathe. *Your son!* Sabine felt herself heat with shame and humiliation when she thought of what she and Alexis had done in Galen's sight. The perversion of the scene sickened her.

I'm sorry, my love. Now do you understand why I was so —

How can he be your son? He has nothing of you. Nothing!

He is of my blood, more so than a vampire made by bite. He was born to me and a mortal woman, Sabine, many centuries ago.

Mortal? So he's like Sofian, part vampire, part human?

Yes.

His mother — why didn't you change her?

She didn't want to become one of us. Perhaps if she'd known her life would end so suddenly, her decision might have been different. Not that it would have mattered, after what happened. Our village was attacked by a powerful Northern King. A vampire. He slaughtered the mortals, imprisoned me and stole Alexis. He blames me for it.

But I'm sure you did all you could —

I was a healer, a High Priest, Sabine. Though a vampire, I'd never perfected my fighting skills, and my people suffered for my lack of strength.

If you were a healer, you didn't lack strength!

I couldn't protect what was mine. When I finally escaped my underground prison, my village was dust. For centuries I searched for my son, learning all I could about the ways of war. I knew I might have to fight for him, but I never dreamed I'd be fighting against him.

Couldn't you just tell him what happened?

He refused to listen. The Northern King was his father. I was a bitter memory. He's mimicked the savage bastard who raised him. All my teachings have blown away with the ashes of our village.

You know he plans to kill you when we reach his kingdom.

I know.

We need to escape.

I need to destroy him. It will kill me to do it, but his evil has to end.

Galen, I'm so sorry about what I've done.

You've done what you've had to, Sabine. You've kept us both alive. Can you forgive me for subjecting you to him?

There's nothing to forgive. I only wish I could ease your suffering.

You do. Just these brief moments when I feel you so deep within me provides comfort and strength. I love you, Sabine. Whatever happens, never forget how much.

The King's slave women were often allowed the run of the ship, though they preferred their own quarters due to the lustful looks and comments of the crew. Sabine noticed only Calypso seemed exempt from their lewdness, and this further confirmed her belief that Alexis favored her for more than just sex.

Though the other vampires — save the King and a few members of his crew — only ventured topside during the night, Sabine spent most of her days gazing over the rail with Calypso, remembering what it was like to be free. Her thoughts always fixed on Galen, and they mentally communicated as often as they could.

"Look at that." Calypso pointed into the dark blue water one afternoon. The dorsal fins of several sharks circled the ship. "Unusual for such cold water."

Sabine wrinkled her nose. "Those things are deadly, even to our kind. My brother told me stories of a shipwreck and how several men — vampire and mortal — were eaten alive."

The women watched the sharks in silence for several moments. Finally Calypso asked, "Did you have someone at home? A husband or lover?"

It was an overcast day, soothing on vampiric eyes. Sabine recalled how Galen had exposed her to the day, of how they enjoyed sharing it together almost as much as the night. If only he was with her now. He'd been cooped in the brig for far too long, and Sabine was greatly concerned for his welfare. Though he told her he was well and no longer tortured, she knew neglect and lack of contact with others could be nearly as tormenting as the King's evil needles.

"Someone," Sabine murmured. "No. I had no one in my homeland. Did you?"

Calypso shook her head. "The males of my kind didn't appeal to me. Most of them have so little fire. They tend the house and care for the children, but rarely offer excitement."

Sabine's brow furrowed. "I'm not sure I'll ever understand your clan. I'm accustomed to men acting like men, not nursemaids."

"It leaves the women more time for important things like hunting and planning defenses."

"Couldn't such work be shared among you?"

"Not with men. Better to keep them tame or else they'll try to take over everything." As Calypso spoke, her voice faded, and Sabine followed her line of vision to where the King stood wearing only trousers and boots, the muscles of his bare torso rippling in the moonlight as he practiced with his sword.

Sabine noted lust in Calypso's eyes and didn't blame the woman in the least. Alexis was almost as stunning as his father. Both were like tall, sleek stallions — all raw bones and muscle.

"Attractive, isn't he?" Sabine whispered.

"He's like a carnal beast in legends." Calypso moistened her lips with the tip of her tongue. "A man like that is too dangerous for everyone's good. Were he in my village, we'd have him in chains."

"Where he belongs."

Calypso nodded, her gaze followed the King's every movement. "He's skilled with a sword."

"In every direction," Sabine muttered.

The women looked at each other and smiled before Sabine left Calypso admiring the King while she walked to the other side of the ship.

Suddenly a man repairing a mast — one of the few vampires aboard who could endure sunlight — bellowed, "Lookout below!"

Sabine turned in time to see a thick piece of wood drop from the mast. It struck Calypso in the head, knocking her overboard. Fearful that her friend would drown or worse, be consumed alive by the sharks. Sabine rushed across the deck, but the King was quicker. He dove overboard. The crewman leapt from the mast, grasped ropes and rushed to the rail.

"Lower the ropes!" Sabine shrieked as the sharks' fins sped closer then disappeared beneath the water. She had one leg over the rail when the King surfaced, supporting Calypso.

He fastened her to the ropes while the men hauled her upward. The King used his vampiric claws to climb the ship's wooden side. On deck, Sabine squatted beside Calypso whose eyes were just beginning to focus. Blood seeped from a cut on her head where the wood had struck her, and her forehead had already begun to bruise. The King knelt beside Calypso, gathering her close and inspecting her head.

"I'm fine." Calypso tried to push him away, but he swept her into his arms and headed below.

"You should have the ship's physician see her." Sabine followed at his heels. "She's only mortal, you remember."

"Keep to your own affairs, wench!" Alexis snarled.

"She needs a trained healer to look at her!" Sabine grasped his shoulder.

Alexis glared at her. "The ship's physician was killed during the last battle!"

"Then let Galen see to her!"

The King paused, fury turning his eyes red. His chest rose and fell with agitated breathing, and she knew the thought of asking anything of Galen must have sickened him.

"Will you put me down, you stupid boar," Calypso muttered, brushing blood from the side of her face.

Alexis' jaw tightened and he shook his head in disgust before turning to his cabin.

Several of the crewmen had awakened and stared at their captain and the women.

"Bring Donovan to my cabin. Now!" Alexis ordered the nearest man who hurried to do his bidding. The King turned to Sabine. "I said to go about your business."

"Let her stay," Calypso said.

Alexis strode to his cabin, ignoring Sabine who followed him, her heart pounding. It would be the first time in a month since she'd seen Galen.

* * * * *

Lantern light caused Galen to squint as soon as he stepped into Alexis' cabin. The brig had been completely dark—accommodating to vampire eyes, yet after so many months without light, he'd lost some of his tolerance.

Still, the woman he'd been asked to tend was mortal, and Galen knew the lantern light was for her benefit. The scent of the injured woman's blood had reached him even in the brig, and after so many weeks starved of the life-giving liquid, he felt almost faint. It took him a moment to master his bloodlust, though his teeth ached and his mouth watered for even a swallow.

His eyes first focused on Sabine who stood at the foot of the bed. Her heartbeat sounded as fast as his own, and above both of theirs, he heard Alexis'.

Alexis motioned for the guards who'd brought Galen to leave. By the time the doors closed behind them, Galen's vision had adjusted and he approached the bed. A tall, sinewy mortal woman sat up, back braced against the headboard, a hand pressed to her bloody forehead.

As Galen reached for her, Alexis grasped his wrist and snarled, "If anything happens to her, you're shark food."

"I said I'm fine!" the mortal snapped.

"You'll sit there and do as you're told!" Alexis turned his furious eyes to her and stepped aside for Galen. "A crewman is coming with water."

"Good." Galen inspected the injury. "Needs stitches. Don't you have a physician on this vessel?"

"He's dead."

Galen raised an eyebrow. "Killed him, too, did you?"

"In the mood for more torture?"

"If you weren't such a stubborn brat, you might learn something more important than how to destroy villages."

"Maybe I could learn to run from my duties, like you."

Galen felt torn between choking Alexis to death and shaking some sense into him, but he was far too old for anyone to give him sense.

A crewman entered with a bucket of water and a box of supplies from the ship's last healer.

"Good. There are herbs here to deaden the discomfort."

"The last thing I want is something to fog my mind more," the woman said. "To hell with your herbs and just do what you have to. This is nothing compared to half of the injuries I've had in battle."

"She comes from a tribe of warriors," Sabine spoke for the first time. The sound of her voice caused Galen's insides to twist and his breath to catch in his throat. Though her voice had sounded in his mind, it seemed like forever since he'd heard its gentle tone on the air.

"MeeKoran?" Galen asked Calypso. "I recognize the mark on your wrist."

Sabine glanced at the circular symbol tattooed on the back of Calypso's wrist. She'd always thought it had been a form of decoration, never having guessed it indicated her clan.

"You know my people?" Calypso's eyes widened a bit.

"I've had dealings with them."

The King watched the exchange between Galen and Calypso, his teeth gritted. He snapped, "Keep to your work. You don't need to speak with my slave."

"You son of a bitch!" Calypso hissed. "You should have let me drown and kept me out of my misery!"

"I saved you because I like self-punishment!"

"Hold still!" Galen ordered. "I'm trying to stitch you up."

Calypso quieted, but remained glaring at Alexis who shot her angry looks as well. Galen sensed much more than fury between them, however.

He loves her, Sabine's voice sounded in his head. *She seems to be his only weakness.*

At least he's able to love somebody, Galen replied.

Such a weakness is important. It could be used to work against him.

I've corrupted you, Sabine. You've become as conniving as any pirate.

I learned from the best?

Had their situation not been so grave, Galen might have smiled at their playful sparring, but Alexis' gaze roamed over them, and Galen tugged his mind free of Sabine's.

"Finished." Galen wiped his hands and cleaned the tools he'd used.

"There's nothing wrong with her then?" Alexis tried to appear aloof, but Galen saw genuine concern deep in his eyes.

"I don't foresee any lasting damage."

"I told you there's nothing wrong with me." Calypso stood, and Alexis shoved her back onto the bed before stalking out of the cabin, slamming the door behind him.

Calypso muttered some curses in her own language before turning back to Galen. "Thank you for your help."

Galen nodded, but immediately focused his attention on Sabine. He was about to speak when Guards stepped inside to guide him back to the brig.

I love you, Sabine, he thought.

I love you, too, Galen. I miss you so much.

Galen's insides warmed at her words, yet any happiness was short lived. Moments later, he was chained in the brig. He recalled the expression of hatred in Alexis' eyes and doubted he'd ever become accustomed to such an expression in eyes that had once looked on him with utter trust and affection.

Alexis was a grown man—a vampire with centuries of living behind him. Galen had to stop remembering the child he'd lost and realize, once and for all, only an evil man remained. A man Galen knew he must destroy.

* * * * *

Sabine's stomach twisted as she watched Galen leave with the guards. He'd appeared very pale, even for one of their kind, and his hunger for blood had been almost tangible. She marveled at his restraint both for blood and toward Alexis. She could scarcely believe they were father and son.

"What's wrong?"

Sabine turned to Calypso who stared at her from the bed.

"Nothing."

"It upset you seeing Captain Donovan. I can understand that. What confuses me is that he doesn't seem to be the beast you described."

"You've obviously spent too long with the King."

"Alexis is a bastard, all right, but sometimes he has decent moments."

Sabine folded her arms across her chest. "You don't hate him as much as you say, do you?"

"I hate him as much as you hate Captain Donovan." Calypso grinned, and Sabine's stomach fluttered. The mortal was far more observant than Sabine preferred.

Chapter Thirteen

❧

Narcisse had always claimed tragedies struck in numbers. It seemed once again, her brother was right. Only a day after Calypso was nearly devoured by sharks, a deadly storm stirred the water and winds.

It happened at dusk, fierce winds that sank most of the fleet, claiming the lives of hundreds of Alexis' warriors.

Sabine and the harem women felt the first stirrings as they were tossed across the hold.

"We'd better get topside," Calypso said as the women dressed. "Feels like we might capsize."

Sabine's heartbeat quickened as the women marched out of the hold. The other holds were emptied of crewmen who must have gone above to try to secure the ship.

"Galen!" Sabine gasped, twisting through the hurrying women as she sought the brig.

"Sabine!" Calypso bellowed, catching up to her. "Where the hell are you going?"

The ship rocked violently, throwing both women against the wall. With the next toss, Sabine used her vampire strength to catch Calypso in one arm and hold them upright by digging the claws of her other hand into the wall.

"I have to make sure Galen got out!"

Calypso didn't seem at all surprised by her friend's concern for the prisoner, but tugged Sabine toward the opposite end of the ship. "Brig's this way."

Halfway to their destination, the floor seemed to fly out from under them and they landed in a heap.

Calypso lifted her head. "I'd say we're going down, my friend."

"Try and save yourself," Sabine said, continuing toward the brig.

"I live for this kind of excitement." Calypso continued guiding Sabine, though she'd already caught Galen's scent and didn't need any further assistance.

"You might just die for it."

"If that's my fate."

"Sabine!" Galen shouted from behind a door bolted with metal.

"Galen! Are you all right?"

"Get off this ship! Forget about me!"

"Oh spare us!" Calypso raised her eyes. "There's no time for chivalry, Captain Donovan! Sabine, it's no use doing that!"

Sabine grasped the bolt, claws scraping as she pulled, her fingers bleeding. Galen began kicking the door from the opposite side, and the bolts started to give.

"Back away!" Sabine shoved Calypso aside as the door flew off its hinges.

Galen rushed through, chains still dangling from his manacled hands. The barbs had torn his wrists bloody.

"What the hell is this?" Alexis snarled. "Slaves freeing prisoners?"

"What are you doing here when your ship's sinking?" Sabine hissed.

"First rule of the sea, bitch. The Captain always goes down with the ship. Though I don't intend to be a stickler for tradition in this case."

"Do you have the keys?" Calypso grasped the King's arm.

"Did you think I was about to let him drown and deny myself the pleasure of killing him personally?" Alexis bared his teeth as he flung the key at Galen, grasped Calypso's hand and fled.

Sabine wasted no time releasing Galen, and together they raced after Alexis and Calypso. As they clawed their way to the top of the ship, they noted only the stern poked out of the water.

"There!" Galen pointed to a dingy Calypso and Alexis were climbing into. In the moment before she and Galen jumped into the fierce, icy water, Sabine noted several of the harem women and two crewmen were already in the dingy.

When they reached the dingy, one of the crewmen yanked Sabine on board. Galen pulled himself up only to be struck in the face by Alexis' fist.

"Stop it!" Calypso bellowed, leaping on the King's back. He easily shrugged off her mortal strength and turned to Galen who kicked him in the stomach, then the head, knocking Alexis unconscious.

"Toss him over," the crewman near Sabine muttered, and she almost agreed. She glanced at Galen and saw hesitation in his eyes.

Not again! Sabine's mind spoke to his.

Before any of them could make another motion, a massive wave washed over the dingy, and Sabine found herself floating in cold black water.

* * * * *

Sabine awoke shivering. In spite of the brilliant morning sunlight, the shoreline air was cold. The tide licking her calves and feet was frigid. Calypso lay a short distance down the beach. As Sabine pushed herself to her feet and rushed toward her friend, she heard the warrior woman's heartbeat and felt relieved.

"Calypso." Sabine knelt beside the mortal and shook her shoulder gently.

Calypso raised herself onto her elbow and blinked seawater from her eyes. "Damn, this has been a rotten couple of days."

"Are you hurt?"

"No. You?"

Sabine shook her head. The women stood, looking around in every direction. Sabine knew they both sought the same thing, survivors, particularly Galen and Alexis.

"Do you think they're — "

"No. They're alive. I can smell them." Sabine smiled. Galen was alive! And so, unfortunately, was Alexis.

"Alexis, too?" Calypso looked so hopeful that Sabine might have been glad the bastard had survived.

"This way." Sabine ran, forcing herself to keep to a slow lope to accommodate Calypso's mortal speed. She shouted, "Galen! Galen!"

"Sabine!" His voice sounded over the wailing wind as she turned toward the middle of the island where trees thickened to a forest. He tore though toward the women, swept Sabine into his arms and kissed her. "Thank God! I lost you when the dingy capsized!"

"I love you, Galen. I love you so much!" Sabine said between kisses.

Alexis' scent grew stronger, and Sabine and Galen turned to the opposite end of the beach. Alexis raced toward them, his speed far more vampiric than human. Calypso was only able to take a few steps toward him before he reached her. They stood inches apart, gazes fixed on eachother. Sabine heard their heartbeats and caught the scent of their bodies as they heated in spite of the cold weather.

Suddenly Alexis' gaze shifted to Galen. "So we found them. Now death." He tugged a silver dagger from a sheath about his waist.

"No!" Sabine snarled, lunging at Alexis, but Galen grasped her and shoved her hard. She landed on her rump in the sand.

"Stay out of this Sabine," Galen ordered as the men circled each other.

"Alexis, stop being a fool!" Calypso snapped. "We're stuck on this island and the last thing we need is to fight amongst ourselves!"

"She's right," Galen said. "Think about it. We have no supplies and it's winter. If we work together, we'll survive more comfortably."

"Well that's fitting! All you ever cared about was comfort in your own life." Alexis snarled, incisors exposed. "I'll cut your throat and we can drink your blood until we get off this rock!"

"Don't be so sure it won't be your blood we're drinking!" Galen's lips curled back over his own fangs. He raised his hands, claws gleaming in the sunlight.

"Damn the both of you!" Calypso bellowed. "I'm not a vampire, so if I don't get warm soon, I'll be dead! I plan on living, so I guess I'll start looking for food and shelter myself. I recommend you do the same, but if you want to kill each other, go ahead!"

"I'll go with you." Sabine stood. She and her friend walked into the woods.

Moments later, the men joined them, Galen beside Sabine, Alexis beside Calypso.

"I thought you wanted to fight to the death?" Calypso glanced up at Alexis, an eyebrow raised.

"I'm not about to let you alone on this island. You're still my slave."

"Oh spare me, Alexis."

Sabine slipped her hand into Galen's and thought, *Your son is a terrible danger to you.*

Galen glanced at Alexis who ignored him. *I know.*

"Our main concern is survival," Sabine said to the group.

"How much of a look at the island did you get?" Calypso asked the men.

"There are some animals in the wood," Galen said. "And a freshwater spring."

"There are caves to the east," Alexis added. "We could use them for shelter, and I suggest we head there now so we can dry off. Especially for the mortal's sake."

"I wonder if we're the only survivors from our dingy?" Sabine asked. She felt heartsick when she thought of the harem women drowning.

"I saw two of my mortal slaves on the beach," Alexis stated. "Dead."

"That's what you get for bringing your women with you," Galen snapped.

"You're a fine one to talk!" Alexis hissed at his father, glancing from him to Sabine. "You brought your whore with you!"

"She's my betrothed!" Galen shoved Alexis so hard and quick that the other vampire didn't have time to react. Alexis staggered almost to his knees.

"Your betrothed?" Alexis' look of rage turned to one of mirth. He turned his gaze to Sabine and smirked. "What a marvelous actress you are, beauty. You had me convinced you loathed his entrails."

"I'd have done anything to keep Galen alive—and I did!" Sabine seethed. "I had to be desperate to bed you!"

"You weren't exactly my preference, either." Alexis turned to Calypso who tossed him a look of disgust and walked ahead.

Soon they reached the caves Alexis had spoken of, and while Sabine and Calypso gathered wood to start a fire, Galen scouted around the island and Alexis hunted for their supper.

"Do you think they'll end up killing each other?" Calypso asked as they lugged twigs to the cave.

"I couldn't blame Galen if he did kill Alexis. I'm sorry, Calypso. I know how you feel about him, but—"

"It doesn't matter what I feel about him. He deserves to die." Calypso dropped her wood and ran a hand through her damp blonde hair. "I should hate the bastard more than I do. If my clan could see me now. I'm a disgrace."

"For being in love?" Sabine shook her head.

"I'm not in love!"

Sabine raised and eyebrow.

"I'm not. But you! All this time betrothed to Captain Donovan! And speaking of deserving to die, I don't blame Alexis for wanting him dead. What kind of a father takes his own freedom over his son's life?"

"What?" Sabine looked at Calypso as if the woman had lost her mind.

"Alexis was stolen from his village when he was a boy. The warlord who took him said he offered Galen freedom in exchange for Alexis. Galen chose to offer up his son to the Northern King—a far more powerful vampire."

"That's what Alexis told you?"

"He never spoke of it to the other women," Calypso said. "But he told me once. I know Alexis has caused suffering, but he also suffered at the hands of the Northern King."

"Galen didn't abandon him! He was imprisoned. He spent years escaping and centuries more searching for Alexis. He tried to explain, but Alexis wouldn't listen."

Calypso held Sabine's gaze for a long moment, as if assessing whether or not to believe her. "Captain Donovan didn't seem like the sort of man to trade off a child, but one can never be sure."

"I'm sure. Galen would never have done such a thing. Alexis has tortured him without mercy, yet when Galen had the chance to kill him, he let him go. Only a parent's love could allow such leniency. You know the truth when you hear it, Calypso."

The warrior woman sat back on her heels for a moment, shivering from the cold. Together, she and Sabine began the time consuming task of starting a fire.

* * * * *

Galen returned sooner than expected. He dragged a large piece of a ship's tattered sail behind him.

"Galen!" Sabine wrinkled her nose. "That thing stinks!"

"But it's protection from the weather until we find something better." He tore the sail into four large, rough-edged squares and sliced a hole in the middle of each. Handing one each to the women, he said, "Put this on."

Calypso, whose teeth were chattering and skin blue-tinged, tugged it over her head and sat close to the fire. Sabine and Galen, also cold but whose bodies were far more adaptable than mortals', also donned theirs.

Sabine was about to join Calypso by the fire, but Galen said, "Don't get too comfortable, either of you. We have to move."

"Move where?" they demanded in unison.

"I found a cave a couple of miles away. It has a natural hot spring and is very warm. We're better off staying there." As Galen spoke, he tore smaller pieces of sail and fashioned crude shoes that they could tie on their feet, as they'd kicked off theirs while struggling in the ocean.

"What about Alexis? He won't know we moved," Calypso said.

"I'll find him," Galen told her.

"At least it's not far. In moments we'll be there." Sabine's voice faded as she glanced at Calypso, who stared at her with a cocked eyebrow. To vampires' speed, a couple of miles was not more than a trot down the road, but to a half frozen mortal without warm winter clothes, it seemed a miserable journey.

"I'll take her." Galen approached Calypso and swept her into his arms. "Just hold on tight."

The mortal did as he said. Sabine killed the fire, and picked up the remaining sail cloak and shoes. Then the three of them raced through the forest with vampiric speed.

When they stepped into the cave, warm, moist air struck them. The soothing sound of rippling water echoed in the otherwise silent darkness. A pool filled half of the cave while the other half was of dirt and dewy rocks. It reminded Sabine of the meditation cave in Natassja's village.

Sabine saw clearly in the black cave, but she knew Calypso couldn't. Still, the mortal smiled as Galen placed her back on her feet.

"This is much better," she said. "Warmth."

"I'd better find Alexis." Galen glanced out of the mouth of the cave.

"I hope he caught something good to eat," Calypso muttered. "I'm starved."

"Me too," Sabine said. She was hungry for both food and blood.

Tonight we can take care of the blood, Galen's mind spoke to hers. They exchanged smiles before he went in search of his son.

* * * * *

Galen picked up Alexis' scent a short distance from their original campground. The King had killed a wild boar and was hurrying toward the abandoned cave.

"Where is she?" He dropped his kill and snarled at Galen who stood on top of the cave. "If you and that conniving she bitch Sabine have—"

Galen folded his arms across his chest and didn't attempt to hide his disgust. "I'm not the mad killer. That's your reputation. Calypso is fine. We've decided to move camp to another cave with a hot spring. At least your mortal won't freeze to death."

"Since when do you care about anyone, mortal or not?" Alexis picked up the boar and slung it over his shoulder. He sniffed the air, seeking Calypso's scent.

"This way." Galen dropped from the top of the cave and motioned for Alexis to follow him. After several moments he glanced over his shoulder and began, "Alexis, I know there's anger between us—"

"Anger?" Alexis' teeth bared. "You have as much talent for understatement as you do for lies."

"I've only lied to you once, and that was when you hired me to deliver those slaves."

"You never stop, do you?" Alexis' teeth gritted. "At least I say what I am! A killer? Yes! A slave master? Yes! A warlord? The fucking best there is! But you? You feign piracy, you feign loyalty, you even feign love! Does your woman know? Oh, I forgot. She's just as great a liar as you are."

"I never feigned my love for you. Whatever that evil bastard who stole you told you were lies."

"The bastard who stole me made me a King. What did you ever have to offer me? The life of a priest when our kind are born to rule? If you ask me, he did us a service. At least now we both have some semblance of power."

"I don't need a trail of destruction behind me to show I have power."

"Then why didn't you crawl back to your temple and stay there?"

"Because a priest couldn't find you, but a warrior could."

Alexis uttered a mocking laugh. "So now I'm to believe you've become a rich privateer for my sake?"

"No, I took the wealth to fight you once I realized what you'd become."

"Each word you speak drives you closer to death. If not for the sake of survival, I'd have killed you on the beach."

"I know you're cooperating because of Calypso. Love can make us see reason."

"I don't love her, and I could kill you when you adopt that condescending tone."

Galen felt genuinely surprised. "I'm not condescending."

"You always were when you played the part of the priest. Truth be told, I like the privateer much better."

"I know after what the Northern King told you—as well as my years of absence—it must have been hard to believe I searched for you, but—"

"I don't care what your excuses are. They don't matter. I've forgotten my life before I was taken. There's nothing worth remembering."

"Even your mother?"

Alexis glared at him, eyes tinged red with fury. "When I think of her I see a mortal lying naked with her throat ripped out. Not something I care to dwell on."

Galen fell silent for a moment, the memory of his first wife's corpse always floated in the back of his mind as well. He held Alexis' gaze. "I'm so sorry that happened."

"Spare me." Alexis snarled. "You swore to protect us and she believed you. The fool."

"If I could have died in her place, I would have willingly."

Alexis dropped the boar and sank his claws into Galen's shoulders. His enraged blue eyes gleamed and the tips of his fangs pricked his lips.

"It's true." Galen's own fingers grasped Alexis' arms. "I loved you and her—"

"Shut up!" Alexis shoved him hard into the nearest tree trunk.

Galen pushed away from the tree, shrugging his shoulders to ease the aftermath of the impact. He pointed to a cave several feet ahead. "That one."

"I know," Alexis snapped.

Indeed, the women's scents had grown strong. Galen longed for the touch of Sabine's body and mind. Dealing with Alexis was akin to running an emotional gantlet. Was he wrong to still try reason with a man who had turned so evil? Or was Alexis actually as evil as he seemed? If he was still able to feel, then there was a slim chance Galen could reach him. Galen knew it was a risk he had to take.

* * * * *

When Galen and Alexis stepped into the cave, arguments between them were forgotten at the sight of Sabine and Calypso swimming naked in the spring. They'd built a fire and created torches to light the cave for Calypso's eyes, and the flames created patterns on the black water and their skin.

"Oh, a boar!" Calypso licked her lips. "Can't wait to sink my teeth into that."

"I can't wait to sink my teeth into other things." Sabine grinned in Galen's direction. He growled deep in his throat. It had been too long since he had tasted her sweet blood, and he needed it far more than food.

"Once you get that thing roasting, how about joining us for a swim?" Calypso suggested.

"I killed it." Alexis flung the carcass onto the dirt floor. "You get the thing roasting."

"Somebody get the thing roasting!" Sabine stood and walked out of the water, her bare skin glowing, full breasts bouncing with each step.

Galen's heartbeat quickened and he ached to touch her. Instead, he picked up her clothes and handed them to her. Her fingers brushed his as she took the shift and dress to slip them on. He noted Alexis' gaze only swept her once, before his attention was nabbed by Calypso who followed Sabine out of the pool. The mortal was attractive as well. Though taller than Sabine, her body was just as curvaceous and muscular. The scent of Alexis' lust filled the cave, far stronger than a mortal yet a bit softer than a vampire. Calypso's eyes raked Alexis seductively as she dressed. Perhaps Sabine was right. Calypso could be an effective weapon against Alexis, should it come to that. He had no doubt it would, Galen thought with a saddened heart.

Between the four of them, the boar got skinned and roasted. Its hide would later be used to make clothes and better shoes than the ones made of sail. While they ate, they discussed survival plans. Galen suggested that since the season was cold, they should live in the cave while building a more permanent shelter.

"How long do you plan on staying here?" Alexis demanded. "I, for one, will not be content to set up a happy home on this rock when my kingdom is probably not a week away. We were nearly there when the damn storm hit."

"I'd rather be marooned than go back to your kingdom!" Sabine snarled.

"I second that." Calypso waved a finger in the air.

"We should still work on building a raft or boat," Galen said. "Unless we do plan on staying here forever."

"Sabine and I will take care of food and shelter," Calypso said. "You and Alexis can work on the boat."

"Since when do I take orders from you, slave?" Alexis tossed her a scathing look.

"It makes sense." She spoke as if to a child. "It saves time. Besides, as part of a rite of passage in my tribe, all girls are left alone in the wilderness with nothing more than the clothes on their back, shoes on their feet, and a day's worth of food and water. Sabine and I will have no difficulty."

"It's settled, then," Galen said.

"Well, if everyone is so quick to take the slave's advice—"

"It's good advice," Sabine said.

"Oh, the lady has spoken. Now we can all be sure the plan will work!"

"If you weren't so hateful, you might actually find something in life to be happy about," Sabine said.

Alexis hissed at her, fangs bared, and everyone finished the meal in silence.

None of the boar went to waste. Even the bones and sinew were used to create needles and thread to better sew the sail into clothing and shoes. When they decided to catch a few hours' sleep, Calypso and Alexis disappeared behind a large rock in the center of the cave, and Sabine curled into Galen's arms.

"I'm worried, Galen," Sabine said. "What if we're lost forever?"

He smiled and stroked her hair. "Sabine, I promise you, we're not lost forever. Do you know how many times I've been in similar situations? Besides, Alexis was right. We had nearly reached his kingdom. I'm guessing we're on one of the islands that are part of the Northern Archipelago."

"Narcisse sailed there with you once. He told us about it."

"Yes. We had trade plans with one of chieftains of a larger island." Galen kissed her. "Sabine, even if we were marooned, I can think of no one else I'd rather be with."

"Unfortunately Alexis has to be with us." She wrinkled her nose. "I'm so afraid he'll try to kill you."

"He's spent his life trying to kill me," Galen muttered.

"I know he's your son, but you can't keep giving him chances. One day he'll end up destroying you."

"What if I can reach him, Sabine?"

She shook her head and stroked his face. "He's too accustomed to his evil ways. He doesn't want to be reached."

"Maybe. I don't know."

"I do. Galen, he tortured you. He had sex with me in front of you. He—"

"Speaking of sex, doesn't he ever stop?" Galen's teeth clenched. The sound and scent of Alexis and Calypso making love filled the cave. The enticing aroma of her mortal blood wafted on the humid air.

"There's one way to forget about what they're doing." Sabine's eyes glistened with wicked humor as she tugged down Galen's trousers, lifted her skirt and straddled his hips.

Immediately, his hands settled on her waist, fingers massaging. She scratched his chest with her claws before unfastening the ties on her dress and pushing her breasts through the opening. As she leaned forward, Galen raised his neck and caught a plump nipple between his lips. His tongue caressed the nub before he bit, causing her to gasp with desire. Her hands supported his neck as she pressed him close, panting his name as he sucked first one nipple then the other.

She wiggled her hips, velvet flesh teasing his cock that had sprung to life at the first touch of their bodies. Her wet pussy enveloped his hardness and he growled. Sabine gyrated, and his hips followed her rhythm.

Suddenly he pushed her onto her back and drove into her with lust pent up from weeks of separation. During the meal, the vampires had drunk some of the boar's blood, but it was nothing compared to the taste of Sabine. His teeth sank into her shoulder as he pumped into her. Her fingers bit into his back, and he felt their bodies bead with sweat from the heat of the spring as well as their fevered movements.

"Sabine, I've missed you so much," he panted, tearing his mouth from her flesh and slowing his thrusts to prolong their first burst of pleasure.

"I love you, Galen," she murmured. Her legs locked around his waist. "I need you so much! Please, Galen, please!"

Her plea excited him more than he thought possible and he surged into her, feeling her arms tighten around his neck. She raised herself higher so she could bite him while his cock rammed her. He bit her again and a ferocious growl of fulfillment vibrated in his chest as he came, long and hard, into her quaking body.

They collapsed on the cave floor, tongues still lapping blood, their bodies a panting mass of fulfilled desire.

* * * * *

"Sabine, I have to tell you something important," Calypso said. They'd been traveling for hours, deeper into the woods and far from the shoreline where Galen and Alexis worked on building a boat.

"What is it?"

"We're not exactly lost."

Sabine's brow furrowed. "What do you mean?"

"This island is familiar to me. I wasn't sure at first, but the two peaks you can see from the shoreline cannot be mistaken. Members of my clan should be here, undergoing the Winter Rite. It's a passage to the highest rank of warrior among us, the Elder."

"You mean we're not alone? But we've smelled no one—"

"They're probably far across the island, and underground. If we stay here long enough, they will be discovered—or we will."

"They could help us get off. Alexis is sure to give them trouble, though."

"Once my people get Alexis, he'll be tried for his crimes against us."

"Will they execute him?"

"Maybe," Calypso murmured.

"How do you feel about that?"

"It doesn't matter how I feel. If his crime had only been against me, I would let him go, but he destroyed one of our trade ships. That's how I was captured. He has committed crimes and needs to pay for them."

"I'm not so sure I could send Galen to his death, no matter what he did."

"It's a code of honor among my people. I am still one of them. What I might feel for Alexis is insignificant. I'm going to find my tribe, Sabine. Come with me, and you will be welcome."

"Unless you have an army here, Alexis has the strength to destroy even a group of mortals."

"I know."

"But he can be trapped."

Calypso's gaze met Sabine's.

It seemed they were to be rid of Galen's son sooner than she imagined. She only hoped that for once Galen's love for his wayward child wouldn't disrupt his reason.

* * * * *

After nearly two hours of hiking, the forest opened into a clearing through which ran a narrow river. Sabine caught the scent of humans before the canoe, paddled by two leather-clad women, floated from a cover of overhanging trees.

Calypso jogged toward the bank, shouting in her own language. The women turned, their faces surprised, and paddled toward the shore

Sabine joined her friend and listened to the exchange between the warriors. Like Calypso, the other MeeKorans were tall and blonde—one with green eyes, the other blue. They carried daggers and bows, and both studied Sabine with wary expressions.

The blue-eyed one stared at her and spoke.

"What did she say?" Sabine asked.

"She wants to know how you can walk by day, if you're a blood drinker."

"Tell her I'm rare."

Calypso relayed the message, and by the length of her speech, Sabine guessed she embellished on their situation.

"They want Alexis," Calypso finally said. "Though they're from a different clan, several of their women were on board my ship when it was attacked. Both their clan and mine have been seeking revenge ever since. They say they're glad to see me because most were believed to be dead."

Though Calypso sounded calm, Sabine noted mourning in her eyes. She touched her shoulder. "I'm so sorry."

"I hate him," she said through clenched teeth. "Yet part of me doesn't."

"He seems to affect people that way," Sabine murmured, thinking of Galen. "We need to return soon or the men will miss us. If you want to stay with your companions, I'll try to keep Alexis away."

Calypso shook her head. "He would come for me. Besides, the MeeKorans would never allow him to get away."

"You're right. I have to let Galen know what's happening."

"They want to attack immediately."

"Ask them to give me time," Sabine said.

Calypso translated, then turned back to Sabine. "Because of what you are, they don't trust you, but out of kinship with me, they will allow until sunrise two nights from now before they attempt to take Alexis."

"How many of them are there?"

"Six in total. That's the most allowed to undergo the ritual together."

Sabine shook her head. "He'll kill them if they try to take him. Galen is the only one among us with the physical power to capture or kill Alexis. We'll need his help for this to work without human bloodshed."

As Calypso spoke, the warrior women appeared offended, but they nodded in agreement.

"What if Galen can't take him?" Calypso said. "It is a real possibility that Alexis might kill him. He's already captured him once."

"Because Galen let him live when he should have killed him."

"Exactly. Galen is obviously hesitant to kill his son. Hesitation with Alexis means death."

"If it appears to be a fight to the death, I have an idea about how to rattle Alexis into losing. He has a major weakness."

Calypso uttered a mocking laugh. "He has no weaknesses. Believe me. I've tried to find them."

"Yes he does. The question is, did you mean it when you said your loyalty to your clan is greater than your feelings for Alexis?"

"What do I have to do with it?"

"Absolutely everything."

* * * * *

"I agree to your plan," Galen said. "But I ask one thing."

Sabine placed her arm around his waist, gazing up at him as they stood side by side on the beach. Sunrise illuminated the sand and water, and if their situation hadn't been so precarious, Sabine would have thought the island one of the most beautiful places in the world. Yet the previous day, she and Calypso had spoken to the MeeKoran warriors and had convinced them to hold their attack for two nights. The women were proud and strong, yet Sabine knew Alexis would destroy them.

"You know I can deny you nothing, Galen."

"Let me talk with Alexis alone."

"It won't do any good, but if it will give you peace of mind, you must try."

"I just—" Galen paused, chin lifted as he sniffed the air.

Sabine did the same, and fear made her body tingle as she shouted, "The fools!"

Galen sped across the sand, Sabine at his heels as they raced toward the scent of mortals, mortal rage, mortal fear and mortal blood.

They climbed over a craggy ridge dividing the beach to where Alexis stood, fangs bared, three of the MeeKoran warriors surrounding him. The other three lay on the bloody sand.

A gash marked Alexis' bare back and the shaft of an arrow protruded from his chest. His eyes spat fury at the warriors. Calypso stood in front of him, the only barrier between the vampire and her people.

"Stop, Alexis!" she snapped.

"It seems you lie as well as everyone else, bitch!"

"Did you think your attack on our ship would go unpunished?"

"You think I won't kill you as easily as your companions?" he raged.

"No," she held his gaze, "I don't think you will."

"Back away, sister!" shouted the warrior standing behind Alexis as she raised a gleaming dagger.

"Alexis, these are silver weapons!" Calypso bellowed.

Sabine caught the plea in her eyes and understood her fear. Though she had no way of knowing silver didn't affect a vampire born of one mortal parent, she had reason for concern. Alexis wouldn't heal from any wound as quickly as a full vampire.

Sabine felt Galen's battle of emotions as he stood beside her, fists clenched.

The warrior flung the dagger, but Alexis had seen it coming from the corner of his eye. He caught it and hurled it back at the woman, striking her in the chest. She dropped to the beach.

Calypso attacked with the remaining two, but Alexis shoved her aside, kicked another in the stomach, and grasped the remaining warrior by the throat, one hand crushing her wrist until bone snapped and her sword fell. The MeeKoran screamed as Alexis sank his teeth into her shoulder.

"No!" Calypso leapt at him, clinging to his back and sinking her fingers into the open wound. Alexis growled and flung aside the warrior he'd bitten. She sat on her knees, trembling from blood loss and pain.

Alexis managed to toss Calypso off his back as Galen leapt at his son. Sabine began dragging the injured MeeKorans to safety.

"I knew you'd interfere!" Alexis snarled at Galen.

"Alexis, this has to stop!" Calypso approached.

"I should have killed you!"

He could have killed her, Sabine thought. Even though Calypso had sided with her people against him, even though he was wounded, Alexis still couldn't bring himself to harm her.

"Demon," the woman Sabine had hoisted over her shoulder murmured weakly.

"Yes, he is," Sabine muttered as she placed the woman beneath the shade of an overhanging cliff, then went to retrieve the others.

"Alexis, those injuries are serious," Galen said. "Let me help you."

"Help me?" Alexis smirked. "I trust you less than I do her!" He pointed in Calypso's direction. "I'd rather die than accept your help!"

Galen took a step closer, and Alexis used his foot to launch one of the fallen warriors' swords into his hand. He lunged at Galen, and Sabine screamed. Galen was just as fast as his son, however, and sprang out of the way. He landed in a crouch and took a sword from the open palm of an unconscious warrior. He blocked an overhead blow and lashed out with his foot in an attempt to knock Alexis off his feet.

Alexis jumped to avoid the blow, and when he landed, Galen faced him. Their swords clashed as Alexis began driving Galen toward the rocks leading up a cliff.

"Alexis, don't do this!" Galen shouted.

"If it's the last thing I do, I'm going to kill you!"

"You don't want to kill me!"

"The hell I don't!" Alexis' eyes seemed to glow red in the sunlight.

"Galen!" Sabine picked up two daggers and chased the men.

"No, Sabine!" he bellowed. "Don't interfere!"

Sabine stopped, heart pounding, eyes stinging with tears. He was right. She couldn't interfere in what was sure to be the final battle between father and son.

* * * * *

"If you wanted to kill me, you wouldn't have risked your own life to unchain me when the ship was going down!" Galen said to Alexis.

He blocked the King's overhead blow and dodged a sword thrust. Even above the shoreline wind and the clash of steel, he heard the pounding of Alexis' heart, or was it his own?

"Shut up!" Alexis snarled.

"Did you ever think you hate me so much because you still feel something for me?" Galen's foot snapped out in a kick that staggered Alexis.

They stared at each other, teeth grinding.

"I feel nothing for you but hate!"

"You loved me once."

"I was a stupid child! The Northern King taught me to be a man—something I never could have learned from you!"

"He taught you to be a killer, not a man!"

"We're all killers! It's inside us, human and vampire. And all my life, I've wanted to kill you!"

"It doesn't have to be this way, Alexis!" Galen said as the blows began again. He didn't attack, merely defended himself. Perhaps it was just his own desire, but he thought he saw a flicker of emotion in Alexis' wild eyes. "I love you, Alexis! I always have. I always will!"

"God, I'm going to cut out your tongue! Lying bastard!"

"Why would I still be lying?"

Alexis paused for a moment, sword raised. Galen's own weapon remained in a defensive position. Both were panting, eyes aching in the sunlight as their vampiric natures rose to accommodate the battle.

"You're my son, Alexis. No matter what happened to us, no matter what you've done or what I've become, I love you."

A muscle flicked in Alexis' jaw and moisture welled in his eyes. "But you'll kill me if you have to."

"Don't drive me to it."

A wicked grin spread across Alexis' face and he spun, sword aimed at Galen's head.

A shriek from the beach caused both to pause in the fight. Sabine stood, Calypso twisted in her arms, fangs tinged red with mortal blood she'd drawn from her friend.

Alexis turned from Galen and leapt from the ridge onto the beach to reach Calypso. Galen followed, landing on his back. He struck Alexis in the temple, rendering him unconscious with a blow that would have killed a mortal. For a moment he sat, panting, his hand on Alexis' back.

Sabine and Calypso hurried over.

"Is he alive?" Calypso asked.

Galen nodded. "That was dangerous, ladies."

"Don't I know it." Calypso touched a hand to her neck where Sabine had bitten. "Didn't hurt as much as I thought, though."

"If I had more time, you might have even liked it," Sabine told her.

Three of the MeeKorans approached, bloodstained and holding their injuries.

"He has to die," said one of them.

"He must be tried," Calypso stated.

"Our sisters are dead!"

"Because you didn't give us the time you promised! Galen would have brought the King to you, but you couldn't wait!"

A tall, red-haired warrior nodded, though her face remained stern. "You're right. He will stand trial. And then he will die."

"I know he's earned whatever punishment he receives." Galen rolled Alexis onto his back and inspected his injuries.

"Galen, you cannot save him from whatever comes." Sabine touched his arm. "You've done all you can. He might have been a good child once, but he's a man. Evil, twisted and beyond redemption."

"I know." Galen sighed, slipping a dagger from his boot and raising it above Alexis' chest. His throat constricted and tears stung his eyes as he prepared to finish what he'd started centuries ago.

Chapter Fourteen

ഔ

"Are you sure those herbs will keep him unconscious?" Sabine asked Galen.

They, along with Calypso, drifted on the ocean toward the MeeKoran homeland. There, Alexis would be tried by Calypso's clan.

"I'm sure," Galen said. "I've brought enough to keep him asleep for a couple of days."

"We'll reach my village long before then," Calypso said. "And you said his injuries should almost be healed by then?"

"Yes."

"I never knew he was part human. And my people will be interested to know that silver isn't effective against all of your kind."

Galen glanced at Alexis who lay on the bottom of the boat. With his eyes closed, he didn't appear so hateful, and for the fist time, Galen began to see something of himself in the dark, chiseled face. "You might one day regret stopping me from killing him."

"Perhaps," Calypso said.

"I still don't understand why you did stop him," Sabine said. "Your clan will put him to death anyway."

"Most likely." Calypso looked at Galen. "Are you sure you want to stay and watch? I know you feel for him, in spite of what he is. He's still your son."

Galen nodded. It wasn't that he wanted to watch the trial, but he was compelled to do so.

Sabine's hand slipped into his and she squeezed it.

I love you, Galen. I'm so sorry it didn't work out between you and Alexis.

No, my love, I'm sorry for all you've gone through because of us.

Sabine rested her head against his shoulder, and Galen inhaled the scent of her hair, the enticing aroma of her flesh. Soon they would be back on their own island.

* * * * *

Two days later, they arrived at Calypso's homeland. The first snow of the season had begun to fall as the villagers dragged ashore the bodies of the two women killed during the fight on the island. Galen carried Alexis, still unconscious, over his shoulder.

In the village, Galen helped the women fashion bonds strong enough to hold Alexis in prison until his trial. Since Alexis' attack on their ship, during which Calypso had been taken prisoner, the MeeKorans had studied their enemy, and now each warrior carried at least one silver weapon. Galen melted down one of the daggers to form barbs for the insides of manacles, and he secured Alexis in bonds similar to the ones in which his son had chained him.

They were also surprised to learn that a troop of MeeKoran warriors had joined Galen's men, led by Sophian and Cass, in a raid on Alexis' kingdom. The vampire and the wolf had taken Galen's fleet north, hoping to rescue him, and had met the MeeKorans on the way. According to Calypso's people, the Northern Kingdom was now under the control of Galen's warriors. Search parties were still underway to find him and Sabine, and as soon as Alexis' trial ended, Galen and Sabine would travel farther north to join their friends.

Once Alexis was secure, Calypso brought Galen and Sabine before the leader of her clan.

A sinewy woman of late middle years, the clan leader, Zorina, stared at them with penetrating brown eyes.

"You have done my people a service, and you have returned one of our finest warriors," Zorina said.

"I'm afraid I'm the cause of much of your trouble," Galen said. "The Northern King is my son."

"Yet you have brought him to justice. You know he will die for his crimes, yet your honor overpowers your heart. It is the sign of a true warrior."

Sabine felt Galen's sadness. In his search for Alexis, he had been forced to become a warrior. Ironic how his heart had brought him to such an end.

"Eat. Drink." Zorina motioned for two young girls to bring refreshments. "The trial will be on the morrow."

"I think I would like to rest before eating," Sabine said, sensing Galen's need to leave the eyes of the tribe.

Calypso brought them to a small yet comfortable hut where they discarded their clothes and slipped onto the cot.

Sabine's breasts crushed against Galen's chest as he held her. She lifted her head and stared into his eyes. He made a motion to speak, then seemed to think better of it. Her mind drifted toward his, and she sensed the intensity of his emotions. There would be no words strong enough to express how he felt on the eve of his son's death, nor could she speak words powerful enough to offer true comfort.

Instead she kissed him. Her tongue gently stroked his lips, his cheeks, his teeth. Her eyes slipped shut, and she allowed her hands to roam over his face and arms. She traced his ribs and curled her fingers in his chest hair.

Galen's hands warmed her waist and back. They cupped her buttocks and slipped between her legs, stroking the curls nestled there. His fingertips dipped into her warm pussy, caressing until her body turned to liquid. Then he rolled her onto her back and thrust into her. Sabine closed her eyes and clung to him, their thoughts entwined each feeling pleasure and pain, completely wrapped in one another.

I love you, Sabine!

I love you!

She heard his breathing grow ragged as his teeth sank into her shoulder. Moaning, she licked his neck and bit as his thrusting increased, driving them both to a bittersweet climax.

* * * * *

Galen knew the instant Alexis awoke. Neither his acute vampiric senses told him, nor an emotional kinship with his blood child. The entire village knew by the inhuman roar and string of curses that caused warriors to grasp weapons and mothers to bolt their doors for the safety of their children and husbands.

Galen and Sabine leapt out of the cot where neither of them had been able to sleep.

"You don't think he's escaped, do you?" Sabine asked as they raced to the prison hut just outside the village square. A scaffold stood behind the small yet secure prison made of stone. Two guards stood outside, swords poised for defense, but Galen could see others through the open door.

"He won't get through those bonds. They're even thicker than the ones he had on me."

The guards raised their swords when Galen and Sabine tried to step inside. Though they could have tossed the mortals aside, they respected the MeeKorans' authority and remained outside. Still, he saw Alexis clearly, hauling on his bonds until his wrists bled, his eyes aflame and fangs gnashing at the guards.

"You bitches better pray I don't get loose!" he snarled. "I'll bleed every last one of you! Especially you!" Alexis jabbed his finger in Calypso's direction. She stood at the front of the group.

"That's why he risked his own life when he thought I was going to kill her," Sabine muttered.

"You!" Alexis caught sight of Galen and Sabine. He hauled on the bonds and growled. "These chains are your doing. I know it!"

Calypso motioned for the guards to allow Galen and Sabine inside. Though they had yet to discover her position among the MeeKorans, she seemed to be a warrior of some rank.

Galen stepped closer, Sabine beside him. "This is the last thing I wanted, Alexis."

"Spare me!"

"We won't," one of the guards snarled. Alexis lunged at her only to be jerked back by the chains.

"These chains better hold." A wicked smiled spread across Alexis' face. "For your sakes."

"Ignore him," Calypso stated, causing Alexis to toss her a furious look. "Everyone go. His trial is in a few hours."

"My trial! That's rich! A horde of weak, mortal bitches trying the likes of me!"

As Galen followed the others out of the prison, he resisted the urge to glance back at Alexis. The King had created his own end, and they both would have to live with it.

* * * * *

The trial took place early the following morning. Galen aided the guards in dragging Alexis to the scaffold where Zorina and a jury of three Elders—warriors of the highest rank among the MeeKorans—listened to Calypso and several other warriors who had been involved in Alexis' attacks. When the time came for the King to speak in his own defense, he refused, but stood silently, gaze fixed on the horizon.

Galen and Sabine watched with the rest of the crowd who shouted for the demon's death. Zorina silenced them by raising her hands.

The clan leader said, "The time has come for us to decide the prisoner's fate. The chosen Elders will signify his guilt by remaining seated, his innocence by standing."

All three Elders remained fixed in their seats, their faces solemn.

Zorina continued, "The punishment is—"

"Wait!" Calypso stepped forward.

The crowd murmured and Galen's brow furrowed as he and Sabine exchanged looks.

"You wish to be heard Elder?"

Elder! Galen and Sabine felt each other's surprise. Calypso *was* high up.

"Am I right to assume the prisoner will be executed?" Calypso walked up the scaffold steps and faced Zorina.

"It is the law."

"Then I ask for the Matriarchal Release."

More murmurs swept through the crowd.

"Don't do it, Calypso!" someone shouted. "No father is better than one like that!"

Zorina drew a deep breath and released it. "He murdered our sisters. He took you as a slave. You have no obligation to a child born of such a union."

"It is still my right."

"It is."

"Then I take him as my slave under the Matriarchal Release."

"What the hell are you talking about, wench?" Alexis snarled.

The guard nearest him struck him across the face with the butt of her sword. He growled.

"It is settled. Take the demon back to the prison where he will remain until Elder Calypso provides a suitable cage for him."

"Cage?" Alexis bellowed. "I thought you were going to kill me!"

Zorina dismissed the crowd with a wave of her hand. Before she left the scaffold, Galen heard her whisper to Calypso, "I am not pleased with your decision."

"I understand," Calypso replied.

"You're supposed to kill me!" Alexis shouted. "Damn all you bitches to bloody hell!"

"Galen," Sabine gazed up at him, confusion in her eyes, "does this mean what I think it means?"

"We'd better find out."

Together they walked to the scaffold where a large group of guards had already begun dragging Alexis back to prison.

"Am I right in guessing you're pregnant?" Sabine asked Calypso.

"Yes," the warrior woman replied. "By law, if the father of a MeeKoran woman's child is placed on trial, she may use Matriarchal Release rather than see him executed. That means he becomes a slave of the tribe."

"What?" Alexis bellowed, his lips curled back. "What do you mean slave? What do you mean pregnant?"

"I know you're many things, Alexis," Calypso approached, arms folded across her chest, "but I didn't think stupid was one of them. Tell me, what part of pregnant don't you understand? Surely it can't be the conception."

"This might be a good experience for you." Sabine couldn't help grinning in the face of Alexis' rage. "See how slavery feels from the other side."

"Fuck you all!" Alexis roared as Galen joined the guards in dragging him to prison.

"As a slave to the MeeKorans, you can be sure you will— fuck us all," Calypso told him.

"Perhaps that's an even better way to pay for our sisters' deaths." One of the guards prodded Alexis' crotch with the tip of her spear.

"I'm still not pleased," Zorina stated, "but this should at least prove interesting."

"Will it ever," Calypso said under her breath as she and Sabine exchanged smiles.

They joined Galen as he stepped outside the prison.

"You're really carrying his child?" Galen asked.

Calypso sighed, nodding. "This is the last thing I imagined. For some reason, I couldn't let him die."

"I wish he was a different kind of man," Galen said. "If you need anything, you know where to find me. It's still my grandchild."

"Thank you for the offer, Captain Donovan, but MeeKorans are independent. We'll be perfectly fine."

"Which is more than I can say for Alexis." Sabine looked both disgusted and amused as she peered into the prison's barred window.

Inside, the MeeKoran warriors had slashed off Alexis' clothes so he stood naked and chained to the wall, growling and gnashing his fangs as two women felt every inch of his muscled chest and thighs while a third knelt between his legs, licking the length of his cock. The King appeared momentarily panicked as he glanced down at the redhead sucking his growing erection. In spite of his fury, she seemed to be doing her job all too well.

"Yes." Calypso's own jaw tightened, and Sabine noticed a bit of jealousy in her eyes. "Let him know what it is to be a slave. The MeeKorans despise him, but they'll use his body well. Men like him are unheard of here."

"So I've noticed," Sabine murmured. Indeed, the only men she'd seen in the village were slender, meek and obedient to the dominant women who used them as house servants and nursemaids.

"We have a ship leaving for Alexis' conquered land," Calypso said. "I'll take you to it so you can rejoin your people."

"Finally." Sabine sighed, edging closer to Galen who slipped his arm around her and squeezed.

Epilogue

ᏽ

A troop of Galen's men met him and Sabine as the MeeKoran ship on which they traveled docked in the largest bay in what had once been Alexis' kingdom.

"We thought you were dead!" Cook grinned as he embraced each of them.

"You should know by now we're not that easy to kill," Galen told him. "Where's Cass and Sofian?"

"Sofian is still out searching for you. He and the others are to return at the end of the week to report any findings. They'll be pleased to know you're both safe. Did the bastard King drown?"

"No," Galen said, "he's prisoner of the MeeKorans."

"Prisoner?" Cook's brow furrowed. "They should execute him right away. Humans, no matter how careful, always have trouble controlling an imprisoned vampire."

"I think in this case imprisonment might be exactly what he deserves," Sabine said.

"Even if he escapes, his kingdom is gone."

"Cass has taken over leadership," Cook said. "Pretty damn good at it, too. But wolves usually are, particularly those with alpha blood. He wanted to look for you, too, but this kingdom needed a strong hand until everyone accepts that Alexis has been overthrown. Not that we've had much trouble. Most of the people here didn't like him any better than we do. Oh, before I forget, Sabine, your brother is here."

"Narcisse?" Sabine's belly tightened with both excitement and apprehension. So much had happened since she'd last seen her brother.

"He's been out searching for you as well. Just returned hours ago and planned to leave again as soon as he gathers fresh supplies. He's been very worried."

"I have to talk to him. Where is he?"

"At the palace, just over the hill."

Together, Galen and Sabine hurried toward the frost-covered hill.

I wonder how angry Narcisse will be, Sabine thought. *I hope everyone is well at home, after all that happened, and I wonder if Leona had a boy or a girl.*

It will all be answered soon, my love.

They paused for a moment at the top of the hill and gazed at the tall castle of pale gray rock stretching toward the sky.

When they reached the gate, both Cass and Narcisse awaited them.

"Sabine!" Narcisse dragged his sister into his arms and held her so tightly she nearly lost her breath.

"Narcisse! I'm so sorry about everything. How is the village? How is Leona?"

"We've started rebuilding, and Leona is fine. We have a daughter." Narcisse held Sabine at arms' length. "God, you've changed."

"I have. It was so horrible, Narcisse."

"But now you can come home."

"Home?" Sabine's brow furrowed. "I—"

"You bastard!" Narcisse approached Galen, fangs bared, fists clenched. "My village was destroyed and my sister—"

"Narcisse, please!" Sabine stepped between them. "I love him!"

Narcisse paused, eyes darting from Galen to Sabine. "They said you're engaged, but I couldn't believe you really wanted to marry him, especially after what happened."

"Narcisse, I never intended for your home to be destroyed, and I certainly never intended to harm Sabine in any way. I was desperate. I needed only a moment of your time to help me, but then you weren't there and Sabine offered to save my life. Not that it's enough, but I sent men to help your village rebuild."

"I know." Narcisse ran a hand through his hair, some of his anger fading. "They've done well, and I've begun to recruit my own army of our kind. Debray land has never been home to any vampire but us, yet I have no wish for it to be ruined again by a group of immortals." Narcisse touched Sabine's cheek. "You really want to be with him?"

"I never dreamed of loving a man so much."

"Then I wish you both an eternity of happiness." Narcisse kissed her cheek. "If you ever want to return to Debray land, it will always be there for you."

"Thank you." Sabine embraced her brother.

Cass, who had been observing silently, cleared his throat. "It seems this is cause for celebration. This is a rich land, Galen, and I'll have them prepare a feast in the great hall."

"You've taken to this life rather easily for a priest." Galen folded his arms across his chest and cocked an eyebrow.

"I like this land, Galen." Cass inhaled deeply, eyes closed. "Can you smell the wildness, the freshness? My birthplace isn't far from here. My pack lives just across the tundra. From what I hear, they've been fighting off Alexis and his predecessor for years. Leave it to them to be arrogant enough to tangle with wolves."

"The people here have asked Cass to bring peace between this kingdom and the wolves," Narcisse said. "He should do it."

"I'm not sure if I'm the right man to bring peace," Cass said. "Not anymore, but I would like to stay here. I'm afraid part of this world is in my blood, Galen."

"Then stay." Galen placed a hand on his friend's shoulder. "I know how long you've contemplated returning home, and now you're close enough to do what is in your heart. Though we'll miss you on the island, you're a wolf, Cass. One last thing, you promised to marry us."

Sabine looked up at Galen. "Are you thinking what I am, Captain?"

He nodded. "I don't want to wait another hour before marrying you, little miss."

"And Narcisse is here to give me away." Sabine smiled at her brother who offered her his arm.

Cass cocked an eyebrow. "It seems I have a wedding to perform when we reach the hall."

The wedding took moments, and afterward Galen swept Sabine into his arms and carried her to an upstairs chamber where they shed their clothes and tumbled into bed.

"Galen," Sabine said between kisses, "I want to get home to our island as soon as possible."

"So do I." He growled, teeth nibbling one of her nipples.

"But first I want to visit Castle Debray and see Narcisse and Leona's baby."

"I want to make one of our own."

She giggled. "That too."

"We'll leave tomorrow evening, but right now I want us to fuck like savages."

"That's what I've always loved about you."

"My longevity?"

"Your crudity."

I love you, little miss.

And I love you, Captain Donovan. Eternally.

The End

About the Author

&

A lifelong fan of action and romance, Kate Hill likes heroes with a touch of something wicked and wild. Her short fiction and poetry have appeared in publications both on and off the Internet. When she's not working on her books, Kate enjoys dancing, martial arts, and researching vampires and Viking history.

Kate welcomes comments from readers. You can find her website and email address on her author bio page at www.ellorascave.com.

Enjoy An Excerpt From:
INFERNAL

Copyright © KATE HILL, 2005.

Dulcie stepped into the large, brightly lit kitchen. Though she disliked how bright humans kept everything, she'd grown accustomed to their preferences. Matthew had little difficulty with it, having been raised by a mortal family. Still, the sun irritated his eyes so much that during the day he usually wore sunglasses.

He stood by the sink, talking to one of his hospital's fellows, Nancy Brenner. Dulcie smiled, glad Nancy was there. For the first time that night, she sensed Matthew relax. Nancy had no idea her boss wasn't human, but Dulcie doubted it would matter. She was a pleasant young woman with a full, freckled face, kind brown eyes, and the pudgiest fingers Dulcie had ever seen on someone so slim. She was a good friend to both Matthew and Dulcie.

Yet Nancy didn't capture Dulcie's attention at that moment. Matthew did. Even after eight years of marriage and a string of previous affairs, Dulcie thought he was the most attractive man she'd ever seen. Though not perfectly handsome or a pretty boy, he possessed magnetism that outshone classic looks. Well over six feet and rangy, he moved with the grace of a great cat, fluid but with underlying power. Impeccably dressed in a dark blue designer suit that accentuated his broad shoulders and long, lean legs, he leaned against a countertop as he talked. The red silk tie knotted at his throat made Dulcie quiver as she thought about what he'd probably do with that tie later in their bedroom. The clean cut of his dark, curly hair formed a perfect square against his smooth, strong neck. His high forehead looked almost primitive, yet the sapphire eyes beneath shone with keen intelligence and decency. His nose—straight, slightly snubbed—was his cutest feature, and his mouth was his most erotic. He turned to her and smiled.

"We were just saying now would be a great time to get out of here," Nancy murmured to Dulcie.

"Sounds like the best idea I've heard all night," Dulcie replied, glancing at Matthew as he slipped the wine glass from her hand and placed it on the countertop.

He whispered close to her ear, "I told you this was a bad idea."

"Yes, you did." Dulcie tilted her head against his shoulder. "At least the night is still young."

"Well, I'm going while the going's good." Nancy edged her way toward the door. "See you tomorrow, Matthew. Dulcie, maybe we can get together for dinner at the end of the week?"

Dulcie waved to her. "I'm there." Once Nancy had gone, Dulcie looked up at Matthew. "Want to go outside for a minute before saying goodbye to our charming hostess?"

"I detect sarcasm in your voice."

"Do you blame me?"

"Not in the least," he whispered, his voice only audible to her keen vampiric hearing. "Lana is a jealous snob. Always has been. Robert's not too bad. I can almost condone his affair with Jacqueline."

They stepped through the sliding glass doors onto a concrete porch tastefully decorated with white lawn furniture. The Blacks had just built the large, suburban home, but Dulcie thought the spacious Colonial Matthew had renovated looked much more attractive. She'd been thrilled to move out of her condo and in with him after their marriage. He'd added on a studio for her, completely surrounded by glass picture windows since he knew how much she loved to paint by moonlight.

As they walked through the Black's dark backyard, shadowed even more by trees, a soft-rock love song drifted from the CD player inside the house.

"Sound familiar?" Dulcie slipped her hand into Matthew's as they walked behind some tall bushes.

"How can I forget?" He drew her into his arms. "The song we danced to at our wedding. Care to dance it again?"

Smiling, she nodded and drew a deep breath at the touch of his hand on her waist. He grasped her other hand and led her in gentle, swaying motions across the grass. His movements slowed as he tilted her face up to his for a kiss.

Enjoy An Excerpt From:
GOD OF THE GRIM

Copyright © KATE HILL, 2005.

Matthew's gaze fixed on the doorway of his house as Geneva, dressed in a hobo costume, approached the well-lit front porch. Two large, carved pumpkins sat on the steps. Matthew squinted to see the detailed faces, knowing Dulcie had carved them. She usually had one in every window, but this year there were only two. He hoped she was well. His stomach clenched at the thought of seeing her. As Geneva walked up the wooden steps and rang the doorbell, he willed his breathing to regulate.

He hid behind a weeping willow tree in a yard halfway down the street, against the wind so she couldn't catch his scent. Making the bus trip from New York to Boston was dangerous, but on this night of all nights, he *had* to see her. Halloween was their special holiday. Memories of past years filled his mind. Dulcie always looked so beautiful in a black satin nightgown. How he loved tearing it from her exquisite body and devouring her. He could almost feel her hands and teeth on his skin. His cock pulsed as he imagined thrusting deep inside her warmth. Repressing a shiver, he longed to hold her again and tell her how much he loved her. But he would have to be satisfied with seeing her. It had been such a painfully long time...

The door opened and she stood, wearing a black turtleneck that clung to her full, firm breasts. Black jeans molded to her shapely hips and thighs. High-heeled black boots adorned her feet. Her thick hair hung loose down her back. How soft it felt against his palms!

"God, she's so beautiful," he whispered.

"Trick or treat!" Geneva quipped, holding up a pillow case.

"Hello." Dulcie smiled at her, dropping treats inside.

"Can I have the other kind?"

Matthew's jaw tightened. *Stop being a brat, Geneva.*

"Sure you can," Dulcie said. Suddenly her head lifted, and she stared directly at Matthew's tree. He hid behind the trunk, his heart pounding and his mouth dry. He hoped she hadn't seen him and prayed she had.

"That's a cool wig," Geneva said to Dulcie.

Matthew shot the tiny hybrid a scathing look. *Jealous little bitch*!

The door closed, and she was gone. Closing his eyes, he swallowed past the tightness in his throat. Perhaps seeing her had been worse after all.

"You bastard!" Geneva roused him from his self-pity with a kick in the shin.

He hissed. "Why did you have to make those stupid comments to her?"

"Why didn't you tell me she was so beautiful?" Geneva snarled, drawing back her foot to kick him again.

He picked her up, pinning her arms to her sides, and held her against the tree, her feet dangling. "You little bitch! Can't you ever be nice?"

Geneva smiled snidely and shouted. "Help! Help! Daddy, don't hit me anymore!"

Matthew dropped her hard on her rump. "Shut up, Geneva! Are you trying to get me caught?"

"No one can catch you, Matthew Winter. I should know that by now."

He walked away, Geneva at his side. "Did you put it in the candy tray?"

"Yes, I tossed it in the tray before I left. You know, I don't like her. I'm going back to egg her house." Geneva turned on her heel, but Matthew caught her shoulder.

"Hey, that's *my* house, too."

"Oh, yes. I forgot." Geneva thought for a moment. "Why should I care? I should egg your face for not telling me what she looked like."

"Why does it matter to you what she looks like?"

"When I had the illusion that she was ugly, the thought of you married was easier to deal with."

He raised his eyes to heaven. "Let's go. We have to catch a bus back to New York."

"I'm going to trick or treat a little more while I'm here. This is a rich neighborhood. I bet everyone gives full-size chocolate bars." Geneva looked in the bag at Dulcie's treats. "Nice. Candy. A package of chocolate chip cookies and...what the hell is this? Dental floss?"

Matthew smiled and gazed back at his house. "She remembered."

"Don't tell me the damn dental floss is your idea?" Geneva scoffed. "Figures."

"All that candy is bad for the teeth, not to mention what it does to a person's cholesterol—"

"Eat this." She shoved a piece of chocolate at him, and he took a bite. "Good. Now I know you never talk with your mouth full, so maybe it'll save me the health lecture."

Matthew gently shoved the back of her head as they continued down the winding street.

* * * * *

The doorbell rang and Dulcie reached for the tray of candy, then paused. A small black box with a miniature red bow sat amidst the chocolate, cookies and sample-sized dental floss.

Where did it come from? Was it a bomb from Jay's men? If so, how did they get inside?

The little girl! It must have been. When she'd opened the door, she thought she caught Matthew's scent from the little hobo but had passed it off as a psychological reaction to her missing him so much. She knew the girl was a hybrid. It wasn't all that unusual to see a young child who'd been changed into one of their kind, so she hadn't thought anything of it.

Suddenly Dulcie knew the box wasn't from Jay. With trembling hands she opened the lid. Inside rested a single, perfect black pearl attached to a delicate gold chain.

"Matthew," she whispered, removing the pearl. Beneath the cotton at the bottom of the box was a folded note, the handwriting painfully familiar. It read:

I love you.
Happy Halloween.

She threw open the door, tossed the candy tray at a startled group of children and jumped in her car.

The little hobo couldn't have gone far, and she guessed Matthew was with her.

For hours, she combed her neighborhood and the surrounding ones, but as dawn neared, she realized that Matthew, if he had been close by, had disappeared.

Sadly, she returned home and lay in bed, her fingers caressing the black pearl at her throat as the sun rose outside.

Why an electronic book?

We live in the Information Age—an exciting time in the history of human civilization, in which technology rules supreme and continues to progress in leaps and bounds every minute of every day. For a multitude of reasons, more and more avid literary fans are opting to purchase e-books instead of paper books. The question from those not yet initiated into the world of electronic reading is simply: *Why?*

1. *Price.* An electronic title at Ellora's Cave Publishing and Cerridwen Press runs anywhere from 40% to 75% less than the cover price of the exact same title in paperback format. Why? Basic mathematics and cost. It is less expensive to publish an e-book (no paper and printing, no warehousing and shipping) than it is to publish a paperback, so the savings are passed along to the consumer.

2. *Space.* Running out of room in your house for your books? That is one worry you will never have with electronic books. For a low one-time cost, you can purchase a handheld device specifically designed for e-reading. Many e-readers have large, convenient screens for viewing. Better yet, hundreds of titles can be stored within your new library—on a single microchip. There are a variety of e-readers from different manufacturers. You can also read e-books on your PC or laptop computer. (Please note that Ellora's

Cave does not endorse any specific brands. You can check our websites at www.ellorascave.com or www.cerridwenpress.com for information we make available to new consumers.)

3. *Mobility.* Because your new e-library consists of only a microchip within a small, easily transportable e-reader, your entire cache of books can be taken with you wherever you go.

4. *Personal Viewing Preferences.* Are the words you are currently reading too small? Too large? Too... ANNOYING? Paperback books cannot be modified according to personal preferences, but e-books can.

5. *Instant Gratification.* Is it the middle of the night and all the bookstores near you are closed? Are you tired of waiting days, sometimes weeks, for bookstores to ship the novels you bought? Ellora's Cave Publishing sells instantaneous downloads twenty-four hours a day, seven days a week, every day of the year. Our webstore is never closed. Our e-book delivery system is 100% automated, meaning your order is filled as soon as you pay for it.

   Those are a few of the top reasons why electronic books are replacing paperbacks for many avid readers.

   As always, Ellora's Cave and Cerridwen Press welcome your questions and comments. We invite you to email us at Comments@ellorascave.com or write to us directly at Ellora's Cave Publishing Inc., 1056 Home Avenue, Akron, OH 44310-3502.

THE
☥ ELLORA'S CAVE ☥
LIBRARY

Stay up to date with Ellora's Cave Titles in
Print with our Quarterly Catalog.

To recieve a catalog,
send an email with your name
and mailing address to:

CATALOG@ELLORASCAVE.COM

OR SEND A LETTER OR POSTCARD
WITH YOUR MAILING ADDRESS TO:

CATALOG REQUEST
c/o ELLORA'S CAVE PUBLISHING, INC.
1056 HOME AVENUE
AKRON, OHIO 44310-3502

ELLORA'S CAVEMEN
LEGENDARY TAILS

Try an e-book for your immediate
reading pleasure or order these titles in print from

WWW.ELLORASCAVE.COM

ELLORA'S CAVE
THE BEST IN TODAY'S ROMANTICA™

MAKE EACH DAY MORE *EXCITING* WITH OUR

ELLORA'S
CAVEMEN
CALENDAR

www.EllorasCave.com

Cerridwen, the Celtic Goddess of wisdom, was the muse who brought inspiration to storytellers and those in the creative arts. Cerridwen Press encompasses the best and most innovative stories in all genres of today's fiction. Visit our site and discover the newest titles by talented authors who still get inspired - much like the ancient storytellers did, once upon a time.

Cerridwen Press

www.cerridwenpress.com

Discover for yourself why readers can't get enough of the multiple award-winning publisher

Ellora's Cave.

Whether you prefer e-books or paperbacks,

be sure to visit EC on the web at www.ellorascave.com

for an erotic reading experience that will leave you breathless.